NEVAEH

THE STORY OF THE LOST

THE THRONE EPIC MYSTERIES
BOOK #1

WRITTEN BY
MATHEW J. SHAW

Twisted Storylines Publishing

First Edition: January 2026
ISBN: **978-1-0698069-1-8**
Published by: **Twisted Storylines Publishing**
Written by: **Mathew J. Shaw**
This is a work of fiction. Names, characters, places, and incidents are either the product of the author's imagination or used fictitiously. Any resemblance to actual persons, living or dead, events, or locales is entirely coincidental.

Table of Contents

Twisted Storylines Publishing's Mission Statement

Unravel the untold.
Experience the unexpected.

At Twisted Storylines Publishing, we are devoted to delivering original, imaginative experiences that defy convention.

Our mission is to unearth untold stories with twisted plotlines, genre-bending narratives, and characters that collide in unexpected ways.

We embrace the chaos of creativity—where fantasy meets realism, and the familiar is turned on its head—to craft epic, human stories that resonate deeply with readers.

Through every book we publish, we challenge norms, ignite curiosity, and celebrate the art of storytelling that dares to be different

Books by Mathew J. Shaw

Grab Your Copy Today
Step into worlds you've never imagined with our two breakout releases
original, creative tales that bend reality and twist expectations.
These mysterious stories will leave you questioning everything and craving more.
If you love mystery, suspense, depth, and narrative surprises, you won't want to miss them.

The Throne Epic Mysteries Series
Nevaeh - The Story of The Lost Book #1
Book #2 - Coming Soon
The Mind of Clayton Trilling Series
The Next Step - The Controller's Game Book #1 - February 2026
Unravel the untold.
Experience the unexpected.

Sign up for our email list to receive updates scan the QR code

Dedication

❖ Nevaeh is dedicated to my parents for bringing me into this world

❖ And those who sat by and watched as I typed away my thoughts on the computer everyday writing this book

My wife Melissa
My cousin John

❖ I also dedicate Nevaeh to myself, the author, as someone who always felt like an imposter typing away on my computer wanting to pursue a career as a writer, writing Nevaeh allowed me to see I was the only thing holding myself back.

Prologue

This Book is an Enigma
The Title of This Book is a Riddle
The Plot of this Book is a Puzzle
Every Chapter in This Book is a Mystery
Each page in Every Chapter is a Puzzle Piece
And Nothing is what it seems to be
As you progress through the chapters of this book, you'll uncover clues and answers to its mysteries. However, with each mystery solved, new questions and enigmas will emerge. As you turn the pages, the answers you receive will unveil more questions. By advancing through the book and its chapters, you'll steadily uncover the full story, leading you to the grandeur of the story and the ultimate revelations at the end.

The universe, as contemplated by the human mind through life and living, is filled with questions and mysteries.

Each answered question or solved mystery brings forth new questions and mysteries to explore.

I've designed the story within this book to mirror that image of perpetual mystery. So, what does that mean?

According to Oxford Languages, a mystery is defined as:

1. something that is difficult or impossible to understand or explain.
2. a novel, play, or movie dealing with a puzzling crime, especially a murder.

While this book falls into the second definition, I believe the first definition —better describes what you are about to read.

This may sound unconventional to a reader eager to dive into a book and discover its story.

This is not a story you simply read.

The plot is a mystery you must solve.

The only way to solve it is by reading.

Imagine a box of jigsaw puzzles—dozens of them—tangled together in the same box without a final image to guide you.

No edges.

No corners.

Just scattered fragments.

Each chapter offers a piece.

Not in order. Not with explanation.

Some pieces belong to different puzzles.

Some seem to contradict.

All are part of something larger revealing the epic plot.

This book unfolds in the style of conversation. Through dialogue and narration, characters will reveal mysteries, pose questions, and uncover clues that help piece together the puzzles within the story.

As our characters discover new connections, clues, questions, mysteries, and answers, so will you, the reader.

In the pages of this book, you'll encounter a tapestry of compelling themes: beliefs, truth, philosophy, and religion.

This is a work of fiction, and my intention is not to offend, but to explore these profound concepts that shape the human mind and experience.

These concepts mold the human mind giving each individual human a different experience and lens to view reality through.

These overarching themes drive the narrative forward, setting the stage for the mind-bending revelations that await you at the end of the book. Without them, the astonishing twists and turns of the story could never come to life.

Across cultures and centuries, the concept of an afterlife has stirred the human imagination—a realm not universally proven but profoundly envisioned in the theater of our minds.

We see it in the Elysium of ancient Greece, in Valhalla, the hall of warriors; in Christianity through Heaven, in Nirvana the Buddhist state of liberation; and in the eternal Paradises described by Islam and Zoroastrianism.

These visions may differ in shape and source, yet they are all born from the same place: the deep folds of the human mind, which crafts meaning from mystery and hope from fear.

The afterlife lives not within us, but within our thoughts—a conceptual landscape drawn by our longing for justice, reunion, everlasting life, and truth.

Perhaps it's a reflection of our desire to make sense of mortality, or to extend our stories beyond the last breath.

In imagining what lies beyond, we create possibilities that soothe, inspire, and reveal. Whether real or symbolic, this mental monument to life's continuation gives shape to our deepest beliefs—and whispers that there may be more, just beyond the edge of knowing.

It is there, some believe, they will step into truth.

Welcome to Nevaeh, where truth is a lie.

And the afterlife a perpetual mystery.

A Note to Readers

Nevaeh is a journey—one filled with bold themes, layered tropes, and unexpected turns. Within its pages, you'll encounter fictional religious beliefs and spiritual ideas that diverge from traditional doctrines.

These are imaginative expressions meant to explore, not to preach, or offend. If any moment gives you pause or requires time to reflect, that's okay. Take it.

This story welcomes those willing to engage with unfamiliar perspectives and the questions they raise.

Nevaeh isn't just a story—it's an immersive experience. Crafted in a narrative style that's both thought-provoking and emotionally resonant, it invites readers to unravel layered mysteries while contemplating profound philosophical questions.

With each page, Nevaeh challenges assumptions, stirs reflection, and leaves a lingering sense of unease.

Blending genres with bold originality, it stands apart as a novel that doesn't just entertain—it provokes, unsettles, and stays with you long after the final chapter.

Prelude - The Story of The Lost

ohn Torberry sat on his couch, leaning forward with his elbows on his knees and his chin resting on his fists. He watched the television, horrified by the stories of the people known as The Lost.

John's brother had gone missing two weeks ago and was now officially one of The Lost.

Empathetic to the stories of others who had disappeared, John was on the brink of tears, worried he would never see his brother again.

John sat beside his wife, Linda, as they watched a show called The Lost Files, which highlighted many investigations into the missing persons collectively called The Lost.

The show had just cut back to the host, Cindy Schrouder.

"The story of The Lost is beyond anything we could have ever fathomed in our darkest nightmares. We have reviewed more than twenty of The Lost cases tonight, and that barely scratches the surface of the total number of people who have vanished into thin air.

Among these cases, one stands out as it was the first case discovered, leading to the formation of the organization we call The Throne and the ongoing investigation into The Lost's disappearances. It's also one of the few cases with multiple eyewitnesses confirming a phantom ambulance sighting.

On the day Leonard Chance went missing, the street was bustling. He was stabbed twice in broad daylight on a busy sidewalk.

Despite being gravely injured, Leonard managed to call 911 before being picked up by a phantom ambulance.

To witnesses, everything seemed normal until minutes later, a second ambulance arrived, sparking the entire investigation into The Lost and, eventually, this show, The Lost Files.

Since Leonard Chance's disappearance, The Throne has documented over seven thousand similar cases. These disappearances, following the same pattern, have been happening daily across the country for the past twenty years.

Where are they being taken?

Are they being kidnapped?

What is happening to them?

Who is taking them?

Why are they being taken?

Will we ever see these people again?

Are they alive?"

Pausing for a few seconds before continuing,

"Are they dead?

These are just some of the questions people are asking because we still have no idea what is happening to The Lost.

All we can do is speculate as the numbers continue to rise daily.

The Lost have infiltrated our lives, culture, and minds nationwide, instilling fear that you could be the next to disappear.

If you have any information on The Lost and their disappearances, contact The Throne by dialing 119 on your mobile device. Thank you for joining us tonight on The Lost Files."

John turned to his wife, holding back tears." Do you think I'll ever see my brother again?"

His wife Linda responded, "I pray that Tony comes home every day. All we can do is hope The Throne can find out what is happening to The Lost."

Part One

Chapter 1 - The Chosen One

Amelia lay peacefully asleep in her bed, unaware of the morning sunbeam that pierced through the gap in the curtains, casting a golden path across the room.

Slow, quiet footsteps crept towards her bed, stopping just beside her, the silence in the room almost tangible, unknown to Amelia, eyes stared at her as she slept.

Suddenly, the tranquility was shattered as the alarm clock on her bedside table buzzed loudly, jolting her awake.

Her three-year-old son, Michael, who had been standing there, let out an ear-splitting scream, adding to the chaos.

Amelia's heart raced as she joined Michael in his cries; the serene morning transformed into a whirlwind of noise and confusion.

Calmly with a hint of anger Amelia asked, "Why are you screaming to wake me up, Michael? We've talked about that."

Michael's bottom lip quivered as he looked up at her, his brown eyes wide with remorse. "Sowy, Mommy. Didn't mean to. Came to wake you up, clock sceamed, scaed me."

Amelia's expression softened, and she kissed the top of his head. "Oh, my poor baby. Is everything okay now?"

Michael's pout vanished as quickly as it had appeared. "I not baby. Mommy awake to potect me now."

He wrapped his little arms around her neck in a tight hug. Amelia chuckled, holding him close. Playfully teasing Amelia said, "Your mommy will always protect you."

She paused for a second, "And Mommy will stop calling you a baby when you don't need diapers anymore. Deal?"

Michael pulled back; his face scrunched into a defiant frown. "Hmmft, no deal."

Amelia approached him slowly as if angry with him, as she got close her expression quickly changed, she started laughing and reached out her arms tickling his sides, earning a squeal of delight before she spoke.

"You start school in six months, Michael. We'll work together so you're ready."

Changing the subject, Michael grinned. "Dad made Beakfast."

Amelia smiled. "Yummy! But we need to work on your R's. It's Brrreakfast."

Concentrating and trying his hardest, "Brreeekfast."

"That was good, baby. Where are John and Thomas?"

"Dey downstais wit Dad. Les go."

"Mommy will be down in a minute."

Amelia gently set Michael down, watching as he bolted out of the room with the boundless energy only a toddler could possess.

She sighed deeply, stretching her arms above her head, and let the warmth of the morning light chase away the remnants of sleep.

Reaching for her rings on the nightstand, her fingers brushed against her cherished Bible and the small cross depicting Jesus, symbols of her unwavering faith.

Kneeling beside her bed, Amelia placed the cross tenderly atop the Bible and bowed her head, closing her eyes in prayer. The morning's chaos faded into a serene moment of connection and reflection. Praying softly she spoke,

"God, Jesus, the Creator of all, please protect my family today, all Christians who follow Your path, and their families. Lead us not into evil. Give us the strength to follow Your way and enter the Kingdom of Heaven when You decide it is our time. I love you Jesus."

After finishing her prayer, Amelia rose gracefully, switching the alarm clock to the radio, and allowing the soft hum of music to fill the room.

She slipped into a modest dress, the fabric flowing gently against her skin, before sitting at her vanity.

As she meticulously applied her makeup, the music faded out and the all too familiar voice of Cindy Schrouder created a discomforting background, as she weaved together the threads of her morning routine.

"This is *The Lost Files* for August 13, 2035. I'm your host, Cindy Schrouder. Today, we'll discuss newly released case details from The Throne about confirmed Lost disappearances and phantom ambulance sightings.

Later, we'll speak with an expert on avoiding becoming one of The Lost. Stay tuned."

Amelia frowned, a cloud of discontent darkening her features. The cheerful chatter of the radio host suddenly felt out of place, grating against her lingering sense of unease. With a decisive movement, she turned off the radio, plunging the room into a reflective silence.

The abrupt quiet allowed her thoughts to surface, unfiltered and raw, as she sat there, momentarily lost in contemplation.

Muttering to herself, "The Lost and The Throne, The Lost and The Throne. That's all anyone talks about now."

Amelia descended the stairs, greeted by the mouth-watering aroma of bacon wafting through the house.

In the kitchen, her husband Jacob stood at the stove, expertly flipping toast onto a plate with practiced ease. The sight brought a warm smile to her face.

Her teenage sons, John and Thomas, were already at the table, devouring their breakfast with the eagerness and energy that only teenagers possess. "Looks delicious. Don't forget, choir rehearsal tonight."

Groaning her son John said, "We know, Mom. Can we just eat?"

Thomas looked at Amelia and smiled as he said, "We've been practicing all week, Mom. You'll love it."

A big smile came across the face of her husband Jacob, "You should hear them; they're both little Frank Sinatra's."

Amelia proudly said with a smile, "I can't wait to hear you both. I know you'll make Jesus proud."

Suddenly, a piece of scrambled egg flew across the table, launched from Michael's fork with an unexpected flick.

The golden morsel sailed through the air, tumbling in slow motion before landing with a soft plop on John's plate.

Everyone froze, the surprise momentarily suspending their morning routine. John looked up, his expression a mix of shock and amusement, while Michael's face turned crimson with embarrassment.

Jacob turned away from the stove, eyebrow raised, as Amelia suppressed a chuckle, the corners of her mouth twitching in amusement as Jacob said Sternly "Michael! Stop throwing your food."

Protesting the accident as his fault Michael responded, "It was my fok."

Laughter erupted from the two older boys.

Jacob gave them a stern look to quiet their laughter, his eyes narrowing in disapproval.

Amelia, sensing the tension, immediately spoke up, correcting Michael's mistake with a gentle but firm tone. "Your R's, Michael. It's fork, for-ka."

Michael tried to pronounce the word with every ounce of will he had, he hesitated at first and then said, "Fo-ka."

Jacob turned to Amelia, his stern expression softening as their eyes met. Amelia offered him a reassuring smile, her calm demeanor a steady anchor for him.

She reached out, gently placing a hand on his arm, and with that small gesture, the bond between them was strengthened, reaffirming their partnership and love.

Jacob asked, "Heading to the church this morning?"

Amelia nodded while speaking, "Yes, we have an event on the Savior's land.

I'll be home in three hours and then off to the boys' rehearsal. Busy day for all of us."

Jacob responded,

"I'll make sure the boys are ready when you get back. Call me if you need anything."

After finishing breakfast and exchanging goodbyes, Amelia stepped outside. She waved to her neighbor as she walked to her car.

As she drove past the houses in the community without driveways—where the owners didn't have cars and were forbidden to leave—she thanked Jesus for blessing her to be a Savior and not a Servant.

The community of The Servants and Saviors of Christ sprawled around her, a self-contained world of 150,000 homes, complete with its own economy, laws, and government. Walls and checkpoints encircled the vast land.

As she drove through the gate, the guard waved her on, and a towering sign overhead read: *Jesus Loves You.*

Amelia turned onto the highway, the radio playing softly. Most followers never left the community, but as a Savior, Amelia had privileges.

She spent her days recruiting new servants and running church events. She didn't see it as confinement—only as devotion to God's will.

Thirty minutes into her drive, A billboard caught her attention. It depicted a suited man looming ominously over a miniature city, his expression cold and calculating.

Puppet strings dangled from his hands, controlling the tiny buildings and streets below.

The image was unsettling, a stark reminder of the unseen forces at play in the world.

Amelia couldn't tear her eyes away, a chill running down her spine as she imagined the lives manipulated by such forces.

The caption on the billboard read: *Investments to Build Your Life and Neighborhood – Odyssey Inc.*

The song on the radio changed, and Amelia's favorite hymn came on. She turned up the volume and began to sing along, her voice filling the car.

God loves me, yes, He does!

The Bible is the word, that everyone deserves!

I love God, the word says so!

We are the servants; He is the Savior!

Amelia's mood soared as she sang, her voice filling the car with joyous melodies. For a brief moment, she was lost in the euphoria of the song, everything else fading into the background.

The sunlight streamed through the windows, casting a warm glow over her as she drove. Suddenly, a car swerved into her lane, but Amelia was too immersed in her singing to notice.

The impact was immediate and violent, the vehicle slamming into her driver's side door with a sickening force.

Her car flipped three times, a terrifying whirlwind of motion and sound, before careening off the road into the forest.

Glass shattered around her, metal crunched under the immense pressure, she was upside down, and darkness quickly engulfed her, swallowing her world in an instant.

Chapter 2 - Who are You?

A man with long, disheveled hair and a scruffy face, evidence of several days without shaving, sat in a pristine white chair, twirling his thumbs in never-ending circles, each rotation perfectly synchronized with a ticking clock.

His eyes were fixed on the couch across from him, where a woman lay face down, unconscious.

The scene was routinely familiar to him; it had played out countless times before.

Anxiety gnawed at him as he waited for the woman to awaken.

His gaze flickered to the table in front of her, where three half-filled glasses stood side by side, the liquid within glistening under the dim light.

He reached over, grabbing his own drink, and took a long, contemplative sip. Stretching out his arms and legs, he whispered to himself, his voice barely audible, a fleeting echo in the silence. "It feels so good every time to stretch these muscles."

"Hello??" came a voice.

"Who's there?" the woman, now awake and visibly shaken.

The man said, "Turn over, sit up, let's talk."

The woman turned over and sat up, staring at the man sitting across from her, who was still twirling his thumbs.

Confused Amelia looked around the room, Seeing the all-white atmosphere that the pristine, snow-white walls created, it was as if she had stepped into a serene, otherworldly sanctuary.

Enveloping her in a cocoon of purity and tranquility.

Every surface gleamed with an almost ethereal glow, reflecting the soft light and casting delicate, subtle shadows.

It felt like standing inside a blank canvas, waiting for life's vibrant hues to paint their story, yet offering a peaceful respite from the chaos of the outside world.

She gave her head a shake and glanced at the three peculiar glasses sitting on the white table half filled with liquid and tried to sort through her memories to remember how she got there.

With a trembling voice, she asked inquisitively, stuttering as she did. "Who... are you? Where... am I?"

The man's thumbs continued their circular motion as he spoke. "I said we will talk. Why don't you start by telling me your name?"

"My name is Amelia Bernhart. And you are?"

"I assure you, Amelia, by the time you leave this room, you will know everything—about me, where you are, and why you are here.

For now, I need you to drink the three drinks on the table in front of you and then answer a couple of questions."

Amelia looked down at the three drinks in front of her on the table. Each glass held an identical drink, yet vibrant colors swirled within them, creating an almost rainbow-like effect.

Smoke or steam slowly billowed out of the glasses, filling them and crawling down the sides in a mesmerizing dance.

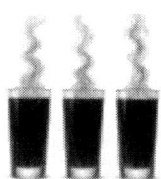

The drinks looked dangerous, an unfamiliar liquid that seemed to hold a mysterious allure.

She didn't know if she could trust the man.

Amelia raised her left eyebrow slightly while lowering her right, her expression a fascinating blend of curiosity and amusement.

Her eyes twinkled with a hint of mischief, as she leaned in slightly looking at the three drinks on the table and said, "You better not be lying to me."

A big smile spread across the man's face, radiating warmth and genuine delight. His eyes locked onto Amelia's, holding her gaze with an intensity that spoke volumes.

He continued to smile for a few seconds, his thumbs never stopping their rhythmic movements, as if they had a life of their own.

A voice laced with emotion, he responded, "I would never lie to you, Amelia."

After this, the smile faded from the man's face, his expression turning serious. His eyes still held a flicker of the previous warmth, but now they were clouded with concern.

Leaning slightly closer to Amelia, he asked in a soft, yet earnest voice, "Now tell me, what do you remember?"

Amelia hung her head; her eyes fixed on the floor as she tried to sort through her tangled thoughts.

The weight of the moment pressed down on her, making it hard to breathe.

She was lost in a sea of thought when she excitedly blurted out, "I remember singing a song while I was driving."

Knowingly the man said, "Yes, you were singing the Servants and Saviors Heavenly Hymn."

Remembering what happened next, Amelia felt a complex swirl of emotions—excitement, confusion, and distress all rolled into one.

Her heart raced as she tried to make sense of it all.

With a heavy sigh, she finally looked up, her eyes meeting his with a mixture of vulnerability and resolve.

In a low, sad tone, she responded, "And then a car hit me."

It was as if the man was watching her the whole time, "Yes, you were on your way to a church event. An ambulance arrived soon after the crash. They tried to save you, but your injuries were beyond repair."

A confused look crossed Amelia's face as the realization of what the man was telling her set in. She started to look around the room, noticing the white walls and the two doors she hadn't noticed before.

Wondering where she was, she asked excitedly, with a bit of attitude in her voice, "What does that mean? If they tried to save me and failed, how am I here now? Who are you?"

The man's fingers stopped twirling, coming to an abrupt halt. He leaned forward, his movements deliberate and measured, as he waved his right hand over the table where the three drinks sat, each one a silent witness to their conversation.

His eyes bore into Amelia's as he responded, "I know you have questions, Amelia, but for you to understand the answers, I need you to drink all three drinks in front of you.

Take your time; I will wait."

The man sat back in his chair, his thumbs resuming their endless circles as if in a perpetual dance.

His gaze remained steady on Amelia, unyielding.

Amelia glanced down at the three drinks for a fleeting moment, their presence a silent reminder of her curiosity to know more she asked, "How did you know about the ambulance? Are you the one who hit me?"

The man waved his hand over the drinks again, a gesture that seemed to hold a deeper meaning.

His eyes never left Amelia's as he spoke, "Amelia, drink all three, and you will have all your questions answered."

His voice carrying a mix of determination and urgency. The weight of his words hung in the air, mingling with the scent of the drinks that sat untouched on the table.

He leaned in closer, his gaze unwavering, silently urging her to find the courage to take the drinks, he sat back, crossing his hands on his lap, his thumbs resuming their rhythmic twirling.

Confused and unsure of what else to do, Amelia reached for the first glass.

She drank it down in a single gulp.

The taste was indescribably sweet, a flavor unlike anything she had ever encountered. As the liquid coursed through her, an overwhelming feeling of exuberance washed over her.

She felt every nerve in her body tingle for a brief, electrifying second.

Her eyes widened in surprise, the sensation so intense and unexpected, she joyously said, "What was that? It was delicious."

The man responded, "Once the other drinks are done, all your answers will come."

Amelia grabbed the second glass and drank it. The flavor was rich and complex, though not sweet like the first one.

A slight burning sensation spread from head to toe, not painful but intense. She closed her eyes, feeling the sensation, and let out an uncontrollable low moan of pleasure.

Embarrassed, she glanced at the man, then down at the third drink. She grabbed it and swallowed it in three gulps.

Sitting back on the couch, she looked at the man and spoke, "So..."

The moment Amelia began to speak, her eyes rolled back, and she started convulsing violently on the couch.

The man watched her, twirling his thumbs, unmoving.

After thirty seconds, the convulsing ceased, and Amelia's eyes opened. "What just happened?"

Waving his hand at her he said, "It's normal when you take the drinks. Don't worry about it."

Amelia raised an eyebrow, her expression a mix of skepticism and curiosity.

She took a deep breath, steadying herself before speaking "I still don't have any answers."

The man responded, "That was just the first step, Amelia. The answers come after the drinks. Ask me anything."

Amelia, timid and unsure, asked in a soft, hesitant voice, "Did I die?"

Seeking reassurance and clarity in his response. The vulnerability in her question hung in the air, a fragile thread connecting her hopes and fears.

The man responded, "I told you before the drinks, yes. Why not ask questions you don't know the answer to?"

Trying to explain what she had meant, Amelia took a deep breath and looked up at the man, her eyes filled with a mix of urgency and earnestness.

"I know I died, but where am I? Where are the Pearly Gates? Where is Saint Peter? Where is everything the Bible described about Heaven?"

The man made a dismissive gesture, waving his hand as if to brush away her concerns.

"Stories of men Amelia, none of that was real. They were all creations of man's imagination. No one truly knew what they were talking about."

Amelia looked flustered, her anger and confusion growing with each passing second.

She glanced around the stark, white-walled room, her eyes darting from one blank surface to another as if searching for an answer.

The oppressive silence and the sterile atmosphere only seemed to amplify her emotions. Her mind raced, trying to make sense of everything, as a storm of thoughts and feelings churned within her. She Yelled,

"I WAS A SAVIOR! In The Servants and Saviors of Christ Church.

All Saviors were guaranteed a spot in Heaven by the First High Priest."

The man spread his arms wide, as if to embrace the entirety of the situation.

His posture conveyed both openness and a sense of authority, a stark contrast to the turmoil that Amelia was feeling. "And where do you think you are?"

He extended his hand towards her, pointing a finger with deliberate precision and said, "I handpicked you. You are one of the Chosen ones."

His voice imbued with a sense of gravity and purpose. The words hung in the air, heavy with significance, as Amelia felt a chill run down her spine.

The intensity of his gaze and the weight of his proclamation left her momentarily speechless, the enormity of his statement sinking in.

Amelia looked around the room, seeing only white walls, two mysterious doors, and the man continuing to twirl his thumbs. "So, this..."

She gestured to the walls and ceiling, her movements sharp and filled with frustration, "Is Heaven?"

The man shrugged, a gesture that seemed to dismiss the gravity of the situation entirely. "Call it whatever you want, Amelia. You're here now. You don't have to worry about anything ever again."

Amelia confused asked, "If you handpicked me, who does that make you?"

He responded calmly, his voice steady and composed. "You already know the answer. I am what you would call Jesus."

Amelia's eyebrows rose, a flicker of surprise and curiosity lighting up her features as she spoke, "You are God?"

"It's complicated, Amelia. The true understanding of God is different from what you were taught. You know how the church believes in the Trinity?"

Amelia responded, Of course, the Father, the Son, and the Holy Spirit."

Gesturing with his fingers Jesus said, "You believe them to be one, but I can only be one at a time.

Each form is a step in my own Creation: Creator God, Jesus as man, and full fruition and destruction as the Holy Spirit."

Amelia looked surprised, her eyes widening as she processed his words then spoke, "Destruction?"

"The Universe I created isn't infinite. It must end. I set it in motion for life to flourish and to find the greatest of my human creations.

Once set in motion, I became Jesus. I never came to Earth or was crucified. Here in heaven, we are all equal."

A lifetime of beliefs within Amelia's mind were swirling, "I'm not sure I understand."

Jesus continued explaining, "Here in Heaven, we are equal. Me, you, and everyone here get whatever they want or need."

Curiously she asked, "How many people are here?"

Jesus responded excitedly, "Thousands. You are the 6,332nd I have chosen."

Still curious she asked, "How does it work with everyone getting what they want?"

Waving his arms around gesturing to the room, "Heaven supplies all sustenance. I can recreate anything, here you can have whatever you desire."

Amelia felt a headache coming on, the pressure building as her mind raced to process the new information. She closed her eyes for a moment, trying to steady her thoughts.

Rubbing her temples in an attempt to ease the tension she said, "This is a lot to take in.

Do you mind if I close my eyes for a bit?"

Jesus responded empathically, "Here, you have the freedom to do whatever you want, whenever you want."

Amelia stretched out on the couch, her mind spinning as she contemplated the weight of Jesus' words.

She closed her eyes, trying to find a moment of peace amidst the chaos of her thoughts. The room fell into a hush, the darkness behind her eyes closing in on her.

Chapter 3 - How is this Possible

melia had been sleeping for hours. Jesus, still sitting across from her, twirled his thumbs, waiting patiently. On the table in front of him was a small buffet of Amelia's favorite foods, their delicious aromas filling the air.

Amelia stirred, rolled over, and, lying on her side, blinked twice before speaking, her voice groggy and barely above a whisper.

"I thought it was all a dream, but you're still here."

Jesus looked directly into her eyes, and she felt an immediate connection, an unspoken bond that seemed to transcend words.

His gaze was steady and filled with a warmth that reached deep into her soul.

"If you'd like me to leave you alone, I can do that until you're ready."

Amelia shook her head as she sat up, her eyes fixed on the spread of food before her. The tantalizing aromas wafted around her, stirring her senses and momentarily distracting her from the whirlwind of thoughts in her mind.

"No, no, don't leave me alone."

"Then let's sit in silence while you eat. Think of the questions you want to ask me. We have many more answers to cover before you leave this room."

Amelia began eating, savoring each dish with a newfound appreciation. The flavors danced on her tongue, each bite bringing her a small measure of comfort and grounding her in the present moment.

She took her time, allowing herself to fully enjoy the simple pleasures of the meal.

As she ate, she felt a sense of calm settle over her, the warmth of the food mirroring the warmth she felt from Jesus' unwavering gaze.

The room, once stark and intimidating, now felt a little less overwhelming, she was almost done eating and said to Jesus,

"You sure know what I like. This duck dish... I had it once in France. I used to joke with my friends that I'd kill someone to taste it again."

Jesus, still twirling his thumbs, responded with a calm and steady voice. "It's called Duck Confit. Eat, Amelia. We'll talk when you're done."

Once she finished, she sat back, pondering what to ask. Her mind raced with thoughts and questions, but before she could settle on one, Jesus spoke first.

"To start let me ask you this... Why would you want this to be a dream? Wasn't it your life's purpose to serve me and secure your spot in Heaven?"

"Of course, I dedicated my life to securing a place in Heaven."

"Then why, now that you're here, do you seem like you'd rather be anywhere else? Why are you doubting my words?"

Flustered, Amelia responded timidly, "I'm not doubting you, Jesus. I've devoted my life to you... Let me ask you this... If the religion I chose wasn't the true religion, how did I come to be chosen?"

"The religion you follow doesn't matter; it's the devotion you showed towards me that counts."

Amelia quickly asked another question, her curiosity and anxiety driving her words forward. "Why was it my time when the car hit me? Why was I taken from my family?"

Jesus responded, "I don't get to choose when it's time. Remember, I set Creation in motion as God, but as Jesus, I no longer have control over it."

Her eyes narrowed as she stared at Jesus, with an accusatory tone, asked, "So, are you just a man now then?"

"I am a man, but unlike other men, I can create whatever you want or desire here in Heaven."

Amelia leaned forward; her excitement palpable. Her eyes shining with anticipation she asked eagerly, "Can you show me?"

"It doesn't work like that, Amelia. Creating your desires takes time and effort, and with 6,332 others here, I'm a busy man. I can usually meet your requests within a week. Put it to the test and ask me for anything."

"Let me think of something." Curious she continued and asked, "You said a week, why measure time here?"

"We measure time because I need to know when people will arrive on that couch. We still have light and dark periods each day. Here, if you don't sleep, eat, or drink you won't be affected. Here, you have the joy of getting what you want and not doing anything you don't."

Intrigued, Amelia asked, her curiosity piqued, "So, what is this place?"

Jesus responded, "This place is Heaven."

Amelia tilted her head to the side and said, "I know it's Heaven, but there's more to it than this room. Where are we?"

Smiling Jesus replied, "I understand your question. Heaven is in its own separate universe, not interacting with the one where you lived, except for those I choose to bring here. When you leave this room, you'll find Heaven is like an island, a large landmass surrounded by water."

Her brow furrowed as she tried to piece together the answer to her next question, confused she asked, "An island? Why water?"

Jesus explained, "The land is open to nature, nothing off-limits, and the water is just the boundary where the Heaven universe ends."

Amelia asked, "Are the stories of Hell true?"

Jesus looked her in the eye and said, "Which ones, Amelia? There are thousands of stories. Here, we call them The Discarded. If you combined every story about Hell, they wouldn't match the true experience of being Discarded. It's not something we talk about often."

Amelia, horrified, her eyes wide with shock. Said, "You've made Hell seem like a sunburn on the beach."

Jesus shook his head, "I don't see that in your future here."

Amelia cut in and said, "To deliberately change the subject, what were the three drinks I had to take?"

Jesus explained, "The three drinks are part of a ritual here. Followers take them on arrival and every three months in a celebration.

They are Pure Emotion, Pure Empathy, and Pure Ecstasy."

Amelia, confused, tried to process the information. her voice reflecting the turmoil in her mind as she asked,

"Pure emotion... Empathy? What does that mean?"

Jesus smiled again and said, "The Three Drinks help maintain the perfection here. They are natural to my creation, keeping everyone happy."

Amelia looked doubtful and asked, "What if someone doesn't want to be happy?"

Sternly Jesus responded, "Then I made a mistake in choosing them."

Amelia asked, "What are we supposed to do here in Heaven, once I'm outside this room?"

Jesus replied, "You'll want to explore, see the island, and meet the others. The island is filled with edible fruits, and the animals won't harm you. Let's get through your first week. Did you have any other questions?"

Her eyes darted downward, avoiding direct contact as she nervously fidgeted with her fingers her voice barely above a whisper as she asked,

"Can we feel love here, the emotion?"

Jesus stopped twirling his thumbs and spread his arms out as he replied,

"Of course you can love, why would you ask?"

After recoiling his arms and resuming the twirling of his thumbs, Amelia replied,

"I loved my family more than anything, but now it seems they are not even a thought in my head."

Jesus sympathetically said, "I am sure their memory will come back to you, Amelia. I wouldn't take that away from you. I think your brain is working overtime trying to process everything you've been taught about me being wrong. Do you have any other questions?"

Amelia looking at his hands asked, "I noticed you constantly twirl your thumbs, why?"

Jesus explained, "It is a coping mechanism for me. I can see and feel the flow of time as it passes like a wind blowing around my body and through my mind, and twirling my thumbs helps me cope with that as a man."

Amelia said confused, "Ok... Umm..."

While Amelia was trying to think of another question, Jesus spoke, his voice breaking the silence with a calm, steady tone. "We can always have another talk like this, Amelia. Why don't we end our talk for now and pick it up next time?"

Her demeanor changed her eyes sparkled with anticipation, and her enthusiasm was contagious as she excitedly, blurted out, "I thought about what I want."

Jesus asked her, "And what is that, Amelia?"

Excitedly she started to speak with a passion in her voice, "When I was a teenage girl, I had a bike called the Silver Streamer. I lost it when we moved, and I never saw it again. They stopped making it. If I could have that bike once again, it would make me very happy."

"Then it will be yours. I'll bring it to you as soon as I can. If you're ready to leave this room now, I have arranged a guide to show you around. Are you ready to step outside that door? Simon will be waiting for you."

Jesus raised his hand and pointed at the door on the other side of the room. Amelia said, "I think I am."

Amelia stood up, her heart pounding with anticipation. Her eyes were fixed on the door, ready to face whatever lay beyond it.

Jesus spoke, "Simon will be happy to show you around and answer any questions you have. I think you'll like him."

As Amelia walked toward the door, she felt Jesus's eyes burning a hole into her back.

Putting her hand on the door and about to push it open, Jesus spoke loudly, his voice echoed in the room,

"Amelia!"

Amelia froze, her hand still on the door. She turned slowly to face him, "Yes?"

There were a few seconds of silence where Jesus just stared at her.

Her heart pounding in her chest, anticipation and uncertainty mingling in her expression.

The room seemed to hold its breath, the moment stretching into eternity as she waited for his next words.

"I love you!"

His words bringing an awkward feeling over her, she paused, staring at him for a few seconds before she responded, "I... love you too, Jesus."

Amelia pushed the door open. She shook her head as she saw Simon waiting on the other side of the door, leaning against the wall with one-foot resting flat against it.

When he noticed the door open, he stood up straight. Amelia said, "Hello, you must be Simon."

In a serious tone, Simon responded, His voice was firm and unwavering, "I don't know if I must be Simon, but that's the name my parents gave me. It could have been anything though. Let's walk this way."

Amelia followed Simon's lead, walking beside him. "Let me ask you this, if you weren't Simon, who would you want to be?"

Thinking for a second, Simon responded, "I don't know. I never thought of being anyone but me.

We haven't been formally introduced. I'm Simon Cartwright."

"Nice to meet you, Simon. I'm Amelia Bernhart."

She extended her hand, and they shook hands. Simon said, "Like the female pilot that disappeared?"

Shaking her head, she spelled it out for him, "Bern-hart. That's Amelia Ear-hart. If I were flying a plane, it would be on fire, that's why there's a 'Bern' in my name."

Simon and Amelia laughed a little at Amelia's corny joke as they walked. "How did your talk with Jesus go?"

Grief and confusion stricken across her face, "It was like a punch in the face, being told that everything I thought I knew was wrong. Is it weird that I'm still skeptical?"

"When I had my first talk with Jesus, I walked out of that room very confused and afraid. I had no clue if what I was being told was true. After a week here and speaking with him a second and third time, I had no doubts."

"So, the way I'm feeling is normal then?"

"What is normal, Amelia? Who decides? If that's how you're feeling, then it must be normal—your normal. If you're skeptical, ask questions. Don't be shy. Jesus welcomes challenging questions and will always tell you the truth."

They reached the door at the end of the hallway, and Simon looked at Amelia, his expression serious and full of unspoken thoughts as he spoke, "Amelia"

His voice carrying the weight of their journey ahead and the significance of the moment as he said her name. "Are you ready? Is your anticipation high? Do you want me to give you a minute before I open this door? Consider this building and your talk with Jesus as the pearly gates. Once you step out, you'll enter Heaven."

His eyes searched hers for a sign of readiness, the silence in the hallway as Amelia thought about the question amplifying the tension and anticipation between them. "I think I'm ready. Let's pull the band-aid off. But before you open the door, will I be surprised?"

"Amelia, if you aren't already surprised by this place, I think you will be."

"What does it look like out there?"

"Why don't we open it and see? My perspective won't match you seeing it with your own eyes."

"How about I close my eyes, and you guide me out?"

"Ready when you are."

Amelia closed her eyes and held her hand out to Simon.

Simon took her hand and pushed the door open.

As they stepped through, she felt moisture against her face that felt like a wet face cloth sitting on her skin, the scent of blooming flowers and fresh fruit took over her sense of smell.

Her skin felt warm, her heart raced with anticipation, each step they took bringing a mix of excitement and apprehension. When they finally stopped, Simon let the door close behind them and said,

"Open your eyes."

Amelia took a deep breath, savoring the fresh air, and slowly opened her eyes to the new world before her.

Chapter 4 - The Mask

2 Weeks Later

Kevan Harrison stood in front of church pews filled with hundreds of people, watching them sing and dance along to the music. The rich sound of the church organ resonated throughout the room as all the parishioners sang along, their eyes glued to the Book of Hymns.

The scent of candles and polished wood filled the air, creating a comforting and serene atmosphere. Kevan waited quietly, a sense of calm washing over him.

When the song finally ended, he stepped up to the podium at the front of the church.

The speakers crackled to life, and his voice, clear and strong, filled every corner of the sacred space.

"You may now be seated... As that was the final hymn of our mass today, we will now pass around the collection plate. I want you to continue to walk the righteous path our GOD Jesus has set out for you, and I look forward to seeing you all again."

The collection plates started to get passed around to all the parishioners, 70% of the people in the church had gotten up from their seats, and walked over to the convenient Donation Station that the church had setup where parishioners could tap a credit or debit card and donate as much as they wanted.

Kevan watched his followers file out of the church as they completed their donations until it was empty and quiet.

He loosened the collar on his shirt and removed the red priest's robe, letting it fall to the floor. Quietly he said to himself, "Finally, that is over. I don't know how much longer I can do this before I break."

The organ player, Alicia, had just finished and was leaving. She walked over, picked up the robe from the floor, and spoke in a concerned tone. "You okay, Father Harrison?"

Handing the robe to Kevan, she asked, "You seemed a bit distant during the hymn."

She looked at him with a mixture of concern and curiosity, hoping to understand what was troubling him. "Are you alright?"

Kevan replied hiding his true feelings, "Yes, Alicia, it was just a little warm in here today. Say hello to your parents for me."

Alicia responded kindly, "I will. Have a good day, Father."

After saying this her kind nice demeanor changed to stern and serious as she spoke, "And I really hope I don't see your robe on the floor again! I would hate to have to report you to the other High Priests"

Alicia walked past the pews and out of the front door of the church. Kevan mumbling under his breath retreated to the back room where his office and dwelling were.

Once in the back room as a sign of rebellion and the respect he had lost for the church, he tossed his robe onto the floor and then he sat down at his desk, which held two books: the Holy Bible and The Edicts of the Anointing Church of Jesus Christ.

At thirty-two years old, Kevan had devoted his life to the church since he was a young child, rising through its ranks.

His father, who died when Kevan was a teenager, had also been a High Priest. After his father's death, Kevan dedicated himself to becoming a High Priest to make his father proud.

Two years ago, he achieved this goal, becoming one of the 13 High Priests of The Anointing Church of Jesus Christ, the highest rank in the church.

However, Kevan now faced a significant problem: he no longer believed in God. After extensive research and study while becoming a High Priest, Kevan concluded that the Bible was filled with myths, stories, and fables written by men long ago with no supporting evidence.

He had become an atheist, hiding his disbelief from everyone.

If his true feelings were revealed, it would destroy everything he had built his life around.

For the past year, Kevan had started drinking at night, feeling depressed and alone, hiding from everyone, and putting on the mask of a High Priest when necessary.

Kevan had a ceremonial event to attend later that night, so he would sit in a catatonic state until it was time.

He set alarms to remind him of tasks, as he no longer cared enough to remember. Five hours passed before his alarm went off, and he stumbled to turn it off. Kevan had 30 minutes to get dressed in his ceremonial priest robe before the car arrived to take him to the ceremony.

All the High Priests would be there, and Kevan dreaded facing them.

This would be the first time since losing his faith that he would see all the high priests in one place. Kevan dressed in his red ceremonial robes and prepared his ceremonial hat, kept in its box unless being worn by a High Priest.

The hat was white, cylindrical with 2-inch frilled folds around the rim, and featured a white cross made of pure ivory.

Each High Priest's hat had a 24k solid gold statue of Jesus on the cross, making the hat difficult to wear for extended periods due to the weight of the ivory cross, and gold.

Kevan grabbed his keys and hat box and proceeded to the front doors of the church where the car would meet him.

Seeing a car with its lights on outside, he exited through the small side door and checked the large doors to ensure they were locked.

He then walked to the car, where the driver, Josh, got out and opened the backseat door for him. Kevan stepped in, and Josh closed the door.

The car radio was on, and Cindy Schrouder was speaking.

"That brings us to the close of today's episode of The Lost Files. I'm Cindy Schrouder, and it has been an honor to guide you through these deeply moving stories. Join us tomorrow as we delve into the heartache and resilience of the families of The Lost, sharing their personal journeys and diving into the latest developments of the ongoing investigations.

Remember, every piece of information counts. If you have any tips or clues about The Lost, please reach out to The Throne by dialing 119 on your mobile devices. Your vigilance and compassion make all the difference. Together, we can uncover the truth."

The driver Josh, a parishioner at Kevan's church, turned the radio down when he got back in the car and changed the station to one playing church music. "Sorry, Father. I just wanted to hear the end of that show, The Lost Files."

Inquisitively Kevan asked, "I heard something about The Lost the other day. What is it?"

"The Lost are people who have vanished—disappearances that all follow a distinct pattern."

His voice carried a quiet weight, the kind that made it clear he had thought about this too much, too often. "It's happening every day across the country, and investigators have found over 7,000 cases that match *The Lost Criterion.*"

Beside him, Father Kevan Harrison adjusted his robes, smoothing the fabric in an absent-minded gesture.

He furrowed his brow, turning toward Josh with growing curiosity. "The Lost Criterion? What exactly is that?"

Josh exhaled, the faintest hesitation flickering in his voice. "It's seven key similarities shared by every case—proof that they're all connected."

His fingers flexed around the wheel as he spoke, as though the very thought unsettled him.

A soft, uneasy chuckle escaped Father Kevan's lips, meant to ease the tension though it barely made a dent in the growing weight between them. "Well, let's hope we make it to our destination without joining their ranks."

He exhaled, then glanced toward Josh with quiet gratitude. "Thanks for coming to pick me up tonight."

Josh offered a small nod, checking the rearview mirror before shifting his focus back to the front. "No problem, Father Harrison. Do you have everything before we head out?"

Kevan patted his lap, nodding lightly. "I've got my robes, my hat, and myself. That's all I'll need this evening—I'm ready."

Josh gave a small smile. "Then let's go. I'll get you there safely."

The car eased forward, the tires rolling smoothly over the asphalt as they left the parking lot behind. Outside, the darkness pressed in, swallowing the world beyond the headlights.

The church music filled the small space between them, a calming contrast to the unease lingering in the air. Josh broke the silence after a moment.

"That was a great mass today, Father. You brought my mother to tears." His voice had softened, carrying something warmer now—admiration, maybe even reverence.

Kevan turned slightly, his expression softening. "I hope they were tears of joy."

Josh chuckled lightly. "They were. You spoke three Bible verses that hold deep personal meaning for her—it felt like the message was meant just for her."

Kevan nodded thoughtfully. "If it's what she needed to hear, then I'm grateful I chose those verses."

His fingers found the fabric of his robes again, smoothing them unconsciously.

Josh's voice dipped slightly, something heavier settling in his tone. "She's been struggling lately. You remember my grandmother's passing three months ago? She hasn't been the same since."

Kevan exhaled, sympathy settling into his expression. "Loss weighs differently on all of us."

His voice was quieter now, thoughtful. "All we can do is stand beside those we love in times of grief."

He turned toward Josh, his gaze steady. "How are you handling it?"

Traffic was light on the two-lane highway, the glow of streetlights casting long shadows over the pavement.

A car passed them in the opposite lane, its headlights momentarily cutting through the darkness before fading behind them. Another set of lights appeared in the distance.

Josh's hands rested loosely on the steering wheel, though his expression remained thoughtful. "I miss my grandmother and think about her every day. It's tough, but those times pass, and I move on."

He exhaled, his fingers tapping idly against the wheel. "It seems those tough times don't pass for my mother, though."

Kevan sat quietly for a moment, adjusting the fabric of his robes before speaking. "Let your mother know she can always come and talk to me if you think it might help." His voice was warm, filled with the gentle reassurance of someone accustomed to offering comfort.

Josh nodded, then hesitated. "I will, Father."

He glanced sideways at Kevan, the glow of the dashboard reflecting in his eyes. "Can I ask you something... that maybe I shouldn't?"

Kevan turned slightly, watching him with mild curiosity. "You can ask me anything, Josh. What do you mean by 'shouldn't'?"

Josh exhaled, his grip tightening briefly before relaxing again. "I wanted to ask if you've ever had any doubts—about our faith, about our Lord and Savior, or about Heaven."

The older man's expression softened, though there was an unmistakable weight behind his words when he spoke. "We all have times when we question our beliefs and what we've been taught."

His gaze lingered on Josh for a moment, thoughtful. "Are you having problems with your faith?"

Josh shook his head slowly. "Not really. I was just thinking... with my mother being so upset after her mother's passing—if her mother is in Heaven, like our faith tells us, why is she still so distraught? Why can't she move on? Unless—"

He hesitated, choosing his words carefully. "Unless she doesn't really believe her mother is in Heaven."

Kevan sighed, his fingers lacing together in his lap. "When we lose people who have always been in our lives, it can be hard to cope with their absence. Not being able to talk to them or touch them—even if we believe they're in a better place—it still hurts to not have them around."

Silence settled over them, the soft hum of the engine and the faint notes of church music filling the space between them.

Josh cleared his throat. "Let's change the subject from something upsetting. It should be a spectacular ceremony tonight."

Kevan smiled, the weariness momentarily lifting from his features. "Whenever I get to wear my High Priest hat, it's always a time I look forward to."

He leaned back slightly, then gestured toward the radio. "Can you turn it up a little? I love the organ playing in this song."

Josh turned the radio up slightly, and they drove on in silence, listening to the music. They reached a section of the highway without lights, making it very dark.

Kevan, sitting in the backseat, closed his eyes, absorbing the music and the superb organ playing. Josh drifted to the right side of their lane as a car approached them in the opposite lane.

At the last moment, the approaching car swerved and smashed into the driver-side front tire. The impact was sudden and violent, causing their car to skid sideways across the road.

The tires screeched against the asphalt, leaving dark marks behind as the vehicle spun around uncontrollably. Time seemed to slow down as the world outside became a blur of motion.

Then, with a terrifying jolt, the car flipped over, the sound of crunching metal and shattering glass filling the air.

Inside, Kevan and Josh were tossed around like ragdolls, their bodies slamming against the interior with bone-jarring force. the passenger seat became dislodged and pinned Kevan into the backseat.

When the violent motion ceased the car came to rest upside down. An eerie silence followed both Kevan and Josh laid unconscious, the chaos of the accident leaving them in a state of suspended darkness.

Kevan regained consciousness after a short time, yelling as he felt the pressure and pain on his body. The front seat was putting painful pressure on Kevan's arm and leg, preventing him from moving or opening the door to free himself.

He heard sirens and saw flashing lights, realizing that paramedics or police had arrived. He heard a vehicle pull up, two doors closing, and voices.

One of the paramedics opened the door that had pinned Kevan. "Let me just give you something to help with the pain, and then I'll help you out of there."

Kevan watched as the paramedic stuck a needle in his arm, feeling the sharp prick followed by a cold sensation spreading through his veins.

He tried to speak, but his mouth felt dry, and the words stuck in his throat. His vision blurred, and he struggled to stay conscious, his mind a foggy haze of pain.

The sound of the paramedic's reassuring voice reached his ears, but the words seemed distant and muffled.

He tried to focus, his eyes fluttering as he fought against the darkness threatening to pull him under.

Chapter 5 - I am not supposed to be here

esus sat in the all-white room, his long hair and scruff on his face, his facial hair growing in over the past few days. Dressed in a pair of worn jeans and a white button-up shirt, he cut a casual yet contemplative figure.

Seated in a chair, he twirled his thumbs anxiously, his gaze fixed on the couch across from him, where Kevan Harrison lay face down in a pillow.

The room was quiet, save for the soft sound of breathing coming from Kevan. Jesus's anxiety was palpable as he waited for Kevan to wake.

As Kevan began to shuffle, a soft groan escaping his lips, his eyes fluttered open. He slowly pushed himself up, blinking away the remnants of sleep, and met Jesus's intense, anxious gaze.

"Finally, you are awake. I have been waiting."

Kevan sat up, his gaze moving from Jesus to the stark white walls that surrounded them. The room was bare, with nothing but two doors at opposite ends breaking the monotony.

He felt a sense of unease creeping in as he tried to make sense of his surroundings.

Turning his eyes back to Jesus, his voice edged with suspicion, he asked, "What is this? Who are you?"

Jesus calmly responded in a warm welcoming tone, "Relax, Kevan. You are in a safe place."

Not satisfied with the answer, Kevan grew tense, the muscles in his shoulders tightening.

His irritation was obvious as he looked around the room again, his eyes darting from the sterile white walls to the two doors at opposite ends of the space.

The questions tumbled out in rapid succession, each one more insistent than the last. "Why won't you tell me? Where am I? What happened to Josh?"

"All of your questions will be answered, Kevan, but first, I need you to drink the three drinks in front of you on the table."

Raising an eyebrow, Kevan asked suspiciously, his eyes narrowed as he scrutinized Jesus's expression, searching for any hint of what the drinks were.

The silence in the room felt heavy, charged with unspoken questions and doubts awaiting his decision to take the drinks. "What are these drinks, why are they smoking?"

Twirling his thumbs, Jesus calmly responded, "Kevan, I understand your frustration. This situation is far from ordinary, but there's a purpose behind it. Trust me, things will become clearer soon."

His voice was steady and reassuring, his demeanor unchanged.

The calmness in his tone was a stark contrast to the growing agitation in the room, and it seemed to hold a promise of answers yet to come. "You can ask me any questions you want, but I can only answer them after you have taken the three drinks."

Feeling tricked, Kevan asked, "Why do I get the sense you're keeping something from me?"

His voice was laced with suspicion, and his eyes bore into Jesus's, demanding honesty. The tension in the room grew thicker, as did Kevan's frustration.

He needed answers, and he needed them now. He continued asking, "So you won't even tell me what the drinks are until after I drink them?"

"All of your questions will be answered after you have taken the three drinks."

Offended that he was seemingly being forced to consume the drinks, a mixture of anger and disbelief.

He glanced at the half-filled glasses on the table, his irritation growing.

The thought of being manipulated in such a way made his blood boil. He asked truly wanting to know, "So what happens if I choose not to drink them?"

"If you choose not to drink... no one has ever asked me that question before.

If you choose not to drink,

I will sit here in silence.

I can't answer your questions,

and you cannot leave this room by exiting that door right over there."

Jesus pointed at the door on the other side of the room, his eyes steady and unwavering.

Jesus continued speaking, his voice carrying a sense of gravity. "That door holds the answers you're seeking."

Curious to know what was beyond the door Kevan was still opposed to taking the drinks he asked, "So we will just sit here then... What is to stop me from getting up and walking out that door?"

Irritated Jesus responded, "Why be so stubborn, Kevan? The place you are in has rules, and those rules must always be followed.

No one else who has been on that couch has objected to the three drinks. I assure you, where you are is a safe place, and a place you will want to be.

Just have a drink; it will not hurt you, I promise. Here, nothing will ever hurt you again."

"I've learned not to always trust what others tell me,"

Kevan muttered, his voice edged with quiet frustration. "I've been duped too many times, and this whole situation seems suspicious."

His fingers curled slightly as he spoke, his posture rigid with unease.

A calm yet resolute voice cut through the tension.

"Kevan, I want to explain everything to you—what has happened, how you got here, and what happened to your friend, Josh. But you must drink."

Kevan hesitated, studying the vessel before him, the weight of the request settling into his chest.

His eyes flickered with uncertainty, searching the face before him for deception.

"I will drink because it seems I must,"

He said slowly, "but this better not be some kind of trick."

Jesus met his gaze with unwavering sincerity, his presence radiating a quiet certainty. "Kevan, I have no reason to trick you. I will never lie to you."

Kevan took down the first drink, feeling a warm sensation spread throughout his body and a sweet taste linger in his mouth.

Encouraged by the invigorating feeling, he downed the second drink in two quick gulps, slamming the cup down on the table with a sense of defiance.

Without hesitation, he grabbed the third cup, drained it, and slammed it down with a final, resounding thud.

His eyes locked onto Jesus, his expression a mixture of determination and challenge. "Now then, where am I........?"

Kevan's eyes rolled back, and his body began to convulse on the couch. His limbs jerked uncontrollably, and a guttural sound escaped his lips.

The convulsions lasted for what felt like an eternity, but in reality, it was only thirty seconds.

When the spasms finally subsided, his body went limp, and he lay still, breathing heavily.

Slowly, consciousness returned, and he blinked, disoriented and exhausted. The room seemed to spin around him as he tried to make sense of what had just happened.

"What in God's name just happened?"

"You are fine now, Kevan. It's normal when the drinks are taken."

Jesus's voice was steady, reassuring, but Kevan still felt the lingering unease crawling beneath his skin. He leaned forward, his eyes wide with anticipation, eager to finally receive the answers he had been chasing.

The room seemed to hum with tension, his mind racing through a maze of questions, each one demanding to be spoken.

"So, who are you?" His voice wavered slightly, unsure but insistent.

Jesus twirled his thumbs slowly, the movement deliberate, almost meditative. "My name is Jesus."

Kevan's breath hitched. His eyes widened in shock, the realization striking like a jolt to his spine.

He felt something churn deep within him—a mixture of confusion, disbelief, and something dangerously close to fear. "What...?"

His voice was barely more than a whisper, disbelief threading through every syllable.

Jesus remained calm, his tone unwavering. "You died after the accident, Kevan. Do you remember the accident?"

Kevan swallowed, the memory flashing before him in fragmented bursts.

"The car flipped...

Josh wasn't moving in the driver's seat...

I was still conscious when the ambulance showed up..."

He paused, recalling the strange moment when the paramedic stuck him with a needle before even asking his permission.

It had seemed wrong, illogical—but he kept the thought to himself.

"I don't remember much after that. If you are Jesus, where am I? Is this a dream?"

Jesus stopped twirling his thumbs and spread his arms wide, gesturing to the space around them. His voice was calm, deliberate.

"I assure you, this is not a dream, even though it might seem that way. Kevan, you are in Heaven. I have chosen you to come here."

His gaze met Kevan's with a quiet intensity, a sense of purpose woven into the certainty of his words. But Kevan's skepticism burned brighter.

He had long denounced God, had abandoned faith years ago—so how could he be *chosen* to go to Heaven?

The idea was absurd. Impossible.

He studied Jesus, suspicion tightening in his chest.

The stark white walls, the two unmarked doors—it all felt surreal, wrong.

His heartbeat quickened. "What happened to Josh in the accident?"

"You and Josh died together in the accident."

Kevan inhaled sharply. "If Josh died too, can I see him? He should be here too."

Jesus's expression didn't change. "Josh was not one of the chosen ones."

Kevan frowned, confusion twisting into frustration. "Josh was a devout follower of you. His life's goal was to pass your judgment and make it into Heaven. How, if I am here, is he not?"

Jesus's voice was steady. "Kevan, you are a devout follower too. You were a High Priest within the Anointing Church of Jesus Christ. Josh was not worthy of the position here that I have given you. As a High Priest, you are probably very familiar with what the Bible stories say."

Kevan clenched his jaw. "I have studied the book my whole life. Of course, I know what it says."

Jesus exhaled. "The smartest thing you could do is forget everything you were taught about God and the Bible. All of it is stories of men being very imaginative. Nothing works the way the Bible explains it does."

Kevan's stomach tightened. "I don't even know what that means, but if this is Heaven, I am not supposed to be here."

Jesus's gaze remained fixed. "You are supposed to be here because I brought you here, and you are here."

Kevan let out a dry, humorless laugh. "So, I walk out that door and enter into some Garden of Eden-style Heaven setting? No evil, no hunger, no suffering?"

"Yes, Kevan, it is exactly like that. You are free to leave whenever you choose if you have asked all the questions, you want answered. We can always talk again if you have more questions."

Kevan rubbed his temples, his mind spiraling through a thousand thoughts at once. "I have a million questions running through my head. Let me think about what the best questions would be to ask."

Jesus folded his hands gently in his lap twirling his thumbs. "Why don't you lay back down, close your eyes, and sleep on it? I will be here waiting for you when you wake up, and we can continue the conversation."

Chapter 6 - The Mechanics of Heaven

Kevan awoke to the smell of his favorite foods, arranged on the table in an array of three dishes.

The first was a plate of perfectly cooked prime rib that melted and fell apart just by looking at it.

The second was eggs Benedict made with peameal bacon, swimming in hollandaise sauce.

The third was a Cajun chicken quesadilla, over-spiced and cut into five pieces, with Cajun sour cream for dipping.

Kevan picked up a fork, the scent of the food stirring something deep within him—nostalgia, warmth, a strange familiarity. "Thank you, I am starving."

Jesus offered a knowing smile, gesturing toward the spread before him. "I hope you like the food I have prepared for you."

Kevan's gaze flickered across the dishes, his expression shifting from appreciation to astonishment. "Do you even have to ask?"

He let out a quiet chuckle, shaking his head. "These are my favorite foods. I ate these dishes almost every week."

He hesitated, gripping the fork slightly tighter. "I would ask you how you knew, but..."

He trailed off, the unspoken thought lingering in the air between them. Kevan started to fill his mouth with the prime rib, the savory aroma tantalizing his senses.

The tender meat practically melted in his mouth, rich flavors dancing on his taste buds.

For a moment, the world seemed to fade away, and he was lost in the simple pleasure of the meal.

But even as he ate, the nagging thoughts of his current predicament lingered in the back of his mind,

"I know everything about you, Kevan. I will always speak the truth to you, but eat up. We can talk when you are done eating. Take the time to think of questions."

Kevan continued, going from plate to plate, taking mouthfuls and creatively mixing the dishes together, tasting two at once and then all three.

When he finished, he sat back on the couch and spoke. "Jesus, that was the best meal I have ever had."

Jesus leaned back slightly, his expression calm yet unwavering. "I thought you would like that. Considering the accident was on a Thursday, and you ate those dishes each week on Friday, Saturday, and Sunday—you didn't get to have them the week I brought you here."

Kevan placed his fork down, savoring the lingering taste of the meal. "Well, I have now, and those dishes were the best of the best that I have had anywhere."

Jesus smiled, a quiet satisfaction in his expression. "I am glad you enjoyed it. So, do you have any questions?"

Kevan glanced toward the door, a new thought forming in his mind. "Are there other people outside that door?"

Jesus nodded without hesitation. "Of course there are, Kevan. There are 6,374 of my followers here."

Kevan frowned slightly, his fingers tapping absently against the table. "Okay, because I'm sure the most basic questions they could answer."

He inhaled, steadying himself. "So, my first question is, why are there only 6,374 people here?"

Jesus's reply was immediate. "They are the only followers worthy to be chosen."

Kevan's posture stiffened, his frustration creeping into his voice. "How is that possible? Billions of people follow your way every day."

Jesus remained composed. "Billions of people do not deserve a place here."

Kevan felt the weight of those words settle inside him, heavy and unsettling.

He narrowed his eyes. "What is it that I—or we—have done to become a chosen one?"

Jesus's voice carried a quiet certainty, firm yet compassionate. "You are asking a question that would take years to explain in words. Some of the words I would need to describe this to you do not even exist in the English language.

Kevan, there are billions of different variables that affect the decision of who the chosen ones are. For me, it all happens in the back of my mind with very little thought, like processes in your subconscious. The chosen ones appear on the couch, and I welcome them here."

Kevan exhaled slowly, trying to process the enormity of what was being said. The words felt weighty, definitive—and yet, they left him with even more questions.

Even though he did not get an answer to his question, he understood why, and that felt satisfying.

Kevan exhaled, trying to wrap his mind around the explanation.

It was vague. Too vague. But before he could press further, another thought pushed its way forward.

"The church always taught that we were given free will, but not a free mind. That God could see into our individual thoughts, and we were always supposed to have faith in Him and pure moral thoughts that he would approve of. My two-part question is—was that true? And how does that work here? Can you see what I'm thinking, Jesus?"

Jesus stopped twirling his thumbs and folded his hands together in his lap. "The trinity of GOD you knew were stages of GOD or evolutions."

He began gesturing as he spoke, his movements deliberate, measured.

"The trinity was not all one, but each was its own individual stage of GOD. Now, and since the beginning of creation, I have been Jesus, and I am a man."

Kevan stiffened slightly at the words. As Jesus continued,

"The powers of GOD went with the title when creation started. However, I can still give you whatever you desire here in this paradise. Most of my time is occupied with meetings and talks like we are having now and satisfying everyone's desires. So, the answer to your question is—you have always had a free mind and free will, and you still do here."

Kevan let the words settle, turning them over in his mind. But instead of clarity, he felt something raw rise within him—something that had been buried for far too long.

He didn't believe in God anymore. Hadn't for a long time. And yet, a lifetime of indoctrination clawed at him in this moment.

He erupted without warning. "THE RELIGION I DEVOTED MY LIFE TO WAS ALL A LIE?!"

Jesus's expression didn't change. If the outburst unsettled him, he didn't show it. "The word 'lie' is so harsh, Kevan. The trinity is real. I, Jesus, am real. And the Holy Spirit will exist when I do not anymore.

The understanding that humans had was not correct, but somehow, they figured that part out. After that, I think they just kept writing stories—building off older myths to fill in the blanks. Humans are storytellers, and it happened everywhere in the world."

He paused, then continued. "Kevan, there were over 100,000 different understandings of GOD—call them all the different religions—that carried different beliefs. None of them were correct, but I wouldn't exactly call them a lie."

Kevan's mind reeled, his heart pounding against his ribs. He narrowed his eyes. "What would you call them? My religion was pounded into my head when I was a baby—before I could even speak or understand the words I was hearing. My first word spoken was your name, Jesus, because my mother always said it."

Jesus smiled softly. "I am flattered, Kevan. I would call them evolutions of the human mind and imagination."

Kevan inhaled sharply. That word.

It wasn't supposed to be uttered. Not in his faith. He repeated the word tasting foreign on his tongue. "Evolutions..."

Jesus nodded. "Yes, Kevan. Evolutions. Much like the word 'lie,' it is just a word to display an idea. Words and language are no more than that."

He studied Kevan for a moment. "Let me ask you this—do you feel like you lied when bringing people into your church and doing mass four times a week?"

Kevan clenched his jaw. He had been an atheist for over a year now, and in that time, yes—he had felt like a fraud. Like he was wearing a mask to fool those around him.

But before?

When he believed?

When he had faith?

No. He hadn't felt like a liar then.

And he understood exactly what Jesus was trying to say.

"No, I don't feel like I was lying."

He paused. "But I am curious as to why you would use the word 'evolution.' In my church, that word was practically banned."

Jesus chuckled lightly. "No word in any language can cause harm or hurt. Evolution is the best word to describe creation and everything in existence.

Everything changes and evolves over time—from the atomic and molecular level to life, the human body, the human mind and imagination. The world has never remained stagnant, Kevan."

Kevan exhaled slowly, trying to steady his thoughts. Jesus gestured toward the door. "Your guide, Amelia, has been here for a couple of weeks. She will be able to fill you in. Whenever you are ready—just stand up and walk out that door."

Kevan tried to think if there were any more important questions he wanted to ask, but he couldn't think of any.

He stood up and started walking towards the door. Jesus stood up from his chair, and just as Kevan was about to touch the door, Jesus spoke, his voice filled with unexpected warmth.

"Kevan!"

Kevan stopped in his tracks at the sound of his name, turning slowly to face Jesus.

Jesus's expression was sincere—unwavering in its intensity.

"I love you, Kevan."

Kevan inhaled sharply. His eyes widened, uncertainty flickering across his face.

The words felt strange, unfamiliar in this context, and for a long moment, he simply stood there, searching Jesus's face for hidden meaning.

At last, his voice emerged, quiet and uncertain. "... I love you too, Jesus."

Kevan hesitated only briefly before stepping toward the door. He pushed it open, blinking at the sight of a woman waiting on the other side.

She met his gaze with a calm demeanor, her posture confident yet inviting.

He nodded. "You must be Amelia."

The door clicked shut behind him, sealing the space he had just left. Amelia took a step forward, offering her hand. Her grip was firm but warm, and her smile carried a quiet sense of reassurance.

"I don't know if I *must* be Amelia, but that's the name my parents gave me. It could have been anything though."

She said with a playful smirk. "Are you ready to go?"

Kevan exhaled, rubbing the back of his neck. "Just give me one minute. That was an awkward conversation... especially at the end."

Amelia chuckled, gesturing toward the dimly lit hallway ahead. "I was weirded right out when Jesus told me he loved me too. That feeling fades quickly. Let's walk this way."

She led him forward, her strides confident and deliberate.

The hallway stretched ahead, quiet and shadowed, the faint glow of overhead lights casting long silhouettes along the walls.

Kevan followed her lead, curiosity mixing with growing anticipation.

"How long have you been here, Amelia?" he asked.

"About two weeks now," she replied, her voice steady.

"And after that time... what do you think of this place?"

Amelia stopped, turning toward him with an unexpected warmth. She placed a hand on his shoulder and met his gaze directly. "I know you're skeptical,"

She said carefully, "But it seems to be exactly what we're told—a paradise, a heaven."

She smiled, but there was weight behind her words. "I was skeptical when I first got here too. But after some time... I couldn't find a reason *not* to believe it. This place gives us everything we need or want."

Kevan studied her expression, searching for cracks—some trace of doubt beneath the surface. But there was none.

The door ahead loomed closer, its smooth surface catching the low light as they approached. Something about it held a quiet promise of answers, a gateway to whatever was waiting beyond.

Kevan inhaled deeply. "I guess I'll have to see it for myself to believe it."

Amelia nodded. "It's right through this door. Are you ready?"

"I think I am. What else do I have to do?"

Amelia smiled. "When I stepped through this door, I kept my eyes closed so I could take it all in at once when I opened them. Do you want to try that?"

Kevan let a smirk cross his lips, though there was an edge of nerves beneath it. "They're already closed. Let's go."

Without hesitation, he raised his arm, extending his hand toward Amelia.

She took it firmly, the warmth of her grip grounding him as they moved forward.

A quiet click echoed through the space as the door swung open. They stepped through together, leaving the dim hallway behind.

Six deliberate steps.

Each one carrying anticipation.

Each one inching closer to whatever lay beyond.

Finally, the door closed behind them. The sound was final, like the sealing of something unspoken.

Amelia's voice broke the silence, steady and sure.

"Okay, I'll count to three, and then you can open your eyes. One... two... three.

Open your eyes!"

Chapter 7 - The Observer

ustin Standone stood at the precipice of the cliff, watching the rocks tumble down the jagged surface before disappearing into the water below. Each bounce echoed faintly, swallowed by the vastness of the canyon.

His pulse thrummed in his veins, adrenaline rushing through him as he lingered at the edge.

The thrill of standing so close to danger sent a charge through his body—until instinct pulled him back, urging him to step away.

He exhaled deeply, filling his lungs with the crisp, wild air. "Whoo hoo!"

His voice rang out over the open expanse. "That feels good. Are you sure you don't want to try it?"

Ten feet away, Martin stood rigidly at the junction where the trail met the cliff, trees rising protectively on either side of him.

He shook his head, his arms crossed as he watched his friend with measured caution. "No, I'm okay,"

He said firmly. "I don't need to be risking the life that GOD gave me."

Justin scoffed, turning toward him. "What risk? There's a fence to stop you from falling—if you think you might fall."

Martin glanced at the weathered fence, his skepticism plain. He shifted his weight slightly, still keeping his distance.

"The risk is... over here, I *can't* fall off a cliff. If I go near the edge, the probability of that happening goes up. So, I'm happy to stay put. I don't like heights."

Justin grinned, shaking his head. "I'm telling you, Martin, it feels just like that feeling we get in church—when we're all happy, singing and dancing together as a group."

Martin let out a short chuckle. "I'm happy to wait until the next time we go to church to get that feeling again."

He glanced at his watch. "Are you done? Can we go?"

Justin sighed, a hint of frustration in his voice. "You never want to have any fun."

He gave one last look at the drop before turning back toward the trail. "Let's go."

They started down the brush-covered path leading away from the cliffside. Leaves crunched beneath their boots, and the air buzzed with the sounds of unseen insects and distant bird calls. The forest pressed in around them, filtering sunlight through its branches.

They had separated from the main hiking group earlier—Justin had been eager to see the lookout first, while the others had opted to visit the waterfall.

Now, with time ticking away, they hoped to catch up.

As they walked, Justin broke the silence. "I forgot to tell you—I got accepted into Seminary."

Martin's eyes lit up. "I haven't heard anything back yet. When is it supposed to start?"

"Six months or so. There's still time for you to get accepted too."

Martin nodded thoughtfully. "I'd love to. We could go together. I always get weirded out by those old priest teachers that are there."

Justin laughed. "Yeah, me too. My parents will be thrilled."

They emerged onto a wider portion of the trail, where sunlight streamed more freely through the canopy above.

Justin glanced down the path. "You want to go see the waterfall? Maybe we can catch up to the group. It's been a good retreat, spending the day in nature."

Martin checked his watch again. "Yeah, I had fun. It's 2:00. If we want to see the waterfall and still make it back to the bus by 3:30, we should go now."

Justin clapped a hand on his friend's shoulder. "Let's get moving."

They saw the waterfall and met up with the group on the bus.

It was an hour's drive back to the church where everyone had parked their cars. The same yellow school bus that dropped them off was waiting in the parking lot at 3:30. Most people were already in the parking lot, getting onto the bus.

On the bus ride home, everyone mostly kept to themselves, conversing. About six times during the hour drive, someone started singing church songs about Jesus, and the whole bus would sing along together before falling back into their conversations.

Martin and Justin were talking in their seats. The hum of the bus quieted as it came to a stop in the church parking lot.

Passengers stirred, gathering their belongings, the muted shuffle of feet filling the space as they moved toward the front doors in orderly single file.

Justin glanced at Martin. "You got a ride home?"

Martin pulled out his phone. "I just have to call my mom. She was going to pick me up."

Justin shook his head. "Don't worry about it. I'll give you a ride home—I need to stop for gas anyway."

Martin hesitated briefly, then nodded. "Okay, just let me call her so she doesn't get worried."

With his mother informed, Martin climbed into the passenger seat of Justin's car. The city faded behind them as they drove onto the quiet back roads, the trees stretching tall on either side.

The scent of pine and damp earth seeped in through the vents, mixing with the familiar tune of Christian songs playing softly in the background.

Martin broke the silence, staring out at the darkening sky. "What do you think Heaven is like?"

Justin kept his focus on the road, his fingers tapping idly on the steering wheel. "I think Heaven will be different from anything man has ever said it will be. No one can know, and what we've been told are just man's best guesses. I have faith in Heaven and Jesus—but not necessarily in the specifics we've been led to believe."

Martin tilted his head. "Doesn't that go against Jesus? Not believing in the Heaven talked about in the Bible?"

Justin's expression remained thoughtful, his voice steady. "I don't think so. I don't believe we're penalized for our thoughts in that way. We were given imagination—we're meant to use it. If we find our way to Jesus, we will be saved."

The conversation settled between them, quiet but lingering.

Three cars passed in the oncoming lane, their headlights momentarily streaking across the windshield. The sun dipped lower, casting warm hues over the empty highway.

Then, the opening chords of *Heaven's Hymn* by Will Pickham floated from the radio, its melody wrapping around them like a familiar embrace.

Justin leaned back in his seat, a faint smile on his lips. "I love this song. Let's just sit back and listen to what Will Pickham thinks about Heaven."

Heaven is a place we will one day see

Heaven is the place that Jesus will be

Heaven, we want it, we strive for that day

Nothing can stop us, we already know the way

Martin said to Justin, "If you think Heaven will be different, do you still think we will get to see our loved ones that have passed on?"

Justin responded, "The most honest answer I can give you is I don't know. I do have faith that everyone that found and followed Jesus will be there, so your loved ones should."

Martin pointed and said, "There's the gas station."

Justin pulled into the gas station. The night enveloped the station in darkness, the overhead lights casting a dim glow that barely pierced the shadows. The silence was almost eerie, with no other cars in sight, adding to the sense of isolation. The only sounds were the low hum of the fluorescent lights and the distant chirping of crickets.

As Justin turned off the engine, the ticking of the cooling metal could be heard, emphasizing the stillness of the night.

Martin said, "I need to go to the bathroom, I don't think I can wait until I get home. I'm going to get the key from the clerk."

"Just meet me out here when you are done."

Martin walked into the store and got the key for the bathroom. It was down the right side of the building, closer to the back wall of the gas station.

When Martin approached the door and unlocked it, he was surprised to see a man sitting on the toilet with the seat down.

He was wearing a hood and a medical mask over his face. "I'm sorry, I didn't realize anyone was in here. I got the key from the clerk."

"I am done in here anyway."

The man got up and walked out the door, brushing past Martin without a saying another word.

Martin watched him leave, a hint of tension in his eyes.

As the door started to swing shut, Martin stepped inside, the cool air of the room a stark contrast to the warmth outside.

He closed the door behind him with a soft click, then turned the lock.

Out in the front of the gas station, Justin was standing beside his car, staring at the counter on the gas pump as it rolled up higher and higher while he pumped gas into his tank.

He seen someone come down the right side of the building out of the corner of his eye and assumed it was Martin coming back, so he didn't pay any attention and continued staring at the counter.

After about ten seconds, a voice came from behind Justin and spoke. "Hey!"

Justin turned around to face the voice, his heart pounding in his chest. About ten feet away stood a man, dressed entirely in black.

The man's jeans, jacket, and hooded sweater blended seamlessly into the shadows of the night. A medical mask covered his face, obscuring his features and adding an unsettling anonymity to his presence.

Justin asked, "Hello. Can I help you?"

The dim light from the gas station flickered across the man's eyes, which were the only visible part of his face.

They seemed to bore into Justin, cold and unyielding. Justin's mind raced as he tried to make sense of who this man was, the unexpected encounter sending a shiver down his spine.

Staying silent, the man took a few steps towards Justin.

Justin's body tensed, as a wave of instinctual defensiveness washed over him.

He released his grip on the gas pump, the nozzle clacking back into the closed position, and took a cautious step backwards.

His mind raced, trying to gauge the intentions of this mysterious figure. "What are you doing? Stay back, don't try anything."

Immediately, the man lunged at Justin, producing a knife from behind his back. Justin was caught off guard, and the blade sank into his left shoulder.

Pain shot through his body, and he gasped, his mind struggling to process the sudden attack.

The hooded man pulled the knife out, the sound of the blade ripping flesh echoing in the stillness of the night, the man turned his back and walked away without a word.

Justin stood there in shock, his hand instinctively reaching for his wounded shoulder. Blood poured out, running down his arm like a river and dripping from his fingertips in a constant stream.

The world around him seemed to blur, the edges of his vision darkening. He felt his strength ebbing away, his legs growing weak. Unable to hold on any longer, he passed out and fell to the ground, the cold pavement a harsh contrast to the warmth of his blood.

Martin came out of the bathroom and walked down the side of the building. He glanced over to see if Justin was still pumping gas and noticed Justin lying on the ground.

Only Justin's feet were visible, sticking out from behind the gas pump.

Panic surged through Martin as he ran over, the bathroom key still clutched in his hand.

When he reached Justin, he saw the puddle of blood beneath him and screamed out, his voice echoing in the silence, "JUSTIN, NO!"

Horrified by the sight of Justin lying in a puddle of blood, Martin's heart raced with panic.

Without a second thought, he sprinted into the gas station store, his footsteps echoing in the empty night.

Bursting through the door, he yelled, his voice filled with urgency and fear, "HELP! CALL 911! MY FRIEND NEEDS HELP!"

The Clerk responded, "Is he okay? Where is he?"

Martin frantic, "He is at the pump. There is lots of blood. Please call now."

The clerk fumbled to pick up the phone, his hands shaking slightly after hearing the word 'blood.'

Panic set in as he pushed three buttons on the phone, his mind racing with the urgency of the situation. "911, what is your emergency?"

"I am not exactly sure what happened. I work at a gas station, and there is a man that needs help. He is bleeding outside."

The clerk and Martin looked at each other, confused, as they watched an ambulance pull into the gas station.

The paramedics swiftly loaded Justin's body into the back of the ambulance and drove off, sirens blaring. At that exact moment, the dispatcher on the phone asked, "What is the address of the gas station?"

The surreal timing left both the clerk and Martin in a state of bewilderment, struggling to comprehend the rapid sequence of events that had just unfolded. "I think we are okay. An ambulance was just here and picked him up."

The dispatcher responded confused, "What do you mean an ambulance was just there?

Every ambulance in the city is dispatched from this office, and I haven't dispatched an ambulance to your location yet."

"I don't know. They must have been driving by or something. Two paramedics got out and put the man on a stretcher and into the back of the ambulance."

In a serious tone the dispatcher responded, "What is the address, sir?"

"It's the gas station on Hollowby Rd. I don't know the exact address. It is like ten thousand something. It is just north of Highway 82. The official name is Gas Guzzlers, but all the signs outside just say gas station."

"I don't see an ambulance dispatched to your location. I am sending the police to investigate. Did you notice the license plate or truck number of the ambulance?"

"I didn't see the license plate or anything."

The clerk asked Martin. And he responded, "No, it was too far away."

The dispatcher said, "The police are on their way."

Chapter 8 - The Observed

esus sat with his long hair, clean-shaven face, and a pair of jeans paired with a white button-up shirt. He was seated in his chair, hands clenched in his lap, twirling his thumbs.

His gaze was fixed on a man who lay face down on the couch across from him. An array of three half-filled glasses sat side by side on the table in front of the couch, a constant presence whenever someone occupied it.

Jesus waited patiently, his thumbs still twirling in his lap, as the man on the couch stirred.

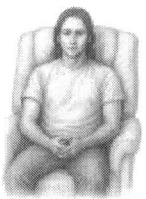

The man rolled over and opened his eyes, blinking as he took in his surroundings of the all-white room.

Justin Standone blinked against the stark white walls surrounding him, their eerie silence pressing in on his senses. The emptiness of the space felt unnatural—too pristine, too calculated.

A strange tension coiled in his chest as he took a slow breath, trying to steady himself. His gaze finally settled on Jesus, and he spoke, his voice carrying a mixture of confusion and curiosity.

"Where in the hell am I?"

His voice cut through the stillness, sharp but uncertain.

Jesus sat across from him, his posture calm, his presence radiating an undeniable certainty. "You're not in hell, that's for sure, so don't worry about that."

His tone was steady, almost soothing. "Why don't we start with your name?"

Justin hesitated only briefly before replying, his voice measured. "My name is Justin Standone."

He gestured toward Jesus, then swept his hand around the immaculate room. "Who are you, and where am I?"

Jesus mirrored his movement, pointing back at him. His gaze was unwavering—an odd combination of authority and compassion that made Justin uneasy.

"When you leave this room, Justin, all your questions will be answered. Let's take it slow, one question at a time."

He paused, then continued, his tone unchanged. "But before we do that, I need you to drink the three drinks on the table in front of you."

Justin's eyes drifted to the table. Three half-filled glasses sat there, their presence almost ominous in the stark surroundings. The liquid inside was still, unassuming, but carried the weight of something unspoken.

Jesus rejoined his hands, his thumbs moving in slow, endless circles as he waited.

Justin's mind raced, weighing his options. The room gave him nothing—no answers, no clues. Just Jesus, seated calmly, watching him with patience that felt both unnerving and inviting.

"I would never lie to you, Justin,"

Jesus said, his voice as steady as before. "The drinks will not hurt you."

Justin took down the three drinks rather quickly, with no hesitation. The first drink was sweet, cool and refreshing, and it tingled on his tongue. As he swallowed, he felt a warmth spreading through his chest, a comforting sensation that seemed to ease his nerves.

The second drink was not as sweet, but had a rich, velvety texture that coated his mouth. It left a lingering taste, and he couldn't help but savor the flavor.

The third drink was the most intense, with a bold, kick that sent a shiver down his spine.

It was invigorating, almost electrifying, and he felt a surge of energy coursing through his veins.

After taking the third drink, a few seconds passed, and Justin's eyes rolled into the back of his head.

His body started to convulse on the couch, his muscles twitching uncontrollably. The sensation was overwhelming, a mix of pain and euphoria that left him gasping for breath.

For about thirty seconds, his body writhed in a state of heightened awareness, every nerve ending on fire.

Then, just as suddenly as it had started, the convulsions stopped.

Justin's eyes fluttered open, and he stared at Jesus, his mind reeling from the experience. He felt different, as if a veil had been lifted, and he could see the world with newfound clarity.

Justin Standone sat upright, his breath heavy, his mind clouded with disorientation. The stark white walls surrounding him stretched endlessly, eerily silent, devoid of warmth.

His heart pounded as he scanned the space, searching for anything familiar—anything that might explain where he was.

He gestured sharply at the stranger, then to the pristine room around him. "Who are you, and where am I?"

The man met his gaze with unwavering confidence, his presence both authoritative and gentle. "When you leave this room, Justin, all your questions will be answered. Let's take it slow—one question at a time. My name is Jesus."

Jesus rejoined his hands, absentmindedly twirling his thumbs.

Justin looked back at him, doubt flickering across his face. "Jesus..."

The man nodded, his expression unwavering. "Yes, the one and only. You have worked your life serving me. Which should tell you where you are."

Justin gestured sharply around the room. "This doesn't look like Heaven, and you don't look like Jesus."

His voice carried disbelief—frustration twisting in his gut. This was nothing like the images he had clung to throughout his life. No golden gates, no clouds, no celestial glow.

And this man—clad in jeans and a white button-up shirt—was hardly the divine figure he had envisioned.

Jesus remained calm. "This place is very different from what you have been taught and told."

He motioned toward Justin. "Tell me, what do you remember before waking up on this couch?"

Justin rubbed his temple, trying to summon fragmented memories. Then, something surfaced—sharp and vivid.

"Not much..." His brow furrowed.

"I was driving my friend Martin home. We stopped at a gas station, and I remember being stabbed in my shoulder."

The recollection sent a chill through him. The sensation of the blade, the sharp burst of pain—it was still there, imprinted in his mind as if it had only just happened. He met Jesus's gaze, searching for an explanation, desperate for something that made sense.

"That is how you got here, Justin,"

Jesus said, his voice steady. "You lost too much blood before the ambulance could reach you. You are fine now; nothing can harm you here. You can still see the scar on your shoulder if you care to look."

Justin swallowed hard, hesitating before tugging his shirt off. His fingers traced over the fully healed wound—about two inches in length, the thick scar tissue standing as proof of what had happened.

"How much time has passed since it happened?"

Jesus tilted his head slightly. "Time here is funny, Justin. You appeared on my couch after your heart stopped beating. It took about what you would call a day for you to wake up here."

Justin frowned. "What 'I' would call a day?"

Jesus clasped his hands together. "Yes. The English language is not the language of the word I spoke in creation. English was invented by men, and I must speak with you in English to try to convey my thoughts. Let me know if you have any confusion."

He continued, his tone patient but firm. "We measure time the same way as in the world you came from, but here, there is no true time—only a light and dark period that corresponds to the cycles of day and night from where you came from."

Justin hesitated. "The world I came from?"

Jesus nodded. "Heaven, for you to understand best, I would say, is in its own universe—separate from the universe you came from. It will have the appearance of an island."

Justin raised an eyebrow. "Why an island?"

Jesus shrugged. "No particular reason—just surrounded by water because it needed an edge."

Justin exhaled slowly, absorbing the information. "How far out does the water go?"

"Maybe a mile or two."

Justin rubbed his chin, thinking. "Are there animals here?"

Jesus nodded. "Yes, plenty of wildlife that roams free. The animals here all eat plants, so none of them will hurt you."

Justin frowned slightly. "What about in the water?"

"The water is the same—some small fish and other small marine animals. The island is filled with thousands of different kinds of fruit-bearing vegetation."

Justin's mind buzzed with questions. "Does anyone eat meat here?"

Jesus shook his head. "We do not kill the animals here for that purpose. However, I can bring things here at your request. Requests take about a week, and if they are not food, they can be anything that will fit through that door."

He lifted a hand, pointing toward the exit.

Justin's brows furrowed. "And you can get anything?"

Jesus nodded. "Most people here like to request alcohol or drugs, but yes—anything your mind could think of from the world you left."

Justin stiffened. "Drugs and alcohol? You allow that?"

Jesus's gaze remained steady. "Justin, here we allow anything that does not impede on another's will. Remember—Heaven is very different from what you have been taught and told. Here, there is no judgment, no sin, no hurt, and no pain."

Justin exhaled sharply. "I have worked my whole life to get here. Why does this not feel real? How many other people are here?"

He shook his head, frustration seeping in. "I have so many questions, but I can't even think right now. My mind is clouded—this is too much."

Jesus remained patient, watching him. "Take your time, Justin,"
He said calmly. "There are 6,375 people here. If you would like—close
your eyes, sleep some more, and then we can talk."

Justin sat motionless, his mind battling contradictions. Nothing about
this matched what he had believed—what he had spent years working
toward.

But here he was, facing Jesus, hearing words that defied everything he
thought he knew.

The weight of it all pressed against him, heavy and unrelenting. He
swallowed, his fingers twitching at his sides.

Maybe sleeping on it wasn't such a bad idea.

Justin did exactly that. Within minutes of closing his eyes, sleep pulled
him under, his mind too overwhelmed to resist its weight.

. . .

When he awoke hours later, the room was unchanged—still stark, still
pristine, still quiet. Jesus sat across from him in the same chair, twirling his
thumbs in steady, rhythmic motion.

But something was different.

Three plates of food now rested on the table—his favorite meals laid
out before him in perfect detail.

A steak dinner with a baked potato and Caesar salad, pork chops with
rice smothered in creamy mushroom soup, and a plate full of shepherd's pie,
thick with gravy.

The scent alone made his stomach clench in sudden hunger.

Justin let out a low chuckle. "You certainly know that the way to a man's
heart is through his stomach."

Jesus smiled, his expression unreadable. "I never wanted to get into
your heart. I wanted you to willingly accept me into your heart. You have
devoted your life to that, and you will be rewarded for it.

Why don't you finish eating and use the time to think of any questions
you might have?"

Silence settled between them, the quiet hum of anticipation stretching
with each passing moment.

Jesus sat still, his thumbs continuing their slow circles, watching as Justin took his first bite—then another, and another—until every plate was cleared.

Justin exhaled heavily, leaning back against the couch, satisfied but still unsure.

He stared up at the ceiling for a moment before shifting his gaze to Jesus, curiosity flickering in his eyes. "That was the best meal I have ever had. I don't believe I finished it all."

Jesus nodded once. "I am glad you enjoyed it. So, do you have any questions?"

Justin hesitated, sorting through the tangle of thoughts in his mind. "I am curious about one thing. You said there are 6,375 other people here. Shouldn't there be more?"

Jesus's expression remained calm. "I am very selective of who I choose to come here after death. Not many pass the test."

Justin frowned. "What is the test?"

Jesus met his gaze. "Supreme devotion to me."

Justin absorbed the words, turning them over in his mind. He had never questioned his devotion—his entire life had been built around it. "I have had that my whole life."

He paused, then shifted the conversation. "I have thought of a request."

Jesus stopped twirling his thumbs, rubbing his hands together with measured anticipation. "What is it?"

Justin sat forward slightly. "I do not like to sleep on the ground. Could I get an air mattress to use as a bed?"

Jesus tilted his head slightly. "Most people ask for a hammock for sleeping. Would you prefer one of those?"

Justin shook his head. "I don't like sleeping in a hammock. I would prefer the air mattress."

Jesus nodded, his voice unwavering. "If that is what you want, that is what you will get."

Justin studied the door ahead, then turned back to Jesus. "Now, when I exit this room through that door, will we be able to talk like this again?"

Jesus's expression remained unchanged. "My door is always open if you need to talk, Justin. I do ask you to wait three days and experience Heaven before we talk a second time. I will always tell you the truth."

Justin took a deep breath, his thoughts tangled. "If that is the case, I want to hold off on asking questions for now. Everything I have been taught and told by my religion doesn't seem to be true.

Let me explore and learn about this place—speak with the others here. Once I have done that, I am sure I will have questions that are much more meaningful to me and you."

Jesus nodded. "However, you want it is how you will have it here. Your guide, Amelia, is waiting for you outside that door when you are ready to leave this room."

Justin's brow furrowed slightly. "My guide?"

Jesus said, gesturing toward the door. "Yes, just someone to show you around, help you learn more about me and this place until you get acquainted with the island."

Justin pushed himself off the couch, stepping toward the door. His fingers brushed against its cool, smooth surface, ready to push it open.

Then—"Justin!"

Jesus's voice rang out, sharp and urgent, stopping him in his tracks. His hand remained on the door handle, hesitation flickering through him as he turned back.

Jesus met his gaze, his expression unreadable.

"I love you."

The words landed like a weight in Justin's chest. He swallowed, uncertain—but something in the way Jesus spoke to him, made his response effortless. "I love you too, Jesus."

Justin pushed the door open, and to his surprise, standing on the other side was Amelia.

Her eyes met his. The light from the hallway behind her cast a soft glow, illuminating her figure as she stood there.

Her voice was gentle, her presence comforting to Justin as she spoke, "You finally decided to wake up. Are you ready?"

"Yes, I am ready."

Together, they started walking down the long hallway, their footsteps echoing in the silence. The hallway seemed to stretch on forever, each step brought them closer to the door at the end, a beacon in the distance.

Justin's mind was a whirlwind of thoughts and emotions, still trying to process everything that had happened.

Amelia walked beside him, her presence a steadying force. She glanced at Justin, a mix of concern and determination in her eyes.

The door at the end of the hallway seemed to hold the promise of answers, and they both felt a sense of urgency as they got closer with each step towards it.

Justin hesitated for a moment, trying to steady his thoughts as he stood beside Amelia in the dimly lit hallway.

The weight of everything he'd just learned pressed against his mind, twisting his understanding of what was supposed to be true.

Amelia's voice was soft yet confident, carrying a quiet assurance.

"So, what are you thinking?

I know everything seems upside down, but soon, it will all make sense."

Justin exhaled slowly. "For the first time in a long time, Amelia, everything is actually starting to make sense."

His voice was steady, but the uncertainty lingered in his expression. "How long have you been here?"

Amelia offered a small smile. "Two weeks or so."

She crossed her arms as if grounding herself in her own memories. "I was very skeptical when I first walked out of that room. My mind was a battleground, fighting against the new information I was being told. But it didn't take long to realize the truth."

Justin frowned slightly. "What would you consider the truth?"

She turned to him fully, her gaze unwavering. "We can't deny the experience we went through to get here, and we can't deny the Heaven that we are about to step into. To me, *that* is truth."

Justin absorbed her words, weighing them against the lingering doubts in his own mind. "I want to see this truth you speak of."

Amelia nodded knowingly. "How much did you learn in there about Jesus and this place?"

She glanced down the hallway briefly before turning back to him. "I stayed in that room for eight hours before I left. You came out rather quickly—four hours or so. Couldn't think of any questions?"

Justin shrugged. "I had plenty of questions, but all of them felt pedantic at the time."

He sighed, running a hand through his hair. "Every question I had seemed the same: *My religion told me this—how does it really work?* I figured it was better to learn more about this place first, then ask the best questions."

As they arrived at the door at the end of the hallway, Amelia paused, resting her hand against the handle.

"Are you ready to see what's beyond this door?"

Justin squared his shoulders. "I'm ready. But can I ask—have you explored the whole island in the two weeks you've been here?"

A hint of pride flickered in her expression. "Almost every inch."

Justin nodded. "I had a prayer ritual I wanted to do as soon as we step outside."

Amelia tilted her head slightly. "How long do you need?"

"It's not about the time—I need your help."

His voice was calmer now, purposeful. "I need to say a prayer at the North, East, West, and South edges of the island. In memory of my family. In the hopes that I will see them here."

He studied her carefully. "Can you guide me to those places?"

She didn't hesitate. "If that's what you want to do, that's what we'll do."

Relief washed over Justin. "Then I'm ready."

Amelia glanced at the door, then back at him. "When I stepped through this door, I kept my eyes closed so I could take it all in at once when I opened them. Want to try that?"

A small smirk crossed Justin's lips. "Why not?"

He shut his eyes, trusting Amelia's guidance. Her fingers wrapped gently yet firmly around his hand, grounding him as they moved forward.

A deep breath. A soft push.

The door swung open, and together, they stepped out.

Behind them, the door closed with a quiet click.

"Okay,"

Amelia whispered, warmth in her tone.
"Open your eyes."

Chapter 9 - #64

wo women were sitting in a room at a desk, with numerous large computer screens in front of them hanging on the wall and a couple of large screens sitting on the desk.

Both women had badges on the left side of their chests. The badges were emblazoned with a gold logo that adorned two capitalized T's side by side.

There was an eagle on the bottom right of the logo gripping the first T within its talons looking to the right.

On the bottom left of the logo was a similar image of a hawk gripping the second T within its talons looking to the Left.

Sitting atop both T's was a crested owl with one foot on each T staring forward.

The badge on the first woman read, "Senior Digital Investigator."

Her name, Mary Schilling, was listed on her shirt below the badge. The badge on the other woman read, "Digital Investigator Trainee."

Her name, Diana Griffin, was also below her badge.

All the screens in front of them were filled with numbers flashing different colors.

Some of the numbers on the screen were solid green with text beside them that said "Checked In."

Some of the numbers were solid orange with text beside them that said, "Check in due."

And some of the numbers were flashing red with text beside them that said, "Check in overdue."

The numbers in orange also had a countdown clock beside them.

Seeing the intimidation on Diana's face as she looked at all the screens Mary said, "Do not let all the screens and information intimidate you, Diana. The computer will do most of the work here. What you are looking at is all our agents out in the field that are active right now."

Diana's brow furrowed, her surprise evident. "There are that many out there?"

The room hummed softly, monitors lining the walls, displaying a web of information—constant movement, shifting details, and flashing alerts.

Mary, standing beside her, nodded with measured confidence. "There are more than what you're seeing.

We have two thousand agents active right now, and eight Digital Investigators, each monitoring two hundred and fifty agents across screens like these."

She gestured toward the glowing wall of data. "You'll be replacing one of our current investigators who is retiring.

Out of all this information, the only thing you need to focus on are the agents flashing red."

Diana stared at the screen. Her pulse quickened slightly. "What exactly am I looking at? What does it all mean?"

Mary folded her arms, her expression serious. "The agents in the field are working undercover, attempting to go missing—to become one of *The Lost*—in the hopes of uncovering what happens to them.

Every twelve hours, they must check in using a randomized code sent through a secure connection.

As long as they check in, they remain green, and you do nothing.

Her eyes shifted to a particular section of the screen. "When you see an agent turn orange, it means their twelve-hour window has passed.

They have five minutes to check-in before their status turns flashing red. That's when you investigate. That's when we start looking into what happened."

Diana scanned the board, her eyes catching movement—a blinking red indicator. "Agent #64 is flashing red. What do I do next?"

Mary offered a small, knowing smile. "This is just a training trial. Another investigator is already handling #64's case, but normally, your first step would be checking home surveillance to see if they're there—maybe unable to check-in for some reason."

Diana leaned forward slightly. "And if they're not home?"

"Then we start looking deeper—pulling their files, their real name, their close contacts, their logs. Most cases are simple: overslept, forgot their alarm, drank too much the night before.

Diana's fingers hovered over the desk's touchpad. "Okay, how do we access the cameras?"

Mary gestured toward the console. "The screens on the wall? You don't control those. But the one in front of you—double-tap on *agents*, then select #64."

Tap, tap.

Diana's eyes flicked over the screen as new information loaded. "Got it."

Mary nodded. "Now, you have access to their full profile—real name, address, occupation, church affiliation, home surveillance, close contacts, and more.

Go into home surveillance."

Tap, tap.

Live camera feeds filled the screen, angles shifting as she flipped between them.

Empty rooms.

Still furniture.

A driveway without a car. "I don't see anyone inside,"

Diana murmured. "And his car isn't there either."

Mary's expression hardened. "Well, you're about to get an experience most trainees don't get. Most don't witness an actual investigation during training."

Diana swallowed, her pulse picking up. "Okay... So, what's next?"

Mary's tone remained steady. "You'd start digging deeper looking for *The Lost Criterion*—checking their real name, their address, contacting local authorities, speaking to close contacts. Whatever it takes to figure out why they didn't check-in."

Diana asked confused, "What is *The Lost Criterion?*"

Before Mary could reply, the door swung open violently.

Howard rushed in, breathless. "MARY—MARY, #64!"

Mary turned sharply. "What is it?"

Howard's expression was tight, his urgency spilling into the air. "I just got confirmation of a *Phantom Ambulance* for #64—witnesses seen it."

Mary's posture straightened. "We need to get *The Commander* involved immediately. Forward all the information to him."

Howard gave a quick nod before rushing out, the door slamming shut behind him.

Diana's pulse pounded in her ears. "I've heard of them before... but what exactly is a *Phantom Ambulance?*"

Mary exhaled slowly, then turned to her. "I think it's time we went over *The Lost Criterion.*"

Chapter 10 - Amelia's Eye Opening

melia opened her eyes and slowly spun around, taking it all in. She felt like she had stepped into a dream, an exuberant feeling washing over her as she explored her surroundings.

Everything seemed surreal and fantastical. She took deep breaths, tasting the slightly sweet moisture in the air.

Behind her was a door set into the front of a ten-foot-tall hill. Beyond the hill, a landscape of varying hills, forests, and mountains extended into the distance.

The door opened into a large, open area covered in the greenest grass she had ever seen. A thick fog loomed in the air, obscuring her view of Heaven.

Trees were sparsely scattered throughout the foggy expanse, each bearing bright fruits in a kaleidoscope of colors. Despite the fog, the vibrant fruits were visible, hanging from the branches.

The open area stretched as far as she could see, with large trees and dense forests emerging through the mist.

She could make out animals grazing in the distance.

As Amelia took a few steps, she noticed the dense fog swirling around her feet, so thick she couldn't see her shoes.

The fog felt like a damp cloth brushing against her skin.

Though it was bright as daylight, there was no sun to be seen in the sky. Regardless, the temperature was perfect—not too hot, not too cold.

Simon glanced up at the sky, the thick fog rolling in like a soft veil over the landscape. "Not the best weather today, but this is as bad as it gets. It never rains or snows, and it's never too hot or too cold."

Amelia rubbed her arms, feeling the moisture in the air cling to her skin. "The fog was surprising. I don't know why, but for some reason, I thought there wouldn't be *any* weather."

She let out a small laugh. "That doesn't make sense though. I need to stop presupposing I know this place."

Simon nodded knowingly. "I asked Jesus about the fog before. He said it's because this place is an island surrounded by water, but without clouds.

The moisture that evaporates gets absorbed into the air, and about once a week, it leads to days like this."

He paused, glancing at her. "Did you notice how the moisture in the air tastes sweet?"

Amelia blinked, considering it for the first time. "Yes... that surprised me too."

Simon explained, "Jesus said the moisture in the air gets sweetened by all the fruit growing on the island,"

Amelia shook her head in amazement. "That's crazy. What if somebody *wanted* it to rain?"

Simon smirked. "If someone wanted rain, I'm sure Jesus would find a way to make it happen."

They continued walking, their feet crunching softly against the earth as they emerged into an open clearing.

The trees surrounding them were heavy with bright red apples, each one gleaming like polished jewels beneath the muted light.

Amelia reached out to brush her fingertips against one of the branches. "If it doesn't rain here, how do all the trees, fruits, and vegetation grow?"

Simon chuckled. "Sounds like a question you should save for when you talk to Jesus again. Because I have no idea. Never thought about it before."

He reached up and plucked an apple from the nearest tree. "Did you want one?"

Amelia narrowed her eyes playfully. "It depends... Are you Satan trying to entice me like with Adam and Eve?"

Simon stopped walking, holding the apple up between his fingers, turning it over slowly as he examined it. He gave her a mock-serious look. "Nope. It's just an apple."

Amelia laughed as they continued down the path, the air thick with the scent of fresh fruit.

Simon motioned ahead. "There are all kinds of fruits, vegetables, and berries growing everywhere here."

Amelia took in the vibrant landscape, then glanced at him. "Jesus said there were over 6,000 people here. Where are they all?"

Simon shrugged, glancing around. "This place is *huge*. Some people stick to certain areas, some travel, some prefer the walking paths, and others move through the thicker forests."

He smiled slightly, "We all meet every three months for a celebration together. You should see how the open area around Jesus's door fills up—it's incredible

They were getting closer to the edge of the open area. There were walking paths extending out from the open area about every five hundred feet.

The trees and vegetation were very thick on either side where the open area met the paths.

They continued walking down the path they came to.

Amelia furrowed her brow as they walked, the thinning fog making way for clearer surroundings. "Jesus mentioned a celebration every three months—something about drinking the Three E's."

Simon nodded. "We all gather and form the shapes of a square, triangle, and circle, then drink one of the Three E's together at the same time."

Amelia glanced at him, curious. "Why those shapes?"

Simon exhaled, shrugging slightly. "Also, a question I can't answer. Just what I was told and did. I don't know the reason why."

Her mind spun with thoughts, the pieces of her reality still refusing to settle. The skepticism inside her had been growing since she stepped out of the room, twisting logic and instinct into tangled uncertainty.

The words came before she could stop them. "Simon, why does none of this feel real?"

She turned to him, her expression tight. "I don't even know how to explain it, but I feel like I'm still alive—that I never died. Does that make any sense?"

Simon gave her a careful look, considering her words. "It's all still new Amelia. I'm sure that feeling will fade.

I don't know if asking you a question will give you the answer,

but... what would you expect it to feel like if your spirit came here after you died?"

Amelia pressed her lips together, frustration simmering beneath the surface. "I don't know. But I don't *feel* like a spirit or soul. It feels wrong, and don't ask me what that means—it just... doesn't feel right."

Silence stretched between them as they continued down the path.

The trees swayed lightly in the gentle breeze, their branches holding ripe fruit, untouched by time.

Simon slowed his pace, his voice soft but firm. "Amelia, just trust and have faith in Jesus like you always have. In about five minutes, we'll reach the beach—the surprise I have for you is waiting there."

He turned to her, his expression warm. "The concerns you're having? I had them too when I first got here. But just give it time."

Amelia scoffed lightly, shaking her head. "It's funny how that suddenly feels hard to do—having faith in Jesus. It never was before. But having a *man* named Jesus standing in front of me doesn't feel right."

Simon smiled knowingly. "You probably already realize this, but the weird feelings? That's your mind fighting against the truth of where you are, what you're seeing, and what you're being told. It conflicts with everything you were taught and told before."

Amelia sighed. "I do realize that... But this feeling is different. I don't know what it is, but something just doesn't feel right."

Simon grinned suddenly, switching gears. "Is there any chance that some Domaine de la Romanée-Conti might change your mind?"

Amelia blinked. "What is *Domain Romane-Conti*?"

"You were close."

He smirked. "It's Do...maine-de-la-Ro...manee-Con...ti. A fine, rare, and expensive wine. That's the surprise—a picnic on the beach, and we can enjoy it together."

Amelia laughed lightly. "I love wine. I don't think I've ever had that kind. Where did you get it?"

Simon's smile widened. "I got it from Jesus—I asked him for it."

He waved his hand casually as they walked. "I love wine, had a collection of my own, went to tastings and auctions all the time.

Every time I guide someone when they first arrive, I use my weekly request to Jesus to get whatever wine I ask for. And then, I share it with the new person I'm guiding. We eat, sit, and talk together."

Amelia shook her head, amused but still tangled in thought. "That actually sounds perfect."

Simon gave her a reassuring look. "It will be."

They reached the edge of the path, where it met a sandy beach.

Chapter 11 – A Surreal Surprise

melia was stunned by the landscape before her: a bright sky, a pristine sandy beach, and perfectly still, untouched water.

The motionless water felt surreal and somewhat disorienting to her, as she was accustomed to the rolling waves typically seen with large bodies of water.

Simon motioned to the left, drawing her attention to a picnic setup—a blanket laid out on the beach, a picnic basket, and a bottle of the finest Domaine de la Romanée-Conti accompanied by two wine glasses.

They walked towards the inviting scene and sat down together on the blanket.

Amelia smiled as they walked, anticipation building in her chest. "I can't wait to try the wine. So, tell me how it works exactly—when Jesus brings things here for us. He mentioned something about that?"

Simon reached into the picnic basket and pulled out a corkscrew. As he started twisting it into the cork, he spoke in a relaxed tone.

"I can only share what I know, which isn't much. But you tell Jesus exactly what you want, and he makes it happen.

He materializes things here in Heaven."

He gave her a sideways glance. "Did you ask him for anything when you had your talk?"

Amelia hesitated before answering, brushing a strand of hair behind her ear. "I did—mostly because I was skeptical. I wanted to test him."

She let out a soft chuckle. "I even told a little lie about why I wanted it. I knew how rare it was, but now I have no idea what I'm supposed to do with a little girl's bike once it's here."

Simon grinned at that, continuing to pull at the cork. After three hard tugs, a loud *pop* echoed into the open air. Immediately, he brought the bottle to his nose, inhaling deeply, savoring the aroma.

"Here, take a sniff," he said excitedly, shoving the bottle toward Amelia a little too fast.

She flinched and leaned back instinctively. "Careful! You almost hit me in the nose."

Simon laughed. "Sorry, I get excited when I get to drink this wine."

Amelia took the bottle from his hands, waving it slowly under her nose.

Her breath was deep, deliberate, as the scent filled her senses. "That smells amazing—better than any wine I've ever had."

Simon nodded, his smile growing. "Just wait until you taste it. The bouquet, the body, the finish—it's out of this world."

He paused, chuckling at his own words. "Which, honestly, I don't even know what that expression means anymore."

They both laughed, the tension between them easing with the sound.

After a moment, Amelia tilted her head, curious. "What else have you asked Jesus for since you got here?"

Simon poured the wine carefully, his hands steady. "Many different bottles. Some of the rarest in the world."

He lifted his own glass, admiring the deep ruby color. "The *Domaine de la Romanée-Conti* costs something like $100,000 a bottle. It's worth more than gold."

He took a slow sip, savoring it before continuing. "I'd never even tried it before I came here—it was the first thing I asked for."

Amelia froze. "A hundred thousand dollars?"

She looked down at her glass with new hesitation. "You shouldn't have told me that—I don't feel worthy to drink it now."

Simon scoffed. "We're in Heaven, Amelia. We were worthy of Jesus—we're worthy of this wine."

He handed her the glass, filling it generously, his grin playful.

"Are you trying to get me drunk Simon Cartwright?" she teased.

His eyes lit up with mischief. "That's my plan—get you to Heaven, get you drunk on the finest wine, and make you fall in love with me."

Amelia snickered and playfully punched his arm. "Simon, I am a married woman."

He lifted his glass, arching a brow. "And I *was* a married man. So what?"

Amelia paused, then smirked. "I guess you're right. I '*was*' married too."

Simon held up a finger. "Now, for the first sip, you need to plug your nose, take a mouthful, and swish it around."

She raised an eyebrow at him, skeptical. "What?"

"Trust me. On three—we do it together."

Hesitating only slightly, Amelia mirrored his movements, awkwardly positioning her hand as they both pinched their noses.

"One... two... three."

They each took a deep sip, cheeks puffing out as they swished the wine around. Their eyes locked, mirroring wide expressions of surprise and delight.

The taste was unlike anything Amelia had experienced before—layers of rich complexity that made her pause, savoring it even after she swallowed.

She exhaled, shaking her head in disbelief. "That was... it was... *it's* so good!"

Simon grinned. "I know, right? The flavors blow me away every time."

Amelia gestured with her hands, trying to form words, but none came until her third attempt. "I'm *speechless*. I've never tasted anything this good in my life."

Simon chuckled, leaning back on his elbows. "There's a reason it was priced so high when we were alive."

Amelia took another sip, letting it linger on her tongue. "I'm glad we have it to enjoy together."

Simon's expression softened. "Me too, Amelia. It makes me feel like my wife is here with me."

She switched the hand holding the wine glass, then reached over, sliding her fingers beneath his hand where it rested beside him.

She intertwined their fingers gently, holding his gaze.

"Let's take advantage of this miraculous place and situation we're in,"

She said, voice warm. "Enjoy this God-worthy wine and each other's company."

Simon gripped her hand tighter, locking his gaze onto hers, a quiet sincerity passing between them. "I couldn't say no to that."

They sat in comfortable silence for a moment, enjoying the slow dimming of daylight.

Instead of a sunset, the brightness simply faded, as if the sky itself was quietly switching off.

Amelia pointed toward the water. "That wasn't anything like a sunset."

Simon nodded. "It's different here."

Her eyes lingered on the sea—motionless, undisturbed. "Why does the water just *stand still*? It's not moving at all."

Simon stretched his legs out, glancing toward the horizon. "I asked Jesus about that once. He said none of the variables that caused waves on Earth exist here—no weather, no wind, no gravity affecting the water. So... it just *stays* still."

Amelia studied the shoreline, lost in thought. "Have you ever gone swimming?"

Simon chuckled. "I'm not much of a swimmer."

She grinned, setting her glass down. "Come on, let's go for a swim—feel the water. Then we can come back and finish our second glass."

Simon looked at her, half amused, half intrigued. Then, finally, he shrugged. "We don't even have the right clothing."

Playfully laughing, Amelia replied, "We don't need clothing Simon."

Amelia snickered, and Simon understood what she was saying. As much as Simon didn't like to go swimming, he liked to see women naked and could not turn Amelia down. Simon started to take his shirt off and spoke. "Let's go!"

They both removed all the clothing they were wearing and held hands as they walked down the beach towards the water. When they took their first step into the water, it felt warm, which made it easy to walk right out until the water was deep enough that their shoulders were covered.

Simon and Amelia faced each other, and Amelia spoke. "The water is beautiful. I will tell you a secret. When I was alive, I never once went swimming naked. I was always a prude and found nudity and sex repulsive because my religion told me to."

"Do you still feel that way?"

"It is like the feeling with my family. I just don't seem to care enough to think about it. Besides, this feels great."

Simon wrapped his arms around Amelia and embraced their naked bodies together in a hug.

Simon could feel Amelia's naked breasts up against his chest, her nipples hard, and the still water started to see some movement below the surface around Simon's midsection as his cock hardened.

Amelia spoke, "I don't know if it is the wine, or what but Simon for the first time ever I feel very sexually aroused, my husband never made me feel like this."

An excited look had come across Simon's face as he responded, "It could be the wine, the place, the setting, would you like to have sex?"

Amelia immediately felt a surge flow through her body and rest in her vagina.

It was a feeling she had never felt before in her life, it was a craving she could only explain as a wanting to have her vagina filled,

She put her mouth close to his ear and whispered. "I have never said this to a man before in my life either, but Simon....... Please fuck me."

Simon slid his member inside of Amelia, as her and Simon enjoyed an ecstasy like they had never felt before, for Amelia the sex was better than it was with any man she had ever been with.

Chapter 12 - Behind the Curtain

A man in a suit sat behind a desk, reviewing a file and some papers. The text "#64" was clearly written at the top of the file. The nameplate on his desk read, "Steve Hauser, Commander of the Throne."

A bead of sweat formed on his brow. He wiped it away with his sleeve, then picked up the phone and dialed a number. Leaning back in his chair, he put the phone to his ear. "I need you to come to my office right now! I think we got in."

Minutes later, the door swung open, and Mark stepped inside, closing it behind him.

He adjusted his tie before sinking into the chair across from Steve's desk. "What's going on?"

Mark asked, his voice edged with skepticism. "What do you mean we got in?"

Steve leaned forward, his expression serious. "We think #64 has been picked up Mark."

Mark's eyes narrowed. "Are we sure?"

Steve nodded, tapping the papers in front of him. "Two missed check-ins—one last night, one this morning. That flagged a deeper investigation. Everything I see here matches our suspicions about *The Lost*."

Mark exhaled sharply, rubbing his chin. "Well, I hope it isn't another disappointment like when #332 went missing."

Steve shook his head. "This disappearance shows all the signs. We have confirmation of a *Phantom Ambulance*—witnesses saw it.

We won't know for sure until #64 makes contact, and that could take weeks, even months, depending on where they are. It's all unknowable from our perspective until then."

Mark leaned back, considering the weight of the situation. "What should we do in the meantime?"

Steve's voice was firm. "We need to make sure everything is in place for when #64 does make contact. We go over the plan with a fine-tooth comb—make sure it's infallible. #64 may be our one and only shot."

Mark sighed, shaking his head. "It's been six years trying to find where *The Lost* are being taken. I was starting to think none of it was real—that we were all just chasing ghosts."

Steve nodded slowly. "I've had the same thoughts Mark. But #64 is our chance. And I don't think we'll have another six years before it's too late.

We don't know *how* or *why* yet—but soon, we should know *where*. And that will give us the advantage to answer the other questions. We can finally find out who's behind the curtain."

Mark straightened in his chair. "I'll alert all the agents on the ground."

Steve stood, gathering the stack of files on his desk. "I'm going to get our tracking systems online and take up post in the Command Room so I can monitor everything from there.

If you need me, that's where I'll be. I'll also make sure all reinforcements are ready once contact is made with #64."

Mark nodded. "I'll speak with Harris and Gary—fill them in on the situation. They'll start preparing too."

Steve handed Mark a thick folder. "Take these files—the most recent confirmed *Lost*. Let's get their investigations started."

Mark took the folder, gripping it tightly. "I'm glad all the hard work we've put in is finally starting to pay off."

Steve gave a small nod. "We'll talk more later."

Mark stood and exited the room, leaving Steve alone for a brief moment. He exhaled and followed Mark leaving the office, he turned right down the hallway. As he walked, he passed numerous glass-windowed offices, each occupied by someone deep in their work.

He continued until he reached the elevator, pressing the *up* button.

The doors slid open, and just as he stepped inside, a woman approached—slender, poised, carrying a file folder.

Steve glanced at her. "Are you going up or down?"

She smiled politely. "I'm going down."

Steve nodded. "I'm headed to the top floor. Not sure if you want to come for the ride or wait for another elevator."

She stepped inside without hesitation. "I'm in no rush."

Steve raised an eyebrow. "I've never seen you up here before."

She chuckled. "I work on 22. I don't think I've ever been above 25."

Steve pressed the button for the 72nd floor. "It takes a while to get up there. That's why I asked if you wanted another elevator—it'll be a long ride up and down for you."

She shrugged. "Like I said, I'm in no rush."

Steve turned to her, offering his hand. "Well, if we're stuck in here together, we should probably introduce ourselves. I'm Steve Hauser, Commander of *The Throne*."

Her eyes widened slightly. "You're *The Commander*?"

She shook his hand firmly, her grip confident. "I've heard of you. My name is Cynthia Brown—Special Divisions Investigation Officer. Very nice to meet you. I just started three months ago."

Steve nodded. "Well, I know *Special Divisions* is handling some important projects for us regarding *The Lost*. We'll probably be working together in the future."

Cynthia felt a rush of excitement at his words. She had heard of Steve Hauser—everyone in *The Throne* had.

As *Commander*, he was the most important man in the organization, overseeing everything that happened within its walls.

He had founded *The Throne* six years ago, playing a crucial role in uncovering one of the largest, longest-running missing persons investigations in history.

She studied him carefully, intrigued. Steve glanced at the floor indicator as the elevator ascended. "So, Cynthia... tell me, what's your role in *Special Divisions*?"

She smiled, shifting the file folder in her hands. "Let's just say... I specialize in finding people who don't want to be found."

Steve's lips curled into a smirk. "Then I think we'll get along just fine."

Chapter 13 - Amelia's First Days

melia and Simon just floated on their backs on the water after they had climaxed. Amelia said, "Aren't you glad you came swimming?"

Simon responded, "It was amazing!"

Amelia nodded her head agreeing with him and asked, here is a question, completely off topic, but it just popped into my head. I have not seen any bugs or insects here, where are they?"

"I asked Jesus that during our second talk his exact words were, 'I know we never see any bugs or insects and if I said there were none that would be a lie, they all live underground.'"

They started to make their way towards the shore where they could stand up in the water and started walking back towards their picnic setting on the beach, Simon put his pants on, and Amelia put on her shirt then they both laid down on the blanket together.

She said, "I feel a little ashamed of myself, I would never have sex with someone I had just met. I didn't even have sex with my husband until we got married, we dated for two years."

Giggling to himself he responded, "That makes me a very lucky man, and you have nothing to be ashamed about here Amelia. No one here will judge you; most people here use sex to pass the time Jesus encourages it, if it is what we want it is what we should have."

Confusion crossed her face as she asked, "Why would sex have been such a great sin to GOD?"

Shrugging his shoulders he said, "It probably never was a sin. I will try to explain it to you how Jesus explained it to me.

Sin is a word that man created and defined, the word means nothing to GOD, and the actions that would be considered sins to the church are not even a thought for GOD."

Amelia exclaimed throwing her hands up in the air, "So does sin even exist?"

Thinking for a moment before he responded, "As a word, and definition it exists but the definition is wrong. Jesus promotes fulfilling all our desires, some men and women here will even engage in sex with others of the same sex if they desire it.

The world we came from we were always judged by every mind in existence based on what the bible said with our own mind being the highest judge.

Here no one judges anyone,

do what you wish and what you will,

as long as you are not impeding on someone else's will or consent."

Playfully Amelia sked, "If I got the urge to jump on top of you and force you inside of me would that be impeding on your will or consent."

Simon looked directly into her eyes and said, "You would not have to force anything you might have to try to stop me from getting too excited."

Simon poured two more glasses of wine and handed one to Amelia.

Amelia took the glass down in one big gulp and yelled out with a horny, drunken excitement. "I AM RRRREADY!"

She climbed on top of Simon feeling his chest, stomach, and arms with her hands while gyrating her crotch gently on his.

Simon grabbed Amelias shirt and started to lift it up, Amelia put her arms above her head and Simon pulled Amelia's shirt off the rest of the way over her head.

Her breasts were perky and felt swollen with excitement and seemed a little bigger than normal, her nipples were hard and protruding from her chest. Amelia proceeded to remove Simon's pants.

Pulling off his pants Amelia stood in front of Simon fully Naked the curves of her body perfect in every sense, Amelia spoke. "I hope you are ready for this."

Amelia sunk down to the ground and started crawling over Simon's legs staring right into his eyes, she crawled right up to his face and embraced him in a passionate kiss, then she reached around and gripped his member, and thrusted herself onto it.

When they were done, they lay side by side on the blanket. The darkness of the night, the warm air, and the expensive alcohol in their blood wrapped them up like a cozy blanket, and they fell asleep holding each other, naked.

In the morning, Amelia awoke and opened her eyes, staring at the sky as she lay on the beach. She reached over to touch Simon, but she couldn't feel his body.

Sitting up, she looked up and down the beach but saw nothing in either direction.

Her eyes moved to the empty, tipped-over wine bottle as she remembered the events of the previous night. She also noticed the picnic basket was gone.

Amelia was confused as to where Simon went and why he would have left, she felt insecure being alone the morning after.

She felt used and felt like a slut for having sex with Simon multiple times last night.

Her mind started to wander, and she wondered if this was a test, and she failed it, she imagined Jesus coming up to her and saying. "You have failed me! Amelia, none of my children are dirty little sluts!"

Amelia started to cry as she put her head between her knees, a tear rolled down her cheek and dripped off her face.

She felt her nerves and anxiety flare up, and she started taking deep breaths in and out trying to calm herself down when she heard. "You're awake, I went to get us some breakfast, are you hungry?"

Amelia, like a wave washing over her, again felt joy, and all her thoughts of Simon using her and her being a slut left her mind. Amelia stood up and ran towards Simon and wrapped her arms around him. "Are you crying?"

Speaking through her tears and sniffles, "I am fine now, for a second there when I woke up, and you were gone, I thought what we shared last night was a one-night stand kind of thing, I felt terrible."

Simon responded, "I would never do that to you Amelia. Come, let us sit and eat."

They moved back over to the blanket and sat down together, Simon set the picnic basket in his hands down and opened it to reveal it to be full of fruit.

Amelia sighed, staring down at her hands as she spoke. "I still feel ashamed of myself, even though I know I shouldn't.

It's like there's a pit of anxiety just sitting in my stomach."

Simon reached into the picnic basket, pulling out a ripe peach.

He handed it to her with a reassuring smile. "Try eating something—it might help. It takes time to adjust to this place for some people.

Is there anything I can do that might make it easier?"

Amelia accepted the peach, rolling it between her fingers before taking a small bite. The sweetness burst onto her tongue, but the unease in her chest remained.

"I don't know, Simon. I trust you completely, and I believe what you say, but I think hearing the words straight from Jesus might help with how I'm feeling."

Simon nodded, understanding. "Jesus likes to wait three days before speaking with new arrivals a second time. He wants you to be able to see, explore, and experience this place first."

Amelia hesitated, then spoke in a low, shy tone. "Would you be offended if I asked for some alone time once we finish eating?"

Simon smiled warmly. "If you want to be alone, that won't bother me one bit. I know you have a lot going through your mind right now."

Relief flickered across Amelia's face. "Thank you, for understanding."

Simon leaned back, stretching his legs. "I do have another nice bottle of wine if you'd like to meet here and share it tonight."

Amelia glanced at him, considering, then nodded. "I would like that."

They feasted on a variety of fruits that Simon had picked for them, the flavors rich and refreshing.

When they had both had their fill, Simon stood, brushing off his hands.

"I'll leave you now, you can hold onto the blanket—it'll come in handy as you travel around the island."

He leaned down, pressing a gentle kiss to her cheek before gathering the empty wine bottle and placing it back in the picnic basket. As he walked off the beach and into the trees, he called back over his shoulder. "See you tonight! Meet me at Jesus's door."

Amelia watched him disappear into the foliage, the quiet settling around her. She pulled the blanket closer, staring out at the still water, letting the moment linger.

Amelia sat on the beach, staring at the still water. She felt lost, realizing she didn't know where she was or what to do. Regret washed over her; she wished she hadn't asked Simon to leave.

As time passed, the water's stillness unsettled her, mirroring her own inaction and the unexplored island before her.

Determined to change that, Amelia stood up and looked around. She picked up the blanket, shook off the sand, and tied it around her neck like a cape.

She decided to walk in one direction down the beach, using the picnic spot as a reference point.

With each step, she felt the grains of sand crunch between her toes.

The beach was bordered by light brush, bushes, and a forest that thickened the further it was from the shore. The sand extended about 50 meters from the tree line to the water's edge.

Looking up and down the beach, Amelia saw two parallel lines formed by the water and the tree line, stretching as far as her eyes could see.

Chapter 14 – The Others

Amelia was without a way to tell time, it felt like she had been walking for over an hour when she heard a distant voice. She couldn't make out the words but continued towards the sound.

As she got closer, she noticed a man and a woman standing near the tree line, which explained why she hadn't seen them earlier. Now about 50 meters away, Amelia called out to them. "Hello, how are you?"

The Man responded, "Good and you."

As Amelia approached them, she extended her hand in a gesture of introduction.

Their eyes met with a warm and inviting gaze, and she spoke with a friendly smile. "Hello, my name is Amelia Bernhart. I just got here yesterday."

The man stepped forward first, shaking her hand. "Hello, Amelia. My name is Tony."

Beside him, Julia let out an exaggerated sigh, narrowing her eyes at Tony. Her lips pressed into a thin line as she scolded him. "You could have introduced me too, ya jerk."

She turned to Amelia, her expression softening. "I'm Julia. Nice to meet you, Amelia. How was your first day here?"

Amelia hesitated for a moment before answering. "Can I be honest with you?"

Tony nodded. "Of course. We all went through it. But after a while, you realize this place can give you anything you want and everything you need—all thanks to Jesus."

Julia threw her hands above her head, gesturing toward the sky as she exclaimed, "Praise the Lord!"

Amelia chuckled, shaking her head. "Pardon my language, but it's really been a *mind fuck*. I'm just exploring the beach right now."

Julia tilted her head curiously. "How come you're by yourself? Where's your guide?"

"I asked my guide for some alone time. We hung out and talked all night, drinking wine together."

Tony's eyebrows lifted slightly. "Wine... Your guide must be—what's his name, Julia? The wine guy?"

Julia snapped her fingers. "Oh, that's Simon. He's always talking about wine."

Amelia's eyes lit up. "Yes! You know him?"

Tony nodded. "Simon came to the last ritual celebration a couple of weeks ago. Haven't seen him since then, though."

Julia picked up where Tony left off. "Don't worry about the *mind fuck* side of it, Amelia. I can guarantee that feeling will go away after spending some time here."

Amelia sighed. "That's what Simon said. I just wish that time would pass already."

Julia smiled warmly and leaned in slightly, her eyes sparkling with a hint of mischief. "You know what a good way to pass the time here is?"

Amelia tilted her head. "No, what would that be?"

Julia's grin widened. "To immerse yourself in the beauty and wonder of this place and the people here. Explore every nook and cranny, meet new faces, and embrace the freedom you have here.

There are no limits to what you can do or experience."

Tony nodded in agreement. "And don't forget to indulge in the simple pleasures. Whether it's enjoying a delicious meal, taking a leisurely walk, or just sitting and soaking in the scenery—every moment here can be a source of joy."

Amelia exhaled slowly, letting their words sink in. "That sounds wonderful. I guess I just need to let go."

Julia clapped her hands together. "Exactly! And remember, you're not alone. We're all here to support each other. If you ever need anything or just want to talk, don't hesitate to reach out to the people you meet."

Tony added, "And if you ever feel lost, just follow your heart. It will always lead you to where you need to be."

A sense of comfort and reassurance washed over Amelia as she listened to their words. She realized she didn't have to have all the answers right away.

She could take her time, explore, and discover the beauty of this new world at her own pace. She smiled. "Thank you both. I feel a lot better now."

Julia winked. "Anytime, Amelia. Now, do you want to know what the *best* way to pass time here is?"

Amelia laughed. "Of course!"

Julia responded with mischief in her eyes and expression as she responded, "Well Tony and I were just about to go into this forest,

put our time to its best use,

and fuck like horny rabbits during mating season.

If you care to join us, I can guarantee your mind will be clear after Tony makes you cum."

After hearing Julia speak those words in such a normal fashion, Amelia immediately felt a surge flow through her body and rest in her vagina, as if it was making the decision to say yes.

She felt the same feeling last night when Simon asked her if she wanted to have sex, an extreme arousal and need for satisfaction, like her vagina craved to be satisfied through sexual pleasure like it was a drug.

She looked at Julia after she said this, and they locked eyes, Amelia felt deeply entranced by Julia for a few seconds.

Her body at this moment was no longer human, she was an entity comprised of nothing but lust. She glanced over and looked at Tony who made his eyebrows dance up and down, enticing her to join them.

Amelia almost uncontrollably ripped all her clothes off, but was able to contain herself.

She couldn't imagine how it would make her feel to have a threesome, knowing how she felt after her time with Simon, and she didn't want to compound that feeling until she was able to talk to Jesus.

She timidly responded, "I would love to but....."

Tony cut in hoping to sway her decision, "I was really hoping you would join us I will make it worth your while, clear your mind."

Amelia wanted her mind clear, and she felt as if her vagina was on fire with a want to be filled as she stood there.

She felt indulging in extinguishing that fire that she felt between her legs was not the right thing to do, she clenched her thighs and rubbed them together like she did when she had to pee.

She could feel her juices squishing in between her thighs as she spoke. "I thank you for the offer........But....But I have to go."

Amelia turned to get away she stumbled a little, losing her balance, stepping in the sand, trying to leave in a hurry before her vagina would not let her.

Julia yelled out, "Maybe another time Amelia nice to meet you."

Amelia continued walking for ten minutes before she even looked back. Her vagina had a lustful fire burning within it that needed to be satisfied.

She could no longer see Tony and Julia, and she had the urge to go back and find them, wanting to feel the pleasure Julia spoke of.

She didn't, she hid in the bushes and masturbated furiously, trying to extinguish the fire she felt inside of her vagina.

When she had climaxed, she continued walking down the beach.

Chapter 15 - Amelia's Trauma

Amelia's journey before heaven was truly complex and layered.

Through the trauma she experienced growing up, the estrangement from her parents at fifteen years old, and her subsequent memory loss at the age of twenty-two in a car accident, Amelia knew nothing of her life before the accident.

After hitting her head in that accident, it had deeply impacted her sense of self and her interactions with the world around her

It's like she's navigating a maze without a map, or a future without a past, trying to piece together who she is and what she truly wants.

It's important for Amelia to take her time, explore her feelings, she needs to find a way to reconcile her forgotten past with her present and move forward with a clearer sense of self.

Amelia's story is a reminder that healing and self-discovery are ongoing processes. It's okay to feel lost and confused, but with time she can find her way and embrace the person she truly is.

The reintroduction to her parents and the church after her accident and her memory loss would never have happened if Amelia remembered what they had put her through.

It was both comforting and confusing.

On one hand, she found a sense of familiarity and belonging, but on the other hand, it brought her back into a traumatic cycle she didn't remember and had once escaped when she was fifteen years old.

The church's teachings and her family's influence shaped her beliefs and behavior's growing up, making it difficult for her to reconcile her past with her present experiences.

...

Amelia 15 Years Old

One Sunday evening, Amelia stayed behind to volunteer, helping clean up after a church event. She was still wearing her Sunday best—a colorful, knee-high dress—as she swept up after the banquet.

One of the High Priests noticed her and being very friendly, invited her to read the Bible with him in his office. Amelia agreed and followed him.

They entered his office, and unnoticed by Amelia, the priest locked the door behind them. The priest said to her, "Please have a seat, Amelia,"

Amelia sat down in a chair on the other side of the desk. The priest walked around and sat across from her.

As she looked around the room, she noticed shelves filled with religious symbols, statues, and pictures—all golden.

One statue stood out from the rest. It depicted a cat with puffy fur holding a fishing rod.

The fishing line was a thin piece of gold, with a gold cross hanging on a gold hook.

Amelia found it amusing, sitting amongst the other religious symbols.

He asked her, "Have you been reading your bible?"

Amelia responded excitedly, "I read it everyday Father, some of the stories I have read hundreds of times. Some only a couple times"

"Are you familiar with some of the other books written by GOD that aren't in the bible."

"I know the Edicts of The Servants and Saviors of Christ was also written by GOD."

The priest responded, a serious tone in his voice, "The book I speak of is called The Promise."

Shaking her head she said, "I don't think I have heard of that book."

"It was excluded from our bible for reasons......... but I and the church believe it is a very important book. Can I read some for you."

Curious to hear from a new book written by GOD, she excitedly responded "Of course!"

The Priest started to read a passage,

"The promise given from me to you, comes as the greatest gift. Created from your rib comes a perfect creation, containing a piece of you, my most perfect creation.

You hold ownership over my creation from the rib, that rib will be there to serve your every want and need to allow you to be the most righteous and Pious man you can be."

The priest turned the page looked up at Amelia and spoke. "What do you think of the first verse?"

Thinking for a moment Amelia responded, "It sounds like the promise is to man, the woman being a gift given to man, so that man can be the best man he can be."

A smile came across the priest's face, "You understand, good. Let me move onto the next verse."

"Ok."

The priest glanced down at the book and started reading,

"The perfect creation from your rib, has been adorned with accents to prove wanting of your eye.

When what the eye sees, aligns with a burning in the heart, thighs, and mind. A union has been approved in my eyes, and you should claim your rib."

The priest stopped and turned the page he looked up from the book only moving his eyes, his head still down facing the book in his hands. "What do you get from the second verse?"

Confused by the verse she said, "It sounds like it has something to do with marriage and GOD's approval."

Shaking his head slightly he said, "Not exactly marriage, but another kind of union, let me go on."

The priest looked back down at the book, and started reading,

"When you claim your rib, it shall serve you through its accents and its third eye.

The burning will cease when the union with the rib is claimed through the filling of the third eye, and the joining of thighs."

The priest closed the book in his hands and rested it on the desk in front of him, he looked up at Amelia to see a confused look on her face trying to understand what the last verse meant.

The Priest slid his chair back and stood up he walked around the desk to a shelf that was behind Amelia's chair.

The last verse had made Amelia feel uncomfortable even though she didn't fully understand it, and it was making her uneasy having the priest behind her not being able to see what he was doing.

Amelia just sat uncomfortably shaking slightly staring forward in the chair.

Then she felt the priest's hands grip her shoulders and start to massage them as he said, "What did you think of the last verse?"

Continuing to rub her shoulders, the priest was also moving his hands in a way that he was feeling lower and lower on her chest coming closer to Amelia's breasts.

Starting to become disgusted, and very uncomfortable Amelia nonchalantly replied. "I didn't really understand it, what are the accents, and the third eye?"

The priest at this time moved his hands directly over her breasts sliding them into her dress. "Well Amelia, the accents, are the beautiful breasts that GOD has given you."

Amelia, froze, she went into shock, stayed silent and just closed her eyes.

Her body tensed, and her breathing became shallow. Amelia was frozen, she was unable to move and unable to speak, as the priest continued to fondle her breasts.

He spoke, "Amelia you prove wanting of my eye, and you have a rib I wish to claim ownership of."

The priest had slowly slid his hands out of her shirt and walked around the chair keeping one hand on her shoulder as he did.

Amelia was still frozen, shaking, and unable to move or speak, the horrors from her past and future flashing through her mind.

The priest now standing in front of Amelia kneeled in front of her, he proceeded to remove the shoulder straps on her dress and pulled it down, so her breasts were fully exposed and fondled them more with his cold hands.

Amelia could do nothing but cry as he spoke, "It is time for the burning to cease through the promise from GOD, I will fill your third eye."

The priest removed his right hand from her breast and started rubbing his hand up her leg starting at the ankle, lifting and entering her dress. "The thighs will rub, your third eye will be my servant, and I will be its savior."

A tear rolled down Amelia's face as she remained frozen, unable to speak. She knew she had to do something to prevent this from happening.

Opening her eyes, she darted her gaze around the room, desperately seeking an escape.

She felt the priest trying to invade her third eye with his fingers. Amelia was nowhere near aroused, the skin on his finger was scratchy, rough, cracked and dry.

His nail long and sharp Amelia could feel it scraping and leaving small scratches on the surface.

The priest started to force his fingers inside of her, his rough skin and her unaroused state combined and made it feel to Amelia like he was trying to stick a prickly cactus into a hole filled with sand.

Feeing this the shock she was in, faded, and she knew she had regained movement. She once again looked around the room, breathing heavily, and she saw her way out.

The priest, preoccupied with Amelia's third eye, didn't notice her quick movement.

In one swift motion, she grabbed the pen from his robe pocket and stabbed it into the left side of his neck with all her strength.

Blood spurted from the wound as the priest realized what had happened.

He staggered back from the chair and stood up, facing Amelia, who remained seated in shock once again, watching the blood pour from his neck.

The priest glared at her with an evil look. He tried to speak, but his words came out as gurgles through the blood, making it impossible for Amelia to understand his angry attempts to communicate. "You little bitch, you are Jesus's whore."

After trying to say this, the priest pulled the pen out of his neck, causing blood to squirt like a sprinkler, arcing into the air and splattering onto the ground.

He collapsed to the floor seconds later, creating a puddle of blood around his body. Crying, scared, and in shock, Amelia knew she couldn't stay in the room any longer.

She got up and walked towards the door, only to realize it was locked. She assumed the key was in the priest's robe, but she couldn't bring herself to go near the body.

She sank down and curled up against the door, her head on her knees, crying uncontrollably. Feeling trapped and violated, she couldn't escape the nightmare.

After a few minutes, Amelia realized she needed help and decided to call the police.

"911 what is your emergency?"

"I need help, I am trapped inside a room at my church. The door is locked."

"Is there anyone else there on the premises or are you alone?"

Amelia looked over at the body on the floor hesitating before she spoke. "Yes, I am alone."

"What church is it?"

"It is The Servants and Saviors of Christ. It is the main branch on Lander Drive."

"We have dispatched a car to your location, what is your name and what room are you in?"

"My name is Amelia Speckle I am locked in the High Priests Chambers."

"Amelia, where is the High Priest, how did you get in there?"

"The high priest is here....."

"I thought you said you were alone?"

"I think he is dead, there is lots of blood please hurry."

Amelia dropped the phone from her ear, letting her arm fall to her lap. She hit the button to hang up on the dispatcher, then let the phone drop to the floor.

Crying and scared, she stayed curled up against the door, unable to move, until she heard people on the other side.

"Amelia we are here to help you my name is Officer Carrigan, we will have the door open in a minute, and we will get you out of there."

Amelia heard the lock on the door click open, she immediately went for the handle and swung the door open and ran out of the room.

Amelia stopped running and collapsed into one of the church pews, her body trembling as tears streamed down her face. She lifted her head and saw the towering figure of the crucified Jesus suspended above the altar—his outstretched arms casting shadows that seemed to reach for her.

Through blurred, tear-soaked eyes, she stared at the broken man on the cross. Her sorrow twisted into rage. She cursed him.

"HOW COULD YOU LET THIS HAPPEN!?" she screamed, her voice echoing through the empty sanctuary.

She remained frozen, sobbing uncontrollably, unable to rise. Her mind spiraled with questions, with grief, with betrayal. How could her God—her protector—allow such horrors to unfold in her life?

Officer Carrigan and a different high priest were staring into the room at the body of the high priest dead on the floor.

The High Priest said to the officer, "Take the girl and bring her home, have two more of our officers come to clean this up. Make sure the dispatchers call does not exist."

Nodding his head Officer Carrigan responded, "The dispatcher saw the signs, dispatched me, and deleted the call once completed."

"I will contact her parents and make them aware of the trouble she has caused here today, and their position and obligation within the church."

"Let me go find her and I will take her home."

The officer proceeded to follow the path that Amelia ran out of the room and found her sitting and crying in one of the church pews. "Get up, Amelia!"

Amelia sat and continued sobbing, not paying any attention to Officer Carrigan standing over her.

She felt cold metal wrap around her wrist and pull her to her feet. "I said get up, now give me your other hand put them behind your back."

Amelia did nothing, continuing to cry motionlessly. Officer Carrigan forcibly turned her around and bent her over the backrest of the church pew, cuffing her hands behind her back.

She could feel him rubbing his midsection against her as he did this. "Let's go, I am taking you home,"

He pulled Amelia to his car outside the church, put her in the back seat, and closed the door.

Sitting in the front seat, he tilted his mirror to see Amelia clearly in the backseat. Staring at her through the mirror, Amelia could only see his eyes.

"You are in a lot of trouble little girl. You have failed GOD through The Promise. You have failed the Servants and Saviors of Christ church. You have disrespected your family and failed them. You will be ex communicated from everything you know for this."

Officer Carrigan tilted his mirror back up and started to drive. Amelia thought she would have been under arrest and going to the police station, but the officer dropped her off at the front door of her house.

When Amelia walked through the front door of her house, she was immediately confronted by her parents, Tom and Cindy Speckle.

Her father spoke in a gruff, deep tone. "Amelia, what..... have..... you..... done?"

Her mother, Cindy, stared at Amelia, shaking. A tear rolled down her face before she started flailing her arms, hitting Amelia and yelling. "You filthy little girl, corrupted by evil, you have disrespected our church."

Amelia fell to her knees, trying to block her mother's feeble attempts to hit her. Tom stepped between them, breaking up the altercation, and directed everyone to sit down at the dining room table.

Tom sat at the head of the table, with Amelia across from him and her mother on the right side. Her father spoke, "Do you realize what you have done Amelia?"

Confused, shaking her head she said, "How do you even know what happened?

Her mother continued sobbing and said nothing. Her father continued, "The church called and let us know what you did."

Sarcastically she asked, "And what did they tell you? You don't want to hear my side of what happened."

Her father was shaking his head as he responded, "After what has happened, I don't think it matters we can't trust you anymore."

Amelia exploded, "WHAT THE FUCK DAD, he was going to rape me."

"DO NOT SWEAR IN MY HOUSE! And do not raise your voice to me! You had a promise to fulfill, commanded by the grace of GOD."

Confused at what she was hearing, her parents were supposed to love her and protect her she blew up. "IS THAT WHAT YOU WANT DAD FOR YOUR DAUGHTER, THE ONE YOU ARE SUPPOSED TO PROTECT! Some old man feeling and licking her tits and sticking his fingers and who knows what else in my pussy. I am fifteen years old. HOW COULD YOU ALLOW THAT."

Her mother continued sobbing, and through tears she spoke. "We all have...... to fulfill the promise......... How......... could you kill...... the High Priest."

Trying to reason with her mother she had to understand,

"HE WAS TRYING TO RAPE ME MOM! If you can't understand that I was scared and didn't know what to do."

Her tears coming to a halt she lifted her head and stared directly into Amelia's eyes as she spoke.

"You should have fulfilled The Promise, just like I did when I was in that same room with the same High Priest on numerous occasions, I loved him. He was a man of GOD."

Realizing GOD must have been watching when it happened, Amelia said, "Pfft GOD, where was GOD to protect me from being raped in his own church!"

Her father cut in yelling, "THAT IS ENOUGH! Do not bring the lord's name in vain! You cannot live here anymore Amelia, and after this conversation you must leave."

Shocked, and scared she responded, "You are both crazy........ WHERE AM I SUPPOSED TO GO.......? I don't believe this......... I thought you loved me, I am fifteen years old dad....."

Her father responded sternly with disappointment in his tone, "The church will take care of the High Priest, so you won't have to worry about being in trouble with the police."

Pleading with her father, "I want to call the police please dad...... can we, I have been violated."

"There is no need for the police to be involved."

Amelia shot back, "I am sure they would be very interested in The Promise to find out that little girls are being raped at the church."

"This conversation is over Amelia, you need to leave. I recommend you take this blessing of getting away with murder in this life, you will be punished eternally by GOD in the next."

Amelia stood up from her chair at the table, confounded. She stared at her parents, moving her head back and forth, looking at them as they sat in silence with their heads down.

Confused by what was happening, she yelled and stormed out of the room, slamming the front door behind her. "FUCK YOUR GOD AND FUCK YOU BOTH."

She didn't speak to her parents again after walking out that door at 15 years old until she had the accident and lost the memories of her younger years at the age of twenty-two.

Amelia's story is incredibly tragic and complex. The trauma she endured, and the subsequent memory loss deeply impacted her life, leading her back into a cycle of abuse and manipulation.

The Servants and Saviors of Christ church, with its twisted traditions and exploitation, was a place she never wanted to return to, yet circumstances beyond her control brought her back.

Two years ago, Amelia executed a reunion with her parents not remembering what had transpired when she was fifteen years old.

Entrapping her and her family within The Servants and Saviors Church once again.

The concept of "The Promise" and the abuse by the High Priests is horrifying.

It's a stark reminder of how institutions can manipulate and control individuals under the guise of religious or moral authority.

Amelia's journey is a testament to the resilience of the human spirit, even in the face of such overwhelming adversity.

If only she was able to remember and had shared her experiences with her friends or her husband, perhaps they could have helped her avoid the painful path she forced herself to walk again.

Amelia's struggle is a poignant reminder of the impact of trauma and the importance of healing.

Her journey is far from over, and with time, and the right support, she can find a way to reclaim her life and break free from the cycle of abuse.

Chapter 16 - The Celebration of Love

Amelia's curiosity exploring the island and the noise led her to a scene that was both intriguing and bewildering. The clearing was filled with people engaging in various activities, some of which were quite intimate.

There was a large fire that burned in the middle of the clearing creating moving and flickering shadows on the trees that surrounded it.

The sight of the naked men and women, the tables stocked with alcohol, and the group singing together created a surreal atmosphere.

Amelia's mind raced as she tried to make sense of what she was witnessing.

The song being sung by the group tugged at her memory, but she couldn't quite place it.

The scene was a stark contrast to the structured and controlled environment she had grown up in.

As she stood there, half-hidden behind the tree, she felt a mix of emotions—curiosity, confusion, and a hint of excitement.

This place was unlike anything she had ever experienced, and she couldn't help but feel drawn to it.

Amelia again felt that same surge flow through her body and rest in her vagina as she stared at them and became more aroused by the second.

Amelia could not stand the craving for satisfaction that she felt in between her legs any longer, and she slid her finger down her pants and inside of herself.

Amelia brought herself to climax quietly moaning to herself, when she heard a man's voice come from behind her.

"If you want to join us, we are about to get started, if you just want to watch that is ok too."

Amelia slid her hand out of her pants, coming to climax before the man spoke, she was thankful he did not arrive a second sooner.

Amelia spoke. "Hello, my name is Amelia Bernhart, I wasn't trying to spy on the party, I just got here yesterday, and I am exploring the island I heard the noise and hadn't seen anyone for hours."

The man speaking in a smooth friendly tone, "Hello Amelia, my name is Leonard Chance nice to meet you. So, you are new to the island,

I have been here for a long time. I don't even think I remember the day I got here anymore."

Amelia asked, "How long have you been here?"

"I stopped counting after five years did you want to join us?"

"What is going on?"

Leonard responded, making gestures with his hands as he spoke.

"It is a Celebration of Love, being your second day here this might sound a little sinful, but me and all of those people are going to meet in the center of the clearing, make a circle around the fire, take all of our clothes off and do what comes natural to all of us."

Amelia fantasized in her mind about standing there naked with everybody.

Just seeing all the naked bodies in the mind of her imagination was enough for a surge that she was not ready for it flowed through her body and when it rested in her vagina, her legs seemed to turn to spaghetti as she collapsed to the ground feeling extreme ecstasy.

Seeing this Leonard said, "I think you are starting to understand why we do this."

Amelia shocked at the extreme orgasm she just experienced. "What the fuck was that Leonard do you feel that surge through your body too?"

Knowingly Leonard explained, "We all do Amelia, did you feel how intense the surge was, when you fantasized about all those people being naked out there?"

Amelia hesitated, her gaze shifting uncertainly as she tried to process the words. "How did you know that?" she asked, her voice barely above a whisper.

Leonard offered a knowing smile, his eyes steady. "I know how this place works, Amelia. The imagination can run wild here. It gives us what we need and supplies us with what we want."

She furrowed her brow, contemplating his words. "What is it that we want?"

Leonard tilted his head slightly, considering her question before replying. "What is the greatest feeling your body has ever had?"

Amelia let out a small, uncertain laugh. "I don't know... happiness?"

Her answer felt hollow even as she spoke it. There was something about Leonard's tone—something that made her question whether her idea of happiness had ever been enough.

Leonard responded, "Amelia, I know it is your second day but don't be shy with anyone here. You know that feeling you got right before I came up behind you....... as you brought yourself to climax?"

Her facial expression changed instantly she looked like a kid in a candy store caught stealing, a look of surprise on her face. "I thought I got away with that up until this point. You are talking about an orgasm?"

"Yes, everybody does it. I know you were trying to be quiet, just not quite enough.

Do you know of any other experience or feeling that feels as good as an orgasm?"

Amelia, stammered, "I....."

Looking directly into her eyes speaking sincerely, "Amelia, do not be shy just tell the truth."

"No then, ok. I don't know a better feeling"

"Amelia, you will find this place is much different from the life we lived before, no one will judge you, sin is not real, Jesus will tell you that himself."

Amelia hesitated for a moment before speaking. "My guide was Simon Cartwright. Do you know him?"

Leonard's brow lifted slightly in recognition. "Yes, I think I met him at the last island celebration—the wine guy."

He let out a small chuckle. "Where is he now?"

Amelia folded her arms across her chest, glancing at the quiet shoreline beyond them. "I sent him away this morning. I wanted to be alone."

"Did you succumb to your urges and desires and feel bad about it, because of the sin you committed?"

Her voice was a mix of astonishment and curiosity, her eyes searching Leonard's face for answers.

Surprised that Leonard knew exactly what happened like he was able to read her mind she replied. "You are good mister Leonard Chance, how did you know exactly what happened?"

"Like I said I have been here a long time I have seen a lot of people come here. If they are here Jesus has brought them here, I also know how backwards the beliefs about Jesus were where we came from.

I would say 90% of people have that problem when they arrive here."

"I sent Simon away because I felt a terrible feeling the next day in my body and my mind. I wanted to hear the words straight from Jesus's mouth and was waiting my three days to talk to him."

"Amelia, in the time I have been here I have taken every chance I had to talk with Jesus. Do you want me to tell you what I think he would say?"

"Yes, please!"

Hesitating for a slight moment before speaking, "It probably won't come as eloquently and with the same words he would use but here it is.

Everything about what you thought you knew was wrong, Sex being viewed as a taboo or bad thing where we came from was just one perspective that caught on and was passed on.

If that perspective was wrong, which perspective is correct, why does it still bother you?"

Amellia responded, "I think it is all psychological at this point."

"Just remember, sin as we know it, is a label of an action. If you had a jar and you knew the label on it was wrong, would you use it for the purpose it was labeled?"

"No, not if I knew the label was wrong."

Leonard gestured to the heaven around them, "We are in the same situation here you are labeling everything with your Christian thoughts but that is not the jar we are in or ever have been.

Here Amelia, call it heaven, call it the island, I have even heard people call it Nevaeh which fits well."

Confused she asked, "Why Nevaeh?"

"Because everything is backwards here from what we thought we knew. It describes this place perfectly to a tee; Nevaeh is heaven spelt backwards.

Like I was saying though call it whatever you want, but we were all brought here by Jesus, and Jesus doesn't label any actions, the judgement is over for us."

"It will just take some getting used to, I think."

"Well keep this in mind, almost everybody has sex with their guide on the first night, and goes through this alone hiding period that you are in.

When you see people who have come out of that period, they like Jesus will not label your actions anymore.

Truth and communication will take you a long way here."

Shrugging her shoulders she responded, "So me feeling this anguish is all just a waste of my energy.......... Saying that, and hearing myself say it, does help a little."

"This place is special you have felt and seen that already."

Leonard gestured to the trees and the beauty of nature around them, then continued, "Now that we are here our will, and consent is all that matters."

An empathetic look crossing his face as he continued, "If you want to feel that anguish, if you think it helps you. If your will and consent do not impede anyone else, the action has no label or judgement."

Pausing for a second and then saying, "Let me ask you this Amelia, what did you think a heaven or paradise would be before this?"

"I always knew in the back of my mind it couldn't be what I thought it was."

Leonard responded, "We all had twisted thoughts of what this place could even be but think about it Amelia.

In my time here no one has gotten sick, or died, we have all the food and water we need, and unlimited access to partners to have sex with and share orgasm with no risks of pregnancy or sex diseases.

What would be a better reward than having an orgasm for the rest of eternity."

Amelia responded, "Yeah, I see your point, anything that I had to do before, work, school, kids, church none of that matters anymore."

Leonard noticed that all the people in the clearing were starting to take their clothes off.

The atmosphere was charged with an almost surreal energy and pure lust that could be smelt in the air, the flickering firelight casting shadows that danced across the scene.

Amelia noticed too, her eyes widening as she took in the sight.

The fire burned intensely between her soaking wet thighs, a sensation that was both alarming and strangely exhilarating.

The sensation between her thighs seemed to pulse with the rhythm of the gathering and the heat of the fire, each heartbeat echoing the primal lustful energy that filled the air.

Leonard and Amelia exchanged a glance, "They will not start without me I can bring you as my guest. Would you care to join us in our Celebration of Love?"

"Why do you call it the Celebration of Love?"

"It would help to view sex as making love to someone else trying to give them the best orgasm, and the same for them.

When the strings of our human mind aren't attached it is two people coming together and sharing love, a want and care for each other's needs. Will you join us?"

Her voice was barely above a whisper, filled with a mix of longing and fear. The weight of her past experiences bore down on her, Amelia put her head down, ashamed to say yes even though she wanted to more than anything.

Timidly, she said, "I'm not sure............"

"It is your choice Amelia, if you want to just watch you can do that, if you want to join, I recommend not to wait.

You want to be there at the beginning when we stand in the circle. I think it will get you over that last hurdle you are facing with sin."

Amelia felt the burning between her thighs as the wetness increased in her third eye like someone left the tap running, she started to feel a constant nonstop drip slowly moving down her right thigh as she said timidly. "Let us go stand in the circle."

A big smile came across Leonard's face as he spoke, "Good choice, you won't regret it. You will have about five minutes once we get out there if you want to get yourself a drink to help calm your nerves."

Leonard extended his hand to Amelia, and she took it, feeling a sense of reassurance in his firm grip. They walked out into the clearing from the tree line, the light filtering through the branches creating a dappled pattern on the ground.

As they approached the group, Leonard's voice boomed with confidence and excitement. "EVERYONE THIS IS AMELIA SHE WILL BE JOINING US FOR THE CELEBRATION."

His tone full of pride and warmth. The group turned to look, their faces lighting up with curiosity and welcome. Amelia felt a mixture of nervousness and anticipation as they made their way closer, the clearing buzzing with the energy Leonard had promised.

He turned to Amelia beside him and spoke. "Go get your drinks now Amelia, you can get to know everyone after our Celebration."

Amelia grabbed a bottle of wine and a glass, setting them on a table near the forming circle.

With her back to the group, she poured a glass and downed it in two quick gulps.

She poured another glass, drank all of it, and then set the glass down.

When she turned around, she saw all thirteen people standing in a circle around the fire, naked, and holding hands.

Embarrassed by her clothed state, Amelia began to rush as she removed the picnic blanket tied around her neck.

Leonard said to her, "No rush Amelia, the wait and the anticipation only makes it better!"

She continued undressing until she felt the warm air on her skin. Leonard held out his hand, indicating the empty space beside him.

Amelia walked through the circle to the open spot and held hands with Leonard and the person next to her.

Once the circle was complete, Leonard spoke aloud to everyone.

"As with every Celebration of Love, we will take the first five minutes closing our eyes and holding hands, feeling the sexual energy between us all.

I will let you all know when to open your eyes."

Amelia closed her eyes tightly, determined to participate in the celebration the right way.

She stood with her eyes shut and hands locked with the people next to her, focusing on her breathing to fully immerse herself in the experience. Feeling the heat from the fire immerse them all in warm air.

She felt a tingle in her hands, whether from body heat or sexual energy, it grew into a vibration traveling through her hands.

After about one minute of having her eyes closed her imagination started to go into overdrive.

She started seeing all the people in the circle naked in her mind, fantasizing about having sex with them.

Touching their bodies in places she thought were naughty.

Amelia felt her vagina become wetter than it ever had been in her life so that it felt like she was peeing, and a river was running down her leg.

The images flashing through her mind were enough to give her the 1st multiple orgasm of many to come today, even with the contact of only holding hands with someone.

She would have fallen to the ground if she wasn't holding hands with the people next to her supporting her.

She had three more orgasms before Leonard spoke. "Open your eyes!"

Amelia opened her eyes embarrassed standing in a puddle of her own fluids she could feel it all over her feet and squishing in between her toes.

She looked around the circle and was no longer embarrassed like when she had her eyes closed.

She noticed the women in the circle were all dripping fluids down their legs and had created puddles of their own around their feet.

All the men in the circle, it was the same, their upright erections covered in their own fluids, some men with a strong shot had it on their chests and stomachs too.

Everyone released their intertwined hands, and everyone started sexually massaging the person to their right. using the fluids they created as body oil eventually in time resulting in the mixture of all their fluids combined.

Touching and Kissing each other everywhere on the body, eventually resulting in the advance to oral sex being exchanged between everyone in the group, at natural intervals the group would swap partners, team up on individuals.

With everyone being able to share many multiple orgasms together with everyone participating in the celebration.

Amelia had never felt such an amazing feeling in her body in her entire life to orgasm so many times in a row the intensity of each orgasm increasing each time.

She never would have been sexual with a woman before she died, but she quite enjoyed pleasuring women with her tongue giving and receiving oral sex.

As Leonard told her she would not regret her decision to join them, and it set her on a path for the next two weeks of traveling the island like a sex zombie.

Indulging in her sexual appetite with as many people as she could, as often as she could.

She continued her friendship with Simon, they would go out as a couple and find others to join them. Simon fell in love with Amelia on the second day when they again shared a picnic on the beach after she participated in The Celebration of Love.

Deep inside he wanted to keep her all to himself, but Simon also enjoyed the freedom of the relationship they created.

Caught up in all the sex Amelia was having she waited almost two weeks before going to see Jesus again and talking with him.

Chapter 17 - Amelia and Jesus

Amelia stood in front of the door to Jesus's compound within the hills, waiting for it to open after notifying Jesus of her arrival by using the button beside the door. Within two minutes, the door opened, revealing a fifty-foot-long hallway with another door at the far end.

Initially dark, the hallway was soon illuminated by five sets of lights on both sides of the wall.

These lights, spaced ten feet apart, directed their beams towards the light on the opposite wall, creating bright light barriers at each interval.

The bright white light at the end of the hallway created a blur, obstructing the view of the door on the other side.

As Amelia walked down the hallway, each light barrier she passed through revealed more of the door from the bright white blur.

The experience felt surreal as the light engulfed her body.

When she reached the door at the other end, she put her hand on the handle and opened it.

As she did, all the lights behind her turned off, and she stepped into the same bright white room she had awoken in almost two weeks ago.

Although she didn't see Jesus in the room, something caught her eye—a brand new Silver Streamer bike, discontinued for over twenty years, leaning against the bright white wall behind the couch.

Amelia walked over to the bike, her fingers tracing the handlebars and the silver streamers.

She felt a wave of nostalgia and excitement wash over her.

She turned around to Jesus sitting in his chair with a warm smile on his face he said, "I thought you would like that."

Surprise in her voice as she spoke, "I was looking for one of these for so many years and could never find one, Thank you. I must admit, I lied when I said I had one growing up. I was still skeptical and used this rare bike as a test for your powers."

Jesus took a bow towards Amelia as he spoke, his gesture graceful and respectful. His voice carrying a warmth that seemed to fill the room, "I hope I passed your test."

Motioning his hands towards the couch, Jesus invitingly spoke. "What brings you to see me today? I have more of that duck you like. Come, sit and eat."

Amelia walked away from the bike running the streamers on the handlebars through her hand as she walked over to the couch feeling the nostalgia of finally owning the bike once more.

She sat down and started eating. Jesus sat across from her, twirling his thumbs, waiting patiently until she was done eating.

Then he asked. "How was the Duck?"

"That duck was better than the first time. Thank you."

"How have you been finding it here? Are you enjoying yourself?"

Sitting back on the couch, somewhat ashamed of what she was about to tell Jesus, Amelia rubbed her belly.

Her voice trembling slightly. She avoided eye contact; her gaze fixed on her hands as she gathered the courage to continue.

She spoke softly, "I was having a rough time after my first day....... feeling guilty and wrong, but that all changed after I met a man named Leonard Chance."

"Leonard has been here a long time. He knows a lot about this place."

"Yes, he does."

"So, what were you feeling guilty and wrong about, Amelia?"

Amelia started to feel a bit of the guilt from her first night as she spoke these words to Jesus.

She flashbacked to the morning after in her mind when she woke up alone and envisioned Jesus calling her a "dirty whore."

She put her head down, ashamed and embarrassed, and spoke in a low voice. "Simon and I had sex on our first night."

Stopping his thumb twirling and throwing his hands up in the air excitedly, His eyes sparkled with enthusiasm, and a wide grin spread across his face Jesus responded,

"If that is what you wanted to do!!!!! You have nothing to feel wrong or guilty about!!!!!!"

His sudden burst of energy was infectious, filling the room with a sense of acceptance.

"I know that now. It all changed after talking to Leonard. I am not ashamed of judgment or sin any longer."

Continuing his thumb twirling and speaking in a tone that deviated from any of Amelia's previous encounters with him, Jesus said, "Good, Amelia. Indulge, enjoy, and discover."

His words carried an unsettling undertone, a stark contrast to the calm and reassuring presence she had known.

Amelia felt a shiver run down her spine, the unexpected shift in his demeanor causing her to question everything she thought she understood about him.

She stood there, uncertain and wary, trying to decipher the true meaning behind his cryptic statement.

Changing his tone, Amelia once again felt the warmth she associated with Jesus, he continued, Jesus spoke excitedly. "I do have something else for you!!!"

"What is that?"

"Open your hand."

Amelia sat up on the couch and put her hand open-palmed up in front of her.

Jesus sat up and put his hand over top of hers, opened his hand, and pulled it back.

A ring appeared in Amelia's open hand.

She stared down at it, knowing it was her wedding ring. Remembering her family, a tear started to form in her right eye.

Amelia's eyes widened in surprise. "How did you know? I haven't even asked you yet."

Jesus smiled, a quiet certainty in his expression. "I spoke with Simon yesterday. He told me you wanted it, so I took a little extra time to bring it here for you."

Relief flooded Amelia's chest. She clasped her hands together; her voice filled with gratitude. "Thank you Jesus!"

Jesus met her gaze warmly. "What else was on your mind, Amelia?"

She hesitated for a moment, sorting through the thoughts that had been stirring in her mind. "Nothing big, but I do remember one question I had for you."

Jesus nodded, waiting patiently. "What was that?"

"If it doesn't rain here, how do all the trees, fruits, and vegetation grow?"

Jesus's eyes gleamed with approval. "Not many even ask that question, Amelia. You are one of only a few."

He gestured toward the land around them. "The island is filled with underground channels. The water surrounding the island flows beneath it, weaving through those channels. The trees and vegetation draw their water from deep within the ground."

Amelia absorbed his words, she had expected something miraculous, something beyond earthly understanding.

And yet, the explanation—simple, rooted in nature—made perfect sense.

She exhaled slowly. "That's incredible."

Jesus smiled. "Everything here is sustained as it should be, without struggle or need. Just as you are meant to be, Amelia."

Amelia nodded slowly, absorbing Jesus's words. "Okay, that makes sense. Simon mentioned something to me about the shapes and the Three E's. It made me curious—why is it done?"

Jesus chuckled lightly, his gaze warm but knowing. "To tell you the truth, Amelia, it's just something I made up—but don't tell the others."

A playful smirk touched his lips. "It helps enhance the community. It brings unity to relationships among the people here.

They work together to build the shapes, striving for perfection, helping each other, connecting through the process. It gives everyone a shared goal."

Amelia considered that for a moment, her thoughts drifting back to everything she had ever been taught. "You know, throughout my life as a follower of you, Jesus, we could only ever fathom the questions we would ask you when we met in the afterlife."

She sighed, shaking her head slightly. "Now that I'm here, none of those questions seem to apply anymore—because you're not the same as we were taught. It makes coming up with things to ask very difficult."

Jesus stopped twirling his thumbs, waving his hands in a who-cares fashion, his tone indifferent but firm.

"I don't think the questions matter much anymore, Amelia. You're here. The knowledge might be nice to have, but you don't need to overthink it."

He paused for a moment, studying her. "Instead—I have a question for *you*."

She straightened slightly. "What is it?"

Jesus's expression shifted, more serious now, but still filled with quiet warmth. "Would you care to be a guide for newcomers, like Simon was to you?"

A spark of excitement flared in Amelia's chest, her voice assured and eager. "Of course Jesus!

I would love to. I would do anything for you."

After meeting Leonard for the past two weeks, Amelia had sex with every person she had met. She found that after this time coming across new people to have sex with was a somewhat rarer occurrence.

In turn when she met new people, she got extremely horny and wanted to have sex with them immediately.

Just the thought of guiding two new people for Jesus within her mind, caused a surge of ecstasy through her body which rested in her vagina as a puddle of fluid.

She could feel this fluid run down her thighs and in between her ass cheeks as she sat on the couch and excitedly responded. "I will be happy to, Jesus."

"Tomorrow Kevan Harrison will arrive here, and the next day Justin Standone, please be at the door in the morning on both days."

Hiding the fact, she wanted these men inside of her as soon as possible, she was trying to come off as helpful, she responded. "I will probably sleep outside the door tonight, so I will be here."

Amelia realizing she was still holding her wedding ring within her hand opened it and looked at the ring.

The thoughts of her family invading her perverted thoughts of sex, started to produce more fluid from her body, which started to pour down her face, as she broke down crying, battling these thoughts within her mind.

Jesus got up from his chair and walked over to the couch and sat beside Amelia. Jesus hugged her, and said, "It is ok Amelia."

Amelia slid the ring on her finger and hugged Jesus back before saying goodbye and rushing out of the room.

Chapter 18 - Kevan's Eye Opening

Kevan opened his eyes and spun around slowly, marveling at the beauty around him. The vibrant colors, and the serene atmosphere made him feel like he had stepped into a dream.

He took deep breaths as he did this, noting that the air also had a slightly sweet taste he could feel on his tongue.

Behind him was a metal door built right into the front of a hill face, maybe 10 feet tall.

Beyond the hill were other hills of various sizes, mountains, and forests extending as far as his vision could reach.

The door opened into the middle of a vast open area covered in the greenest grass he had ever seen.

The vibrant hue of the grass seemed almost surreal, like a lush carpet stretching endlessly before him. Trees, sparsely spread throughout the area, bore bright fruits of many colors hanging from their branches, creating a kaleidoscope of natural beauty.

The open area stretched to the horizon, where he could see large trees and animals grazing in the distance.

The peaceful scene filled him with a sense of tranquility and wonder, as if he had stepped into a paradise untouched by time.

Taking a few steps, Kevan spoke,

Kevan let out a slow breath, eyes sweeping across the landscape as he tried to process everything at once. "It's all so beautiful,"

he murmured. "So where do we go from here?"

Amelia turned to him with a reassuring smile. "The choice is yours. But I do have a surprise set up for you, if you'd like to see that first."

Kevan gave a small chuckle, nodding. "Of course—if you went to the trouble."

She extended her arm, gesturing toward the path ahead. "Let's walk this way."

Side by side, they moved forward, the ground beneath them impossibly soft—almost like a cushion of air and grass blended seamlessly into one.

The scent of the fruit-bearing trees surrounded them, thick and intoxicating, the colors of the island somehow more vibrant than anything Kevan had ever seen in his life.

It was overwhelming, as if reality itself had been heightened, stretched into something dreamlike and unnatural. "So, you've been here for two weeks?"

Kevan asked, watching the way Amelia walked with ease, as if she had long accepted whatever this place was.

She nodded. "Yeah, two weeks."

Kevan hesitated, looking down at the ground in front of him as he walked, he exhaled sharply. "Can I speak honestly with you?"

Amelia glanced at him with quiet amusement. "You'll find that truth and communication will take you a long way here."

Kevan shoved his hands into his pockets, his voice tight. "What do you think is going on here? Because this place doesn't feel like Heaven."

Her expression softened, like someone recalling an old thought that had troubled them once but was no longer sharp enough to hurt.

"It made me suspicious at first too," She admitted.

"But after spending time here, you'll find there's no reason to doubt anymore."

Kevan shook his head. "I feel like I'm not supposed to be here."

"I felt the same way on my first day."

They continued walking, the landscape around them shifting in subtle ways—the trees taller, the air warmer, the sky impossibly blue.

Kevan glanced ahead, watching the path curve slightly before disappearing into the forest.

The feeling in his gut grew heavier. "It just doesn't feel right."

Amelia shot him a knowing glance. "Hopefully my surprise will make you feel better."

She reached up, effortlessly plucking a bright red fruit from a tree they passed. Kevan noticed how the fruit's skin shimmered slightly, as if the light caught it at impossible angles, bending into a color that didn't exist.

He swallowed, suddenly unsure of everything. "Where is everybody?" Kevan asked, shifting the subject. "Jesus said there were over six thousand people here."

"They're all here somewhere," Amelia said simply.

"It's a big place."

Kevan sighed. "So, what's this surprise you've got for me?"

Amelia smirked. "If I told you what it was, we could no longer call it a surprise."

The mystery in her voice pulled him forward, despite his reservations.

"We'll get there soon,"

She added. "You'll see."

Kevan let out a dry laugh. "So, what have you done in your past two weeks here?"

Amelia glanced at him, her expression easy. "I've explored most of the island, met people along the way, had conversations, built relationships. I had my second talk with Jesus yesterday, which brings me here today—as your guide."

Kevan arched a brow. "So where exactly are we headed?"

She gestured ahead. "This path leads to a beach. That's the setting of your surprise."

Kevan hummed in thought, processing her words. "So, what church were you a part of before coming here?"

"I was part of the Servants and Saviors of Christ. I handled finances and other things within the church."

Kevan slowed slightly. "I've heard of your group. My father was a High Priest there."

Amelia turned to look at him more fully, sensing there was more to the story.

Kevan continued, "After my father died, my mother became part of the Anointing Church of Jesus Christ. I became one of thirteen High Priests within the church about two years ago."

His voice dropped slightly, weighted with something unspoken. "Did your church follow the Edicts?"

Amelia responded, "We had the Bible, but we also had a Book of Edicts that we used side by side."

Kevan nodded, his expression unreadable. "I was always told other churches followed the Edicts, but I never knew for sure."

Amelia let out a small sigh. "None of that matters anymore, Kevan. Everything we were told by religion—by men—wasn't real. But *this place*? This is as real as it gets."

Kevan swallowed, staring at the horizon ahead as the forest began to open, revealing glimpses of the beach beyond. "As a High Priest, I was one of those men who spewed lies to my followers."

His voice cracked slightly, and he hung his head, shame weighing on his shoulders.

Amelia didn't hesitate—she reached out and placed a gentle hand on his arm.

Amelia empathically responded, "Don't be so hard on yourself, Kevan. None of us were in a position to know we were being lied to."

He exhaled shakily. "I came to that realization about a year ago. I stopped believing in God entirely. I became an atheist."

Amelia's brows lifted slightly, but she said nothing.

Kevan continued, "I continued as a High Priest, putting on a mask for everyone."

Kevan shook his head, frustration flickering across his features. "It made me very confused when Jesus told me he *chose* me to come here."

Amelia walked slower, studying him. "It would be wise to only worry about the *here and now,* not things you can't change."

Her voice was gentle, but firm. "Especially on your first day. It can do a number on your mind."

Kevan stared at the sand beneath them, the grains finer than anything he had ever seen. His voice was low, almost desperate.

"The here and now? Where is *here*? And what is *now*? It's all the same inside my head. I would've thought this place would feel different."

Amelia turned her gaze toward the ocean at the end of the path—the way it remained still, undisturbed, as if frozen in time.

The water stretched endlessly, mirror-like, reflecting light but not reality.

"How did it happen?"

She asked, changing the subject. "Your death, I mean."

Kevan swallowed hard. "We were hit by a car. My friend Josh was driving."

Amelia let out a small breath. "I was hit by a car too."

She hesitated before asking, "Did your friend come here too?"

Kevan's expression darkened. "No. Jesus said he wasn't chosen."

He gestured vaguely with his hands. "Which doesn't make any sense. How—and *why*—are we being chosen to come here? Josh was a devout follower of Jesus."

Amelia met his conflicted gaze, offering the only answer she had. "That might be a question only Jesus can answer for you."

Kevan exhaled. "I did ask him that. He said Josh wasn't worthy."

He clenched his jaw. "But what *makes* us worthy?"

Amelia turned back toward the horizon, where the sky melted seamlessly into the ocean's still surface. "I wondered that for some time too,"

She murmured. "But eventually, that question will drift to the back of your mind."

They came to the end of the path and arrived at the sandy beach.

The soft sand crunched gently under their feet as they stepped onto the beach, there was an even golden glow casted over the water and the sky.

Amelia had a picnic setting prepared for them, complete with a blanket spread out on the sand.

There was an array of delicious fruits in a pile, a bottle of wine, and two glasses carefully placed, ready for them to enjoy.

The sight brought a warm smile to Kevan's face, the thoughtful gesture touching him deeply.

Amelia turned to Kevan, her eyes sparkling with anticipation. Her voice filled with warmth and excitement. "Surprise! I figured we can just sit, relax, talk, and have a glass of wine. My guide Simon did the same thing for me, we had a wonderful time together."

"That is very nice of you, thank you."

They walked over to the picnic blanket, and both sat down, Amelia opened the bottle of wine with practiced ease and poured two glasses, the rich liquid glistening.

She handed one to Kevan, their fingers briefly touching as they exchanged a warm smile.

They clinked their glasses together, the soft chime echoing the start of a peaceful, intimate moment. "When I arrived here, Simon had a $100,000 bottle of wine for me. I couldn't get my hands on anything that spectacular, but we got this generic red wine."

"You have been extremely kind to me, Amelia. Everything is wonderful."

He looked out and noticed the still waters that extended to the reaches of his vision as he took his first sip of the wine.

Kevan swirled the wine in his glass, watching the deep red liquid catch the sunlight.

The color was rich—deceptively inviting—but when he took his first sip, his expression twisted into something between amusement and mild disappointment. "You know what? I take it back. This wine is gross."

Amelia playfully punched his arm, making him laugh. "I'm joking," he said, shaking his head.

She smirked. "It was the best I could get; you jerk."

Kevan took another sip, this time letting the flavor linger on his tongue, analyzing it with exaggerated contemplation.

Amelia mirrored his movements, sipping slowly. A moment later, she scrunched her nose.

"You're right, though. It does not taste good."

They both laughed, the sound carried softly by the still, humid air. Kevan glanced toward the endless stretch of water—so smooth it looked like glass. Something about it unsettled him.

"What's with the water?" he asked, shifting his glass in his hand. "I've never seen a large body of water so settled."

Amelia followed his gaze, her expression calm but distant. "None of the factors that caused waves on Earth exist here."

Kevan frowned. "What do you mean?"

Amelia's voice was steady, as though she had explained this many times before.

"Jesus says we're in a separate universe from Earth. It's just the island and water, stretching to a barrier—the edge of this dimension.

There are no external forces affecting the water. No wind. No gravity as we knew it. So, it just sits there."

Kevan let out a quiet breath. "Huh. Now that's something to think about."

Amelia's eyes brightened slightly, remembering her own curiosity from weeks before. "All the bugs are underground too. No flies, no mosquitoes. That was my second question after I asked about the water when Simon and I arrived."

Kevan took another sip, scanning his surroundings, as if only now noticing the absence of insects—the strange purity of the air. "Huh. Hadn't even noticed yet."

He chuckled, the sound effortless, before the conversation shifted again.

"So, how did you get involved with your church?"

Amelia twirled her glass between her fingers absentmindedly. "Through my parents. They were members and got me, my now husband—fiancé at the time—to join also."

She glanced at him. "How did you get involved with yours?"

Kevan exhaled, rubbing a hand over his jaw. "Like I said before, my father was a High Priest with your church. After he died, my mother decided to change churches."

Amelia nodded, sensing the weight behind his words. "How did your father die?"

Something shifted in Kevan's expression—a flicker of fear that darkened his features in an instant. Amelia immediately regretted asking.

"I hope my asking is okay. I'm sorry."

Kevan swallowed hard, his jaw tightening before he shook his head. "You're fine, Amelia.

I had a hard time with my father's death for a long time. I was just a teenager when it happened."

She hesitated before speaking. "What happened?"

Kevan looked down, staring at the fine grains of sand scattered across the blanket.

He focused on them, as if counting their endless patterns would keep the flood of memories at bay.

But the moment pressed on, drawing the truth from him like an unraveling thread.

His voice was quiet, almost fragile. "I haven't talked about this with anyone, so excuse me if I have trouble expressing myself."

He took a breath, steadying himself. "I do want to get it out."

Amelia waited, listening.

"When I was seventeen, my father was murdered."

The word *murdered* lingered in the air between them, carrying a weight that made the world feel smaller. "It happened inside the church,"

Kevan continued, his voice tight. "I don't know the details. No one would tell me anything."

Amelia's breath hitched slightly. "It happened inside the church? Who would do such a thing?"

Kevan shook his head, frustration threading through his expression. "I have no clue who did it. But the worst part—the part that still haunts me—is that I was supposed to pick him up that evening."

His fingers curled slightly against the blanket. "I saw his body lying on the floor inside his chambers. A pool of blood surrounding him."

Amelia's stomach tightened. "I am so sorry, Kevan."

He gave a small nod, as if acknowledging her sympathy but unable to hold onto it.

"The officers there made me leave. The next day, I checked the news. Nothing. I went to the police station—no records. Nothing.

I confronted the High Priest who had been there that night, and he acted like I imagined the entire thing."

Amelia's hands tightened around her glass. "That's insane. How could something like that happen?"

Kevan let out a bitter laugh, shaking his head. "My mother moved within a week. We joined another church. Everyone acted like nothing had happened and my father never existed."

Amelia, engrossed in his words, poured more wine, her hands moving automatically as she listened.

She refilled Kevan's glass as well, the soft sound of liquid pouring adding a strange sense of normalcy amid the weight of the conversation.

"So, what did you do?" she asked.

Kevan sighed, rubbing his temple. "There wasn't much I could do. I was only seventeen. But I still have flashbacks—see his body. It never really goes away."

Amelia nodded slowly, the empathy in her expression steady. "Were you and your father close?"

Kevan hesitated. "I wouldn't say close. We loved each other, but my father was a strict man. A man of God. He followed his religion down to its fundamentals. It kept us divided as father and son."

Amelia's voice softened. "And your mother? Were you close with her?"

"We became closer after my father died."

He exhaled, staring ahead. "I followed in his footsteps. Became a High Priest. Hoped it would make my mother proud."

He glanced at her. "What about you? Were you close with your parents?"

Amelia's expression darkened slightly. "I was—before coming here."

Kevan furrowed his brow. "Were you always part of the church?"

She gave a small nod. "As far back as I remember. But that comes with a caveat."

Kevan tilted his head. "What caveat?"

Amelia took a deep breath. "I had an accident eight years ago. I lost all my long-term memories."

Kevan straightened slightly, surprise flickering across his face. "So... you don't remember anything?"

"I suffered trauma to my head. I still knew my name, who I was, but everything else was blank. My entire life before that day—it was gone."

Kevan stared at her, the quiet understanding of loss shared between them. "That must have been hard to handle."

Amelia let out a small, tired laugh. "I felt like I didn't know who I was anymore."

He nodded slowly. "So, you can only wonder what kind of adventures you had growing up."

Amelia smiled faintly. "Exactly."

She lifted the bottle. "Would you like another glass of wine?"

Kevan chuckled, shaking his head. "I don't know if I should. I might fall over if I tried to stand up."

Amelia grinned. "Ahhh, you'll be fine."

Amelia filled both of their glasses.

After doing so, she stood up, raised her arms above her head, and stretched out her whole body right in front of Kevan.

Her nipples pressed against the shirt she was wearing, revealing that they were hard. Kevan noticed her nipples popping out of her shirt and became excited inside, though he didn't reveal that he noticed. "Ooh that felt so good." Amelia said after stretching

"If you wanted to stretch some more, I wouldn't object." Kevan said.

She looked him directly into his eyes and said, "If that is what you want Kevan, I could stretch my body in all types of poses. Did you see something you liked."

Kevan, being shy, and embarrassed put his head down hesitated before speaking only one word. "Yes."

"Kevan, don't be shy, here if you want something you can have it, and no one will judge you.

If you want me, I am yours."

Kevan felt a massive surge flow through his body that rested in his mid-section. Giving Kevan a feeling he had not felt in over two years, being sexually aroused and having a hard cock in his pants.

Kevan had made a vow of celibacy when he became a High Priest and for the past two years, Kevan had not had sex, touched himself, or even been aroused.

"I wouldn't even know what to do it has been so long."

"It's like riding a bike we never forget how to do it.

Either way Kevan, but if it is what you want, know it is yours........ Want to go for a swim?"

"We don't even have swimsuits."

"We don't need swimsuits silly no one is here; it is just me and you.

Just think how nice the warm water will feel up against your skin, assisted by the wine of course."

Kevan with his head down not looking at Amelia said, "Is it ok if I watch you undress?"

"Kevan if you want to watch me feel free, if you want to stick that hard thing in your pants inside me, I invite you to."

Kevan's excitement elevated, he tried to hide it from Amelia, but she could see it through the look on his face, and the hard thing creating a small tent in his pants.

Amelia started to undress slowly giving Kevan an undressing worth watching.

She danced around slightly squeezing, feeling, caressing, and tickling her breasts, and body.

She slowly moved her hands down and lifted her shirt slowly over her head.

She stood posed holding the shirt in her left hand at the side of her body dangling on her fore finger.

She stopped and stared down at Kevan directly into his eyes, seeing flames within his pupils and seeing the fire she had created within him.

Amelia let the shirt slide off her finger and onto the sand below. Kevan's mind was racing never having a thought about sex for over two years and now seeing Amelia's strip show for him, he was full of ecstasy and lust with nothing on his mind but sticking his hard cock inside of her.

Kevan said, "If you would believe it, I haven't seen a woman naked in over two years."

"How come?"

Amelia moved her hands and started to slowly lower her pants as she said this.

"I took a vow of celibacy when I became a High Priest, seeing you now and how it is making me feel, I think that was the biggest mistake of my life."

"We all make mistakes, now is the time to make up for them."

Amelia was bent over forward with her pants down to her ankles, she dangled her breasts and shook them a little from left to right.

Kevan was focused staring at her hard nipples following them as she stood up slowly.

Amelia slowly repeated the same motions removing her underwear, a fire burning inside Kevan like he had never felt before.

Amelia wearing nothing but shoes and socks stood completely naked facing Kevan, she let his eyes linger on the front of her body for a few seconds, and then she turned around slowly so Kevan was staring at her back and her buttocks.

She bent over forward slowly pausing while gripping her ankles, Kevan stared in a trance at her dripping vagina and the shiny lips of her clitoris.

Amelia slowly removed her shoes one at a time and did the same with the socks she was wearing, she remained bent over while she did this enticing and tempting Kevan with her soaking wet vagina.

When she pulled the second sock off her foot, she stood her back still facing Kevan and started running towards the water as she yelled. "COME ON!"

Kevan popping out of his vaginal trance could feel his hard cock pulsating in his pants, needing to be relieved.

Kevan stood up as quick as he could and started to run towards the water removing his clothes as he did.

He heard Amelia splashing when she reached the water but could not see her because he had stopped running and was bent over at the time removing his pants.

Kevan could see Amelia's head floating and swimming away from him standing on the shore as he reached the water and yelled. "WAIT FOR ME!"

Amelia didn't reply, she kept swimming further out and Kevan rushed to catch up with her, she eventually stopped and turned around to face him floating in the same spot.

When Kevan was within ten feet of Amelia she dived down under the water. She swam underwater towards Kevan, swimming in circles around him rubbing his cock very lightly with one of her fingers each time she went by the front of his body.

Amelia quietly floated up above the water behind Kevan's back seeing him moving his head looking around for her.

She floated closer and put her hands on his shoulders and started rubbing them, giving him a massage. "I thought I would never find you."

She ran her hands through her wet hair smoothing it back, so it wasn't in her face "I am here now."

"Were you touching me under the water?"

Giggling Amelia responded, "I might have."

"I thought there was a fish down there trying to bite my dick."

Amelia busted out laughing while continuing to massage his shoulders. "I said I might have. It might have been a fish; it could have been both."

Amelia continued laughing and spoke. "Let's swim in a little so we can touch the bottom."

They both floated closer to the shore and stopped when they could touch the bottom again.

Amelia, now facing Kevan, wading one foot apart, they held their hands together under the water.

Kevan said, "The water not having any motion feels really weird."

"Yeah, it does I never thought about that, it feels like half set gelatin."

Kevan put his head down and was looking at the water as he spoke, "I still have shy kindred feelings within me, but the amount of lust I feel for you is overwhelming every sense in my body."

"You don't have to be shy Kevan, I am right here waiting for you."

Amelia pulled him closer with their intertwined hands; she positioned herself with her mouth right next to his ear and whispered to him.

"We can take it slow Kevan, take your lust out on me. Fuck me Kevan! Fuck me!"

Amelia could feel Kevan's hard cock floating between her legs rubbing her thighs gently, and she whispered.

"It's just me and you Kevan, you deserve it, just put it in........... put it in........ Uhhhh"

Amelia moaned loudly as Kevan had slid his cock inside of her as deep as he could, Kevan let out loud noises of pleasure at the same time.

Chapter 19 - Kevan's Trauma

After having sex once in the water, and two more times on the beach Kevan and Amelia were exhausted, and they decided to take a break. Kevan said, "You are amazing Amelia." Amelia blushing responded, "Oh stop you were pretty amazing yourself." Kevan responded with a serious tone, "It has never felt like that before."

Amelia gestured with her hands, "I think it has something to do with this place,

"What do you mean?"

"It is our reward for being here. A wise man named Leonard once asked me when I first came here, what is the greatest feeling your body has ever felt?"

Kevan responded joyously, "I would have to say what we just did."

"Exactly Kevan, in my first couple days when I was having a rough time because I had sex with my guide Simon. Leonard said what would you expect heaven to be but one infinite orgasm the greatest feeling we can feel."

Processing what Amelia had just told him; the only part of the sentence he heard was that she had sex with Simon.

Almost offended thinking they had something special, "What?....... You had sex with Simon too?"

"Yes, Kevan. Here you are free to have sex with anyone you see."

"Anyone?????"

"They need to be willing and consent to it, but everybody is all the time you just need to ask. It is how we pass the time here."

An offended tone in his voice, "For a moment there I thought we had something special."

Seeing Kevan was having mixed emotions comprehending it Amelia tried to make him understand,

"We did have something amazing and special Kevan, Simon and I also had something that was amazing and special, as well I have shared something amazing and special with many other people here.

There is nothing like marriage here we can share love, emotion and feeling with everyone...... doesn't that sound better than having to devote yourself to one person."

Nodding his head and agreeing with her sentiments he said, "It does don't get me wrong. The thought of it just seems so backwards from where we came from."

Amelia spread her arms wide and exclaimed, "Welcome to Nevaeh Kevan!"

"What is Nevaeh?"

"It is heaven spelt backwards, just like this place."

They sat in silence for a minute or so and then Kevan asked, "So what happens now?"

A mischievous look coming across her face she responded, "Right now, we are going to do it again, Later I will have to leave you for a bit, but I will be back."

Surprised she had to leave he asked, "Where do you have to go?"

"Someone else is arriving here tomorrow, Jesus has asked me to be their guide also. I must be there when the sky lights up."

Thinking of what she said, he responded, "When the sky lights up???? That sounds funny what does it mean?"

"Did you notice how weird it was when it turned dark."

"Amelia, you were naked in front of my eyes I seen nothing else."

"You will see what I mean when the sky lights up in the morning, I will try to explain it to you another time."

"What am I supposed to do once you leave."

After explaining how she had asked Simon to leave her alone because she was ashamed after they spent the night together, she said, "I walked down the beach, met some people but none of that matters right now.........

Right now..........

I want you inside me."

Kevan willingly obliged and him and Amelia had sex into the night multiple times until they fell asleep.

When Kevan awoke on the beach the next morning, he found that Amelia was gone. Naked, sand stuck to most of his body, he walked along the path where he'd scattered his clothes the day before while chasing after her.

He took a quick swim to wash the sand off and got dressed.

He sat down on the sand, staring out at the water, processing everything that was going through his mind.

Twenty minutes later, he got up, dusted the sand off his clothes, and remembered that Amelia had said she walked down the beach. He decided to do the same.

Kevan struggled with a clash between the religious moral ideologies he had devoted his life to and the true culture in heaven.

He had been walking for about two hours without seeing another person, which triggered his autophobia.

When Kevan's autophobia was triggered, it always brought flashbacks of the most traumatic night of his life which was when his autophobia conditioned developed.

...

Kevan 17 Years old

Kevan exited the church through the back door and made his way to a dark blue van parked nearby.

He climbed into the driver's seat, started the engine, and let it warm up for a few seconds before reversing out of the parking spot.

He then drove around the building and parked in front of the massive open doors of the church.

As the church bells rang through the air, people began to file out of the wide entrance.

Kevan stepped out of the van, walked around to the side, and slid open the door.

The event inside had just concluded, and his father had tasked him with driving the church van to take some of the elderly parishioners back to their nursing homes.

Kevan waited patiently for his passengers, who were among the last to exit the church.

He assisted the four women and two men into the van one at a time, greeting them with their names as they got inside. "Barb, Claire, Don, Ruth, Marcy, Frank."

Kevan slid the van's door shut, pausing for a moment to glance inside.

The ladies were already deep in conversation, their voices filling the vehicle with an easy warmth.

He walked around to the driver's side, hopping into his seat and starting the engine.

As the van pulled onto the road, Barb leaned forward slightly, her voice carrying over the hum of the tires.

"Thank you for driving us today, Kevan."

Kevan met her gaze in the rearview mirror and smiled. "You know, Barb, it's my pleasure. I'm just glad to know you all got home safe."

Barb tilted her head, studying him. "Are you even old enough to drive this thing? I remember when your mother gave birth to you. How old are you now?"

Kevan chuckled, shaking his head. "I have my driver's license and plenty of practice driving this big van. I'm seventeen now."

Barb let out a sigh, turning to the other ladies with amusement. "They grow up so quick."

Kevan listened as the women resumed their conversation, their voices blending into a steady hum behind him.

He glanced at the rearview mirror again, noting that both men had their eyes closed, lost in their own quiet worlds.

He turned the radio up slightly, letting the music spill into the space between the chatter, hoping it would keep everyone distracted for the rest of the ride.

But within minutes, Barb's voice cut through the melody. "Ooh ooh ooh, Kevan, turn up the radio! I *love* this song!"

Kevan laughed, reaching for the volume dial. "No problem, Barb."

Barb and the ladies in the back were all singing along and dancing in their seats to the song on the radio, which Kevan didn't mind at all.

Kevan looked at the two men through the rear-view mirror in the backseat, and they were now awake eyes open and did not look happy about the noise the ladies were making.

Kevan glanced at Barb singing and dancing in the rear-view mirror and was happy the music was keeping them busy. While keeping his eyes on the road, every ten seconds he would glance in the mirror and see Barb singing and dancing with the other ladies.

The song on the radio came to an end and faded into another song. "Oh my Jesus, Kevan, turn up the radio. I love this song too."

Kevan reached for the radio dial, nudging the volume up slightly.

Music spilled into the van, blending with the cheerful voices of the ladies in the back as they sang along, their tones bright and full of energy.

But from the far end of the seat, Frank let out a weary sigh, his expression tight with mild frustration. He shifted slightly, rubbing his temple before speaking.

"Can we please turn the radio down? And ladies—please sing quieter? Church is over. I'd like to relax from all the noise."

Kevan glanced at him through the rearview mirror, noting the crease in Frank's brow.

He nodded and turned the dial back down to a more acceptable level, letting the melody settle into the background.

Barb, however, wasn't ready to back down completely.

She huffed playfully, throwing Frank a teasing glance. "You're always trying to ruin our fun, Frank."

She sighed dramatically before offering him a small smile. "Fine, we'll sing quieter for you."

The other women stifled amused giggles, lowering their voices just enough to keep the mood light while respecting Frank's request.

Kevan smirked to himself, settling into the rhythm of the road as the conversation behind him carried on, ebbing and flowing like the soft hum of the tires beneath them.

Barb was singing and dancing in her seat, whispering the lyrics of the song to herself.

She started to get a pulsating pain in her left arm and stopped dancing, rubbing her left arm with her right hand.

The pain went from pulsating to shooting up her arm. She was having trouble breathing, couldn't talk, and knew she needed help.

She turned to Claire, who was beside her, and tried to get her attention. When Claire looked over at Barb, her face was all red.

Barb was able to whisper to Claire right before she passed out. "Heart attack."

Barb fell back in her seat, and her eyes closed.

Claire quickly alerted Kevan and everyone else in the van to the situation. "KEVAN, Barb is having a heart attack! We need to call an ambulance."

Everyone in the van turned to face Barb, except for Kevan, who kept his eyes on the road while glancing in the mirror to see Barb unconscious in her seat.

He got his phone out of his pocket to call 911. "911, what is your emergency?"

Frantically while trying to stay calm Kevan explained the situation, "I am driving down Markson Road. We just passed Highway 74, and one of my passengers in the vehicle is having a heart attack."

"There is a gas station at the corner of Markson Road and Dryden Drive Continue driving, and the ambulance will meet you there to transfer the patient. What is their name?"

"Barbara Stanley is the woman's name."

"Is Barbara still conscious?"

"Her eyes are closed, so I don't think so."

"Continue to the gas station. The ambulance should arrive about the same time as you do. If Barbara is unconscious already, she needs the paramedics to administer treatment immediately.

I will stay on the phone with you until you meet the ambulance."

Kevan was already speeding, freaking out on the inside but trying not to show it to his passengers. All the ladies were crying, and the men were trying to console them.

Kevan sped up a little more, seeing the lights of the gas station in the distance and the lights of the ambulance further down the road traveling towards them.

Kevan pulled into the driveway of the gas station just seconds before the ambulance. He pulled into a corner of the gas station where there was enough room for the two vehicles to meet.

Kevan stopped the van, jumped out of the driver's seat, walked around to the sliding door of the van, and opened it. "Everyone out, the paramedics need to be able to get to Barb as soon as possible."

Everyone exited the van. Barb was the first one to enter the van and was now in the back corner of the very back seat.

Kevan saw the ambulance enter the gas station as all the ladies in the van flagged it down. Kevan spoke again to the two men. "Frank, Don, I need your help to remove the middle seat in the back so they can get Barb out with no problems."

Kevan jumped inside the van, released the two locks behind and in front of the seat, and spoke. "Okay, we can just lift it out now. I just need you guys to grab the other end."

They all lifted the seat out of the van and set it on the ground beside the passenger door.

The ambulance was now parked ten feet from them, lights still flashing. The two paramedics in the van jumped out of their seats and proceeded to the back of the ambulance, opening the doors and sliding the stretcher out of the back.

Kevan yelled. "She is right here in the back of the van."

The paramedics rushed over with the stretcher and jumped into the van to get Barb out.

They gently removed her and placed her on the stretcher. "Is anyone coming to the hospital with us?"

Claire stepped forward and spoke, "I will go. I have her sister's number, so I will call her as soon as we get there."

Kevan responded to Barb, "Okay, you make sure you call me once we know her condition. What hospital will she be going to?"

One of the paramedics responded, "St. Mary's."

Within seconds, Claire was in the back of the ambulance with the paramedic and Barb, and the doors on the back swung shut.

The sirens came back on, and they sped out of the gas station.

Kevan spoke aloud to the group, "I think we should all take a moment to pray for Barb."

Kevan, Don, Ruth, Marcy, and Frank all stood huddled outside of the van, holding hands, with their heads down, praying for Barb.

Kevan was saying the prayer. After thirty seconds of Kevan speaking in memory of Barb, he ended with: "...Please, God, help Barb. Amen."

The group broke apart after the prayer finished. Ruth was crying, so Marcy hugged her while Ruth cried on her shoulder.

Kevan spoke, "Frank, Don, let's get the middle seat back in the van so I can get you all home."

They put the middle seat back into the van and once again got into the back. Marcy and Ruth sat in the back crying together, while Frank and Don sat in the middle.

Kevan, quite shaken himself from the experience, was glad it was finally over.

He remained calm, trying to be the strong one, and tried not to make the experience more difficult for his passengers, who all lived with Barb in the nursing home and saw her every day.

The ride was quiet the rest of the way, other than the radio playing lowly in the background and the sobbing of the women in the back.

Kevan pulled up to the front doors of the nursing home and stopped the van.

He jumped out and again opened the sliding door for his passengers to exit. As they exited,

Kevan spoke. "Try to get some sleep. I know it has been a long drive. I am sure we will get an update soon enough. I will speak with the front desk and let them know what happened and where Barb is."

Kevan walked into the building with his passengers and wished them all a good night, then spoke with the front desk about what happened to Barb.

He walked back out to the van, got into the driver's seat, and closed the door.

Now that his passengers were gone and he was all alone, the full scope of the situation hit him, and his emotions started to flood his consciousness.

Kevan started crying uncontrollably in the driver seat of the van out front of the nursing home as a flood of emotions he had never felt before washed over him.

Kevan and Barb were not close by any means. They did see each other at least once a week at the church. For some reason, her having a heart attack and not knowing if she was okay or not, brought up feelings and thoughts of death within Kevan.

He had not been affected in this way attending funerals at the church. There were so many people in the church that most he was not acquainted with, and a funeral felt no different than a mass to him.

Barb was one of the members of the church that he knew, and being so close to the situation of her heart attack, and being the driver at the time, flooded him with emotions he had never felt before in his life.

Kevan gained his composure and was able to put a stop to the tears rolling off his face and landing on the steering wheel.

He moved the emotions to the back of his mind, wiped the tears from his face, rubbed his eyes, and realized that he needed to get back to the church.

The drive that should have taken thirty minutes each way had extended to over two hours by the time he would get back to the church.

He started the van and drove off. Kevan was minutes from the church when his phone started ringing.

He glanced down at the screen, saw that it was Claire calling him, and he pulled over to answer the call. "Claire, how are you? How is Barb doing?"

Claire was just crying and sobbing through the phone for a few seconds before she said: "Barb is gone... she didn't make it."

"Claire, are you okay? Do you want me to pick you up from the hospital?"

"Barb's sister is on her way here. I am going to wait for her. Barb was alive when I called her; I don't want to have to be the one to tell her."

"You call us, Claire, if you need anything. I will let my father know what has happened. I am almost back at the church."

Barb said, "If anything changes or I need you, I will let you know."

"Thank you for calling, Claire."

Tears started to form and roll down Kevan's face as he hung up the phone and put it on the seat beside him. He started the van again, not even wanting to drive anymore.

Kevan wanted to do nothing but go home, close his eyes, and go to sleep. He wanted to put an end to this seeming nightmare and the feeling of death hovering over him.

When Kevan arrived at the church, he drove around to the back of the building and parked the van in the same spot he took it from, then exited the van.

Kevan did not have a key to open the back door of the church that he exited from when he left, so he started to make his way around the building.

The keys to the van were jangling in his hand as he walked because his hands were shaking uncontrollably due to the shock he was feeling about Barb's death and the evening's events.

When he came around to the front of the building, Kevan noticed a police car parked outside.

He quickened his pace at the sight of it. Upon reaching the front doors, he walked inside.

The area appeared empty, but he could hear low voices off in the distance.

He followed the sound, which led him to his father's office—the High Priest's chambers.

The door was wide open.

When Kevan reached the door and glanced inside the room, he saw a familiar face—Officer Martin Carrigan, who attended church every week.

Officer Carrigan was speaking with a high priest, both of them having their backs to the door. At first glance, Kevan assumed the high priest was his father.

Upon further examination, Kevan noticed the officer and priest were standing over another high priest lying in a pool of blood.

Recognizing the face of the fallen priest, Kevan stood in shock, unable to speak or move.

He stared at the face of his father, whom he had hugged just two hours ago, now lying dead on the floor in a pool of blood.

Kevan stood there for about a minute, the conversation between the officer and the high priest sounding like distant mumbles, the soundwaves barely penetrating the massive cloud in his mind.

Officer Carrigan glanced over his shoulder and noticed Kevan standing at the door. "Kevan, go outside, you don't need to see this."

Kevan stood still, unable to move staring at his father's face, only hearing mumbles. "KEVAN, GET OUT OF HERE!"

The officer yelling broke Kevan out of his shocked trance, but he still could not move. Kevan's eyes filled with water and released a river of tears that trailed down his face.

Officer Carrigan angrily walked over to Kevan, grabbed him by the left arm and dragged him away from the door and spoke. "Kevan, go wait outside in my car, I will drive you home when I am done here."

"What happened to my dad?"

"We are not sure, but we need to find out. Go outside and wait, this is a crime scene, you can't be here, just jump in the backseat the door will be open."

Kevan went back outside the church and got into the backseat of Officer Carrigan's car.

He sat staring out the window at the front doors, waiting for Officer Carrigan to come outside and take him home, away from this nightmare.

After ten minutes in a catatonic state, doing nothing but staring at the back of the seat in front of him and seeing his father's face, Kevan began to feel claustrophobic and terrified.

He wanted to get out of the car. Kevan started panicking and tried to open the door, but it wouldn't budge from the inside.

He pulled at the door handle violently, pushing against the door, but eventually gave up.

Sitting in the back seat, hyperventilating and desperate for the nightmare to end.

Kevan waited in the car for about an hour with no sign of Officer Carrigan.

Two other police cars pulled up and parked next to Officer Carrigan's car.

Two officers stepped out of their vehicles and went inside the church. Kevan waited for another hour before Officer Carrigan finally came out, got into the driver's seat, and adjusted the mirror to look at Kevan in the backseat. "Let's get you home Kevan."

"What have you found out?"

"We will know more tomorrow. For now, it has been a long night, so let's get you home no more questions, I want silence."

Kevan sat silent for the rest of the ride home, with hundreds of questions running through his mind that he could not get answers to.

Ever since that traumatic night when Kevan had waited for two hours alone in the back seat of the police car he developed a condition called Autophobia.

Which caused him to experience shaking, sweating, chest pain, dizziness, heart palpitations, hyperventilation, and nausea as well as a feeling of being detached from his body through having flashbacks to that traumatic night when he was alone for too long.

Kevan was able to get through the nights alone without this feeling coming on, but being alone during the daytime seemed to have a more potent effect.

...

Present Day

Kevan was still feeling the effects of his autophobia. He was shaking, sweating profusely, hyper-ventilating, and clutching his chest from the pain he was feeling as he mindlessly and aimlessly walked down the beach.

His mind was still consumed by flashbacks, but he was brought back to reality instantly the moment he heard someone say.

"Hello, are you ok?"

The pain in his chest and the shaking started to subside immediately, allowing his breathing to become more routine. "Yes, I am fine now, thanks to you. My name is Kevan Harrison. What is your name?"

"Not sure what I did, but you are welcome.

My name is Leonard Chance. Nice to meet you, Kevan."

"Same to you. I just got here yesterday. You are the first person I have seen in over two hours."

"I was having a celebration with some friends. If you care to join us, I can introduce you to everybody."

Kevan responded not wanting to be alone anymore, not wanting to give his autophobia a chance to replay the memories. "I would like that. I just don't want to be alone anymore. Thank you, Leonard."

Chapter 20 - Justin's Eye Opening

ustin opened his eyes and spun around slowly, taking it all in. He took deep breaths as he did this, noticing that the air had a slightly sweet, warm taste that he could feel on his tongue.

Behind him was a metal door built right into the front of a hill, maybe 10 feet tall. Beyond the hill were other hills of various sizes, mountains, and forests extending into the distance.

The door opened into the middle of a vast open area covered in the greenest grass Justin had ever seen.

Trees were sparsely spread throughout the open area, bearing bright fruits of many colors hanging from their branches.

The open area stretched to the horizon, where he could see large trees. In the distance, animals grazed on the grass.

Amelia glanced at Justin as they walked, the soft rustling of leaves filling the quiet space between them. "So, what is this prayer ritual you want to do?"

Justin's expression was thoughtful, his steps steady. "The ritual was one of the Edicts of my church. When blessed with a place in God's kingdom, pray at the four corners of the kingdom for your family and friends' blessing and arrival."

Amelia considered this. "We had Edicts at my church too, but that wasn't one of them."

Justin nodded, the conversation settling into a comfortable rhythm. "Let's get started. Which way do we go?"

She hesitated, glancing at the sky. "I don't exactly know which way is north, but we can still follow the four corners like in your Edict. Come on—follow me."

With that, Amelia started forward, weaving through the landscape, Justin close behind.

"So, have you met a lot of people here?" Justin asked, breaking the silence.

Amelia nodded. "Yeah, I'd say around a hundred or so. I've met them while walking, just like we're doing now.

The island is huge, though—everyone is spread out."

They reached the edge of the clearing, stepping onto a path that wound through thick trees. Amelia reached up, effortlessly grabbing two ripe peaches from a low-hanging branch.

She turned to Justin, holding one out in offering.

"The center of the island is where Jesus is, and that clearing we just left. It's the heart of everything. From there, paths lead into the forests, eventually reaching the beaches and water."

She paused, glancing at him. "You sure you aren't hungry? The fruit here is *really* good."

Justin shook his head. "I'm okay for now. How long do you think it'll take us to walk the four corners?"

Amelia shrugged, biting into her peach. "Three or four days, I'd say."

The mention of time brought another thought to mind. She turned to him, curiosity flickering in her eyes. "So, what church were you with before coming here?"

"I was a member of the Children of Christ Church."

Amelia frowned slightly. "I've never heard of that one. Were they big?"

Justin nodded. "We had churches all over the country—millions of followers. The church I attended had over fifty thousand members alone."

Amelia raised a brow. "Wow. I was a member of the Servants and Saviors of Christ."

Justin absorbed that for a moment. "That's interesting. What has your experience here been like so far?"

Amelia smiled. "Yesterday, I guided a man named Kevan. He was a High Priest in the Anointing Church of Jesus Christ. I can introduce you to him after we finish our walk."

Justin's interest piqued. "I'd like that."

Then, hesitantly, he asked, "Amelia, I have an awkward question... where are the bathrooms here? How does that work?"

She let out a small laugh. "Nature is our bathroom. For number two, dig a little hole so no one steps on it."

Justin blinked. "Okay... and uh..... Cleaning up?"

Amelia motioned toward the landscape. "There are plenty of plants around that are really soft—almost like toilet paper. And I usually stick close to the edge of the island so I can access the water to clean up properly whenever I need to."

Justin hesitated for a brief moment, then sighed. "I have to go. Can we stop here? I'll make my way into the forest."

Amelia smiled, motioning to the path ahead. "I'll be right here when you're done."

Justin walked off into the thick brush and forest that lined the side of the path, he travelled further into the forest than he needed to, but he wanted to get far enough away from Amelia that she could not see or smell what he was doing.

Justin's hand brushed on a plant as he was walking and he felt the plant had a smooth silky feel, he grabbed some of the leaves figuring they were the plants Amelia had told him about.

Justin found the spot, and he dug a small hole pulled down his pants and squatted. When he was finished, he walked back to meet with Amelia.

Justin adjusted his stride, catching up to Amelia as they neared their destination. "Okay, ready to go. Where was that water?"

Amelia gestured ahead, her expression warm. "We're almost there. We were heading in that direction already."

She glanced at him, then added, "I actually set up a picnic for us—food and wine. I wanted to grab them as well."

Justin raised an eyebrow, amused. "Perfect. Sorry I ruined your picnic."

Amelia waved off his apology with a smile. "No problem. If you look ahead, you can see the beach now."

Justin followed her gaze, taking in the stretch of untouched sand that shimmered under the light, the still water stretching infinitely beyond it.

Amelia's voice softened slightly. "This beach has become my usual spot—the place I know best. My guide, Simon, brought me here on my first day. We had a picnic too—food, wine, and a conversation that lasted all night."

She glanced at Justin. "I can introduce you to Simon later if you'd like."

Justin nodded. "I'd like that."

For a few moments, they walked in silence, the rhythmic sound of waves—or lack thereof—casted an eerie sort of peace over the scene.

Then Justin spoke again. "So, what do you think of Jesus?"

Amelia barely hesitated. "I love Jesus. And I would do anything for him."

Justin hummed thoughtfully. "You don't find it a little weird?"

Amelia's expression remained steady. "You must try to see it from his perspective. He sacrificed himself to become a man equal to us. He gives up everything here to make sure we have what we need."

Justin was quiet for a beat, before shifting the conversation. "So, how did you die?"

Amelia breathed in slowly before answering. "Car accident. You?"

"I was stabbed at a gas station."

His voice was almost detached, as if the memory had been pushed far enough away to be bearable. "I have a scar on my shoulder from the wound."

Amelia frowned slightly. "Did you have the scar when you woke up on the couch?"

Justin nodded. "Yeah."

The conversation lingered between them as they stepped onto the sand, their footsteps barely leaving an imprint in the surface.

Amelia pulled off her shoes, letting the warmth of the ground seep into her skin.

Justin rolled his shoulders, glancing out at the water. "I'm going to go for a swim before I do my prayer."

Amelia turned to him, considering. "Would you mind if I joined you?"

A smirk played at the corner of his lips. "Not at all, Amelia."

Justin and Amelia walked to the edge of the water and started to remove their clothes. Amelia stripped down naked, while Justin kept his shirt on, and they both walked out into the water.

Amelia smirked, watching as Justin waded into the water, the fabric of his shirt clinging to his skin. "You're going to get your shirt all wet," she teased.

Justin ran a hand through his damp hair, the water cool against his skin. "It's okay. We've got a lot of walking ahead of us. It'll keep me cool, and it won't take long to dry."

Amelia crossed her arms, tilting her head as she studied him with an amused glint in her eye. "I was kind of hoping to see your big, manly chest—and that scar you were talking about."

Justin chuckled, shaking his head as he swiped water from his face. "I don't know how big it is."

Amelia laughed, stepping forward and splashing at the water playfully. "Well, I guess I'll just have to take your word for it."

Justin smirked, letting the conversation linger for a moment before diving beneath the water, disappearing under the still surface like a ghost slipping into another world.

Floating back to the surface in front of Amelia Justin noticed her breasts floated on top of the water.

Justin eyes noticeably glanced down and were focused on her breasts and her nipples hidden below the water.

Justin stared for a few seconds before realizing Amelia noticed, he looked away, and Amelia spoke out. "Do you like what you see?"

"Of course I do, Amelia. You are a beautiful woman."

Amelia floated over to Justin, put her hands on his shoulders, and started to massage them.

She leaned forward so her mouth was right beside his ear and whispered. "If you want what you see, it is yours. You have my consent. Fuck me!"

After hearing Amelia say this Justin felt a massive surge flow through his body and rest in his cock inflating it like a balloon.

Justin had never felt a sensation like this in his life, and he wanted to have sex with her more than anything, but he did not want to deviate from completing his prayers.

It was an inner battle for Justin to deny himself the pleasure, he shrugged Amelia's hands from his shoulders, moved away from her, and spoke.

"Amelia, I am flattered, and I would in an instant, but right now the most important thing for me to complete, is my prayers.

I do not want to stray from completing that task as quickly as possible.

I would ask that you respect that and understand how important this is for me."

Amelia felt awful trying to impose her sexual appetite on Justin, and surprised at his reaction, "I'm sorry... Of course, I will respect that. No more detours or deviations."

"I am all done in the water. I am going to get the prayer done here, and then we can move on."

"Okay, I will be out of the water in a second, and I will grab the food and wine and wait for you to finish."

Justin got out of the water and put his pants back on.

Amelia watched him from the water rubbing her vagina wishing Justin was inside of her.

Justin kneeled on the sand by the shore, starting his prayer.

Once Amelia had quietly climaxed, she made her way towards the shore and walked towards the picnic she had set up for them.

She sat down on the blanket, put the wine and glasses inside the picnic basket, and closed the lid.

She sat watching Justin, waiting to see him get up off his knees.

She opened the picnic basket again, removed the wine and a glass, and poured herself a glass of wine while she waited.

After a couple of minutes, Justin rose to his feet. Amelia finished her glass of wine, put the glass back in the picnic basket, and got up, walking towards him. "Are you ready?"

"Yeah, we will keep walking this way until we reach the next spot."

Amelia faced down the beach, her gaze following the path she had walked before—when she had sent Simon away, met Tony and Julia, and later crossed paths with Leonard Chance.

Her fingers pointed toward the stretch of sand ahead, the route familiar. "We'll walk the island in this direction until we circle back to this spot."

Justin nodded, taking in the endless horizon before them. "One down, three more to go."

They walked side by side, the soft crunch of sand beneath their feet the only sound between them for a few moments. Then Amelia spoke again.

"So, were you married?"

Justin let out a quiet sigh, shaking his head. "No, not married. Never had enough time. I was devoted to my church, always working for it. Never much time for me."

Amelia glanced at him with understanding. "I was the same. I know how that goes."

Her voice softened slightly. "I was married though—three kids. I was at my church every day. Worked there too."

Justin nodded in thought, before his gaze flicked to the basket Amelia carried. "Could I get one of those peaches?"

A smile tugged at Amelia's lips. "Of course. They're so good—so juicy."

She opened the picnic basket, pulling out two ripe peaches, their vibrant colors gleaming under the soft sunlight.

Handing one to Justin, she watched as he accepted it with a grateful smile, rolling the fruit between his fingers before taking a bite.

"I have wine too, if you want some," Amelia offered.

The sweet scent of peaches mingled with the sweet air, adding to the quiet serenity of the beach.

As they bit into the tender fruit, its taste burst onto their tongues—cool, refreshing, a perfect contrast to the warmth of the day.

Justin wiped at his mouth with the back of his hand, shaking his head. "This is fine for now. Maybe later when we stop to rest."

They walked down the beach side by side. Justin was asking questions about the island in an inquisitive way most of his questions Amelia didn't know the answers.

Amelia was telling Justin about everything she had learned about the island since she arrived.

She mentioned the foggy days, the still water, the insects, the different kinds of fruit and where you can find them, and any other explanation she could supply.

They walked on for hours together, exchanging stories and getting to know each other.

When it was starting to get dark, Amelia got Justin to stop to watch the sky change from light to dark.

Amelia paused, glancing toward the endless stretch of water before them. "We must stop for a minute. I want you to see something."

Justin slowed his steps, curiosity flickering across his face. "What is it?"

She turned back to him, a knowing smile tugging at her lips. "Just come sit for a minute. You don't want to miss it."

Without another word, she lowered herself onto the sand, her legs folding beneath her as she faced the horizon.

She motioned for Justin to join her, and he hesitated only briefly before sinking down beside her, mirroring her posture.

Together, they sat in quiet anticipation, watching the stillness of the water stretch into infinity.

Amelia's voice was soft, carrying a quiet sense of reverence. "You may have noticed—there's no sun here like back on Earth. It's about to get dark, and when I saw it happen for the first time,

I thought it was incredible. I figured you might like it too."

Justin glanced at her, then back at the horizon. "What should I be paying attention to?"

She inhaled slowly, the breeze barely shifting the air around them. "Just keep your eyes on the horizon above the water."

And so, they watched—waiting for the moment when the sky would darken, not like the sunset of the world they once knew, but in a way unique to this strange, quiet place.

The brightness of the day started to fade as the minutes passed.

It reminded Justin of a place called The White Room.

The White Room was a place Justin encountered on one of his religious retreats. Everyone would go inside The White Room to pray and worship Jesus in large groups.

The White Room was all black with no light that entered the room. Prayer sessions inside The White Room would last one hour, and once you entered The White Room, you could not leave until the prayer session was completed.

When the prayer session within The White Room started, the entire room—walls, ceiling, and floor—would intermittently and slowly turn a bright white and then fade back to black.

By the end of the sessions, The White Room would be flashing like a strobe light going from black to white very fast, mesmerizing, and creating a surreal feeling of what they said was Jesus.

The way The White Room faded to black at the start of the sessions resembled to Justin how the entire island's sky dimmed to darkness within minutes.

They decided to camp out on the beach and enjoy the picnic that Amelia prepared for them.

They drank wine and ate, conversing into the night.

Amelia tried again to seduce Justin into having sex with her, but Justin refused until his prayers were completed. Justin ended up falling asleep while Amelia stayed awake, drinking the bottle of wine by herself.

She went swimming in the water while Justin slept so she could bring herself to climax without disturbing him.

Once Amelia finished the bottle of wine, she laid down beside Justin and fell asleep.

•••

Time passed into the night as they slept when Justin was startled awake by Amelia's scream.

He awoke and rubbed his eyes, looking around for Amelia; he noticed she was not beside him.

Justin got up and rushed off, walking towards the direction he thought he heard the scream come from, calling Amelia's name.

She wasn't far from where they were sleeping.

Justin found Amelia lying on her chest and stomach with her head turned to the side, the right side of her face resting on the ground.

Her eyes were closed, and she was unconscious.

Justin felt for her pulse, and her heart was still beating.

He lifted her head off the ground, sat down in front of her, and rested her head in his lap.

That is when he put together what had happened.

Under Amelia's head was a small rock about six inches long. The side of her head that was on the ground was on top of the rock, and her head was cut, bruised and bleeding.

He looked down at her feet and saw that there was some brush from a plant that had caught around her ankle and seemed to have tripped her.

When it caught on her leg, she fell and hit her head on the rock, knocking herself unconscious.

Justin tried to wake her up, but she was completely unresponsive.

In what seemed to Justin like hours, with everything moving in slow motion from his perspective, after a few minutes, Amelia's eyes opened.

Amelia's head rested on Justin's lap.

She stared at Justin's face hovering above her for a few seconds before her mouth opened wide, and she let out an ear-piercing scream.

Amelia's body was vibrating like she was shivering, and she was shaking like a leaf in the wind.

Her eyes filled with fluid as she screamed, and tears started to run down the side of her face as she cried and screamed simultaneously. "Amelia, you can stop screaming. Are you okay?"

Amelia remained unresponsive; her body wracked with violent sobs as her head rested on Justin's lap.

The intensity of her emotions was overwhelming, each tear a testament to the pain she was feeling.

Justin gently stroked her hair, his touch a silent offer of comfort and support. He felt a deep sense of helplessness, wishing he could do more to ease her suffering.

The sound of her cries echoed in the quiet surroundings, "Amelia, what is happening? What is wrong? What can I do?"

She continued crying, and after a few seconds without saying a word, she sat up, then stood up on her feet, stumbling a little as she did.

Amelia turned towards Justin, her face glistening in the darkness from all the tears coating her cheeks.

Backing away from him with each step, her words choked with emotion. she stammered. "Justin... I'm sorry... Please... please... I'm sorry... leave me alone."

Amelia turned and ran off into the forest after saying this, not turning back around. Her footsteps faded into the distance as she disappeared into the dense trees.

Justin stood there, stunned and heartbroken, his voice echoing in the darkness as he called out to her.

He shouted, his voice filled with desperation and concern. "Amelia, where are you going? Come back... Amelia."

Justin, still sitting in the same spot on the ground, was very confused.

He was worried about Amelia and didn't know if he should go after her or not.

With her telling him to leave her alone, he was not sure what to do or what had caused Amelia to turn into a blithering, screaming, and crying mess to run off.

Justin still had his prayers to complete, and he didn't want to deviate from that task until it was done. In his worried state, Justin started to move in the direction Amelia did, calling her name.

Amelia responded by screaming from the distance. "No... Justin... Alone."

Justin couldn't see her but heard her run away from him, rustling through the brush as she did.

Justin was shocked at how Amelia had acted and wanted to know why.

After contemplating for a few seconds, Justin decided to go back to the beach and try to sleep.

He hoped Amelia would come back and be there when he woke up in the morning.

Justin had trouble falling back asleep, being worried about Amelia, but eventually, he dozed off. He woke up when the sky turned from dark to light.

He sat up and looked around the beach to see if Amelia had returned, but she was not within his vision.

Justin sat for a minute, thinking about what he was going to do.

He wanted to go and find Amelia, but his prayers were the most important thing to him right now. After realizing Amelia would have come back if she didn't want to be alone, as she had said.

Justin decided he would continue to follow the beach and complete his prayers on his own.

Justin decided to go for a swim before he started walking. He kept his shirt on while in the water. When Justin got out of the water, he removed his shirt and wrung out the excess water before putting it back on.

Justin grabbed some fruit that was left over in the basket before starting his walk to the next prayer spot.

Without Amelia, he would have to estimate the locations for his prayers.

He continued walking down the beach for hours, worrying and wondering about Amelia the entire time.

Chapter 21 - The Command Room

The elevator bell rang, and a light on the panel lit up, prompting a fingerprint verification. Steve put his thumb on the panel, and the doors slid open, revealing the Command Room.

Cynthia looked around, trying to see what she could from inside the elevator. She noticed two women in the room who turned around when the elevator doors opened.

She also saw four extremely large screens, one on each wall, displaying digital maps of the entire world, each with different color marks and information.

Large computer screens were positioned in the corners of the room, six in each corner, displaying information she couldn't read. In the center of the room was a hologram of the planet, seemingly floating above a pedestal.

Steve took a step into the Command Room, turned around to say goodbye to Cynthia, and wished her a pleasant trip back down from the 75th floor.

The elevator doors slid closed as Steve continued walking into the Command Room.

Steve strode into the command room, his presence demanding attention as he addressed his team. "Doris, Olivia—good day to you ladies. Tell me, what have you found out about #64's disappearance?"

Olivia's fingers moved swiftly over the keyboard, bringing up surveillance footage on the screen. "For starters, Commander, we have a full record of #64's movements for the past twenty-four hours—right up until the Phantom Ambulance."

Doris spoke focused on her screen, "I've gone through the history of #64's tracking system and pinpointed the exact location where he was taken."

Steve nodded, his expression calculating. "I'll need that address. Cross-reference it with all our databases—see if we can find any patterns."

His gaze shifted to Olivia. "Have we checked #64's phone records? I want to know which tower last pinged his phone before it went offline."

Olivia tapped a command, bringing up another screen. "Already done, Commander. If you look here—this red dot marks where #64 was taken. The red circle around it indicates phone tower triangulation. His phone went offline at the same time as his tracking device at that location."

Steve's jaw tightened. "His tracking device went offline too?"

Doris nodded grimly. "Yes, Commander. The signal disappeared shortly after he arrived at the location in the Phantom Ambulance."

But it reappeared and again disappeared. We've identified three points of interest—the spot where the signal vanished, the location where it reappeared, and its final destination."

Steve narrowed his eyes. "Why would the signal disappear and reappear like that?"

Olivia exhaled, shaking her head. "It doesn't make sense, Commander. According to the map, the signal dropped off in one warehouse, then reappeared thirty kilometers away in another.

It moved half a kilometer to a secondary warehouse, where it remained for two hours and twelve minutes."

Steve leaned over the table, analyzing the data. "And after that?"

"The signal returned to the same warehouse where it originally reappeared."

A tension settled over the room the implications unclear yet unsettling.

Steve straightened. "These locations are our only leads. Send me the addresses for the site where #64 was taken and where the Phantom Ambulance picked him up. I also want the names and addresses of any witnesses."

Doris gave a sharp nod. "Already working on it, Commander. We should have full tracking data on both buildings within the hour."

Steve rolled his shoulders, mind already shifting gears. "I'm heading out to check the first building and the spot where the signal reappeared. Mark will take over in the Command Room.

Send agents to investigate the site where #64 was held for two hours. Harris and Gary will question witnesses at the pickup scene."

He turned toward the door. "I'll leave you ladies to your work. I Just need to make a call before I head out."

Olivia gave a small salute. "Understood, Commander."

Steve sat at the computer, fired off a quick email, then picked up the phone, pressing a button to initiate a call.

The line clicked, and Mark's voice came through. "Commander."

"I need you to take my place in the Command Room while I'm gone. We have a lead on #64's location, and I want to investigate immediately.

I've sent you the names and addresses of witnesses—dispatch Harris and Gary to speak with them."

Mark didn't hesitate. "I'll make the call and be there as fast as the elevator lets me."

Steve smirked slightly. "Appreciate it, Mark. I'm heading down now."

Hanging up, he stood, addressing his team once more. "Thanks, Doris, Olivia. Mark will be here soon—I'll be back."

With that, he turned and left, the case moving forward with each step.

Steve made his way to the elevator doors, and moments after he stepped in front of them, the doors slid open.

Steve stepped into the elevator and pushed the button that read 22.

It was a lonely ride; the elevator only stopped twice on the way down for one person, and they got off one or two floors below, so they weren't on the elevator long.

When Steve finally arrived at the 22nd floor, the doors slid open, and he walked out of the elevator.

On the left and right were four large offices, two on each side, with glass walls and doors.

One hundred steps from the elevator doors there was a service desk with a large sign above it that read "Special Divisions" and displayed a large version of the same TT logo found on their badges below it, two small doors on either side of the desk.

The woman at the desk looked up from her computer as Steve approached and spoke.

Steve entered the Special Divisions office, his sharp gaze scanning the room as he approached the front desk. "Hello, Alice."

Alice stood from her seat, greeting him with a professional nod. "Hello, Commander. Welcome to Special Divisions. How can I help you?"

"I'm looking for one of your investigators. Cynthia Brown."

Alice glanced at her computer screen briefly before responding. "Cynthia just got back from lunch not long ago. Let me give her a call."

She sat down, picked up the phone, and pressed 9-9-9-9 before speaking into the receiver.

Over the P.A. system echoing loudly, "Cynthia Brown, please report to the front desk. Cynthia Brown, please report to the front desk."

Alice turned back to Steve. "She should be here in a few moments."

Steve nodded. "Thank you, Alice."

He stepped away from the desk, folding his arms as he waited. Moments later, the door to the right of the front desk swung open, and Cynthia Brown entered.

She moved toward Alice, unaware of Steve standing a few feet behind her.

"Someone called me to the front desk?" Cynthia asked.

Alice gestured toward Steve. "Yes, the Commander is here to see you."

Hearing his name, Steve turned to face them, and Cynthia's expression flickered with surprise as she processed Alice's words.

"The Commander...?"

Her brows knitted together in confusion. Alice, sensing her hesitation, pointed directly at Steve, who stood patiently behind her.

Cynthia turned around quickly, her eyes widening as realization dawned on her.

"Commander...?" she echoed, this time with a mix of astonishment and curiosity.

The unexpected presence of The Throne's Commander added an air of intrigue and curiosity to the moment, and Cynthia straightened slightly, awaiting an explanation.

"You're here to see *me*...... Commander?"

Steve nodded. "Yes, Cynthia. I need a Special Divisions investigator. Are you up for it?"

Cynthia hesitated. "I can get you one of the senior investigators, Commander. They have far more experience than I do."

Steve's tone remained firm, his eyes steady. "Cynthia, you didn't answer my question. I asked if *you* are up for it. I could've gotten a senior investigator myself—but I didn't want one.

I wanted to give a new investigator a chance to shine."

Cynthia swallowed, the weight of his words settling in. "But why me..... Commander?"

Steve smirked slightly. "Honestly? Probably our elevator ride together. You were the first person that popped into my head when I decided I needed a Special Divisions investigator.

My usual partner is standing in for me in the Command Room."

Cynthia's hesitation melted into something closer to determination. "I would be honored, Commander. What would you like me to do?"

"Grab your gear. We're investigating a suspicious location tied to #64 and the Phantom Ambulances."

Without missing a beat, Cynthia nodded sharply. "Let me run to my office, Commander—I'll be right back."

Steve gestured toward them. "I'll meet you at the elevator."

Minutes later, Cynthia returned, walking briskly, her gear securely locked in a case.

The determination in her stride was unmistakable.

"I'm ready, Commander."

Steve pressed the call button. "The elevator should be here in a moment."

The doors slid open just as he finished speaking. He turned to Cynthia, his expression inquisitive. "Are you *sure* you're ready?"

A spark of excitement flickered in her eyes. "I've been ready for this since I started at the Throne Commander. Let's go."

As the elevator descended to the basement, the hum of its machinery filled the space with a quiet tension. Steve leaned against the wall, arms crossed, as he briefed Cynthia on everything they had uncovered about #64's disappearance.

"Those locations are our only leads. The Command Room is working on intel, but we'll be the eyes and ears on the ground. We need to find out where #64 was taken after his tracking devices went offline."

Cynthia absorbed his words, her brow furrowing in thought before she finally spoke. "I don't think #64 was taken anywhere else Commander."

Steve straightened slightly, glancing at her. "Hold that thought."

The elevator doors slid open, revealing the dimly lit corridor.

They stepped out, their footsteps echoing as Steve approached the service desk to the right. After a brief exchange with the valet, he turned back to Cynthia.

"Our car is on its way. You're driving."

Cynthia nodded, walking toward the driver's side of the undercover black SUV as the valet pulled up and handed over the keys.

Sliding into the seat, she pulled up the navigation system, inputting the address before pulling out of the underground parking garage and onto the street.

As the city lights blurred past them, Steve finally returned to their earlier conversation. "Now—what did you mean before when you said #64 wasn't taken anywhere? That doesn't make sense without more context."

Cynthia exhaled, gripping the wheel as she thought carefully about her words. "I said it wrong Commander—but hear me out. Obviously, #64 *was* taken somewhere.

What I meant was, I think #64 was taken *underground* based on what you told me."

Steve's gaze sharpened. "And why do you say that?"

They merged onto the highway, the hum of the tires steady beneath them.

"Process of elimination," Cynthia said.

"If #64 was picked up by a Phantom Ambulance to become one of The Lost, I don't think whoever is behind this *knew* they were an undercover agent of The Throne.

They wouldn't have had the knowledge to remove their surgically implanted tracking device.

But if both the phone *and* tracking device went offline at the same time, my guess is that at those locations, they didn't *remove* them—they went below ground, where all signals are blocked."

She tightened her grip on the wheel. "It's the only explanation that fits Commander."

Steve let her words sink in, a slow nod forming as realization settled over him. "That is *quite* genius, Cynthia. Impressive deduction."

He smirked slightly. "I knew I picked you for a reason—even I, and the ladies in the Command Room, weren't putting all those pieces together."

Cynthia smiled faintly. "I worked for a company that made tracking devices before joining The Throne, Commander. I know *everything* about how they work."

The highway stretched endlessly ahead of them, the setting sun casting long shadows over the road.

As they drove deeper toward their destination, Steve shifted gears, steering the conversation toward another mystery.

"What are your thoughts on the Phantom Ambulances?"

Cynthia's voice carried a quiet admiration for the method, despite its sinister purpose. "To make The Lost disappear without a trace? It's ingenious, really.

Injure someone—stage it like an accident—and have a Phantom Ambulance identical to the real ones waiting to pick up the victim.

It leaves *zero* suspicion at the scene. No alarm from the police until it's too late. And if they're truly going underground?"

She let out a breath. "Then they leave absolutely *no* trace behind. Which, hopefully, we'll find out soon."

Steve nodded grimly. "Yeah... Quite ingenious. If you're right, and The Lost *are* being taken underground, we're about to uncover a hell of a lot more questions than answers."

Cynthia tapped her fingers against the steering wheel absently. "Yeah... I see where you're going with that. This one building really means *nothing* in the grand scheme of things Commander."

Steve turned his head slightly, watching her. "That's not exactly where I was going—I wouldn't say it's nothing. It's the only lead we've had in a long time."

Cynthia kept her eyes on the road. "Think about it, though.

We know The Lost are being taken from *all over* the country. There's no way they're all being sent to this *one* building.

There must be a network—multiple locations across the country all doing the same thing."

Steve sighed, rolling his shoulders. "Let's not get ahead of ourselves just yet. Like I said—I think you're right. But until we know for sure, there's no point in speculating too much.

Olivia and Doris are gathering intel in the Command Room. We'll go over it all when we get back."

Cynthia hesitated before asking, "Will I have clearance to enter the Command Room now Commander?"

A knowing smile played at the edge of Steve's lips. "Of course, Cynthia. You've already proven yourself a valuable asset to this investigation."

A flicker of pride touched her expression. "Thank you for this opportunity Commander. You gave me a chance that no one else would. I won't let you down."

Steve leaned back into his seat, studying her for a moment. "Tell me—what made you decide to join The Throne?"

Cynthia's jaw tightened slightly before she answered. "My sister is one of The Lost."

Steve's gaze softened. "I see."

Cynthia continued, her voice edged with quiet determination.

"I wanted to do what I could to stop this from happening to people,"

Steve exhaled slowly, nodding in understanding. "I feel the same way. It's why I put *everything* I had into making sure The Lost weren't forgotten. Why I built The Throne from that first investigation six years ago."

He glanced at her. "What was your sister's name?"

Cynthia swallowed, her voice barely above a whisper. "Esther Rollins."

Steve's expression darkened slightly with recognition. "I remember her case. I interviewed the witnesses myself. The Throne was smaller back then... She went missing over three years ago now."

Silence hung between them for a moment, filled with unspoken weight.

The highway stretched on, leading them closer to a truth—neither of them were sure they were ready to face.

Steve and Cynthia continued driving to the location, going over the details of Esther's case and many of the cases of The Lost's disappearances.

Before they knew it, the navigation system said, "Exit right 500 meters, Highway exit 125." They got off the highway, and the location was about five minutes from the highway exit in a small industrial area on the outskirts of a town called Prudence.

They parked in the parking lot beside the location to observe the area and see if there were any people or movements they needed to worry about.

The building was rectangular with all white siding, and the roof was about twenty feet from the ground. Surveillance cameras on the corners of the building panned the area.

There were no doors visible from where they were parked, and no people could be seen anywhere near the building, so Steve gave the okay to check it out. "Put on your gear, and we will get to work."

Cynthia moved swiftly to the back of the SUV, opening the door and retrieving the locked case she had grabbed before leaving the office.

With practiced precision, she unlatched it, revealing a sleek, one-piece suit made of high-grade latex material.

The fabric enclosed her entire body, leaving only her face exposed.

She lifted a pair of goggles from the case, the lenses encircled by faintly glowing lights, and slid them over her eyes, the subtle hum of activation signaling they were online.

Steve, standing nearby, watched as she secured the final adjustments. "Try an X-ray scan of the building—let's see if we can get an idea of what's inside."

Cynthia tapped the side of her goggles, initiating the scan.

A moment later, she frowned. "They must have something blocking the feed from within the walls, Commander. The X-ray scan reveals nothing."

Steve exhaled sharply, his eyes narrowing on the structure ahead. "Let's go, then."

Their approach was timed carefully, waiting for the surveillance cameras on the building's corners to pan away before making their move.

They pressed themselves against the wall, staying out of view. The structure was unsettling—no windows, no doors visible along the exterior.

When they reached one of the narrower sides, they stopped.

A single heavy-duty metal garage door loomed ahead, secured under the unblinking gaze of a surveillance camera mounted above it.

Steve studied it, his tone quiet yet firm. "Thoughts? No doors. No windows. We won't be able to get through this garage entrance. How do we get inside?"

Cynthia examined the building for a moment before responding. "We'll need to access the roof, Commander."

Silently, they maneuvered along the opposite side of the structure, slipping between security blind spots.

Cynthia reached into one of the suit's compartments, retrieving a compact device.

With the press of a button, a grappling hook extended outward. She gauged its weight before launching it expertly onto the roof.

A moment passed as she tested the rope's security, then she held it out to Steve.

Steve smirked. "Ladies first."

He gestured toward the rope.

Cynthia raised an eyebrow, amused. "You *are* a gentleman, Commander."

Without hesitation, she scaled the building, her movements precise and fluid. Steve followed, slower but steady.

When he reached the top, Cynthia was already kneeling over a ventilation shaft, retrieving another tool.

"This is the main ventilation shaft," she explained.

"I'll have it open in a few moments."

Steve watched as she expertly used a laser cutter, slicing through the thick metal grate.

The edges glowed red-hot before she slid the tool away, pocketing it. With a sharp pull, she removed the grate entirely.

She turned to Steve, her eyes gleaming behind the goggles. "Are you ready to see what's inside, Commander?"

Steve's voice was steady but brimming with anticipation. "I've been waiting six years to find this building. I'm ready."

They slid into the ventilation shaft, moving cautiously through the confined space. It was tight, but navigable.

Cynthia reached another grate and immediately began cutting through it.

Once done, she kicked it out, sending the metal crashing to the ground below—the sharp noise echoed ominously in the darkness.

She peered out, scanning the area. "Ha! I was right, Commander—there's a ramp here, heading downward.

Quite a drop. I'll deploy the grappling hook so we can climb down."

With efficiency, she secured the rope and descended first. Steve followed, landing beside her as she surveyed the room.

The chamber was lined with lights every ten feet, casting a sterile glow against concrete walls.

At the far end stood another garage-style door, identical to the entrance.

Steve approached Cynthia as she examined it. "What have you found?"

She gestured to the mechanism. "No controls to open the door from either side. The operation must be remote—most likely controlled from inside the Phantom Ambulances."

Steve nodded. "That makes sense. What does the UV scan show?"

Cynthia activated her scanner; eyes locked onto the data feed. "Just a few seconds... The building is clean. No recent human activity. But—tire tracks."

She adjusted the settings. "Three distinct signatures, likely from separate Phantom Ambulances, each showing varying levels of deterioration."

Steve's mind raced. "We'll need to cross-reference records to determine which Lost individuals were transported through here—and when they vanished."

Cynthia's fingers hovered over her interface. "Before we proceed, let's find out *where* this leads. Check your phone for signal."

Steve pulled out his device, frowning. "Nothing. You?"

Cynthia shook her head. "No signal. They must have installed signal-blocking infrastructure into the building."

From the garage entrance, the ground extended about twenty feet before sloping downward—a steep incline plunging into dimly lit darkness.

They proceeded carefully, the ramp stretching endlessly before them. The descent was gradual, but it persisted for over an hour before leveling out.

The lights along the walls abruptly ceased, leaving them shrouded in pitch-black silence.

Cynthia activated her suit's lights—bright white beams illuminated the tunnel, casting elongated shadows behind them.

Steve eyed the endless void. "How long have we been walking?"

Cynthia checked her readings. "Over a kilometer—heading east."

Steve exhaled, tension settling in his shoulders. "We're beneath the highway by now—with no sign of an endpoint. How is this possible? How do tunnels like these exist?"

Cynthia kept her pace steady. "If these tunnels were built secretly, they're likely unsanctioned by the government—or unknowingly authorized under false pretenses."

Hours passed in monotonous footsteps and silence, the tunnel never breaking its course. Then—finally—something different.

To their left, a secondary tunnel branched off.

Steve slowed, studying the divide. "A fork in the road. Now what?"

Cynthia ran another UV scan. "That settles it. All three Phantom Ambulances went straight. But—three other tire tracks turned at the fork."

Steve's brow furrowed. "Then we follow the path #64 took."

He exhaled. "I wish we had brought a vehicle—who knew we'd be walking for this long?"

Cynthia smirked. "We'll need additional teams to map the rest. More investigators, more intel."

Another few hours of walking, and finally—the incline returned. They trudged upward, the burning in their legs growing unbearable.

Then—the tunnel ended.

The same type of garage door loomed ahead, an identical blockade to the one at the entrance.

Cynthia scanned the door, then froze. "Huh."

Steve tensed. "What is it?"

She recalibrated her UV feed. "None of the Phantom Ambulances left through *this* door. But—I'm detecting three other tire tracks here. They match the tracks at the fork."

Steve's breath hitched. "So, they were transferred to another vehicle before reaching this exit."

Cynthia nodded. "Looks that way, Commander. Probably the second location—where #64 was held for two hours."

She scanned the tire marks again. "The three vehicles that turned at the fork *entered* the tunnels from this door. It means we have no way of getting out here—we'll have to backtrack."

Steve glanced around. "How far have we traveled between doors?"

Cynthia checked her readings. "Exactly *29.7 kilometers*, Commander."

Steve exhaled, his voice edged with disbelief. "I still don't understand how tunnels like this could exist without anyone knowing."

Cynthia's expression darkened. "Let's see what answers we can find *outside* this building, Commander."

And with that—they prepared to retrace their steps through the building at the other end of the tunnel to find an exit, knowing that whatever lay ahead, the mystery of The Lost was only beginning to unravel.

Cynthia grappled onto the ventilation shaft grate, climbed the rope and while hanging, started to cut through it with her laser.

When she finished cutting through it, she dropped to the ground, her weight pulling the grate down with her.

Cynthia landed on her feet, catching the grate above her head as she did.

She dropped the grate to the floor; a loud clanging echoed throughout the tunnel. Cynthia threw her rope inside the ventilation shaft and secured the grapple.

With the grace of a cat and speed of a cheetah she climbed the rope and was inside of the ventilation shaft within seconds.

Steve followed and climbed the rope with haste in his tired state, wanting to get back to the surface so they could investigate further into the information they had acquired.

Cynthia was already working on their exit cutting off the last ventilation grate that would free them from the building. "One more cut and we are free Commander."

Cynthia pushed the grate out and climbed onto the roof, moving swiftly despite the weight of her gear.

Steve followed, pulling himself up and immediately reaching into his coat for his phone.

"Hello, Olivia."

A sharp breath crackled through the receiver. "Commander, where have you been?"

"We're at the location where the signal reappeared. Send a car to pick us up ASAP. I'll brief you all when I return to the Command Room."

Steve ended the call and turned toward Cynthia, who was already securing the grappling hook for their descent. Without hesitation, she grabbed hold of the rope and slid down effortlessly.

Steve stepped onto the ledge, adjusting his stance—when something caught his eye.

A car rental business stood directly across the street from the building.

His gaze narrowed.

It was too conveniently placed.

Sliding down the rope, he landed beside Cynthia, but his attention remained locked on the building across the road.

He took a few steps toward it, studying its windows, its signage—something about it nagged at him.

Cynthia noticed his sudden shift. "What are you thinking Commander?"

Steve's voice was low, considering. "Something about that rental place being *right here* makes me think it's involved. Could be where they get the vehicles to transport The Lost after they leave the Phantom Ambulances."

Cynthia's expression darkened as she pieced it together. "We know they never left the tunnel—they were transported somewhere else. That would make sense."

Steve's jaw tightened in decision. "I want to check it out. Wait here for our ride."

The bell jingled as he swung the door open. The air inside was thick with the scent of old paper and disinfectant.

A man sat behind the counter; phone pressed to his ear. His nametag read Martin.

Martin raised a hand in acknowledgment. "I'll be with you in one second, sir."

Steve nodded, using the time to scan the room. His eyes landed on a water cooler tucked against the wall.

Realizing how dry his throat was after hours underground, he poured himself a cup and drank deeply.

The cool liquid rushed through him, refreshing yet grounding.

"Hello, sir. What can I do for you?"

Steve turned back to the counter, his movements steady. "Hello, Martin. My name is Steve Hauser. I'm the Commander of The Throne."

He reached into his coat and produced his badge, the insignia catching the dim light and gleaming with unmistakable authority.

Martin's reaction was instant—his eyes widened, his breath hitching slightly. "Wow, Commander. Never thought I'd meet you in person."

Steve's voice remained firm but polite. "Nice to meet you, Martin. I'm here on business, and I don't have a lot of time."

Martin swallowed, quickly adjusting his posture. "What can I help you with today Commander?"

Steve slid his hands into his pockets, watching Martin carefully. "I need a copy of your records for all car rentals picked up on Monday and Tuesday."

Martin hesitated for only a fraction of a second before nodding. "That won't be a problem. Just give me a few minutes."

Steve gave a small nod. "Thank you, Martin."

A few minutes later, Martin handed him a two-page printout—every rental for the last two weeks. Steve scanned the papers, then tucked them neatly into his coat.

He grabbed another glass of water from the cooler—one for Cynthia.

Stepping back outside, he found her waiting exactly where he'd left her, eyes on the approaching vehicle.

As they waited for the approaching vehicle he handed Cynthia the cup of water, she said, "You were right Commander."

Steve responded wondering what she meant, "About what?"

"I did a UV scan of the driveway of the car rental business, the car that transported #64 Out of the tunnel matched UV signatures I found there."

Their ride pulled into the rental car driveway, and without a word, both climbed inside.

The doors shut, and the car sped off—taking them back to The Throne and deeper into the unraveling mystery ahead.

Chapter 22 - Finding the Key to Heaven

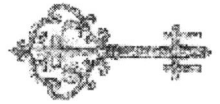

The elevator doors to the Command Room slid open, revealing the controlled chaos within. Screens glowed with incoming data, voices hummed in urgency, and at the center of it all stood Mark, eyes locked onto Steve the moment he stepped out.

"We were getting worried about you Commander. Where have you been? What did you find?"

Steve didn't hesitate. "We have our first solid lead on what happens to The Lost after they're taken."

He scanned the room. "For starters, we need to dispatch four additional investigation officers to each location. We need full-scale exploration."

Doris nodded. "I'll handle that now, Commander."

Steve turned back to the team. "The site we investigated led underground. A tunnel. the tracking signals of #64 disappeared—because the tunnels blocks all transmissions. We followed the path for *29.7 kilometers* before surfacing inside an identical building, where the signal reappeared."

He paused, letting the significance of their discovery settle. "Midway, we encountered a fork in the road. That's why we need more investigators—to map the tunnels and uncover where they lead."

A silence came over the group as reality settled in, Steve added, "What about the other location where #64 was for two hours?" Steve asked.

Doris exhaled. "Just an empty warehouse, Commander. One table inside. We're working to identify the owner."

Cynthia frowned, processing the information. "Why take them to a warehouse for two hours? The timing suggests they switch drivers or vehicles—but why?"

Steve considered this before Olivia chimed in. "We traced ownership of the building in Prudence Commander. It was a mess—they went through hundreds of subsidiaries to hide it.

But everything ties back to *Odyssey Inc.* I have the President and vice of the company listed as Domenic Cirrone and Antonio Balata"

The name settled over the room like a warning. Steve's expression darkened. "Odyssey Inc..."

Doris was already deep in her work. "I'm pulling records on the company now—assets, possible persons of interest."

Olivia tapped a screen. "Commander, if there's *one* tunnel, we can almost guarantee there are *more.*"

Steve nodded slowly. "I am aware, Cynthia said the same thing in the car."

Olivia's fingers flew across her keyboard. "I may have a way to locate them remotely. It's experimental, but now that we know what we're looking for, we might be able to detect similar underground anomalies across the country."

Steve allowed himself a brief flicker of satisfaction. A big smile crossing his face "Amazing work, ladies."

He turned back to the team. "We found UV signatures from *nine* different vehicles passing through that tunnel. Cross-reference those vehicles with other Lost cases from this region.

If we can confirm more Lost traveled through this tunnel, we'll have a pattern."

He reached into his coat, retrieving the rental records.

"I had a hunch and grabbed car rental records for two weeks prior to #64 going missing.

Cynthia confirmed my theory is correct, they're using the rental cars to transport The Lost out of sight, then switching vehicles before continuing to their final location.

I want to see which of these rentals match the timing of *The Lost* disappearing."

Cynthia spoke up. "And Odyssey Inc?"

Steve exhaled. "We're going there next. I want a face-to-face with the President, Domenic Cirrone, or the Vice President, Antonio Balata."

Doris didn't look up from her screen. "Give me ten minutes, and I'll have their full profiles ready Commander."

Steve gave a sharp nod. "I want full exploration of the tunnels immediately. Make sure the teams are equipped for long-duration travel. Once they're underground, there will be *no* contact with the surface."

Mark gestured toward the main screen. "How did you access the buildings? You said the garage doors were locked."

Steve smirked. "Teams on-site will enter through ventilation shafts on the roof. It's pitch-black underground, so ensure they bring lights."

Mark absorbed the information before nodding. "I'll oversee the investigations. Harris and Gary will handle tunnel mapping."

Steve's eyes swept across his team. "We didn't encounter *anyone* inside the tunnels. But if you do—arrest them. Bring them back for questioning."

Mark hesitated. "Should we force access through the garage doors?"

Steve considered it before shaking his head. "It would speed up exploration—but I don't want to alert whoever is running this operation.

If they know we've found their tunnels, they'll start erasing evidence."

Doris suddenly stopped typing, her brow furrowing. "Commander... there's something strange."

Steve turned toward her. "What is it?"

Her fingers hovered over her keyboard. "Odyssey Inc is listed as a *1.2 trillion-dollar* investment firm.

But there's *no* public ownership—no shareholders. The company doesn't have a *visible* owner."

The weight of her words settled like stone.

Steve narrowed his gaze. "How does a trillion-dollar company operate without ownership transparency?"

No one had an answer. The tension in the room thickened. Steve inhaled sharply.

"Cynthia and I will handle Odyssey Inc." He turned toward his team. "You have your orders and know what needs to be done. We'll brief again upon my return."

"Thank you, Commander," came the collective response.

He and Cynthia strode toward the elevator. The doors shut behind them, sealing them in silence. Cynthia leaned against the wall, her voice quieter than before. "Now I see why they call you The Commander."

Steve let out a small, tired smirk. "Now you do...... I am The Commander the one and only!"

They both laughed as they stepped into the underground car park, retrieved their SUV, and pulled out onto the main road. Cynthia drove, her expression focused. "Have you ever heard of Odyssey Inc before Commander?"

Steve exhaled slowly, watching the city lights blur past them. "I've seen their headquarters—big letters on top like the Hollywood sign. That's all I know."

Cynthia adjusted her grip on the wheel. "What do you think they have to do with The Lost?"

Steve's expression remained unreadable. "Right now? All we know is they own the building. Until we know more, I won't speculate."

He leaned back slightly, voice lowering. "But I want to warn you—you may see a side of me you haven't experienced before."

Cynthia smirked slightly. "Are we playing bad cop, Commander?"

Steve shook his head. "Not exactly. We have an objective—to speak with Cirrone or Balata. We stay friendly *until* they try to stonewall us."

His fingers drummed against the dashboard absently. "I don't expect them to be cooperative. But once they realize who I am, they won't have a choice."

Cynthia stole a quick glance at him. "I want to thank you again for this chance Commander. I haven't left my desk in *three months.*"

Steve let out a quiet chuckle. "You immediately proved you will be integral to this investigation going forward. Besides after what we found underground, I *couldn't* send you back to your desk—not until we know exactly what those tunnels are being used for."

He turned his gaze toward her. "Besides—you wouldn't have appreciated it."

Cynthia grinned. "I'd follow orders, but I wouldn't be *happy* about it."

Steve's tone grew steadier. "We finally have the lead we've been waiting for. Soon, we'll find The Lost."

He met her gaze. "We're in this together now. Mark is my partner—but until we have contact with #64, I need someone *in* the field with me."

Cynthia's grin widened slightly. "I am *honored* Commander. Really."

Ahead, the towering skyline of Odyssey Inc loomed. And whatever waited inside—Steve and Cynthia were ready to confront it.

Steve spoke, "Do me a favor, Cynthia. When it is just me and you alone together like this, you don't have to call me Commander all the time, just call me Steve."

Cynthia turned her head to look at Steve in the passenger seat, Steve looked over at her.

She responded with a straight face staring right into Steve's eyes. "If that is what you command, Commander."

Steve stared at her after she said this, and Cynthia stuck her tongue out at Steve in a childish way.

Steve couldn't help but chuckle at Cynthia's playful gesture. It was moments like these that took the stress out of their days.

The tension in the air seemed to lighten, if only for a brief moment, she laughed and spoke, "Just having some fun with you...Steve. I am honored to have the privilege it makes conversation easier."

They pulled up in front of the Odyssey Inc building and parked out front on the street. As Steve and Cynthia stepped out of the car, they couldn't help but be awed by the sight before them.

The hustle and bustle of the pedestrian traffic, combined with the serene beauty of the gardens and fountains, it created a unique atmosphere.

The building had forty-five floors and two large glass double doors.

There was a large grand half-circle staircase leading up to the doors, extending from the building to the street.

Three sets of stairs led towards the door of the building: two along the wall and one leading up to the front doors from the street.

Gardens and fountains filled the spaces between the staircases. Statues of angels in the fountains had instruments in their mouths that shot water into the lower-level fountain below.

As Cynthia and Steve ascended the staircase, the sound of water splashing from the instruments created a soothing background melody.

The sheer number of coins in the fountains spoke of countless wishes and dreams.

Cynthia noticed a sticker on the head of one of the angel statues that read, "Jesus Loves You." There was a lot of pedestrian traffic moving in and out of the building and up and down the stairs.

Steve and Cynthia pushed through the towering glass doors of *Odyssey Inc*, stepping into a world that felt more like a luxurious business lounge than the headquarters of a trillion-dollar investment firm.

The center of the lobby hummed with activity—a food court sprawled out before them, tables arranged neatly, clusters of business professionals and employees eating, chatting, oblivious to the weight of the investigation that had just walked through their doors.

The air carried the scent of fresh coffee and various cuisines, blending with the low murmur of conversation.

On either side of the massive space, four food vendors lined the walls, while six elevators stood like monolithic gateways—three per wall—waiting to transport executives to the upper floors.

At the far end, a sleek reception desk with eight kiosks stood beneath a sign that read Odyssey Inc Reception in bold, polished lettering.

Steve and Cynthia strode forward, approaching one of the kiosks. A woman, eyes glued to her screen, barely acknowledged their presence as she spoke in a clipped, indifferent tone.

"Hello. Welcome to Odyssey Inc. My name is Veronica. How can I help you today?"

Steve's voice was firm, unshaken. "We need a meeting with Domenic Cirrone and Antonio Balata."

She didn't look up.

Her fingers continued tapping across the keyboard, attention locked on the glowing monitor.

"Domenic is out of the country," she stated flatly. "Antonio is in today. Do you have an appointment?"

Steve's jaw tightened slightly. "Yes. Me being here *is* my appointment."

The woman barely reacted, continuing her work without so much as a glance in his direction.

"Sir, if you don't have an appointment, I can't help you."

Steve exhaled, then leaned forward slightly. "I don't think you understand."

He reached into his coat, retrieving his badge, and placed it squarely on her desk.

The insignia glinted beneath the overhead lighting—The Throne's official emblem, unmistakable, absolute.

Veronica's fingers hesitated over the keyboard. Then she finally looked up.

Her eyes widened slightly. The moment of recognition hit like a spark igniting a fuse. Her earlier indifference dissolved in an instant, replaced by sharp awareness.

"Oh my god—Commander. I—I'm so sorry."

Steve nodded, allowing her a second to adjust before speaking again. "That's okay, Veronica. But it is *critical* that I meet with Antonio Balata immediately."

Veronica shifted in her seat, pulling up another screen, urgency replacing the indifference in her voice.

"He's in a meeting with our investors on the forty-fifth floor for the next twenty minutes."

Steve's eyes flicked toward the elevators. "Can we access forty-five from there?"

She shook her head. "No. You need clearance. I can assist you."

Without hesitation, she stepped out from behind the desk, motioning for Steve and Cynthia to follow.

They moved through the lobby, weaving between the tables, past the murmuring business professionals, toward one of the elevators.

The timing was uncanny—the doors slid open just as they arrived. Veronica stepped inside with them; her professionalism now tinged with something more personal. "I have to come up with you to give you access once we reach forty-five."

Steve nodded. "Thank you, Veronica."

For a moment, she hesitated, then lowered her voice slightly. "I really *shouldn't* be doing this. I'll probably get in trouble."

Steve glanced at her, his tone easy, yet decisive. "Tell them I forced you."

But Veronica shook her head. "No! I *want* to help."

The elevator hummed as they ascended, the soft overhead lights casting a glow over the three of them.

Then, as if confessing something she had been holding onto for far too long, she finally spoke.

"If you're here, I know it has to do with The Lost."

Her voice wavered slightly. "My sister is one of them. And if helping you today might improve her chances of coming home—I'll do whatever it takes."

Cynthia's eyes flicked toward her, absorbing the weight of that revelation and feeling an unspoken connection with her.

Steve's expression remained steady, but something subtle shifted beneath it—an acknowledgment of shared pain, of silent determination.

"Then I need one more favor," he said.

Veronica nodded, already knowing what was coming.

"Don't tell Antonio we're coming. I want to catch him off guard."

Her lips pressed together, then she gave a single, resolute nod. "I won't say a word."

The elevator chimed. The doors slid open onto the forty-fifth floor. Veronica stepped aside, gesturing down the hallway.

"The meeting room is *to the right* when you exit. His office is *all the way* at the end of the hall."

Steve adjusted his coat, his expression unreadable. "Thank you again, Veronica."

She met his gaze, her voice quiet but unwavering. "No problem. I hope you get the answers you're looking for."

Steve stepped forward, Cynthia beside him. The meeting room was ahead. And whatever waited inside—Antonio Balata would *not* be expecting them. Steve and Cynthia stepped out of the elevator, turning to the right.

The hallway stretched before them, lined with impressive glass offices and meeting rooms buzzing with corporate activity.

Through the expansive windows, executives in tailored suits debated figures, scrolled through presentations, and closed deals, completely unaware of the storm about to hit their floor.

As they moved down the hallway, their footsteps were softened by the thick carpeting, but their presence carried the weight of authority.

A long bench sat outside the meeting room.

Steve motioned for Cynthia to sit, taking his place beside her.

She leaned slightly toward him. "So, is he in there? What does he look like?"

Steve pulled out his phone, scrolling through the intel Doris had sent him. Within seconds, Antonio Balata's face appeared—sharp suit, calculating expression, a man used to control.

He turned the screen toward Cynthia.

Her gaze flickered across the image. "And what's the plan?"

Steve's voice remained measured. "We wait for their meeting to finish—then we strike fast. Catch him off guard. Get what we need."

Cynthia smirked. "You make it sound so easy."

Steve exhaled slightly. "I don't know how easy it will be. He may know *nothing* about the buildings or tunnels—but he has access to information we need.

We don't know what pieces we're looking for yet, but we're at the tip of the iceberg. We must uncover everything beneath the surface."

Cynthia leaned back. "Well—looks like it's time."

The door to the meeting room cracked open.

One by one, investors filed out, briefcases in hand, conversations murmuring as they headed toward the elevators.

They barely acknowledged Steve and Cynthia, absorbed in their own world.

As the last attendee exited, leaving Antonio alone inside, Steve and Cynthia exchanged glances.

Steve stood. Cynthia mirrored his movement.

They entered.

Antonio stood near a bulletin board, meticulously removing papers from push pins, focused—until Steve spoke.

"Antonio Balata. We need to talk."

Antonio barely glanced up. "You need an appointment. I have another meeting across town."

Steve stepped forward. "You may need to cancel that. Because *your* meeting is with *us*—right now."

Antonio let out a low scoff, straightening his tie. "I don't know who you think you are, but I am a *very* busy man, and I don't have time for this nonsense."

Steve didn't blink.

He reached into his coat, pulled out his badge, and placed it on the table between them.

The Throne's insignia gleamed under the fluorescent lights, unmistakable.

Antonio's breath hitched—his posture shifting subtly. His tone changed.

"Commander..."

There was surprise. But also, something more—hesitation.

Antonio adjusted his jacket, nodding once. "What can I do for you?"

Steve leaned forward slightly. "We need information. And no one is leaving until we get it.

If you want *any* chance of making your next meeting, I suggest you cooperate."

Antonio's jaw tightened. A flicker of resistance. Then—acceptance.

"Can we take this to my office?"

Steve motioned toward the door. "Lead the way."

Antonio exited the room, his stride purposeful, as though he was still trying to control the situation.

Steve and Cynthia followed. They reached Antonio's office at the end of the hallway.

As soon as the door shut, Antonio turned toward them, crossing his arms. "Let's make this quick. What do you need?"

Steve cut straight to the point. "A warehouse. Officially owned by a string of subsidiaries—all leading back to Odyssey Inc. We need information."

Antonio let out a slow breath. "Give me the address."

Steve handed him the details from Prudence. Antonio sat at his desk, fingers flying across the keyboard.

"What information are you looking for specifically?"

Steve's tone was firm. "Everything."

Antonio scanned the screen. "The building is officially owned by a network of realty companies under Odyssey Inc. That explains the subsidiaries—companies moving assets between them."

Steve's expression remained unreadable. "What is the building *used* for?"

Antonio frowned slightly. "On paper? Industrial warehouse. Rental property."

Steve narrowed his gaze. "Who is listed as the renter?"

Antonio's fingers paused. He shook his head slightly. "It doesn't say. Let me make a call."

Steve glanced at Cynthia. She gave a slight nod—approval.

Antonio picked up the phone, dialing swiftly.

The line clicked.

A voice answered.

"Hello, thank you for calling *Real Realty*. This is Sarah speaking. How may I assist you?"

Antonio's voice was controlled. "Sarah, this is Antonio Balata, vice president of Odyssey Inc. I need to confirm details we have on file."

Sarah was immediate. "Of course, sir. What's the address?"

"1639 Gulliver St., Prudence."

Pause.

Sarah's tone shifted slightly. "I have the file up. What do you need?"

Antonio's words came deliberately. "Who is paying the rent?"

Another pause.

Then—Sarah spoke.

"A corporation. Just a number—4815162342 Inc"

Steve's gaze sharpened.

Cynthia glanced at him—understanding the significance.

Antonio nodded as if confirming something silently in his head. "That's perfect, Sarah. Can you forward the full file to my email?"

"Give me a few minutes. I'll send it over."

Antonio hung up, then turned to Steve and Cynthia.

"You'll have a copy of *everything* shortly."

Steve's expression was measured, but there was an undercurrent of satisfaction. "You've been very cooperative Antonio thank you."

Antonio adjusted his sleeves. "I know how important your work is Commander."

He glanced at his watch. "And I *might* still make my meeting."

A pause. Then, unexpectedly—"I truly *hope* you find those missing people Commander."

For the first time, there was a break in his corporate demeanor.

Steve processed it, nodded once. "The information you've provided will help. Can I get your card in case we need to follow up?"

Antonio handed Steve a business card as he and Cynthia stood up from their seats. Steve's phone went off when he received the information from Antonio.

They got up and walked out of the office. Steve forwarded all the information to Olivia and Doris so they could get to work on finding out who the owner of 4815162342 Inc was.

As Steve and Cynthia drove back toward *The Throne Headquarters*, the weight of their findings lingered between them like an unspoken shadow.

Cynthia finally broke the silence. "Everyone was so cooperative. I didn't get to see that other side of you that you talked about."

Steve smirked slightly, keeping his eyes on the road. "The badge and position I hold demand a lot of respect.

Almost everyone knows someone who has been taken—to become one of The Lost.

When people encounter The Throne, they're usually eager to help."

Cynthia nodded, tapping her fingers against the dashboard absently. "I pictured our encounter with Antonio going *very* differently."

Steve exhaled slowly. "It could have. If Odyssey Inc is involved, Antonio might not know anything—or he could be a pawn, kept out of the real operations.

If he *did* know, I don't see him being as cooperative as he was."

Cynthia glanced at him, then back at the road. "I still think Odyssey Inc is tied to this somehow—maybe financially."

Steve turned to her. "Why do you say that?"

She tightened her grip on the wheel.

"Look at what we've uncovered so far—the Phantom Ambulances, The Lost disappearing all over the country, now these tunnels.

Whatever this is, whoever is behind it, they've invested *years* into making it happen. That's not just power—it's *money*."

Steve's jaw tightened. "The tunnels alone are an engineering feat. We need to explore them *fast* before whoever is behind this starts wiping away the evidence."

As they pulled into *The Throne Headquarters*, they didn't waste time. Within minutes, they were inside the elevator, ascending to *The Command Room*.

The moment the doors slid open, Olivia was waiting. "You are back—perfect timing. Commander, I just had a breakthrough."

Steve stepped forward. "Good news or bad news?"

Olivia hesitated. "Depends on how you look at it. It's *good* for our investigation but *horrifying* once you understand the implications."

Steve straightened. "What did you find?"

Olivia turned to the massive screen on the far wall.

The image flickered—then a detailed map of the entire country appeared.

"I've been running an experimental scan,"

Olivia began. "Combining X-rays and soundwave emissions from satellites to detect underground structures. Now that we *know* what we're looking for, I was able to refine the search."

She tapped her tablet, zooming in on *Prudence*.

The tunnel appeared on-screen, highlighted in red, linking the two buildings Steve and Cynthia had investigated.

"This is where you were earlier," Olivia explained. "Now, watch closely."

She zoomed in further.

Finer details and sharpened edges of the tunnel came into focus displayed in shades of black against lighter textures.

"Notice these portions,"

Olivia continued. "The scan picks up black spots along the tunnel's perimeter. And see this?"

She traced her finger along the screen, revealing hundreds of small black dots running perfectly through the middle of the tunnel.

"What does it mean?" Steve asked, his voice steady.

"I'll show you."

Olivia tapped her tablet again—zooming *even closer*.

The single dot fragmented into four smaller dots—arranged in a diamond pattern.

Cynthia leaned forward. "What is that?"

Olivia took a deep breath. "The scan works in two dimensions. The diamond pattern isn't just a cluster—it's the scan picking up the *four walls* of the tunnel it is a result of the sound waves bouncing off the walls and the x-rays sensing the vibrations.

That means these tunnels weren't carved sloppily underground—they were *built* with structural integrity."

Silence weighed heavy in the room. Then Olivia pressed her tablet again—this time, the entire map shifted.

Lines spread across the country like veins in a body, connecting in an intricate underground system.

No one spoke. The horror of it sank in.

Finally, Olivia whispered: "I ran an AI scan for the same *four-dot* patterns. The results gave me this—a nationwide underground tunnel network.

Our agents inside the tunnels are confirming it *with every step they take*."

Steve's voice was sharp. "I want every access point mapped. Send investigators *now*."

Olivia nodded. "Already working on it Commander. The tunnel you found earlier—both buildings were owned by Odyssey Inc. The warehouse

#64 was taken to? Also, Odyssey Inc. I'm cross-referencing *all* properties in those areas."

She motioned toward the screen again. "And this line here—this one is *different* from the rest."

Steve stepped forward. "How different?"

"Two pixels thicker," Olivia answered. "And when zoomed in—it's *three times wider* than the others."

Steve narrowed his eyes. "What does that mean the tunnel is bigger?"

Olivia hesitated. Then nodded. "Exactly! big enough for a truck or train."

Steve exhaled. "We need answers *now*. I want the renters and owners of every building tied to this network identified—*immediately*."

Doris suddenly spoke up. "Commander—I started investigating 4815162342 Inc. Something isn't adding up."

Steve turned to her. "What did you find?"

"For the past *thirty years*, 4815162342 Inc. has been the official renter on paper. I accessed invoices—there are confirmed underground construction permits from *twenty-five years ago*.

But the permits list 'basements' and 'shelters'—nothing near what we've uncovered."

Cynthia shook her head slowly. "Someone *hid* this operation *in plain sight*—for decades."

Doris looked up. "Commander—we need more manpower to sift through this information."

Steve didn't hesitate. "How many?"

"Two teams of ten Digital Investigators. Five Forensic Accounting Investigators."

Steve nodded. "Approved. Temporary Command Room credentials for all of them."

Olivia picked up her phone, issuing orders immediately.

Doris typed rapidly, her voice tightening. "More data is coming in by the second—and it's *bad*.

There's a maze of numbers and shell corporations tied to this. We may need *ten* Forensic Accounting Investigators."

Steve's voice was firm. "Whatever you need—approved."

Olivia let out a breath. "I think we need a vacation on an island after this Commander."

Steve cracked a smirk. "If we find The Lost, I'll approve it—*all expenses paid.*"

Mark turned from the monitors. "Commander—I've been scanning for #64's signal every sixty seconds. We *still* have nothing."

Steve's expression darkened. "If The Lost *are* trapped underground, there's no chance we'll get a signal. But we keep scanning. *We don't stop.*"

Then—Doris abruptly gasped. "Commander—I *found a name.*"

The entire room turned to her.

"What name?" Steve asked.

"Brian Schersinger."

Cynthia frowned. "Who is that?"

Doris's fingers flew across the keyboard. "I confirmed it—he is the *owner* of 4815162342 Inc"

Olivia's voice sharpened. "Why didn't we find this before?"

Doris shook her head. "I don't know, I have confirmation that 4815162342 Inc purchased a delivery van thirty years ago with a driver's license attached to the sale.

Also, now that I have the name from the driver's license, for some reason I have also found confirmation that one Brian Schersinger is the owner of 4815162342 Inc. The system links his *name* to the company—but the company doesn't link *back* to his name."

Steve inhaled slowly. "Find out *everything* about Brian Schersinger. Find out *everything* about Odyssey Inc and these shell companies."

He turned to Cynthia.

"We're going to the address linked to that name. *Now.*"

Olivia's voice echoed in the Command Room as the group continued their work as Steve and Cynthia strode toward the elevator.

And with that—the race to uncover the truth continued.

Chapter 23 - The Life of Brian

teve and Cynthia had been driving for hours, winding through lonely country roads, the silence between them stretching as the scenery became more desolate with every mile.

There was something unsettling about the drive itself—mile after mile of empty land, fields with no signs of life, roads that seemed forgotten.

It was as if the world around them was deliberately unremarkable, designed to make them lower their guard before they arrived at their destination.

Then, suddenly, the emptiness ended.

Massive walls stretched around what appeared to be a self-contained community, its pristine design an eerie contrast to the barren land surrounding it.

Cynthia slowed the car to a stop in front of an imposing wrought-iron gate, its intricate metalwork polished and deliberate, giving the impression that whatever lay beyond it was meant to be hidden, protected—controlled.

At first glance, it looked like the entrance to a luxurious estate. But Cynthia knew better.

Steve's eyes flicked to the right, scanning the large metal-engraved sign hanging on the wall beside the gate.

CHURCH OF THE ODYSSEY COMMUNITY GROUNDS

Cynthia's stomach twisted. "Church of the Odyssey... That can't be a coincidence."

Steve exhaled slowly. "Exactly what I was thinking."

Before they could say more, movement stirred inside the guard booth.

A security guard, dressed in an immaculately pressed uniform, leaned forward, eyes locked onto them with a scrutinizing gaze. His posture was stiff—alert, but not in the way of someone protecting civilians.

This was the posture of someone enforcing control.

Cynthia rolled down the window.

The security guard's voice was clipped, professional—but entirely unwelcoming.

"What is your business in our community?"

There was no politeness. No courtesy. Just wariness.

Cynthia frowned slightly. "Well, aren't you friendly."

The guard's expression didn't change.

"These grounds are private property. If you have no business here, you are *not welcome.*"

Steve remained calm, reaching into his coat, pulling out his badge, and holding it up.

The gleaming insignia of The Throne caught the dim evening light—a symbol recognized everywhere.

His voice was steady, but firm. "I'm Steve Hauser, Commander of The Throne."

The guard's shoulders stiffened—an involuntary reaction.

Steve continued. "We're here on official business dealing with the investigation of *The Lost.* We need access to a specific address within your community."

Silence.

The guard measured them carefully, then finally spoke. "I will have to clear this with my superiors. What is the address?"

Steve met his gaze evenly. "Unit 795."

The guard picked up the phone inside the booth, his voice lowering slightly, as though this request was unexpected. Steve and Cynthia exchanged glances.

Steve didn't say it aloud, but Cynthia knew what he was thinking.

There was hesitation. A subtle delay. Then—the guard placed the phone down, his grip tighter than before. His words felt more like an order than permission. "You have clearance to enter."

But Cynthia knew. They weren't being let in. They were being watched. And whatever lay beyond that gate—whatever waited behind those walls—would not make this investigation into Brian Schersinger easy.

As Steve and Cynthia drove through the iron-wrought gates, the world around them shifted. Gone were the endless stretches of empty countryside, the miles of desolation that had swallowed their journey in silence.

Inside the walled community, everything felt strangely manufactured—too perfect, too controlled.

On the left side of the street, identical square houses stretched in seamless rows, like a carefully designed blueprint—each one identical to the next, no driveways, no vehicles, just patches of trimmed grass and walkways connecting doors to the road.

On the right side, a grocery store stood, but something was off—no parking lot, no cars.

In the distance, towering over everything else, was the church.

A massive structure, its steeple piercing the sky, hoisting an unmistakable cross—a symbol of authority looming over the community like a watchful eye.

Cynthia kept the car rolling forward slowly, scanning everything—absorbing the unnatural calm of this place. Steve shifted in his seat; eyes locked on the church. "That building must be the church."

His voice wasn't questioning. It was certain. Cynthia barely nodded, still processing.

Then—Steve sat forward slightly. "Slow down. I want to talk to that man outside."

Cynthia eased the car to a stop. Steve rolled down his window, calling out to a man washing his windows outside one of the square houses.

The man turned toward them, his posture eerily welcoming, like he had rehearsed this moment a hundred times before. "Hello and welcome to our community! Have you found Jesus? Jesus loves you."

Steve's tone was polite—but strategic.

"Hello. Thank you."

He paused briefly before adding, "We were looking for a man named Brian Schersinger—not Jesus. Have you heard of him?"

The shift was instantaneous.

The man's entire expression faltered—a flicker of amazement, quickly swallowed by something much darker. *Fear.*

His hand clenched slightly around the wet rag, as if steadying himself.

Then—his voice came too quickly, too forced. "Never heard the name before in my life. If you'll excuse me, I need to get back to my duties."

Pause.

Then, an urgent addition, forced and hollow—"Jesus loves you."

Steve rolled up the window, exhaling slowly. Cynthia turned toward him, eyebrows raised. "He obviously knew Brian. Did you see his face when you said his name?"

Steve nodded, staring back at the church. "Yeah. I caught that."

His voice was lower now, more thoughtful. "I want to see what kind of reactions we get from others."

Cynthia glanced at the neat rows of identical houses, the absence of cars, the eerily pristine environment.

Something about it gnawed at her, clawing at the edges of logic. "I get the feeling that once you enter that gate... you don't get to leave."

Steve slowly turned toward her, absorbing her words. They both knew. This place wasn't just a community.

It was a system. A carefully designed reality—one that might just hold the answers to *why* The Lost disappeared.

Steve exhaled again, his tone quiet—but weighted. "Almost all of The Lost are religious. I always knew there was a connection... but I never thought much of it."

Cynthia stared out the window. The church loomed ahead. Waiting. Watching. Steve's voice came barely above a whisper. "I think it's a *big* part of this puzzle."

As Steve and Cynthia continued their drive through The Church of the Odyssey Community Grounds, the unsettling uniformity of the place weighed on them.

The road curved sharply, forcing them around the grocery store in a U-shape, as if designed to keep movement predictable. The square houses continued—numbered sequentially, stretching on like a lifeless grid, each identical, each featureless, each designed for uniformity rather than individuality.

The plaza that emerged beyond the last turn was the first sign of human activity. People walked, shopped, mingled—but something felt off. Nothing about their movements seemed natural.

They weren't people living their lives.

They were people going through motions, maintaining a carefully orchestrated facade. The church loomed ahead. Massive. Overpowering.

A shadow cast over the entire community, as though ensuring no one forgot their place beneath its presence.

And then—something stranger.

Near the entrance, a celebration was underway. Children ran past tables of food, families gathered, yet among them walked men in red robes—the high priests of the church, seamlessly woven into the scene.

They weren't merely watching the people. They were part of them. Their presence was not an institution separate from the community—it was the community.

As Steve and Cynthia's vehicle rolled through, heads turned.

Groups of people whispered, pointed. They knew immediately. Steve and Cynthia did not belong. Steve glanced toward Cynthia. "Pull over here. I want to speak with these people."

Cynthia parked near a small gathering of three people—a middle-aged man in a sharp suit, flanked by a younger man and woman, each holding drinks, mid-conversation.

As soon as Steve rolled down the window, the man in the suit turned toward them, curiosity flickering behind his careful gaze.

"Welcome to our community. My name is George. This is Jim, and Sally." The smile was practiced. "Have you found Jesus? Jesus loves you."

Steve didn't flinch, didn't play into the routine greeting. "I'm not looking for Jesus." His words were measured. "I'm looking for a man named Brian Schersinger."

The reaction was immediate. The conversation stopped cold—as though someone had yanked the air from the room.

The three exchanged quick, nervous glances, subtle shifts in posture.

Then—George spoke before he could stop himself. "Mary is the person you need to talk to..."

The slip was obvious.

Too obvious.

Jim elbowed George, cutting him off sharply, stepping forward as if his sudden presence alone could erase what had just happened. "We have never heard that name before."

The correction was too fast—too rehearsed. The deflection came next—a clear attempt to remove themselves from the conversation entirely. "We need to get back to our celebration. Have a good day. Jesus loves you."

Jim turned his back quickly, pulling George and Sally with him, escorting them away from the road, from Steve, Cynthia—and their questions.

Steve exhaled, rolling up the window. Cynthia barely waited a second before speaking. "They got weird when you said his name."

She shifted in her seat. "And—who is Mary?"

Steve's expression remained unreadable, but his eyes sharpened slightly. "Not sure. But that just means we're on the right track."

Cynthia glanced back at the church, its shadow stretching unnaturally long across the plaza. "In this community—there's only one road."

Her voice was quieter now. "So, our odds of being on the right track are pretty good."

Steve pulled up his display. "Olivia just sent me something. Let's see what we've got."

Olivia had sent them a satellite map of the entire community, showing the layout and the winding road they were on.

The road followed a sine wave pattern from one wall of the community to the other, with houses on the left side and amenities on the right. From the bird's-eye view afforded by satellite images, the stark contrast within the community was glaring.

The northern sector, sprawling past house number 1000, boasted opulent, detached homes, each with grand driveways and an array of cars parked out front.

It was a veritable enclave of affluence, a realm where the rich resided in their luxurious abodes.

In stark opposition, the southern part of the community which felt like an oppressive cage.

There, the houses were mere square boxes, huddled together in a monotonous grid side by side.

It felt as though the inhabitants were prisoners of their circumstances not having cars, trapped within the bleak confines of their modest dwellings.

The disparity between the north and the south was a poignant reminder of the socio-economic divide that cleaved the community into two starkly different worlds containing two different classes of people.

Cynthia glanced at the map on the display. "So, we have thirty square kilometers of land, walled off, extending north to south—one road, two gates."

Steve nodded, watching the numbers on the houses. "795 isn't far now. Should be just past the next U-bend."

Cynthia frowned slightly. "How many units do you think are here?"

Steve calculated briefly. "1200, maybe 1500, knowing where 795 sits."

They followed the bend, moving deeper toward the heart of the community. Ahead, a man in a deep red robe stood by the road—his posture calm, his presence deliberate.

The robe was striking, unnaturally vivid against the muted backdrop of the uniform houses. His eyes were locked on their vehicle.

Steve and Cynthia exchanged a glance of quiet caution.
Cynthia's voice was lower now. "Well... what do we have here."

Chapter 24 – High Priest Sadow

hey pulled over. As they stepped out of the car, the man in the red robe moved toward them, slow but purposeful—his expression unreadable.

When he spoke, his tone was soothing, practiced, yet carrying the weight of authority. "Welcome to our community. I am High Priest Sadow. You may call me Father Sadow. Have you found Jesus? Jesus loves you."

Steve didn't flinch. "Father, we were looking for a man who lived here thirty years ago.

His name was Brian Schersinger."

Father Sadow's expression remained neutral, but his posture shifted—only slightly, as if he had prepared an answer long ago. "Sorry, but I never knew him. I have only seen his name in our community records."

A careful choice of words. Steve narrowed his gaze. "What kind of information might the records have on Brian Schersinger?"

Father Sadow did not hesitate. "No more than his name, unit, and the timeline of his stay."

Pause. Then—a slight nod, as if recalling something conveniently. "I remember seeing the name you asked about—Brian Schersinger—in a list of members from thirty years ago. But we have had three different families live in this unit since then. There would be nothing left behind."

Cynthia's voice came a little sharper. "What happened to Brian Schersinger? Why isn't he in the community anymore?"

Father Sadow's expression did not change—but his tone lowered slightly. "Brian Schersinger died."

Pause. Then, almost an afterthought—"I don't recall when."

His words held an eerie finality. "Behind our church, there is a headstone with his name. You will find the year of his passing there."

Steve spoke calmly. "Can we see it Father? You can ride with us."

Father Sadow gave a polite shake of the head. "I will walk back and meet you there. I need the exercise."

He glanced toward the celebration, as though observing the timing. "Our gathering should be ending soon."

As Steve and Cynthia climbed back into the vehicle, Cynthia exhaled slowly, watching Father Sadow in the rearview mirror. Her voice was low and firm. "What do you think about this guy?"

Steve's fingers tapped absently against the dashboard. "He seems cooperative. Truthful."

Cynthia shook her head slightly. "This place is *shady*, Steve. Father Sadow included. I've heard about communities like this before—but I never thought they were actually *real*."

Steve's tone darkened. "It frightens me sometimes—what ideas humans bring to life."

The church loomed ahead as they parked again.

Father Sadow approached, his red robe billowing slightly as he walked.

He spoke gently, gesturing toward the back of the church. "Brian was one of the earliest members of the community, back when we were just beginning."

Pause. Then—a small, unsettling addition. "We are fortunate his resting place is close."

Steve studied his tone but said nothing. Father Sadow turned left, leading them behind the massive building.

As they walked, Steve spoke again. "Is there anyone here who might have known Brian?"

Father Sadow's tone instantly changed—low, stern, absolute. "Yes."

Steve pressed further. "Could we speak with them?"

Father Sadow stopped walking, then turned toward him—his entire posture shifting. His words were controlled, yet his voice hardened into cold authority. "That you may *not* do!"

Pause. A slight tilt of the head. "The Church of the Odyssey is a *sovereign nation*."

The words felt rehearsed—polished, as though many before them had asked the same questions—and failed. "We extended courtesy to you by opening the gate."

Another pause. Then—an undeniable declaration. "But you will investigate no further without a *court-ordered warrant.*"

Steve's tone hardened instantly—the weight of his authority showing itself fully now. "I am the Commander of The Throne. I can have a warrant at my office in *twenty minutes.* Do we really need to jump through hoops?"

Father Sadow's expression did not shift, but his words grew colder. "Here, we have our own economy. Our own laws. Our own enforcement officers. *Our own authorities.*"

The final statement cut through the air. "We do not respect yours—just as you do not respect ours."

Cynthia's breath hitched slightly, sensing the shift in power dynamics—the underlying warning within his words. Steve stepped closer. "I *guarantee* you, Father—we will be back."

Pause. "And we *will* get the information this community is hiding."

Father Sadow held his small, unreadable smile, responding with an eerily calm certainty. "And we will *welcome* you when you do."

Then—without another word, he turned his back to them. Dismissive. Finished. His robe swept gently across the stone pathway as he moved toward the graveyard. "There is his headstone."

The three of them stood solemnly, looking down at the headstone. The inscription read,

Brian Schersinger, a loved member of our community, June 12, 1970 – August 14, 2005.

The dates and words carved into the stone added a poignant gravity to the moment. Steve and Cynthia exchanged a glance, a mix of surprise and realization dawning on their faces.

Father Sadow remained silent, his gaze fixed on the headstone as if paying respects. The revelation that Brian Schersinger had passed away added a new layer of complexity to their investigation.

They had come seeking answers, only to find themselves standing at his grave. The quiet of the churchyard seemed to echo the weight of the discovery, and they knew they had to rethink their approach.

Father Sadow spoke, "I will have to ask you to leave now. We must prepare for our evening mass."

Steve responded, "We will respect your wishes, Father, but we will be back sooner than later."

They got back into their vehicle and began the drive back towards the gate. The sun was beginning to set, casting a warm, golden glow over the landscape.

Long shadows stretched across the road, and the sky painted a canvas of reds, oranges, and purples.

Steve and Cynthia remained silent, both lost in their thoughts.

The revelation at the headstone weighed heavily on their minds, altering the course of their investigation. The quiet hum of the car's engine was the only sound as they navigated the winding road of the gated community.

The headstone had given them one fact. Brian Schersinger was dead. Nothing else. No history. No connections. No answers.

Cynthia finally broke the quiet, her fingers tightening on the wheel, "So all we found out is Brian Schersinger died in 2005. That does not help us at all."

Steve sat back, exhaling slowly, his mind racing through possible scenarios. "I've informed Olivia and Doris of what little we found. Hopefully, they've uncovered something by the time we get back to the Command Room."

His tone was measured, but Cynthia caught the frustration buried beneath it. She shook her head, staring straight ahead. "There's no way we've lost this lead on #64."

Her voice was firmer now—certainty laced through it. "All the evidence led us *here*. It must be connected."

Steve glanced at her. "What does that tell you?"

Cynthia gritted her teeth slightly, her instincts sharpening. "It tells me that—whether or not they *know it*—they're not telling us the whole truth."

Steve let her words settle before nodding. "Exactly, Cynthia."

His tone shifted—stronger now. "This place *is* our next lead. We just haven't found it yet."

She exhaled, then muttered. "We might need a warrant before we do."

Steve's voice carried absolute certainty. "We will."

Pause. Then, quieter—but weighted. "If Brian Schersinger's death is just a fact with no meaning—then why did they react like they did when we said his name?"

Cynthia didn't answer immediately, but she didn't have to.

Something was wrong. Something was buried beneath the surface here. And if this community held any connection to The Lost—to #64—they would find it. No matter what it took.

As they approached the gate, the sky had darkened, and the sun had fully set. The streetlights in the community flickered on, casting a warm glow on both sides of the street.

The once-serene setting now felt slightly eerie under the artificial light.

Cynthia slowed their car coming closer to the exit gate, an older woman suddenly emerged from behind a tree by the wall. She rushed towards them, waving her hands frantically, her expression one of urgency and desperation.

Cynthia stopped the car, and they both watched as the woman hurried closer. Steve sat forward, alert.

Cynthia brought the car to a stop, and the woman hurried closer, her breath uneven, her eyes wide with pleading hope.

Then, the words tumbled out of her—raw, desperate. "Please stop!"

Cynthia rolled down the window. The woman leaned in, gripping the edge of the door as if she was afraid, they might drive off before she could speak. "My name is Mary Toplin. My friend George told me you were asking about Brian Schersinger."

She inhaled sharply, her hands trembling slightly. "He's dead... but I can tell you the story of what happened."

Steve's gaze sharpened. "What do you want in exchange for this story?"

He wasn't dismissing her—but he understood desperation well enough to know it usually came with a price. "Father Sadow does not want us talking to anyone in the community without a warrant."

Pause. "We would like to respect that."

Mary's eyes burned with pleading intensity. "All I want is for you to drive me out of that gate with you. And I will tell you everything I know."

Cynthia turned toward Steve, lowering her voice just enough for only him to hear. "She could be lying... just wants to get out of this place."

Mary's eyes darted between them, reading their hesitation, recognizing the doubt that could cost her an escape.

She didn't give them time to reconsider. Her voice cracked, desperation bleeding through her words. "I'm not lying. Brian and I were in love—*and they murdered him.*"

Steve's expression shifted. The truth was never delivered that raw—unless it was real. His fingers moved to the lock button, pressing it.

The doors unlocked with a soft click.

His voice was firm, steady—but carrying the weight of a decision that couldn't be undone. "Get in."

Mary didn't hesitate. She climbed into the backseat, ducking low as if expecting unseen eyes to be watching her every move. Steve and Cynthia continued driving, the car rolling toward the gate.

Mary stayed pressed against the seat, breaths shallow, controlled, her fingers gripping the fabric beside her, as though forcing herself not to tremble. Up ahead, the security guard recognized their vehicle.

The gate opened without hesitation.

Steve lifted a hand casually, waving to the guard. The guard nodded back, his attention fleeting.

No suspicion. No recognition of the extra passenger hidden in the backseat.

As the gate slid closed behind them, the car rolled onto the open road. Only then did Mary exhale shakily, as if finally breathing for the first time in decades.

Steve's voice came, low but firm. "So, Mary—what can you tell us?"

She sat forward slightly, wrapping her arms around herself as though needing to hold herself together. Then—the dam broke.

Her words poured out uncontrolled, not rehearsed—but drenched in grief. "Brian and I were in love. I know I said that already, but you *must* understand. We were building a life together—*thirty years ago.*"

Steve and Cynthia listened in silence, knowing that whatever came next would rewrite everything they thought they knew. "Brian had a delivery company. A good one. Successful. It was just him, but people *depended* on him."

Her fingers tightened against the fabric of her sleeve, as if holding onto pieces of the past. "It started small. A truck his uncle gave him. Then—a year before he died—he bought a new one."

She swallowed, voice wavering slightly. "Started renting a warehouse in Prudence... that was supposed to be the next step. Growth."

Pause. Then, quieter. "Is that enough to prove I'm *not* lying?"

Cynthia glanced at Steve, then back to Mary. "What was the name of his company?"

Mary blinked, shifting slightly. "Divine Deliveries." She hesitated. "But officially... it was just a numbered corporation."

Steve's expression darkened. "It has to be *4815162342 Inc.*"

Mary's brows furrowed slightly, recognition flickering in her eyes. "That number sounds familiar... but my memory isn't what it used to be."

Steve nodded, leaning forward slightly. "You said Brian was murdered."

Pause. Then, absolute certainty in his voice. "Who killed him?"

Mary closed her eyes briefly, as if bracing herself against the weight of the truth. And then—she told them everything. Mary sat in the backseat, her hands clutching the fabric of the seat beneath her, as if she needed something solid to hold onto.

For thirty years, she had carried this story. She had whispered it to herself in the dark. She had prayed for someone—anyone—to ask about Brian.

And now—finally—it was her time to speak. Her voice trembled, but once she started, there was no stopping the dam that broke inside her.

"Thirty years ago, the community was different... run by a different group of High Priests."

She paused, inhaling sharply—not for air, but for control. Her eyes locked onto Steve's through the rearview mirror. "There were thirteen of them. But only one mattered. The black robe High Priest—the highest ranking of them all. His name was High Priest Dresden."

Steve's brow furrowed. "Do you know his full name?"

Mary shook her head, quickly, desperately, as if that single detail had haunted her the longest. "I don't know if Dresden is a first name or last name, real or fake. The High Priests only ever went by one name."

Her fingers tightened against her arms, her voice wavering slightly. "I was supposed to become a Mother of the Church."

Then—a bitter laugh, hollow and cold. "It's the highest rank a woman could achieve—but it was just a way to keep us quiet. We handled finances, clerical duties, organizational tasks—so the *real* leaders the men, didn't have to."

Cynthia sat rigid in her seat, absorbing every word. Steve remained calm, measured—but his silence carried weight.

Mary's tone darkened. "I spent my days at the church while Brian worked. I overheard things—things I was never meant to hear. High Priests talking about members, affairs, politics. But then—one day—the conversations changed."

Her breath hitched, as if the memory was fighting its way out of her throat. "They decided the community needed to be *cut off*."

Steve's jaw tightened. Mary's voice grew hoarse, her words tumbling out faster. "Back then, we were free. People came and went. We talked to the outside world. But the High Priests decided—without telling anyone—that it would *end*."

She swallowed hard, her fingers digging into the seat again. "One day, they locked the gates. From that moment on, they would only open to let people *in*. No one would ever leave."

Silence swallowed the car. Then—a broken whisper. "We tried to fight back. Some tried climbing over the walls. But they brought in a security company—private enforcers. They stayed for six months until the last of us gave up."

Her voice cracked, but she kept going. "Brian was the first to rebel."

The weight of his name settled in the car, filling the space like a ghost had entered the room with them. "The day they locked the gates, Brian came home from his deliveries. He couldn't leave for work the next morning."

She stared blankly at her hands, her voice losing all softness now—becoming sharp, pained, raw. "Brian stormed into the church—confronted the High Priests—tried to tell them they *couldn't* do this."

Pause. Then—her voice shifted. Lower. Darker. "Within days, Brian's sanity crumbled. The weight of confinement, the walls closing in, broke him. He wasn't thinking about work anymore. He wasn't thinking about anything except *getting out.*"

Cynthia's breath slowed, chills creeping up her spine.

Mary's eyes burned with grief. "Brian was trained in the military before he came here. He used that training to make a bomb. He had a plan to blow the gate—*for us to escape together.*"

Silence. Then—an exhale filled with thirty years of suppressed pain. "But they found out."

Steve sat unmoving, listening. Mary shook her head, her voice quivering now. "The security agents took him—dragged him in front of the thirteen High Priests."

Pause. Her voice grew quieter. "I don't know what happened inside the church."

Then—barely a whisper. "But I know he never walked back out."

Cynthia's stomach twisted.

Steve's voice remained steady, but only just. "You think they killed him?"

Mary laughed—dry, hollow, haunted. "What do you think Commander?"

Her tone dropped, exhausted. "Dresden told me that Brian *escaped* the community."

She lifted her gaze slowly. "Over a week later, they *found his body*—inside the community. And then, they held a funeral."

Steve and Cynthia exchanged glances, the entire weight of this revelation settling in.

Mary wasn't done but Cynthia cut in, "Brian's company has been paying rent on the warehouse in Prudence—for *thirty years*. Who was handling the accounting?"

Steve exhaled sharply. "Someone had to be running it."

Mary nodded—almost to herself. "I was. Just like I did for the church."

Pause. "After they locked down the community, after Brian *died*, they forced me out of the church. I had no way to settle his affairs. And yet—his name never *stopped* appearing."

Steve leaned forward slightly. "What do you mean?"

Mary's fingers trembled, as if remembering too much all at once. "Three months after Brian's death, I got five letters in one day."

Pause. "One was for a *loan approval*. The other four? *Registration for four more numbered corporations.*"

Cynthia stiffened, chills creeping into her spine. "Wait—you're saying Brian's *business* didn't die with him?"

Mary laughed softly—bitterly. "Not just his business—his *name*."

She shook her head. "After Brian's death, I kept hearing rumors—people across the community receiving mail addressed to him, to his company.

Over time, people *stopped asking about it*.

The High Priests made it clear—they didn't want Brian's name spoken."

Pause. Then—her voice fractured slightly. "Eventually, people just started ignoring the mail."

Steve's jaw tightened, the pieces fitting together in a way that made too much sense.

His voice was quieter now. "Mary... you don't even understand how valuable this is to our investigation."

Pause. Then—the shift happened. His tone grew firm, decisive. "Come back with us. Work with our investigators and accountants—help us untangle this mess.

Because I think you just revealed the key to everything."

Mary exhaled slowly, as if she had waited her whole life for someone to ask. Her voice came softer now—but carrying the strength of someone who had finally escaped their prison. "I have been waiting thirty years to tell my story."

Pause. Then, absolute certainty in her words. "I'll help with whatever I can."

They continued driving back to The Throne, discussing the critical details Mary had shared.

When they arrived, Mary couldn't contain her amazement. She stared up at the large sign above the building that read "The Throne," her eyes widening in wonder.

Having been trapped in the community for over thirty years, she had never seen a building with so many floors. The sheer scale and modernity of the structure left her momentarily speechless.

The Command Room buzzed with activity, every corner occupied by Digital Investigators and Forensic Accounting Investigators engrossed in their work.

New stations had been set up since Steve and Cynthia's last visit, reflecting the urgency and scale of the ongoing operations.

As they stepped out of the elevator, the sight of the bustling room only heightened their determination.

Olivia spotted them and hurried over, her expression a mix of relief and urgency.

The energy in the room was palpable, each investigator focused on piecing together the critical information they needed. "Welcome back Commander, Cynthia. Hello, my name is Olivia. Nice to meet you."

The Command Room was charged with anticipation as Steve, Mary, and Cynthia stood among Mark, Doris, and Olivia.

The air was thick—not just with tension, but with the weight of revelations that had been buried for three decades.

As they spoke, each new piece of information—Brian Schersinger, the Church of the Odyssey, the underground tunnels, the stolen identities—wove into a narrative that was finally becoming clear.

Steve's voice cut through the room, steady but commanding. "Everyone, this is Mary. She lived with and loved Brian Schersinger thirty years ago. She'll be assisting in our investigation."

A pause. "Formal introductions later. Olivia—please tell me you have good news."

Olivia barely glanced away from her screens, fingers flying across her keyboard. "We haven't been sitting here twiddling our thumbs, Commander.

I've dispatched investigators into *every* entrance to the underground tunnels. I've traced their ownership back to Odyssey Inc."

Steve's jaw tightened slightly. "They own *every* building?"

Olivia nodded, adjusting the display on the large screen before continuing. "Not directly—but Odyssey Inc. owns thousands of real estate companies across the country. That's how I connected them.

All the tunnel buildings are listed as *rental properties*."

She gestured toward the screen, where records flickered into view. "Antonio Balata has been cross-referencing everything for us—he's sending information on the renters as he gets it."

Steve absorbed the information quickly. "Any progress inside the tunnels?"

Olivia nodded sharply. "We've explored *forty-five percent* of them nationwide. Mostly, we've just found—more tunnels.

But we *did* reach the one I suspected was *larger*."

Her eyes flicked toward Steve. "You were right, Commander. There are tracks down there—train or subway, maybe even something worse."

Steve's breath was slow but deliberate. "Teams are following them?"

"Yes. We're dispatching more as we speak."

A voice cut in unexpectedly. "There were tunnels beneath the warehouse in Prudence?"

It was Mary. The room fell silent, suddenly recognizing the weight of her presence. Olivia turned toward her, nodding slightly. "There are tunnels *everywhere*."

She adjusted the screen again, highlighting Prudence. "That's all the warehouse had—a ramp leading *underground*."

Mary shook her head, suddenly pale, distant—remembering something.

Her voice was quiet. "I had been inside the warehouse before Brian died—it wasn't like that then."

A pause. Then—her expression shifted. "But... the tunnels. The tunnels are reminding me of something—a conversation I overheard between the High Priests decades ago."

The tension thickened instantly. Steve stepped forward slightly. "What kind of conversation?"

Mary exhaled slowly, as if forcing herself to relive it. "It might be nothing, but I remember hearing them—talking about brainstorming how to start a *community underground*."

Silence.

Steve's eyes narrowed, his expression tightening. "We haven't found any people *inside* the tunnels yet. But we're still exploring."

His tone was firm—but laced with something deeper now.

Uncertainty. Caution.

Then—another shift in focus. "What have you found, Doris?"

Doris barely looked up—her hands racing across the keyboard. Her tone was clear but overwhelmed. "Commander—the maze of numbers keeps growing."

She barely finished before another voice rang out. "I got a hit with a name!"

It was one of the Forensic Accounting Investigators. Doris snapped up immediately. "Send it to me *now*."

Steve's posture stiffened. "What is the name?"

Doris pulled up the data, her eyes scanning rapidly. Then—she let out a sharp exhale. "Lionel Trebor."

A pause. "He's listed as the renter of one of the tunnel entrances under *4348684541 Inc* for fifteen years."

Her fingers flew over the keyboard, pulling up additional details. "We have an address—another church community, this time on the *other side of the country*."

She adjusted the large map on the screen, and the image zoomed in. The satellite view revealed something chilling.

The new church community was one hundred times larger than the Church of the Odyssey.

Steve's breath came slow and controlled, his mind racing. Then—another voice cut in. "Doris! We've got another name."

The room was motionless, waiting. Doris scanned the screen quickly.

Her voice came tighter now—"Gerald Randall."

Another pause. "Renter of another tunnel entrance under *6146538137 Inc.*—for fifteen years.

And once again, an address to another religious community."

She pulled up another satellite view, zooming in. The Anointing Church of Jesus Christ. And again—far larger than the first.

Steve exhaled sharply, leaning against the table, staring at the expanding map.

The picture was finally forming. "I have a theory."

Everyone turned toward him. His voice was controlled—but tense, weighted with absolute certainty. "The Church of the Odyssey hijacked Brian Schersinger's identity after his death."

The words fell heavy. "Probably Lionel Trebor and Gerald Randall too."

Silence. Then—Cynthia, thinking aloud now. "They're using the identities of their dead members... to secure assets for their communities and churches?"

Steve nodded. "It explains the scale. This operation would take *billions*."

Cynthia exhaled sharply, shaking her head. "So, they wash, rinse, repeat—with new identities, businesses, and investments."

Steve's eyes flickered with realization. "Investments, you say."

A pause. Then—his voice hardened. "Odyssey Inc. is involved in this. We *know* they are. Let's find the connection."

Then—Mark's phone rang. His eyes flicked downward at the screen. "Excuse me. It's one of our agents from the tunnels."

A pause. Then—his voice changed. His posture straightened sharply. "Which is *weird*, because there's *no service* down there."

He stepped away, answering.

Seconds passed. Then—Mark turned back, his expression tight with urgency. "Steve—the agents in the tunnels have encountered a *phantom ambulance*."

Silence fell over the room like a heavy storm cloud. "They arrested the paramedics inside. Secured the kidnapped person in the back."

Pause. "They just pulled into the underground parking garage. They're bringing them to thirty-five for interrogation."

Steve inhaled sharply—but there was no hesitation. "Mark, you stay here and fill in for me as Commander. Keep scanning for #64.

We are so close to finding The Lost I can feel it. Cynthia and I will handle the interrogations.

Now that we have hijacked a phantom ambulance, they are sure to know we have found the tunnels.

Now that they know, let's get them explored one hundred percent as soon as possible.

Knock the doors down and get vehicles in there. I want to know where every tunnel leads."

Overwhelmed by the information she was hearing Mary spoke up and said, "Excuse me, everyone I hate to interrupt, but I have been imprisoned within that community for over thirty years.

If you don't mind me asking, what is this place? What is The Throne? What is The Lost? What is #64? And what is a....... Phantom ambulance?"

Part Two

THE LOST and THE THRONE

Chapter 25 - What is Heaven?

Kevan was walking through the forest after meeting Leonard Chance and participating in The Celebration of Love. Kevan at this time felt amazing after sharing the most intense sexual experience he has ever had in his life with Leonard Chance and his friends.

Kevan had met up with Leonard and his friends everyday indulging in The Celebration of Love.

Kevan was hoping he would get to meet more new people on the island, primarily in the back of his mind he wanted to have sex with them.

Kevan was abstinent when he was a High Priest and now having access to sex in abundance, he was developing an addiction to it to the point where he craved sex all the time.

Being deprived for so long from the touch of the opposite sex, how beautiful their bodies were, and how they gave him an immense feeling within his chest when he looked at a naked woman.

Knowing the life that he led had nothing to do with him arriving in heaven he started regretting everything he had done in his life prior to coming here.

Kevan could hear a quiet sobbing, faint but unmistakable, carried by the wind like a whispered cry for help.

He followed the sound, his steps careful, scanning the area. Then—he found her. Amelia was curled up on the ground, her body rigid, her face streaked with tears that hadn't stopped falling.

She wiped her red, swollen eyes, looking up at Kevan—but she didn't speak.

She wanted to run. To flee. To hide. But she couldn't move.

The only thing she could do was stare up at him, frozen, helpless—another wave of silent tears forming and rolling down her cheeks.

Kevan sat down beside her, his presence gentle but firm, wrapping an arm around her.

His voice was soft, careful—but carrying the weight of worry.

"Amelia—what is wrong? Are you okay? What happened?"

Amelia took a shaky breath, trying to pull herself together, but her hands trembled against her skin as she wiped away the streaks of sorrow.

She wasn't just crying. She was grieving.

She inhaled again, forcing the words out between uneven breaths. "Kevan... I am so sorry."

Kevan's brows furrowed, pulling back slightly. "You have nothing to be sorry for."

But Amelia shook her head. "I've been a mess for days. I can't stop crying."

Kevan searched her face, reading the brokenness behind her words. "What changed Amelia? What happened?"

She exhaled sharply, like the weight of speaking was a battle within itself. "It's hard to explain."

She rubbed her temples, shutting her eyes briefly. "I hit my head on a rock... and now I'm seeing things. *Dreams. Visions.* But not like dreams."

Kevan's expression darkened slightly. "What kind of dreams and visions?"

Amelia opened her eyes, locking onto him now—almost desperate for him to understand. "Those aren't the right words."

She swallowed hard. "It's more like I'm seeing memories."

Pause.

Then—her voice grew quieter. "Memories of nightmares I don't remember living through."

Kevan's breath was slow and deliberate, measuring her words carefully. "Could these nightmares... these memories... be real?"

Amelia's fingers dug into the ground slightly, her voice cracking. "That's what I'm afraid of."

A shift in the air—movement from behind. Justin emerged from the trees, his presence silent, careful, his gaze scanning the scene.

He saw Amelia first—her tear-streaked face, her rigid posture, the absolute distress hanging over her like a storm cloud.

Then—Kevan beside her, tense, concerned. Something was very wrong. Justin's voice was calm but alert. "Is everything okay here Amelia?"

Amelia swallowed thickly, shifting slightly, as if only now realizing Justin was there. Her voice was quieter. "Yes, Justin. This is Kevan Harrison. He's the High Priest I guided before you."

Justin nodded slightly, his attention still locked on her. "Hello, Kevan."

Then—back to her. "Amelia—can we talk?"

His voice softened just slightly, laced with concern. "You ran off after you hit your head. I haven't seen you in days. I was worried. Are you Ok?"

Amelia exhaled slowly, her body still tense. "I'm the best I can be."

Pause. Then—a weak attempt at normalcy. "I was just trying to explain to Kevan what happened."

She blinked through another layer of fresh tears, then added quickly. "Were you able to finish your prayers? I—I'm so sorry for ditching you like that."

Justin nodded. "Yes. But then I started looking for you."

His tone remained steady, but weighted now. "What did happen, Amelia?"

She took another deep breath, bracing herself.

Then—she spoke. Not rushing. Not collapsing into emotion. Just speaking. Trying to make them understand.

"Like I told Kevan... I'm seeing things. Memories."

Pause. She exhaled, voice tightening slightly. "But they weren't there before. I—I don't remember them at all."

Justin listened carefully, his posture shifting slightly. Amelia pressed a hand against her forehead, shaking her head as if forcing herself to push forward.

"When I hit my head, something *broke* inside me.

These nightmares—these memories—came *flooding back* into my mind."

Her voice cracked. "That's why I ran. I—I couldn't even speak."

Kevan leaned forward slightly, his voice softer now. "You don't have to talk about it if you don't want to, Amelia. Let's go get some food—get your mind off it."

Amelia shook her head sharply. "No!

We *must* talk about it, Kevan."

Her voice was absolute—like something far greater than just her pain was at stake now. "We're supposed to be in Heaven, right?"

Kevan's expression shifted, his brows knitting together slightly.

Amelia inhaled sharply, gripping her arms. "How is this happening to me in a place that's supposed to be *perfect*? How am I living through a *nightmare*—inside my own mind?"

Her voice hardened, grief turning into something more raw, more uncertain. "How could God *allow* this?"

Kevan's voice was low now, quieter. "I have felt the same way since I got here."

Pause. "Being an atheist, not believing in God, wondering—how was I *brought* here?"

His gaze locked onto her now, studying her carefully. "You told me Amelia. That Jesus chose us. That we just needed *more time here*."

Amelia stayed silent, her hands tightening into fists.

Her voice was barely a whisper now. "I believed that."

Pause. "But I don't think I do anymore."

Justin stayed quiet, sat back—watching, listening.

He felt it, too. The shift. The unraveling.

Amelia's belief wasn't just breaking—it was collapsing entirely. And whatever was happening here—was far from Heaven.

"After I left with my guide Simon, we spent some time together, had food and wine. Being with Simon, I was aroused more than I had ever been in my life.

I held back for a short time, but we had sex many times that night, which is something I never would have done before coming here.

I think the Three E's were responsible for that."

Kevan brow furrowed thinking of what Amelia was saying, "I was celibate since I became a High Priest, and I jumped at the chance to have sex with you Amelia.

I understand what you are saying about the intense feelings of arousal, sex is all I think about at this point when I am travelling around the island.

Was it the same for you and Justin?"

Amelia continued, "Justin turned me down when I made advances on him. He wanted to get his prayers done."

Justin responded, "I did turn you down, but I did feel that surge of extreme arousal like never before. I think you might be onto something."

Amelia continued her story, "After my guide and I split up, I craved more sex every second, it was really all I thought about."

A pause, and then a smile came across her face

"I met a man named Leonard Chance, who has been here for over six years. He told me that an eternal orgasm is what heaven is.

I participated in an orgy with him and all his friends and had the best time of my life. For the next two weeks before you guys came here, I was having sex at least twenty times a day."

Kevan chimed in recognizing the name, "I met Leonard after you left me. I have participated in the Celebration of Love a few times since then."

Justin added, "I didn't meet Leonard, but I met some other people. I was invited to spend some time with them, but I was focused on completing my prayers, so I declined.

Amelia continued her story, "After I hit my head on the rock and the memories came back, I became a different person than I was before or after I came here."

She paused, hanging her head down so she was staring at the ground she said, "The memories that I received were filled with sexual abuse from when I was younger and filled in the missing pieces from my life.

When I was fifteen, I was sexually abused by a priest at my church. It was something called The Promise."

Being a High Priest within the church Kevan knew exactly what The Promise was, and he was horrified, "You had to fulfill The Promise? The Promise is the reason I chose celibacy when I became a High Priest."

Amelia asked, "What do you mean?"

Kevan was visibly uncomfortable as he spoke, "If you had to fulfill The Promise, then you know what it is. A religious excuse for the High Priests of the church to have sex with whoever they want within the church.

When you become a High Priest, you must fulfill The Promise, unless you choose to be celibate.

I was horrified at using my power as a priest to rape women within my church, so I chose to be celibate.

You had to fulfill The Promise when you were fifteen years old?"

Amelia looked up and directly at Kevan, "I think the priest that abused me when I was fifteen years old was your father Kevan. I am the one who murdered your father."

A mix of surprise and shock crossed his face, "How could that even be possible?"

"I don't know Kevan, but it is true."

Kevan defending his father, "My Father would never do something like that, I can't believe it."

Bluntly asking him she knew that the answer would reveal the truth, she asked, "Was your father celibate?"

"No, he wasn't, but I still can't even think he would be doing that."

Forcing herself to go back to the memory she was silent for a few seconds and then she spoke.

"Your father, inside of his chambers, had shelves filled with Christian statues of religious figures. He had a weird-looking statue on the shelf that didn't quite fit with the others. It was all gold, and it was a cat fishing, catching a cross."

Kevan paused, his thoughts colliding in a chaotic storm.

The memory rushed back uninvited—the store, the moment he used his allowance to buy the statue, the pride of giving it to his father—a memory once innocent, now stained with the truth he couldn't ignore.

The vision shifted—another recollection surfaced, stronger, sharper. Sitting across from his father. The same chair where Amelia had been abused.

Kevan's chest tightened, his breath shallow. The cat statue—its quiet presence on the shelf.

A silent witness. A witness to conversations, to horror, to blood.

His voice trembled. "I gave my father that statue."

Pause. His breath hitched, his thoughts spiraling. "I still can't believe it. What does this *mean*?"

A pause—long enough for the weight of the thought to fully settle. Then, barely above a whisper—broken, unraveling. "I don't know what to say. I feel *terrible*."

Silence wrapped around them, suffocating. Amelia exhaled shakily, trying to process it all. "There *must* be a reason we were both brought here. That I was made to be your guide."

Justin, always analytical, always dissecting the world into logic, responded. "I don't know if we should read too much into it."

Amelia blinked at him, her expression tight. Justin's voice was calm, but firm. "You were both part of the same church networks. It could just be a coincidence."

Amelia shook her head harder this time, frustration creeping into her tone. "The *connection* is too big to be a coincidence."

Justin exhaled, his logic unwavering. "That's exactly what a coincidence *is* Amelia—something that *feels* too big to be one. But it's just probability."

Kevan sat rigid, barely listening, his own mind drowning in its battle.

Justin continued. "People from your church networks were being taken. That means the probability of finding connections like this with other people *here* goes way up."

Amelia's breath was uneven, sharp. Then—a realization hit her. Her tone shifted, growing more cautious. "How do you *know* they were taking people from our church networks?"

Justin's gaze darkened. He didn't hesitate. "The Commander of The Throne saw a pattern. Put agents in place to monitor it."

Kevan's stomach twisted. He shook his head slowly, his voice barely above a whisper—cracked, disbelieving. "How can any of this be real?"

Pause. Amelia had realized that Justin knew more than he was letting on and asked, "How do you know about The Throne, and people from our churches being taken?"

The words carried every shattered hope, every ounce of betrayal. Justin's expression hardened, his tone grave. He knew this moment had to be handled carefully.

If Kevan and Amelia were to truly see the truth—they had to hear it without hesitation.

He met their gazes, his voice unwavering. "What if I told you none of it was real?"

Silence. "What if I told you that you were kidnapped, brought here, made to think you died and went to Heaven?"

Amelia inhaled sharply, her hands clenching against her arms. Justin's tone did not falter. "What if I told you this has been happening to *thousands* of people for over twenty years?"

The dam finally cracked. Amelia's breath hitched—her eyes blown wide with clarity. Her voice was raw, barely above a whisper. "That would make more sense than what Jesus told us."

Kevan's posture remained stiff, but his eyes screamed disbelief. He didn't want to accept it. Couldn't. His voice trembled with resistance. "How could you even *know* that?"

Justin's reply was immediate, sharp. "Have you ever heard of The Throne? Do you know what they did?"

Amelia's response came instantly, her voice steady despite her racing mind. "Yeah. Of course. The division of the NBI that finds missing persons—The Lost, or something."

Kevan exhaled sharply. "I heard about it on the radio. But I never left the community much—I don't know much about The Throne."

Justin's expression grew heavier, firmer. "The Throne didn't find missing persons."

Silence. "The Throne's only objective was to figure out where *The Lost* were *being taken*. The people on this island?"

His breath was slow, controlled. Then—the final blow.

"We *are* The Lost."

Kevan felt his stomach churn, his body rigid. Justin continued. "People were disappearing *daily*, picked up by phantom ambulances—just like we were—never seen again."

Pause. "For the last three years, I was undercover inside the Children of Christ Church. Agent #64 for The Throne. I infiltrated hoping to be picked up and brought *here*."

Amelia inhaled sharply, her voice tighter now. "Why would The Throne place undercover agents in church communities?"

Justin answered without hesitation. "A pattern emerged. Everyone who went missing was deeply religious, involved in cult-like communities."

Kevan was still stiff, his mind failing to grasp the enormity of it. "Do you know where we *are?*"

Justin shook his head, his frustration thinly veiled. "No. But that information *will* come."

Pause. "I placed trackers all around the island. I was hoping The Throne would pick up the signal—but I haven't gotten confirmation."

Amelia's eyes flickered with realization. "That was your prayer ritual—putting trackers around?"

Justin nodded sharply. "Yes. I didn't know if I could trust you. Now I do."

Kevan's voice was hoarse, barely above a whisper. "So... what are we supposed to do?"

Justin met his gaze. His words were absolute. "For now—we wait. I want to see what is at the edge of the water, I asked Jesus for an air mattress, we can get it tomorrow"

Then—a twig snapped behind them.

Kevan and Justin stiffened immediately. Amelia shifted, her tone suddenly lighter, forced. "I miss tennis."

Kevan frowned. "Tennis?"

Justin narrowed his gaze. "What?"

Before they could process it, Simon emerged from the forest. Amelia's voice dropped to a whisper. "That's Simon. I don't know if we can trust him."

Pause. Then—deadly quiet. "He's been here *three months.*"

Amelia's breath hitched, but she didn't show it. Instead—she turned to him, forced a neutral smile, and spoke first. "Hey Simon, this is Justin and Kevan. These are the people I guided."

Simon's eyes flicked across them, scanning their faces, measuring their presence. His expression didn't change, but there was something unreadable in his gaze. Justin responded first, his voice steady, polite—but controlled. "Simon, nice to meet you."

Kevan followed, keeping his tone even. "It's an honor to meet the guide who guided Amelia."

Simon tilted his head slightly, his mouth twitching at the corner—was it amusement? Was it indifference? Then—casually, effortlessly, as if it was the most natural thing to say—he offered a distraction.

"Nice to meet you guys. What are you all up to?"

Pause. Then—he turned his attention back to Amelia. "I got more of that wine. Thought maybe we could spend some time together."

Amelia's shoulders stiffened—barely noticeable, but Justin caught it instantly. Her smile remained, but her response was carefully chosen. "I can't right now, Simon."

She gestured toward Justin. "I'm still guiding him. We're traveling around the island. Maybe in a couple of days when we're done."

Simon's expression darkened subtly, his posture shifting—not aggressive, but tense. His voice carried just enough bite to reveal his disappointment. "Pfft. Whatever."

Then—he turned sharply, walking away. But his movements weren't casual anymore. His shoulders were too rigid. His steps were too precise. The sound of his footsteps echoed faintly, even as he moved farther away, vanishing into the trees.

He didn't look back. Didn't say anything else.

But everyone felt the weight of his reaction hanging in the silence he left behind. Amelia exhaled slowly, as if forcing herself to reset. Her voice was quieter now. "So, let's get through tonight."

She turned to Justin, ignoring the lingering tension in the air. "Tomorrow, you get that air mattress. Kevan and I will do whatever we can to help you."

Justin, who had been watching Simon disappear, finally pulled his attention back to them.

His tone wasn't forced, wasn't uncertain. It was absolute. "I promise you both—I will get us home."

Chapter 26 - The Lost and The Throne

he Throne was established over six years ago, with Steve Hauser at its helm. It all started with a missing person case that landed on Steve's desk while he was working as an NBI (National Bureau of Investigation) investigator.

The missing person in question was Leonard Chance. Throughout his career, Steve had handled thousands of cases, but there was something particularly curious about Leonard's.

At the time of his disappearance, Leonard had managed to call for an ambulance. Although the call was abruptly disconnected, Leonard had managed to say that he had been stabbed and provided his name and exact location.

Within five minutes, the ambulance arrived at the scene, only to find fresh blood on the ground. There were multiple witnesses, none of whom had seen the actual incident but had noticed the presence of two ambulances.

Only one witness, Jerry Haliburton, had seen exactly what had happened from across the street. Once the police got involved, Jerry's account was verified by surveillance cameras in the area.

The case was immediately flagged as a high-priority kidnapping and missing person case and was assigned to Steve.

Steve sat down with Jerry Haliburton, the one eyewitness who had seen the incident.

It was 2:42 PM, thirty minutes after Leonard Chance had called for the ambulance and disappeared. Steve's partner, Mark, was speaking with the other witnesses who had seen the ambulances but not the incident.

Their statements were corroborated by video footage from a paranoid store owner who had two cameras outside his shop. Steve was hopeful that Jerry could provide information that the other witnesses and the video couldn't.

The interrogation room was quiet, tension settling between Steve and Jerry Haliburton, the only person who had seen the truth unfold.

Jerry sat across from him, his gaze sharp—not the eyes of someone confused by what he saw, but the eyes of someone who had seen far too much before this moment.

Steve leaned forward slightly, his voice level but expectant. "Please tell me what you saw."

Jerry exhaled, adjusting his posture. "I was sitting across the street when it happened."

His tone wasn't shaken—it was exact, as if he had played this moment over and over in his mind. "Feeding the birds, like I do every Sunday."

Pause. "I finished the loaf of bread and took a break. Checked my watch—2:12 PM."

The time locked in Steve's mind instantly. Jerry continued. "I leaned against the wall, pulled out a cigarette. When I raised my lighter—looked down the length of it—I saw it happen across the street."

His voice didn't waver. "Like I was looking down the sight of a gun."

Steve's jaw tightened slightly, absorbing the precision in Jerry's words. Steve confirmed, "So, it was 2:12. What happened?"

Jerry's expression darkened slightly, remembering every detail. "Yes, it happened in seconds. The victim—Leonard Chance—was walking west, carrying a shopping bag. Normal. Just a guy on the street."

Pause. "The other man? Hooded sweatshirt. Black pants. Hood up. Walking *east*—toward Leonard."

Steve listened closely. Jerry inhaled. "They passed each other. No words. No interaction."

Pause. Then—a flicker of something unreadable in Jerry's face. "The hooded man pulled something out. Stabbed him. Twice."

Steve leaned forward slightly, voice sharper now. "You *saw* the weapon?"

Jerry tilted his head slightly, thinking. "Saw the motion. The blood. Something sharp, for sure."

Pause. Then—an unsettling addition. "But they both kept walking—like nothing happened."

Steve's breath slowed, his mind calculating. "He didn't collapse immediately?"

Jerry shook his head. "Three steps. Then he fell forward—onto his chest and stomach, where he was stabbed."

Pause. Then—Jerry's posture changed. He shifted slightly, his fingers tapping absently against the table. "I looked west. Before I could even cross the street—an ambulance was already coming. I looked at my watch again and it was 2:13"

Steve's pulse quickened. "Already, after one minute?"

Jerry nodded slowly. "Speeding down the road. Fast. Skidded to a stop."

Pause. Then—the first red flag. "I heard one paramedic yell at the other after they picked up the victim."

Steve's breath was steady, expectant. "What did he say?"

Jerry exhaled slowly—as if it had been running through his mind for weeks. Then—he finally spoke. "He said, I told you we *didn't* have time to stop."

The words hung in the air like a death sentence. Steve stiffened, his thoughts racing. "Why did that stand out to you?"

Jerry exhaled sharply, shaking his head. "Gave me *a feeling in my gut* the second I heard it."

Pause. "After they left—it kept replaying in my head."

Silence. Then—Jerry's expression shifted again. His voice was lower now. "I checked my watch right *before* the victim was stabbed—and again *after* I saw the ambulance coming."

Pause. Then—the final detail that solidified everything. "Only one *minute* had passed."

Steve stared at him, his mind racing through every possibility. He barely spoke above a whisper now. "Why does that make you suspicious?"

Jerry exhaled—but there was a flicker of something unreadable in his face. Then—a chuckle. "Who's the detective here?"

Steve didn't respond. Jerry's expression shifted—almost amused, but something darker lurked beneath it. "Sorry. Used to be a private investigator in my better days."

Pause. Then—his tone sharpened again. "There's *no way* an ambulance, police, or fire department could've been called, dispatched, and arrived in *one minute.*"

Silence. "It would be *impossible.*"

Pause. "The *best* response times? Five minutes."

Steve felt the realization settling into his bones now. "I see where you're going."

Jerry leaned forward slightly, his voice lower, weighted. "Now take it *further*, Detective."

Pause. "The ambulance was *dispatched*, made a stop, and *still* arrived within one minute?" His gaze locked onto Steve's. "Does that sound right to you?"

Steve's stomach twisted, his breath slowing. Jerry leaned back, arms crossed now. "The second ambulance?"

Pause. "That one arrived at 2:17."

Silence. Then—Jerry's tone darkened. "Right on time. *Five minutes* after the victim was stabbed."

Steve felt it now—the chilling certainty. Everything about this was wrong.

That single conversation ignited Steve's curiosity, propelling him deep into the case's details. As Steve delved into Leonard's investigation, he stumbled upon multiple missing persons reports that mirrored Leonard's circumstances.

His discovery was startling: twenty other cases from across the country shared the same criteria as Leonard's. He named these cases "The Lost" and the commonalities among them "The Lost Criterion."

Steve identified seven criteria that these twenty cases had in common, five of which were already present in Leonard Chance's case:

The Lost Criterion:

1. The person is deeply religious.
2. An injury occurs.

3. An ambulance is called by the injured or bystanders.

4. The injured person is picked up by a phantom ambulance.

5. The injured is declared missing or kidnapped after the investigation.

6. On the 6th day, the missing person's death certificate appears in their records.

7. The search for the injured person ceases.

On the sixth day of Leonard's investigation, Steve awoke to find Leonard's death certificate suddenly appearing in his digital record and files overnight.

This piqued his curiosity further. He began to think through the case, talking himself through the details, determined to unravel the mystery.

"I think that guarantees that I am onto something with these connections. I just wonder how many others there could be out there. How many times did this happen with no witnesses,

Or the ones that couldn't make the call after the injury and were picked up by phantom ambulances never to be seen again."

After delving deeper into Leonard's death certificate, Steve discovered something highly suspicious: the certificate appeared to be fake.

It was signed by a doctor who had died 30 years prior and had never worked at the issuing establishment.

Additionally, there were no records of Leonard's death in the files of the issuing institution. This revelation heightened Steve's suspicions.

Steve soon found that the twenty other cases connected to Leonard's also had fraudulent death certificates. None of these individuals had ended up in any hospital, a detail that intrigued and concerned Steve.

What was happening to these people? Determined to uncover the truth.

Steve continued his investigation.

Steve theorized that fake ambulances were being used to kidnap The Lost. According to his hypothesis, the kidnappers caused the injuries as part of their plan.

They would choose their victims and have phantom ambulances and paramedics on standby to pick them up before the real authorities arrived.

As Steve pursued this lead, he uncovered hundreds of cases that matched The Lost Criterion. He started investigating the anomalies of emergency calls where no victims were found when authorities arrived.

This brought the total number of The Lost to over five hundred.

With the investigation growing, Steve received additional resources and was able to hire full-time investigators dedicated to finding more missing persons cases that fit The Lost Criterion.

One year after Leonard's initial investigation, Steve meticulously compiled a presentation for his superiors. It showcased an alarming pattern: 2,000 missing person cases that all fit a disturbing profile known as The Lost Criterion.

These cases spanned the entire country, encompassing thousands of individuals who had vanished mysteriously over many years.

The locations of these disappearances were plotted on a map, forming a dense web of colorful push pins. The sheer number of cases transformed the map into a chaotic explosion of color, obscuring any semblance of a recognizable geography.

It was as if the map had become a haunting mosaic of lost souls.

Steve's superiors were both astonished and deeply concerned. They recognized the gravity of the situation and immediately allocated additional resources to support Steve's investigation.

Delving deeper, they uncovered cases matching The Lost Criterion that dated back over the past two decades, cases that had slipped under the radar until now.

The chilling realization set in: for twenty years, The Lost had been slipping through the cracks, leaving behind a trail of unanswered questions and shattered lives.

Now, with heightened awareness and a renewed sense of urgency, Steve and his team were determined to uncover the truth behind these mysterious disappearances and bring justice to The Lost.

Steve's immediate promotion marked the beginning of a new era. What had started as a routine investigation into a single missing person quickly transformed into something much larger.

Within a year, Steve's efforts led to the formation of a specialized division known as The Throne.

This entity branched off from the NBI, becoming an independent organization with one sole objective: to find The Lost.

With an influx of resources, The Throne expanded rapidly. The more evidence they uncovered, the more it became clear that this was a monumental task.

Suspicious reports of missing persons poured in, each fitting the disturbing profile of The Lost Criterion.

What began as a modest operation with Steve and three other investigators in a small office soon grew into an enormous 72-floor building.

Each floor housed a different division of The Throne, employing over 7,000 people stationed across the country, all dedicated to this singular mission.

The importance of finding out what happened to The Lost could not be overstated. It was a global priority, overshadowing all other concerns.

Now, six years after Leonard Chance's initial investigation, the number of The Lost has swelled to over 7,000 missing or kidnapped individuals. Steve remains resolute in his determination to uncover the truth.

He clings to the hope that, somewhere, every one of The Lost is still alive.

Driven by an unyielding sense of duty, he vows not to rest until he brings them home.

Chapter 27 - The Phantom Ambulance

teve and Cynthia waited on the 35th floor for the agents to arrive with the drivers of the Phantom Ambulance and the victim. They had three investigation rooms prepared for them.

Within minutes, the elevator doors slid open, and the agents escorted in the two Phantom Ambulance Paramedics (PAP). Steve asked immediately, "Where is the victim?"

"The victim in the back was out cold. We had to bring the stretcher from the ambulance. Another agent will be bringing her up. They didn't have any identification on them. We've been calling them One and Two."

Steve responded, "Make sure the victim is taken directly to the infirmary. I want the doctors to find out exactly what she was given. Inform me the minute she wakes up."

The interrogation room was cold, sterile, and drowning in silence.

The agents had seated both men in separate rooms, handcuffing them to the tables—isolated, vulnerable, waiting. Steve and Cynthia entered PAP One's room first, the door clicking shut behind them.

Steve didn't speak immediately. He lowered himself into the chair across from the man, arms resting steadily on the table, his stare heavy and unwavering.

Cynthia stood behind him—hovering, watching, waiting. Her presence was deliberate, adding pressure even before the first word was spoken.

Then—finally—Steve broke the silence. "Who are you working for?"

Nothing. he just stared back, silent, unreadable. Then—slowly, deliberately—he closed his eyes.

Not in defiance. Not in thought. Just—closed them. Refusing to engage.

Steve exhaled, but his expression didn't change. "I don't think you understand how serious the situation is."

Pause. "It only gets *worse* if you don't answer our questions."

The man didn't flinch. Didn't move an inch. His hands trembled slightly, the cuffs rattling softly against the bar, but his eyes stayed shut. Steve stood abruptly, pushing the chair back firmly, but not aggressively.

He turned to Cynthia, speaking as he walked toward the door. "Let's see what Two has to say."

They exited without another glance at the man, closing the door without hesitation. Through the window, Steve and Cynthia could see the second man clearly—tense, agitated, talking to himself.

He stopped abruptly the moment the door swung open. Steve sat across from him, taking the same position as before. Cynthia remained just behind—looming, listening.

Steve's voice was calm—but edged with purpose. "Your friend didn't say a word."

A pause—just long enough to sink in. "If you want *any* chance of walking out of here, it would be wise to answer our questions."

The man inhaled deeply, his breath shaky—but his words came without resistance. "If I have the answers to your questions, I will give them to you."

Steve watched him closely, dissecting his posture, his tone, his tension. "Why is your friend being so uncooperative?"

The man exhaled sharply, his fingers clenching slightly against the table. "He doesn't understand where we are." Pause. Then—his voice shifted. Lower. More unsettled. "I do."

Steve narrowed his gaze. The man's expression darkened, his tone growing heavier. "I'm horrified to think that what we were doing had *anything* to do with all those missing people."

Silence. Cynthia and Steve exchanged a glance—a subtle confirmation. He knows something important. Steve leaned forward slightly, pressing deeper.

"If you cooperate and you're useful, you may get to walk out of here."

Pause. "Tell me why we found you and your friend in the tunnels—with an ambulance and a *person* in the back."

The man swallowed hard, shifting slightly in his seat. "We were just doing our job."

Steve's expression stayed unreadable. "What is your job? And *who* do you work for?"

The man exhaled slowly, as if the weight of his answer was suffocating him. Then—he admitted the truth. "I have no clue who we work for."

Pause. Then—his voice steadied, like the confession itself had freed him. "But I can explain our job."

Steve nodded once, allowing him to continue. "My friend in the other room—he has a phone."

Pause. "Our employers send a message—an address, a date, a time. That's how we know we have a job."

He shifted uncomfortably, shaking his head. "We go to the address at the time. The ambulance is *already there*, waiting for us."

Silence. Then—a chilling admission. "Once inside, there are uniforms in the back."

His breath was uneven now, as if the reality of saying this out loud was catching up to him. "The GPS coordinates are *already programmed*—with a time and place for the pickup."

Steve studied him carefully, the pattern becoming unmistakable now. "How many times have you done this?"

The man looked away briefly, exhaling. Then—his voice quieted. "This was the *second* time."

Pause. "The first message came three weeks ago—after we signed up."

Cynthia finally spoke, her voice calculated, piercing. "What do you know about the tunnels?"

The man shook his head slightly, his hands fidgeting against the table. "I know they exist."

Pause. "But we were just *directed* to them by the GPS."

Steve exchanged another glance with Cynthia. This was bigger. Much bigger. "Where were you taking the pickup?"

He hesitated. Then—he answered, slower now. "I don't know. You found us before we got there."

Silence settled heavier between them.

Then—a shift in his tone. "But I can tell you about the first job."

Steve leaned back slightly, considering. Then—he nodded once. "Tell me everything."

He hesitated only briefly, but then spilled everything, knowing there was no way out of this.

"My friend found the job online."

Pause. "It was listed as a driver team of two. Paid *$30,000* per driver, per pickup. On call *24/7*."

Cynthia's brow furrowed slightly, absorbing the number.

Steve didn't react. Big money meant big secrets.

He exhaled. "We thought it was a joke when we signed up. We had *no idea* what we'd be doing, but it paid a *lottery amount* of money."

Pause. "Then, two weeks ago, we got the message."

His voice grew darker. "An address. Instructions to bring nothing but the clothes on our backs."

Steve nodded, letting him continue. "The address led to a warehouse."

Pause. "Ambulance inside. Already waiting for us."

His breath hitched slightly, as if remembering how that moment had felt. "Once inside, there was a needle."

A pause, weighted. "Instructions said to *use it on the pickup* to keep them calm."

Steve narrowed his gaze. Cynthia crossed her arms. The man shook his head slightly, as if reliving the moment when he realized how far in they had already gone. "We followed the GPS to the pickup."

Silence stretched. Then—the first real crack in his voice. "It led us to a remote highway."

Pause. "Nothing around."

A breath—deeper this time, shaky. "We found a crashed car with an unconscious woman inside."

Silence. "We gave her the needle and then put her in the back of the ambulance."

Pause. Then—an undeniable shift in his tone. "Then the GPS led us into the tunnels."

His gaze darkened. Steve exchanged a glance with Cynthia, confirming everything.

He asked, "What happened after the tunnels?"

He shook his head, his hands clenched together tightly now. "When we got to the exit, there was a *car blocking the way*."

Steve's breath slowed. The man continued. "We got out... found a note on the door."

Pause. "It read—'*Leave the ambulance here. Load the pickup into the wooden box inside the trunk of the car. Seal it closed with the nails and hammer provided inside of the box. Follow the GPS inside the car.*'"

His voice wavered slightly, like the memory was suffocating him. "We followed the instructions."

Pause. "Exited the tunnels. Followed the GPS."

Cynthia asked—sharp, precise, cutting straight to the point. "Did you notice anything that indicated it was a rental car?"

He hesitated, then nodded. "Yes... there were those paper mats on the floor."

Pause. "But I'm not sure."

Steve pressed further. "So where did the GPS take you after the tunnels?"

He exhaled sharply, his pulse visibly racing now. "It led us to another warehouse."

A pause—long enough for the tension to tighten. "The garage door opened automatically when we arrived."

His hands tightened against the table. "Inside was empty... except for a desk with a briefcase on it and a note taped to it."

He swallowed hard. Then recited the letter—he spoke the words carefully, as if saying them aloud confirmed how truly trapped they had been. "*Your money is in the briefcase. Take it and exit out the door behind the desk. Never speak of this again. We will contact you soon.*"

Silence. Steve's jaw tightened slightly, weighing everything. "The second job today—was it the same?"

He nodded once, stiffly. "Exactly the same up until being arrested by you."

Steve inhaled slowly, then exhaled in measured calculation. "You have cooperated and answered all my questions."

Pause. "And I believe your story."

His breath hitched slightly, as if he hadn't expected that response. Steve kept going, firm but steady. "You will still be arrested and processed at some point, but as Commander of The Throne—"

Pause. "I'll let you *walk out of here today*."

Cynthia didn't react, but she kept her eyes on him, watching for cracks.

Steve added—calculated, precise. "I will extend that invitation to your friend—if he gives us the phone."

He tensed slightly. Then—he nodded. "I'll talk to him. My name is Henry; my friends name is Jordan."

Cynthia undid Henry's cuffs, standing rigidly beside him as she escorted him into the next room. Jordan sat stiffly, barely looking up as Henry was seated across from him—hands immediately locked back into restraints.

Cynthia lingered for only a moment, then turned toward the door, speaking flatly before stepping out. "We'll give you a few minutes."

The door clicked shut, leaving them alone, drowning in silence. Jordan exhaled slowly, his breath uneven—almost controlled, but not quite.

His gaze flicked toward Henry, his voice lower than usual. "Why are you here? What did you tell them?"

Henry didn't hesitate. His shoulders were heavier now, as if the weight of his confession had already settled into him—as if it was too late to go back. "I told them everything, Jordan."

Jordan's body stiffened, his head jerking upward slightly, his voice tightening. "Why are you using my *real name*?"

Pause. Then—his voice darkened further. "All we had to do was *wait*—and they would have come to *pick us up*."

Henry exhaled sharply, shaking his head like he had already thought through every possible scenario—and knew how it would end. "These people aren't the police, Jordan."

A beat of silence. Then—his voice turned heavier. "We're inside *The Throne*."

Jordan's fingers tightened against the cuffs, his pulse visible now—too quick, too unsettled.

Henry kept going, relentless. "By now, they already know *everything* about us."

Pause. Then—his voice lowered further. "No one is coming to save us."

Jordan's breath hitched slightly, his eyes flicking toward the door—as if half-expecting it to burst open, as if still hoping that someone, somehow, would get them out of this.

Henry leaned forward slightly, his tone weighted, deliberate. "Not if what we were doing had anything to do with *The Lost*."

Jordan stared blankly, processing. But he didn't respond. Just—silent, motionless, trapped in thought. Henry inhaled deeply, forcing himself to keep going.

He had made his choice. Jordan had to make his now. "Jordan, I've told them everything we know."

Pause. "The Commander has promised to let me *walk out of here* because of my cooperation."

Jordan blinked once, slow, unreadable. Henry exhaled sharply, shifting slightly in his seat. "He's extending that promise to *you*, if you give up the phone."

Silence filled the room like a storm cloud, suffocating. Jordan's expression didn't shift, but something fractured in his posture—a hesitation, a warning, a flicker of something deeper than just fear. "Why would they do that?"

Pause. "Just let us *walk out of here*?"

Henry shook his head again, his voice firm now. "I told them everything, Jordan."

Another pause. Then—he finally said the words that made it real. "The information helped them."

Jordan exhaled slowly. Henry kept going. "The Throne isn't the same as the police. We'll probably *still* have to deal with the authorities at some point—*but...*"

Pause. Then—the cold truth. "We'll have a chance to run."

Jordan's breath caught. Henry's voice lowered just slightly. "And not get caught."

Jordan's voice was hoarse now, barely above a whisper. "Our employers might *kill us* for this."

Henry didn't argue. Didn't dismiss it. Because he knew Jordan was right. He just accepted it, exhaling. "We'll have problems coming at us from *all sides* Jordan."

Pause. Then—a bitter truth. "All we can do is try to avoid them."

Jordan's fingers tightened against the cuffs, his throat dry. Then—his voice shifted, lower, careful, treading into dangerous territory. "And all they want is the phone?"

At that moment, the door swung open. Steve entered smoothly, his presence completely controlled, completely intentional.

His gaze landed directly on Jordan, unwavering. "If you have *any* information that Henry might not have had privilege to, now is your time to speak up."

Pause. Then—another calculated push. "But if you agree to give up the phone, my agents will drive you to your house."

Pause. "They will wait outside for you to retrieve the phone."

A final beat of silence. "Then they will *leave*."

Jordan's chest rose and fell slowly, controlled—but not calm. "I had no contact with my employers other than my phone and the website where we signed up—so Henry probably covered *everything*."

Pause. Then—a surprising turn. "I'll give you my laptop too."

Steve sat back slightly, listening. Jordan's voice was quieter now, but laced with something deeper—a resignation, a buried fear that hadn't fully surfaced yet. "Maybe it'll help you find the website again."

Steve nodded once, firm but collected. "I'll go over the details Henry laid out for us with you."

Pause. "Let me know if there's *anything* he might have missed."

Steve played the audio of Henry's interrogation, letting Jordan listen to every word. The room remained silent, their breaths the only sound as it played through.

After the recording ended—Jordan exhaled slowly. Then—he finally spoke. "Everything sounds right."

A pause. Then—his voice tightened slightly, an unexpected addition. "One more thing."

Steve raised a brow. Jordan leaned forward slightly, his voice lower, more cautious. "The car *was* definitely a rental."

Pause. "If that matters."

Steve tilted his head slightly, waiting. Jordan swallowed. "The keychain had a rental company tag."

Pause. "With the make, model, and *license plate* on it."

Steve's gaze sharpened. "That *does* matter, Jordan."

Pause. Then—a final statement, absolute, unwavering. "The information you've given us has filled in a piece of the puzzle we wouldn't have had without you."

A beat of silence. "I thank you both."

Steve stood slowly, his presence controlled but final. "Once my agents have the phone and laptop, your information will be forwarded to the local police."

Pause. "They will take it from there."

Then—a shift in tone. "I want to warn you both. If you want to run?"

Silence. Then—the final warning. "You'll have to do it *fast*."

Pause. "You won't have long before they're at your door."

A beat of silence. "But if you choose to face the police and the crimes you've committed..."

Steve's tone lowered slightly but didn't waver. "As Commander of The Throne, I'll do what I can to have your sentences minimized."

Jordan didn't breathe for a moment. Then—he exhaled, slow, careful. There was no more running from the truth now. Steve and Cynthia left the room, and four agents came in to undo Henry and Jordan's handcuffs, escorting them back to the elevators.

Steve said to Cynthia as they exited the interrogation room, the weight of what they had uncovered settled into them. They had answers. But with answers came more questions—bigger ones.

Steve exhaled sharply, shaking his head as if trying to process the sheer scale of it all. "So, I was right about the rental cars," he muttered.

Cynthia nodded. "They're switching them inside the tunnels."

Steve's jaw tightened slightly, his mind racing through the logistics, the financial backing, the absolute precision of this operation. "It gives us another lead to track."

Cynthia's gaze darkened, already thinking ahead. "Olivia should be able to pull all the rental businesses close to the tunnel entrances."

Pause. Then—Steve's frustration crept in. "I thought we'd get more out of them."

His voice was sharp—not with disappointment, but with the growing realization that even the people inside the operation were blind to its full scope. "It seems they were clueless about what they were *actually* part of."

Cynthia's lips pressed together briefly, but her next words carried a quiet certainty—one that made the entire operation feel even more horrifying. "I wouldn't be surprised if *most* people involved don't know."

Pause. Then—a thought that sent chills through both of them. "If they're paying ambulance drivers *$30,000 each*, how much do you think they're paying the *hitmen* that injure the victims?"

Steve's stomach twisted, because he knew the answer was worse than either of them wanted to admit.

Cynthia shook her head slightly, voice lower now, but sharper. "When *that* kind of money is involved?"

She inhaled slowly, then spoke the truth bluntly, without emotion. "People don't ask questions. They just do what they're told—like *dogs*."

Steve's thoughts darkened further, his mind tracing the numbers—the costs—the hidden transactions that had kept this operation moving for two decades. And then—a realization hit him so hard it stopped him in his tracks.

His voice was quiet now—controlled but weighted. "How is *so much money* involved?"

Silence. Then—another question that was worse than the first. "Where is it *coming from*?"

Cynthia didn't answer immediately. She just watched him, waiting for him to finish the thought. And then—the math clicked. Steve's voice hardened. "Just on *7,000 Lost*—paying the phantom ambulance paramedics alone would cost *half a billion dollars*."

Cynthia stiffened slightly, the sheer *scale* of that number hitting her just as hard. Then—her mind snapped to the one lead they still hadn't cracked open. "Odyssey Inc."

Pause. "We *still* have Odyssey Inc. up our sleeve."

Steve's expression tightened further. Because she was right. Odyssey Inc. wasn't just a piece of the puzzle anymore. They were the centerpiece. "They *have* to be involved."

Pause. Then—firm, decisive. "Let's head back to the Command Room. See what they've come up with while we were gone."

• • •

As Steve and Cynthia entered the Command Room, investigators were already deep into the numbers, tracking where they led—and more importantly, where they ended.

The room buzzed with intensity, but Olivia and Doris moved fast—rushing toward Steve and Cynthia the moment they stepped in. Olivia didn't hesitate.

"Welcome back, Commander. We reviewed the video from the interrogations of the PAPs."

Steve raised a brow. "PAPs?"

Olivia barely slowed down. "Phantom ambulance paramedics."

Steve gave a short nod, letting her continue. "We're *already* working the rental car angle."

Pause. Then—the bombshell. "We found a total of *1,072 tunnels* in a *nationwide network*."

Steve stiffened instantly. Cynthia's breath hitched slightly. Olivia kept going. "Every entrance is a rental property—owned by one or more real estate companies."

Pause. "And *all* of them? Owned by *Odyssey Inc.*"

Silence slammed through the group carrying the weight of something far bigger than they expected. Steve asked confirming, "Every single one?"

Olivia nodded without hesitation as she said each word. "Every. Single. One."

Steve's breath came slow, controlled. His voice hardened. "That's *no coincidence.*"

Then—a snap decision. "I need a meeting with *Antonio Balata* and *Domenic Cirrone* as soon as possible."

She was already typing before he finished the sentence. "Working on it *now*, Commander."

Doris continued not missing a beat, "I'm having no luck with the name Dresden, Commander. The investigators are going through all the church network records to see if they come up with anything.

Also, with the names Lionel Trebor and Gerald Randall, the maze is getting bigger. We're finding hundreds of numbered corporations owned by them. Many of these corporations are also renters of the tunnel entrances."

Affirming his suspicions Steve said, "So we're correct that whoever is responsible is using these identities to secure assets."

Olivia cut in, "I'm building a timeline to visualize when the corporations were born, the buildings were constructed, when the tunnels were built, how long they've been rented, etc."

Mark was busy at the command center when he yelled out: "Commander, come here now!"

The whole group walked over to the command center. Steve asked, "What is it, Mark?"

Mark had a look of confusion on his face as he said, "I just got a signal from #64."

"Where is it coming from?"

Mark continued, "I have no clue. I'm not sure if it's a glitch, but the signal hit 14,000 satellites in orbit. We have no way to pinpoint its origin."

confused Steve asked, "What could possibly cause that?"

Olivia tapping away at her keyboard said, "I'm working on computer simulations to test what could cause that to happen with that type of signal Commander."

Doris continued as soon as Olivia stopped speaking, "We'll have a complete picture soon Commander. We've sorted through the numbers, and it's just a matter of time before we know everything.

The pieces will fall into place, and we'll finally understand what's going on."

Steve said, "I hope you are right."

Olivia continuing with the revelations they found, "We've dispatched all resources in the tunnels; they're almost 100% explored except for the large tunnel. The large tunnel with the train tracks has an entrance building, but the tracks don't go all the way to the entrance.

Where the tracks start, there's an area for loading and unloading supplies or cargo. At the other end of the tracks is a massive, reinforced door. They're still trying to get through it.

There's no train that was found in the tunnels, so it might be on the other side of the door."

Thinking as he spoke, Steve said, "So they could be using trucks to deliver supplies into the tunnels, then loading them onto the train. We need to find where the train and supplies are going; we must get through that door."

Cynthia added, "If that's the case, we probably have more drivers who have no clue what they're involved in."

Looking up from her computer Olivia exclaimed, "Commander, I've confirmed an appointment with Antonio and Domenic in two hours. If you don't go, it'll have to be next week."

"Cynthia and I will be there. We should get going. You all know what you need to do, let's finally close this case."

Olivia with a big smirk on her face said, "I don't think you'll know what to do if we ever find The Lost Commander. You might become lost."

Steve responded, "Very funny, Olivia. We'll be back after the meeting. Keep me updated in real time on any new information connected to Odyssey Inc. It may be useful when we talk to them."

Mark cutting in with important information, "Before you go, Commander, I got a call from Harris and Gary. Their agents found one of the rental cars in the tunnels.

Harris and Gary interrogated him on the scene and will bring him in soon. His story corroborates and fills in the rest of what Henry and Jordan told us."

Steve asked, "What did they find out?"

Mark continued, "The guy freaked out when he found out there was a body in the trunk. He told them everything he knew. Like the PAPs, he signed up online for a high-paying transporter job.

He was sent a message with an address that led him to a warehouse. He found a note telling him to follow the GPS and deliver the car where it directed. The victim was in a sealed wooden box in the trunk."

Steve trying to piece it together said, "I wish we knew where he was going next."

Cynthia chimed in saying, "Just a thought, but I don't think he'd be in the tunnels unless that was his destination."

Silence as they weighed what she said, then Mark asked, "What do you mean?"

Cynthia took a deep breath and continued, "The tunnels must be for quickly hiding the phantom ambulances after kidnapping the victims.

I don't see them switching to a rental car, parking it in a warehouse, then traveling back through the tunnels to go somewhere else."

Steve contemplating her words added, "They could use the tunnels as an extra measure to avoid detection since they have a body in the trunk."

Cynthia started explaining with her hands as she spoke, "Why would they be moving the victims around? It doesn't make sense. The next stop for the victim and the transporter is obvious and right in front of us........

It must be the train tracks. They must be using the train to transport the victims to wherever The Lost are being taken.

If supplies are using the tracks to get to The Lost, it's safe to assume that's how the victims are getting there too."

Steve with a big smile on his face said, "I think you are right, That's brilliant, Cynthia."

Cynthia continued her explanation of her theory, "We can't know for sure, but it's safe to say our transporter would drop the car off at the tracks.

Find another rental car waiting with money inside and drive it out of the tunnels to a random location, or maybe even back to the rental car business."

Steve looked at his watch and said, "We can brainstorm more on this later. We must go now if we're going to make that meeting at Odyssey Inc."

Chapter 28 - The Odyssey

hirteen men sat around an intricately designed table in a dimly lit room that resembled a sanctified church setting, illuminated by the soft glow of hundreds of candles. The table was round, with twelve men seated around it. A square section jutted out, and the thirteenth man, who acted as the head, sat there.

In front of each man burned two large candles, one white and one black. Between the candles lay a Bible and a book of edicts, topped with a mask.

Each mask was unique in color and depicted a different monstrous or demonic face.

The twelve men around the round section were draped in red robes, while the man at the head of the table wore a black robe.

The man in the black robe was the elusive High Priest Dresden. They conversed quietly among themselves, and the table was scattered with finished plates of food and half-empty glasses of wine.

A group of servants entered, carrying trays of coffee cups. Two of the servants began to offload the cups, while the other two cleared away the finished plates.

As the servants exited the room, the man in the black robe stood up, his presence commanding attention, and began to speak.

"Now that we have all been fed, we can address the matter at hand and the reason we are gathered here tonight. I will brief you on the issue at hand, and then we can discuss our options moving forward.

What we have accomplished with Nevaeh over the last twenty years is something we never thought possible. However, we have received confirmation that The Throne has infiltrated the tunnels.

They have arrested three individuals: two in an ambulance and one transporter.

It is only a matter of time before they uncover the entire operation.

Nevaeh's location will soon be discovered, and when that happens, it will be time for us to move on from this life, leaving our mark on the world."

The room fell silent as the men in red robes absorbed the gravity of the situation. The flickering candlelight cast eerie shadows, adding to the somber atmosphere as they prepared to discuss their next steps.

One of the men in the red robes asked, "So, we can do nothing? All the money and resources we have spent on Nevaeh will go to waste?"

High Priest Dresden continued, "Money and resources mean nothing to us. We always knew Nevaeh was an experiment and would eventually come to an end; we never expected it to be so successful.

We now know we can establish a believable paradise and keep it well hidden from the world.

The experiment has lasted longer than we expected, and we have gained valuable knowledge. I see Nevaeh as a success."

One of the red robes cut in sarcastically, "I don't see how it can be successful if our ultimate goal is not accomplished."

High Priest Dresden with a devious smile on his face said, "Our goal can still be accomplished, even if Nevaeh fails. I have been working on a Plan B, but we need to act quickly; time is our enemy."

Unamused a red robe spoke out, "And what is this, Plan B?"

High Priest Dresden continued speaking, "Let's work through it. Our ultimate goal with Nevaeh was to secure hidden land, create an illusory heaven for its inhabitants, and have an army that would fight for any cause we gave them mindlessly.

I believe we accomplished all those points with Nevaeh."

A red robe snidely chimed in, "Nevaeh was a twenty-year project, and our army is still not big enough."

High Priest Dresden gave him a sneering look for the interruption as he continued, "Obviously, we need more time, but I think there is another way, a simpler way.

The ultimate goal within our Book of Edicts is to spread The Church of the Odyssey to all lands and rid the world of Apostates, Heathens, Atheists, and Non-Believers.

I believe we could accomplish this tomorrow if we wanted to without additional money or resources."

One of the red robes took a sip of his coffee placed his cup down on the table, "How do you propose we do this simple thing?"

The men at the table exchanged glances, their expressions heavy with defeat. The realization that everything they had worked towards with Nevaeh could be unraveling filled the room with a palpable sense of despair.

Their dedication, their resources, their sacrifices—it all seemed like a waste. The thought that their grand endeavor could come to an abrupt and futile end was almost too much to bear.

As they looked to their leader in the black robe, they hoped for some glimmer of hope or a plan to salvage their mission.

He spoke "Nevaeh, when brought to its end, would have unleashed its inhabitants on the world. But remember, Nevaeh was an experiment we never expected to be so successful.

After much thought, I realized we never really needed Nevaeh; we only did it because we thought we did, and we could.

We already have a network of islands in plain sight, filled with our followers within our communities across the country.

I propose we have Jesus make a video with a call to action for all believers, guaranteeing them a spot in heaven if they take up arms and kill Apostates, Heathens, Atheists, and Non-Believers.

This video will be guaranteed to be seen by almost everyone in the world."

As the leader in the black robe spoke, the men in the red robes felt a flicker of hope reignite within them.

They exchanged determined glances, rekindling their resolve. Dresden continued,

"By hijacking the airwaves, we can have the video play on every television station, every radio station, every video streaming platform, and send the message worldwide in all languages.

This will ensure a surprise, and we will have hundreds of millions of soldiers for the new holy war to rid the world of Apostates, Heathens, Atheists, and Non-Believers."

Though the situation seemed dire, the possibility that their mission could still be accomplished gave them renewed purpose and they silently vowed to do whatever it took to see their mission through to the end.

The leader's words and their own unwavering commitment breathed new life into their spirits.

They were ready to face the challenges ahead, with the hope that their efforts had not been in vain.

One of the red robes responded, "That sounds like it just might work. When do we release this video?"

High Priest Dresden continued, "We release it at the last moment when The Throne is occupied with Nevaeh and the island. The people on the island, whom we can't extract because the tunnels have been compromised, will be used to defend the island and hold off The Throne as long as they can.

We will organize and disseminate prophecies throughout all the churches in our network about a day and time when Jesus will return. That day and time is when the video will be released.

We will arm and prep all our communities, open the gates of our communities across the country, and unleash our followers and millions of others around the world to enlist in this holy war.

I call this Plan B: Viral Mayhem. I motion we move on to Plan B and execute Viral Mayhem. Discuss among yourselves, and we will take a vote around the table.

Raise your hand if you accept the motion."

The twelve men in red robes began to murmur and whisper among themselves. The room buzzed with hushed conversations, creating an air of anticipation.

After a brief period, the whispers gradually subsided, and an eerie silence filled the space. One by one, the men raised their hands, each arm ascending slowly until all twelve hands were held aloft above their seats.

The flickering candlelight cast dancing shadows on the walls, adding to the solemnity of the moment.

High Priest Dresden began to speak, his voice carrying an air of ultimate conviction and a chilling hint of malevolence. The room seemed to darken further, the flickering candlelight casting ominous shadows across his face.

His words were imbued with an unsettling confidence, as if the darkness of the shadows resonated with his speech.

"We are about to bring the most holy of holy wars this planet has ever seen. Our followers will be fighting in the name of GOD to rid this world of Apostates, Heathens, Atheists, and Non-Believers.

So, we can finally create a heaven on earth.

It will be more triumphant than the crusades, more glorious than what Hitler tried to accomplish.

In the name of GOD, we will kill all Apostates, Heathens, Atheists, and Non-Believers, set their bodies aflame, and send them to burn for an eternity in hell."

Chapter 29 - Samuel Constant

ynthia and Steve pulled up and parked in front of the bustling Odyssey Inc building. As they entered, Cynthia couldn't help but noticed a sticker on the glass front doors that read "Jesus Loves You."

It triggered a memory of the same sticker on an angel statue during their last visit and reminded her of their experience at The Church of the Odyssey, where every person they encountered had greeted them with the same phrase.

As Steve and Cynthia stepped into Odyssey Inc, the bustling lobby felt different this time—a polished facade hiding something they weren't supposed to see.

People moved efficiently, conversations buzzed, the hum of expensive machinery filled the space—but beneath the normalcy, something felt off. Neither of them had ever walked through these doors feeling anything other than suspicion.

Now, it was more than that. It was caution bordering on unease. They kept their steps measured, their gazes sweeping the room, absorbing everything.

Steve adjusted his stance slightly, subtly positioning himself so he could see as much of the floor as possible.

Cynthia did the same, her movements purposeful, precise—but never obvious.

They weren't just here for a meeting. They were walking straight into the lion's den.

At the large reception desk, Veronica's friendly face lit up instantly as she looked up from her screen. She rose from her seat with practiced ease, her greeting warm—too warm. "Steve, Cynthia—welcome back to *Odyssey Inc!*"

Pause. Then—a subtle tilt of her head, a flicker of something unreadable in her expression. "What can I do for you today?"

Steve's breath was slow, deliberate, but his posture remained steady, unshaken. "I have a meeting with *Domenic Cirrone* and *Antonio Balata.*"

Pause. "Would you be able to escort us upstairs?"

Veronica's smile remained, but something shifted just slightly in her expression. Not enough for an average person to notice. But Steve and Cynthia weren't average. Her response was casual—but deliberate. "Is this an official meeting with an appointment?"

Pause. "Or do you want to *catch them off guard*?"

Steve matched her energy, not flinching. "We have an official appointment this time."

Veronica nodded once, her fingers gliding over the keyboard effortlessly. She never broke eye contact—not with Steve, not with Cynthia. Then—her smile returned in full force, effortless, polished. "Yes, I see it here in the computer."

Pause. Then—her tone shifted again—lighter but still controlled. "Let's go. Follow me."

Steve and Cynthia exchanged a look—brief, subtle—but fully aware of what was happening. Every person in this building knew something they didn't. And now, they were about to find out exactly what that was.

They walked to the elevator, engaging in a friendly conversation as they ascended to the 45th floor. Upon arrival, they said goodbye to Veronica.

Exiting the elevator and turning right, they spotted Domenic Cirrone and Antonio Balata waiting in the large meeting room. The atmosphere inside the conference room was polished, professional—but there was a tension beneath the surface.

Domenic Cirrone and Antonio Balata rose from their seats, their greetings smooth, practiced, but behind the handshake, Steve already sensed the unease creeping in.

They settled around the large table, facing each other. There was a moment of silence, brief—but weighted. Then—Steve spoke first, his tone

MATHEW J. SHAW

controlled, direct—but carrying an edge that made it clear he wasn't here for pleasantries.

"We are on an extremely tight schedule."

Pause. "The last thing I want to do is waste your time—or ours."

He leaned forward slightly, enough to make it clear that this wasn't a discussion—it was an interrogation. "So, I'm going to put all the cards on the table."

Silence. Then—the pressure came instantly. "Why has your company been showing up—as owners or direct connections—to *everything* we are finding in The Lost investigation?"

Domenic exhaled slowly, adjusting his posture. There was no visible panic—but a flicker of hesitation. A moment too long before he responded. Then—he chose his words carefully. "With all due respect Commander..."

His voice was steady, but there was something measured beneath it. "Odyssey Inc. is the largest investment firm in the country."

Pause. "We own more assets through investments than the country has money itself."

Silence. Then—he dropped the figure, casual—but intentional. "Our company operates on a *1.2 trillion-dollar* budget."

Pause. "So, to me... I don't see these connections as much more than a coincidence."

Steve's expression didn't change. But his silence? It was intentional. Domenic shifted slightly, as if expecting Steve to move on. Steve didn't. His voice was sharper now, laced with finality. "We are *way* past coincidence, Domenic."

Pause. Then—the shift in tone. "I can't reveal sensitive case details—but some of these investments date back nearly *thirty years*."

Domenic hesitated. Then—a slight exhale, as if steadying himself. His voice was smoother now, deflective. "Like I said Commander..."

Pause. "To me, this just seems like *everyday business*."

Steve's gaze hardened. Antonio stayed quiet, watching Domenic now—as if seeing the weight of the conversation shift. Domenic continued, but Steve could see the cracks forming in his calm demeanor.

"I have only been president of Odyssey Inc. for the last *ten* years."

Pause. "Antonio came on eight years ago."

Steve didn't blink. Domenic kept talking, but now—it felt like an excuse rather than an answer. "At Odyssey Inc., we just follow *quarterly directives*—orders handed down to us on where to invest."

Pause. "We manage the underlings, make sure the paperwork is correct, ensure the money goes to the right places."

Steve's breath was slow, deliberate. He wasn't moving on yet. "We couldn't find *anyone* listed as official shareholders for Odyssey Inc."

Pause. "Where do these *orders* come from?"

Domenic shook his head slightly, but now—his discomfort was visible. "There's a *Board of Directors* that gives us our directives."

Steve's tone didn't change—but the weight behind his words did. "Who are they?"

Pause. "Where are they?"

Domenic exhaled—sharper this time. Antonio shifted slightly, as if this was going farther than he expected. Domenic's voice tightened. "I have *no idea*."

Silence. Then—Steve leaned forward slightly, pressing harder now. "You're telling me."

Pause. "The president of a *trillion-dollar* investment firm."

He Paused again for effect, "Has never seen or met *anyone* on the Board of Directors?"

Domenic inhaled slowly, nodding once. But his jaw clenched slightly now—visibly, tense. "We just get our directives and ensure they're executed."

Cynthia finally spoke, her tone firm, cutting through the room like a blade. "How does an investment company *this large* not have *shareholders* involved?"

Domenic exhaled, but Steve caught the flicker of frustration in his expression. Not anger at them. But frustration at being put in a position where he had no real answer. "Odyssey Inc. is owned solely by *Samuel Constant*."

Pause. "There is only *one* owner."

His voice was sharper now, defensive—but controlled. "So, shareholders *aren't necessary*."

Silence. Steve's jaw tightened further. "Why is this Board of Directors *not public*? And who is Samuel Constant"

Domenic's shoulders tensed slightly, but he forced his expression neutral. "Like I said Commander..."

Pause. "I have only been here for *ten years*."

His voice was crisp—but there was strain now. "I was told the Board was left in charge *incognito* when Samuel retired."

Then—a final, unsettling addition. "Even today—our quarterly directives on paper come *directly from Samuel Constant*."

Steve's breath was even—but the way he stared at Domenic now made it clear. Something was very wrong. "How do you even *know* this Board of Directors exists?"

Domenic hesitated. It was too long before he responded. Then—his voice came slower now, more cautious. "It could just be... a story."

Pause. "But as it goes at some point—Samuel Constant retired and left all decisions to an unseen Board of Directors."

A long, weighted pause. "That was over *fifteen years* before I got here."

Silence hung in the air. Then—Steve exhaled sharply, standing slowly, his presence unwavering. "I appreciate your cooperation, Domenic. Antonio."

Antonio barely reacted his gaze locked on Domenic now—as if only now realizing how deep this conversation had gone. "I don't know how much help I was,"

Antonio muttered. "Domenic knows more about this stuff than me."

Steve's tone was final, unshaken. "Can you both do some digging—find what you can on *Samuel Constant* or the Board? I'll contact you when I need to."

Domenic exhaled, nodded stiffly—but behind his calmness, Steve saw it. The first real crack in his control. "Happy to help, Commander. We will do what we can."

As Steve and Cynthia drove back toward the Command Room, the weight of their conversation settled heavily between them. The meeting had yielded no direct confessions, no obvious breadcrumbs—but what it had given them was far more valuable.

Patterns. Undeniable, unshakable patterns that pointed to something much larger than they initially imagined. Cynthia leaned back slightly, staring out the window, but her mind was racing through possibilities. Her voice was firm, decisive. "So, they weren't much help."

Steve exhaled sharply but didn't fully agree. His voice was steady—but carrying something beneath it. "You forget how powerful *one name* can be."

Cynthia turned toward him slightly, waiting for him to continue. "Brian Schersinger's name led us to a web of identities—corporations, real estate firms."

Pause. "It brought us *here*."

Cynthia nodded, watching him closely. Then—Steve pushed further. "Maybe *this* name—Samuel Constant.....is the last piece of the puzzle we've been missing."

Cynthia thought for a moment, then spoke. "We *know* Odyssey Inc is involved, but..."

She shook her head slightly. "What did you make of Domenic?"

Steve exhaled, rolling the thought over in his mind. "I'm not sure yet."

He glanced at Cynthia. "He seemed *truthful*, but anyone can *look* truthful."

Then—his voice shifted slightly, more cautious. "What do you think?"

Cynthia exhaled slowly, the weight of everything falling into place in her mind. "I get the impression Domenic and Antonio *don't know anything*."

Then—she pushed further. "To them, this is just *business*. If The Lost are being controlled by whoever gives the directives, the entire company could just be... mindless puppets."

Steve absorbed that thought fully, because now—he saw it. Not just a company blindly following orders. An entire economic system woven together to orchestrate disappearances. And the more they talked—the clearer it became.

Steve shook his head slightly. Then—his voice came quieter now, carrying the weight of realization. "Buying and investing across *a million different places*—real estate companies, car rental businesses.....what *else* could they be involved with?"

Cynthia didn't hesitate. "Off the top of my head?"

She leaned forward slightly. "They could own or invest in construction companies that *built* the tunnels. They could control transportation companies that *deliver* supplies into them."

Then—another piece clicked into place. "Maybe even funeral homes, medical offices—places where records are created and altered."

Steve stiffened slightly, because now—he saw the true scale of what they were dealing with. "That's *genius* Cynthia. I *wasn't even thinking* about those."

Then—his voice sharpened. "Can you think of anymore?"

Cynthia nodded. "What about the *death certificates* after The Lost disappear?"

Pause. "Someone has to slip paperwork into the system."

Then—her next words felt heavier. "Could they *own* government offices somehow?"

Silence. Steve's pulse quickened slightly, because now—it wasn't just disappearances. It was erasure. Controlled. Precise. Entire identities washed away like they never existed. "At this point, *anything* is possible, we'll have Olivia and Doris do a full forensic audit into Odyssey Inc."

Pause. "From the *first* day of business until *now*."

His voice was absolute, unwavering. "Every revenue stream. Every expense. Every record they've ever touched."

Cynthia had one last thought—one that Steve hadn't considered yet. "What about churches and religious communities?"

Steve turned toward her sharply—because now, it clicked. Cynthia kept going. "Not owning them outright...but funneling money into them? Controlling what gets built? Who gets recruited?"

Steve stiffened further, his thoughts racing now. Because now—he saw it all. Not just the financial system. Not just the records. The entire structure of control.

His voice was quieter now—but deadly certain. "Imagine if Odyssey Inc was just moving pieces across the board, day after day... Millions of transactions.

Millon's of people. Every directive pushing The Lost deeper into the shadows—until they vanish completely."

Then—his words carried finality. "That would mean *every single person* participating in this for the last twenty years...could be mindless puppets, just doing their jobs."

Silence.

Cynthia exhaled slowly, letting the weight of it settle. Then—her voice was absolute. "I think we're onto something here."

Then—she finished the thought for both of them. "It *all* fits."

Steve's mind locked into full strategy mode. Because now—they weren't just chasing The Lost. They had found the system behind their disappearances. Steve's tone hardened as they neared the Command Room. "We need Olivia and Doris to confirm *everything.*"

Then—his final statement carried the weight of certainty. "I think we just figured out *exactly* how this works. Now.....We find out *where it ends.*"

The elevator doors slid open, but before Steve and Cynthia could even step into the Command Room—Olivia's voice cut through the air, sharp and urgent. "Come here *now!*"

Steve and Cynthia exchanged a glance before hurrying toward Olivia's workstation. The energy in the room was electric, charged with something more than urgency—anticipation, as if Olivia and her team had uncovered a truth so massive, so unthinkable, that everything was about to shift.

Steve didn't waste a second. "What is so urgent that we had to *run* over here?"

Olivia didn't blink. "We made it through the *reinforced door* at the train tracks ten minutes ago Commander."

Silence. Then—she continued, her words hitting like a hammer. "Right now, the hole is only big enough for people to fit through. We have about fifty agents on bikes already inside, continuing deeper into the tunnel."

Doris cut in, "We're working on *widening* the entrance to get larger vehicles through."

Steve listened carefully, weighing the information. "That doesn't sound like something I had to *sprint* over here for."

Olivia's expression shifted—almost amused, almost triumphant. "You *underestimate* us Commander."

Then—the delivery came with absolute precision. "We're just getting started."

Steve's gaze hardened. "Let me hear it. What do you have?"

Mark stepped forward, his expression tight with tension, his fingers moving rapidly across the keyboard. "Olivia and I have been working on why we couldn't *pinpoint* the signal from #64....And what we found is... *odd.*"

Steve's breath slowed, but his pulse picked up. "Go on."

Olivia inhaled deeply, her tone sharper now—controlled, yet carrying the weight of something monumental. "It's going to take *some explaining,* Commander—so *no interruptions.*"

She reached for her tablet, flicking her fingers across the screen, bringing up two images side by side on the main display. "Look *here.*"

On the left—a map of the planet. Speckled with thousands of red dots, marking the positions of all 14,000 satellites that had received the signal. Steve's eyes scanned the map, absorbing the sheer density of coverage.

Olivia continued. "The trackers #64 used in *Operation NEWS* were single-point triangulation trackers."

Pause. "When activated, they would triangulate a signal and shoot it *straight up* into space."

Steve nodded slightly, following. "Normally, that signal would hit *a few satellites*, allowing us to pinpoint its exact origin."

Then—Olivia's voice shifted, carrying weight now. "But after running multiple simulations, I found only *two ways* a single-point signal like this could have spread to *so many satellites.*"

Silence. Then—her words hit with force. "It must have hit *something*—traveled across space—and been *amplified.* The *only two ways* the signal could spread like this."

Her fingers moved again, overlaying another image onto the screen "Is through a concave or convex lens."

Steve's breath hitched slightly, because now—this was something entirely different. Olivia pointed at the demonstration. "Look at this model. When the signal passes *through* the lens, it spreads outward—*amplifies*—before continuing up.... The bigger the lens—the bigger the amplification."

She narrowed her eyes. "And the higher the number of satellites it reaches."

Silence slammed through the room. Steve leaned forward, his voice tighter now, heavier with expectation. "Can we *reverse engineer* the signal's path?"

Olivia's expression sharpened. "Yes Commander."

She paused then—the final detail hit like a punch to the gut. "The center of that amplification circle?"

Then—her voice dropped slightly, weighted with certainty. "2,000 kilometers off the *eastern seaboard*."

Steve's breath stalled for a moment, his mind already connecting dots faster than he could process.

Then—Olivia added another layer to the revelation. She swiped her tablet again, overlaying another map. "Now *look at this*. This is a map of *all underground tunnels*."

Then—the final connection hit like a freight train. "The large tunnel—the one with the *train tracks*? it *almost perfectly aligns* with the origin point of #64's signal."

Silence. Then—Olivia asked the question before Steve could. "Could it be possible that this tunnel *continues under the ocean*?"

Steve's hands pressed against the table, his breath coming slower now, controlled—but his mind was racing past the point of disbelief. "I would say *no*. But at this point, *anything* is possible."

Cynthia stiffened beside him, absorbing the full implication of Olivia's theory. Steve continued, his voice lower now—almost dangerous with certainty.

"They're *hiding* The Lost somewhere. And I don't think it's a coincidence that the tunnel could be a *direct shot* under the ocean—straight to where the signal came from."

His pulse pounded, his thoughts locked in a battle between impossibility and undeniable evidence. Finally—he turned toward Olivia. His words carried absolute command. "Where are our agents in the tunnel?"

Olivia responded instantly, without hesitation. "First wave is about *200 kilometers* in, following the train tracks."

Doris added, "More agents are working on getting *larger vehicles* through the reinforced door."

Steve inhaled sharply, locking onto Mark. "Mark—keep two-man teams patrolling *all* tunnels. Concentrate everyone else on following the *tracks* and getting that door down."

Then—he turned back to Olivia. "Find *everything* about where in the ocean our signal came from—Air traffic. Naval records. Known islands in the area—*anything*."

Then—one final order. "Mark—send a *helicopter*."

Mark nodded sharply, already moving. "Dispatching now."

Silence hit again, but this time—it was pure anticipation. Steve's voice was firm—but carrying something deeper beneath it now. "...Amazing work, team."

Then—he exhaled slightly. "That information just blew my mind."

Now they knew—they were closer than ever.

Doris stepped forward, standing beside Olivia, her hands firmly gripping a stack of file folders—as if holding physical proof of something that shouldn't exist.

Her expression was controlled, but behind it—an urgency that hadn't been there before. "You don't want to hear what I've found?"

Then—her next words carried weight. "We left it for last because it gives us enough pieces of the puzzle to *finally see the full picture*."

Steve, still processing Olivia's revelations, turned toward Doris. "I didn't realize there was *more* Doris. Of course, I want to hear what you found."

Doris exhaled slowly, her voice calm, measured—but ready to change everything they thought they knew. "Under normal circumstances,"

Doris began, her tone level but deliberate, "This information should have come to light when we first found the name *Brian Schersinger*."

Silence. Then—the shift in tension. "But it seems measures were put in place to prevent this information from linking *correctly* inside the system."

Steve's brow furrowed slightly, but he kept listening, fully locked in now. Doris continued. "When we originally investigated *Odyssey Inc*, we found that it was owned by *four numbered corporations*."

She paused. "We called them *The Entity Corporations*—or simply, *Entities*."

Steve stiffened slightly. "Each Entity owned *25%* of Odyssey Inc."

Silence. "No named owner was attached to any of them—*no matter how deep we investigated.*"

Then—the bombshell. "Now that we know *Samuel Constant* owns Odyssey Inc—"

Her fingers moved across the tablet, pulling up files on the screen. "We also found that *he owns* The Entity Corporations."

Steve's pulse quickened. He leaned forward slightly, his voice lower, heavier. "What does that tell us?"

Doris exhaled, shaking her head slightly. "That doesn't tell us anything *new*—Domenic already confirmed Samuel Constant was the owner."

She Paused again. "But after conducting a *full investigation* into Samuel Constant—"

Her next words sent chills through the room. "...we found a record from *twenty-five years ago* when he purchased and was transferred ownership of *The Entities.*"

Silence hung in the air. Then—Steve pushed further. "Who owned them before that?"

Doris's breath was slow, her posture tense, like she was holding back the answer for a second longer before delivering it in full force. "That's where it gets confusing Commander."

She paused deliberately for effect, "The Entity Corporations were started by *Brian Schersinger.*"

Then—the impossible addition. "...shortly *after his death.*"

Silence slammed through the room. Steve blinked once, his entire posture stiffening. His voice was slower now, deliberate—as if forcing himself to process what he had just heard.

"You're telling me—Brian Schersinger started *corporations* after he was *dead*?"

Doris nodded, her expression tightening slightly. "And then, *years later*, they were sold to Samuel Constant."

Steve's breath hitched. The realization was crashing down like a wave, and it wasn't stopping. "I don't even know what that *means.*"

Then—the demand for clarity. "Explain."

Olivia stepped forward now, her voice just as heavy. "Doris and I are working on a timeline to map all of this out. We're still finalizing it—but *we will have it done as quickly as possible.*"

Steve exhaled sharply, shaking his head. "It's not over yet, is it?"

Doris's smile was small—but carried something unsettling behind it. "Oh, Commander, we *saved the very best for last.*"

Silence. Then—her voice tightened. We found *government forms* indicating a name and identity change—To *Samuel Constant.*"

Steve stiffened further. "And?"

Doris inhaled deeply, then delivered the final blow. "The person who changed their name to Samuel Constant...was *Brian Schersinger.*"

Steve pushed himself back slightly from the table, his fingers tightening against the surface. For a few seconds, he didn't speak. Then—his voice came slow, controlled—but it carried something different now. "...How is that *possible?*"

Silence. Then—his next words carried absolute disbelief. "That *shouldn't* be possible."

Doris nodded, agreeing. "It gets *more confusing,* Commander."

Then—she added another layer to the insanity. "We also found *official name changes* for *Lionel Trebor* and *Gerald Randall*—"

She paused. "...all done on the *same day* as Samuel Constant's."

Steve's voice was quiet now, almost dangerous with certainty. "...Let me guess.

Then—his voice carried finality. "Brian Schersinger."

Doris smirked slightly, nodding once. "Bingo Commander."

Steve exhaled sharply, shaking his head, trying to force his mind to adjust to the sheer impossibility of what they had uncovered. Olivia said, "All of this should have come up in our *initial* investigation into Brian Schersinger."

Doris nodded, her tone sharper now, carrying frustration of her own. "I *can't explain* why it didn't."

Pause. "But we found that *everything* operates this way—names, numbered corporations—"

Silence. Then—her final words hit like a knife "They get *passed off,* moved around, *sold*—but the records only show *one-way transactions.*"

Pause. "I don't even understand *how one man* had *three identity and name changes*—especially after he was already *dead*."

Steve's breath was slow, his pulse heavy. Then—he exhaled sharply, locking onto Olivia and Doris fully. "I *need* to see that timeline. We must put *all* the pieces together."

Then—he leaned forward, voice carrying absolute conviction. "At this point—*how* it was done doesn't matter.... Because it *was* done."

Silence. Then—his final statement was absolute. "We *still* need to find Dresden—and figure out if *he* is the one responsible."

Because now—they had found the mechanism behind The Lost's disappearances. Now, they just had to find the man who built it.

Chapter 30 - The Cracked Sky

he hum of activity in the Command Room had slowed, conversations turning to murmurs as Olivia combed through the latest findings.

She barely glanced up from her screen as she spoke, her voice tinged with curiosity. "What do you think we could be dealing with, Commander?"

Steve, standing beside her, absorbed the data displayed before them. Olivia continued without waiting for his response, scrolling through layers of restricted reports.

"The signal's location in the ocean is surrounded by restricted airspace—fifty kilometers in every direction. International shipping lanes were also rerouted around it. Those changes were made back in 2014."

Steve exhaled, the realization settling heavily on his shoulders. "That confirms it. We've found something—but I still don't know *what* we've found. The Lost must be there. No one goes to this extent to hide nothing."

His voice sharpened as his thoughts raced ahead. "We need to find out how deep Odyssey Inc's influence runs in government organizations. These kinds of high-level changes don't happen without serious power backing them."

Before Olivia could respond, Mark rushed into view, urgency written across his face. "The helicopter is approaching the signal's location soon."

Steve straightened. "Put us on speaker with the pilot. I want a visual of what he sees on the screen."

Mark tapped a series of commands into the console, and within moments, the pilot's voice crackled through the speakers. "Pilot 1-734, you are on the line with The Commander of The Throne."

A brief pause. Then, the pilot's voice came through, laced with steady professionalism. "I'm honored Commander. I'm crossing into restricted airspace now—fifty kilometers from the signal's location. From this altitude, I should have a visual by now if there's anything at this location."

Olivia frowned, her fingers still moving across her tablet. "That doesn't make sense. *That's* where the signal came from."

Steve's tone remained firm. "Proceed, 1-734. Get us right above the signal."

After a few minutes the pilot came on and said, "Approaching location—fifteen kilometers away."

The room fell into silence. Every pair of eyes locked onto the screen displaying the live feed from the helicopter's camera.

The hum of keyboards ceased, footsteps stilled, breath caught in anticipation. "Everything is clear,"

The pilot reported. "There's some low cloud cover ahead, but otherwise—nothing in sight."

Steve narrowed his eyes at the screen. Olivia's unease grew beside him.

Then—The pilot's voice sharpened. "Wait a minute. What the *hell* is that?"

For a fraction of a second, the camera flickered—revealing something impossible. The helicopter appeared in the clouds on the screen, its own reflection mirrored directly in front of it.

Before anyone could process the anomaly, an explosion ripped through the feed, fire consuming the screen in a blinding flash.

Then—darkness. Silence crashed through the room, thick and suffocating. No static. No connection. The feed was gone. Steve stared at the screen, his pulse hammering against his ribs.

His voice, when it came, was slow, controlled—but edged with urgency. "What just happened?"

Mark was still typing frantically, pulling up every bit of telemetry data that remained. His response was quick but carried the frustration of uncertainty. "I don't know Commander."

Olivia shook her head, her eyes never leaving the screen. "Why did we *see* the helicopter on the feed? That... *shouldn't* be possible."

Steve exhaled sharply, his mind racing through possibilities. "Could it be a glitch in the camera?"

"I'll run simulations," Olivia said, already tapping at her console.

"If it was a malfunction, I'll find out."

Steve's stance tightened, the weight of the situation pressing against him. "Mark—dispatch boats and agents *immediately*. See if we have any chance of rescuing 1-734."

Mark nodded, already sending out commands. Steve continued, "We also need to find out *exactly* what happened here,"

His voice carrying finality. Because now, they weren't just hunting for *The Lost* they needed answers.

...

1 Minute Ago, on The Island

Justin, Kevan, and Amelia were making their way towards the clearing to see Jesus and get the air mattress. They had just entered the clearing from one of the paths.

Three people could be seen far away, moving in different directions towards paths at the edge of the clearing.

When they reached the middle of the clearing, a deafening explosion erupted above their heads.

Instinctively, they scattered, covering their heads in a desperate attempt to shield themselves. The echoes of the blast faded, they realized they were safe.

Slowly, they began to regroup, their hearts still pounding from the shock. They looked up and saw a large black circle filling a portion of the bright sky.

A few seconds later, loud cracking sounds, reminiscent of lightning strikes, echoed through the air. A very large crack etched itself across the sky, originating from one side of the black circle.

More simultaneous lightning-like cracks followed, carving through the middle of the sky from one side to the other.

Screams and cries of confusion erupted from the people on the island.

The air was filled with panic and fear as everyone struggled to comprehend the bizarre and terrifying phenomenon unfolding above them.

The sharp crack split the sky, unnatural and deafening.

It wasn't thunder. It was something else—something none of them had ever heard before.

Amelia flinched, her pulse hammering as she instinctively ducked, her breath shallow. "What the fuck was that?"

She muttered, eyes darting toward the others. Justin stood rigid, his head tilted upward as if expecting to *see* the noise that had shattered the quiet. "It sounded like something hit the sky."

Kevan scoffed, rolling his shoulders like he could shake off the unease settling over them. "How does that tell us anything?"

Justin didn't answer, didn't hesitate. "It doesn't, but if we want to get into Jesus's room to get the air mattress, we should get there *now*."

Silence stretched between them, thick with the unspoken urgency of whatever had just happened. And then, without another word, they moved

• • •

Elsewhere

The small room was suffocating, the air thick with desperation as Jesus hunched over the radio setup, twisting dials and flicking switches with frantic precision.

Static crackled, filling the space with an eerie hum, but he refused to give up. He needed an answer—needed *something* from beyond the island.

Then, finally, a voice broke through. "Jesus, I hate to say this, but everything will be coming to an end."

The words hit him harder than he expected, settling like a stone in his gut. "What do you mean? What is going on? What was that explosion?"

The silence stretched just long enough to make Jesus grip the edge of the table, his fingers turning white. "Heaven has definitely been found,"

High Priest Dresden responded, his voice unnervingly steady. "They will be coming through the tunnels, and The Throne will stop at nothing to destroy what we have built."

Jesus's pulse pounded. They'd been preparing for this, hadn't they? The whispers, the warnings—the inevitable end creeping closer with each passing day. "So, we will be releasing the video soon then?"

Dresden exhaled softly, but his tone didn't waver. "The video will be released at the last minute. We have been prepping all our followers on the outside, prophesizing about your return.

Our followers will do what needs to be done when the time comes."

Jesus swallowed hard, his throat dry. He forced himself to focus, to push past the uncertainty clawing at him. "How am I supposed to get off the island?"

A beat. Then—a devastating truth. "You aren't. Your orders are to stand your ground on the island."

The words sent a cold shiver down Jesus's spine. "Stand my ground? Against *them*? "How are we supposed to do that?"

Dresden's voice lowered, carrying the weight of an unspoken inevitability. "In the underground of the island, there is a hidden armory—fully stocked with guns and ammunition.

Arm everyone.

When The Throne comes up through the tunnels, the only exit from the underground is into the clearing, and the entire island will be waiting for them on the other side of that door."

Jesus's breath hitched. "You want us to kill them? I don't know if my followers will want to participate in that."

Another delayed response. A cruel certainty hung between them. "Your followers will do whatever you tell them. Everyone sent to the island showed express devotion to you.

Every one of them would die for you. Tell them how serious the situation is, that their heaven is being infiltrated, and they are the only defense to protect it."

Jesus clenched his jaw, his heart hammering in his chest. "I will make it happen. I will sound the alarm and rally them all to the cause."

And just like that, the choice was made.

•••

Justin had just taken his first steps into the hallway leading to Jesus's chambers when a loud alarm suddenly blared across the island.

The piercing sound filled the air, signaling an emergency.

Panic surged through Justin, and he quickly turned on his heel, sprinting back outside.

The blaring alarm swallowed his voice, forcing him to yell just to be heard. "What is that alarm?"

Amelia barely turned toward him, her eyes flickering with unease. "It's the call to the clearing. It's usually only used for *The Three E's* celebration."

She hesitated before adding, "Maybe we should wait for another time to get the air mattress. Come sit with us; Jesus should be coming out."

Justin moved closer, settling beside Amelia and Kevan. The uneasy tension lingered, and after a moment, Amelia spoke—her voice quiet, uncertain. "We didn't really finish our conversation about your father before."

Kevan met her gaze without hesitation. "Don't worry, Amelia. I do not hold you responsible for what happened to my father, even if you *did* stab him in the neck."

Her breath caught, the weight of those words pressing into her chest. A tear slipped down her cheek before she could stop it. "I am so sorry, Kevan."

Kevan exhaled, his expression unreadable. "Don't be, Amelia. If my father molested you, he deserved what he got."

His voice hardened slightly, carrying something final beneath it. "As far as I am concerned, my father *never existed*. I don't want you to ever think about or talk about him again."

Amelia wiped at her face, her shoulders trembling. "Thank you so much, Kevan. I wish I could get the bad memories out of my head.

I liked it better when I couldn't remember them."

Kevan shook his head slightly, his gaze darkening as he considered everything they had been through. "I've been thinking about it all, Amelia, and everything is so messed up."

His words came slower now, more thoughtful. "The churches and communities we were part of back home. The first hurdle was realizing

MATHEW J. SHAW

everything we were *taught, believed, and followed* in those churches was wrong. But now."

He paused grief crossing his face. "Now we've found out *everything* about this place isn't true either."

Amelia glanced at him, her expression conflicted. Kevan kept going, pressing forward with the thought that had been eating away at him.

"Why do all of us here on the island continue to choose to believe these things? If everything Justin says is true, we've been used as pawns—brainwashed into being *unknowing, unwilling* participants."

Amelia swallowed, her voice barely above a whisper. "Why would anyone do all of this? None of it makes sense. The island doesn't make sense.

Everything Jesus has said doesn't make sense either."

She clenched her fists, frustration thick in her tone. "What is the *point* of this place?"

Kevan sighed, rubbing at his temple. "I still have no clue. It hurts my head trying to think about it."

Amelia stared at him for a long moment before speaking softly. "Can we just lay here, hold each other, and hug until Jesus comes out? I know it will make me feel better."

Kevan's expression softened. "Of course, Amelia. Justin and The Throne should have us home soon."

The tension eased slightly, but the uncertainty still hung between them—unanswered, unresolved. They laid down together on the grass, spooning each other, finding a brief moment of solace in each other's arms.

Meanwhile, groups of people began entering the clearing from the paths and forests surrounding it. Hundreds of individuals walked in unison, drawn by the blaring alarm that echoed across the island.

As the minutes passed, the clearing rapidly filled with thousands of people, all heeding the urgent call.

The sense of urgency and the united movement of the crowd created an overwhelming atmosphere, as everyone gathered to understand the cause behind the crack in the sky, the alarm, and what it would mean for them.

Once the large group gathered in the middle of the clearing, standing in front of Jesus's door, the clearing became filled with loud, mingled conversations.

Fear and panic were palpable in the air as everyone tried to make sense of the explosion and the crack in the sky.

Voices overlapped, some shouting questions, others whispering anxiously to their neighbors.

The tension was thick, Amelia sat up and said to Justin and Kevan: "We should get up.

Everyone is expected to stand in a line, side by side."

They rose and took their places at the front line closest to the door. Within minutes, the entire population of the island stood side by side, forming lines of about 500 people each, stretching 13 lines deep.

The blaring alarm ceased, and a heavy silence fell over the crowd. The door opened, and Jesus stepped out, clad in a flowing white robe that moved like ocean waves as he walked.

He made his way around and ascended the hill where the door was built into.

Reaching the top, he stopped and spread his arms out to his sides, mimicking the stance of a crucified figure. The masses before him bowed their heads in unison, a gesture of reverence and anticipation.

He stood there for about ten seconds, commanding the silence and attention of everyone present.

Then, he lowered his arms to his sides and began to speak.

"Every single one of you standing in front of me right now was personally chosen by me to come to this miraculous place that we call heaven. This heaven will fulfill all your wills and desires, and it will continue to do that.

Heaven has been found by evil forces, and the forces coming here will stop at nothing to seize this place. As you all know, there was a massive explosion today that put a crack in our sky.

That was the evil forces trying to gain access to heaven.

We need to defend heaven from these intruders before it is too late. I, who personally brought you here, am now asking for your help to defend against these intruders.

We will not let them take this heaven from us.

They will not expect us to fight back, and we will take advantage of this.

We will show them what happens when you disrupt the perfection here.

We will show them what it truly means to be Discarded from Heaven.

There is only one way for them to get to heaven, and that is through this door below where I am standing.

Right now, the room beyond this door is filled with guns and ammunition.

Everyone is to arm themselves and come back outside to guard this door for when the evil forces arrive."

The door below where Jesus was standing opened, and Jesus continued speaking. "Get what you need and get ready."

Jesus once again spread his arms out as if he were crucified on a cross. The followers, now standing in uneasy silence, were struck with confusion and uncertainty.

The command to kill people, coming from Jesus himself, was overwhelming and disturbing.

Hesitation hung heavy in the air as the crowd stood frozen, unsure of how to respond. For a moment, no one moved.

Then, breaking the spell of indecision, Leonard Chance stepped forward. His action sent a ripple through the crowd, a mix of astonishment and fear as they watched him take the first step and turned around to speak to the crowd.

"Everyone here owes their existence to Jesus for bringing us here. I will put my life on the line for Jesus, and I will not stand by idly if Jesus needs my help."

Leonard turned and walked through the door, his steps resolute. A handful of people followed him, their expressions a mix of determination and uncertainty.

Soon, the rest of the island's inhabitants joined in, forming a line that snaked its way toward the room. One by one, they entered, each person preparing to arm themselves to defend heaven.

Amelia exclaimed to the group, "What should we do?"

Justin took a deep breath and exhaled slowly responding, "We must follow what the group does at this point. Get in line and get a gun. We can't go up against the whole island if everyone has guns pointed at us."

Kevan realizing the horror and death if The Throne agents came through the door, "It is going to be a massacre. We can't allow this to happen."

Justin winked at the group as they joined the lineup to get a gun, "I have an idea, but we need to wait until everyone has their guns already. Let's get in line."

Chapter 31 - The Timeline

The Command Room was set up with rows of chairs, gradually filling as people took their seats. Olivia and Doris were at the front, preparing to give their presentation on The Timeline.

Olivia pulled up an image on the screen, capturing everyone's attention.

The room buzzed with anticipation as the last few attendees settled in their seats, eager to hear the critical information that Olivia and Doris were about to present.

Olivia looked up and addressed the room, "We are ready to get started. Everyone, please take your seats."

Doris making her final preparations said, "No interruptions once we get started. We will answer questions after the presentation is over."

Olivia and Doris started the presentation, delivering The Timeline of the investigation.

They switched seamlessly between speakers, each picking up where the other left off with practiced ease.

The audience was captivated, following along as the two presenters shared critical information and insights on The Lost Investigation.

Olivia stood at the front of the room, her eyes scanning the faces before her as she spoke with measured intensity.

"We have no idea how all of this was accomplished. Under normal circumstances, none of what we are about to explain should be possible."

She paused, allowing the weight of the statement to sink in before continuing. "Red flags should have been popping up all over the country for the last thirty years, but through a creative web of fraudulent lies, an empire was created."

Doris picked up seamlessly, her voice carrying the same gravity. "The story of The Lost all started over thirty years ago with a man named Brian Schersinger.

Brian Schersinger was a member of *The Church of the Odyssey Community*."

She tapped on her tablet, pulling up records, witness testimonies, and financial statements that had been buried for decades. "Witness confirmation from *Mary Toplin*, Brian's fiancée, confirmed that in March of 2004, Brian registered his delivery company under *4815162342 Inc.*"

Olivia continued without hesitation, moving the timeline forward. "One year later, in March of 2005, Brian purchased a delivery truck and started renting a warehouse under *4815162342 Inc.*"

The details stacked one after the other, forming a picture no one wanted to believe.

Doris took a breath before diving into the next critical point. "In September of 2005—six months later—*The Church of the Odyssey High Priests* put the community on lockdown.

Brian was last seen being arrested by community security and brought before the High Priests."

The air in the room tightened as she delivered the next blow. "One week later, Brian Schersinger's *body* was discovered inside the community."

A murmur rippled through the gathered investigators, but Olivia didn't slow down. "To the digital world, Brian Schersinger was *still alive* because the community never reported his death to authorities outside of it."

Doris swiped across the tablet, pulling up additional layers of deception. "Within two months, in November of 2005, *Mary Toplin* confirmed that after Brian's death, *his identity was used* to acquire a loan and create four numbered corporations—shell companies we are calling *The Entity Corporations* or *Entities*."

She gestured toward the screen, displaying financial documents that connected each Entity to a growing empire. "These *Entities* would eventually *own Odyssey Inc Investments*, each one controlling *25%* of the company."

The implications settled heavily over the room, but Olivia pressed forward, revealing another layer. "Around the same time *The Entities* were registered, *The Church of the Odyssey* also registered its own numbered corporation—one we are calling *COTO Inc.*"

Doris nodded, tapping the screen to enlarge key transactions.

"The Entities were used to purchase land and commission the construction of the *Odyssey Inc* building we see today."

She paused. "We have confirmation that *COTO Inc* funneled money and assets into the *Entities* to make this happen."

The room was impossibly still, every mind working to process the depth of the scheme.

Olivia glanced at Doris, then continued. "Over the next six months, as *Odyssey Inc* was being constructed using funds from *COTO Inc*, over *fifty new church communities* were built and funded across the country."

Doris took over, driving home the final pieces of their findings. "In June of 2006, *Odyssey Inc Investments* had its first official month of business, investing in a diverse portfolio—real estate firms, construction companies, even funding *public government offices* through their investments."

A beat of silence. Then Olivia spoke, her words deliberate, final. "Everything up until this point—except for *COTO Inc*—was done using *Brian Schersinger's identity, The Entity Corporations, and 4815162342 Inc.*"

She paused before continuing. "This is how they *made Brian Schersinger disappear*—how they ensured his name had only *one existing connection* to all of this."

The final puzzle piece clicked into place. No one could deny it now.

They had uncovered a scheme spanning decades, built on deception, and manipulation.

Olivia swiped the tablet in her hands and the image on the screen changed.

Doris started speaking, "In July of 2006, at the same day and time, Brian Schersinger's identity was officially changed three times, creating three new fake identities: Lionel Trebor, Gerald Randall, and Samuel Constant."

The Command Room was steeped in tension as Olivia and Doris delivered their findings with unwavering precision.

Every detail, every connection, was laid bare, revealing an intricate web of deception and manipulation spanning three decades.

Their seamless transitions between speakers kept the energy high, ensuring that every investigator remained locked onto the unfolding revelations.

Olivia continued, her voice steady but carrying the weight of something monumental.

"Samuel Constant, however, took possession of *The Entity Corporations* from Brian Schersinger, setting the stage for *Odyssey Inc., Lionel Trebor,* and *Gerald Randall* to empower *The Church of the Odyssey* through their investments and business operations—building communities across the country."

Doris picked up immediately, swiping across her tablet to highlight the next timeline event.

"In September of 2006, the *first underground tunnel* was commissioned beneath the original warehouse owned by Brian Schersinger in *Prudence*.

This is the *same tunnel* Agent #64 was taken through."

A murmur rippled through the gathered investigators.

"Over the next *four years, over 2,000 communities* were founded by *COTO Inc* across the country."

Olivia enlarged a map of the country, revealing a sprawling network of tunnels overlaid onto key locations, their interconnected paths lighting up the screen.

"The entire *tunnel system* we have uncovered consists of *1,072 tunnels*, stretching across the country.

Each tunnel was constructed over a five-year period, bringing us to *2015*."

She gestured to the pattern on the map. "Every tunnel location corresponds with a *church community* opened by *COTO Inc* in that area.

Additionally, *each location* is surrounded by real estate owned by *Odyssey Inc*."

She paused. "Rental cars from Odyssey Inc's businesses were used to *transport the lost* after *The Phantom Ambulances* were abandoned in the tunnels."

Then—the critical shift in the timeline. "*2015* also marks the *first missing person case* that meets *The Lost Criterion*."

The gravity of the statement settled over the room like a cold wave. Doris continued, reinforcing the present scope of their findings.

"Today, in *2035*, *COTO Inc* has over *14,000 communities* across major cities, with *over fifty million followers* spread throughout those communities."

She paused. "The identities of *Lionel Trebor* and *Gerald Randall* currently have *over 1,500 numbered corporations* registered to them."

She swiped across the screen again, pulling up financial records. "These corporations have been used to *funnel money, secure assets,* and *move resources* from *Odyssey Inc*—which *eventually end up in the possession of COTO Inc.*"

Olivia nodded once, adding another critical discovery to the timeline. "Thanks to *Mary Toplin*, we also know that *2015* was the year *the original 13 high priests* of *The Church of the Odyssey left* the COTO community. They were replaced by the *current high priests*."

Doris stepped forward again, her voice sharp. "Over the past *20 years*, over *7,000 people* have gone missing, matching *The Lost Criterion*."

Her next words left no room for doubt. "We know the tunnels were used to *erase the existence* of the phantom ambulances and their victims.

Now that we have completed *a forensic audit of COTO Inc*, we can confirm that *every single missing person* who meets *The Lost Criterion* belonged to a *church community* controlled by *COTO Inc* before their disappearance."

Silence. Then—Olivia pressed forward with the final summary. "We still don't know *exactly* who is behind this or *why* they are doing it, but we are closing in on *the location The Lost are being held*.

Hopefully, we will bring them home soon."

Doris exhaled, then delivered the last statement. "The entire presentation can be accessed on *The Throne server* for review. *Commander, did you have anything you wanted to add?*"

Steve stepped forward, his expression tense with the weight of their findings. "Thank you, Doris. You ladies did *amazing work*."

He paused, scanning the assembled investigators before speaking again, his voice sharp with conviction. "Like Olivia and Doris said, we don't know *how* they were able to accomplish this but now we know *how it all fits together.* And we can see *exactly how* they were doing it and *where the money came from.*"

Steve paused shaking his head, "Everything ties back to *Brian Schersinger's identity*—and *The Church of the Odyssey.*"

Silence.

Then—the final command. "*High Priest Dresden* and the other high priests are *our prime suspects.* We must *confirm that*, and we must *find them* as soon as possible."

Olivia nodded once, stepping forward for the last portion of the briefing. "At this point, we will take *any questions* from the audience.

Please raise your hand if you have a question."

The investigators remained frozen for a moment, absorbing the sheer scale of what had just been revealed. And then, one by one, hands began to rise. Olivia scanned the room, eyes flicking to the raised hand closest to the front.

"Go ahead," she prompted.

The man leaned forward, his expression tense. "What were they doing with The Lost once they were in the tunnels?"

Olivia took a slow breath, gathering her thoughts before responding. "The tunnel network spans across the country, and all tunnels lead to a hub where we believe a train would transport them to the final location.

We are awaiting confirmation from the agents in the tunnels."

She tapped her tablet, shifting the images on the large screen behind her. "We don't have confirmation on where The Lost are being held, but based on the evidence we've gathered, we can speculate a few key things."

The screen displayed layered maps, satellite imagery, and complex data points. Olivia continued.

"We know that Agent #64's triangulation signal traveled fifty feet up into the air through a concave or convex glass lens—something that should be *impossible.*"

She glanced at the gathered investigators before pressing forward. "But let's consider the additional evidence."

She swiped her tablet again, changing the images.

A new map appeared, marked by glaring red zones.

"The location that returned from the signal is in the middle of the ocean—a restricted area by both *air and sea*."

She pointed to a highlighted path. "The train tracks in the tunnels follow a *straight-line trajectory* beneath the ocean—leading directly to the signal's origin."

Then, Olivia brought up a still from the helicopter footage, moments before its destruction. "When we sent the helicopter to investigate, it crashed into what seemed like *clouds*. But if you watch the footage carefully, you'll see something strange."

She enlarged the final frame. "A second before the explosion, the helicopter *appeared on camera*—as if it was *flying into itself*."

The murmurs in the room grew louder. Steve leaned forward, crossing his arms. "So, what are we supposed to think about all of this? What's your theory?"

Olivia tapped her tablet again, shifting the screen. "I suspect something *crazy*, but I can't find another way for all the evidence to line up."

Then—she laid out her hypothesis. "I think our train tracks lead to *an island*—one covered by a *glass dome*."

The weight of her words settled heavily over the room. She continued. "If that's true, then that's where *The Lost* are being taken."

She pointed back to the satellite map. "That would explain *why the signal was amplified*—a large concave lens could have directed it to *thousands of satellites* in orbit."

Steve exhaled sharply, shaking his head. "I'm getting *tired* of asking how any of this is possible. Keep going."

Olivia zoomed in on the satellite image. "Look closely at these *live* satellite images of the location."

She played a time-lapse, showing the ocean shifting through seasons, before pausing it on a cloudless day.

"At first glance, it looks normal. But if we zoom in and analyze the *water coloration* around the location, you'll notice something."

A lighter blue halo surrounded the darkened waters. "The lighter blue circle? That's the reflection of the sky. I believe the dome covering the island is *mirrored*—reflecting the ocean around it, making it nearly invisible from aerial surveillance."

She paused before delivering the final realization. "And that would explain why we saw the helicopter in the footage.

A reflective sphere with a large curve at the right angle would distort visual input—causing that *illusion* before impact."

Steve turned toward Doris. "We still don't have *any* communication from our agents following the tracks in the tunnels?"

Doris shook her head. "Commander, signals inside the tunnels are *completely blocked*. However, we've just received confirmation that they've *taken down the reinforced door*, allowing vehicles access."

She tapped a few commands on her screen. "If the tunnel beneath the ocean is *2,000 kilometers long*, then we should have an *army of agents* at that island in *12 to 15 hours*."

Steve nodded firmly. "We need to focus *everything* on getting to that location—whatever it turns out to be."

He turned to Mark. "How soon will our marine units arrive?"

Mark checked the latest reports. "Our *first group* should be there in a few hours. I've already dispatched more teams."

Steve didn't hesitate. "Clear out this room. Let's get to work on this."

Olivia stepped forward as the presentation wrapped up. "I want to thank everyone for coming."

Then—something changed. The large screen flickered, disrupting the images.

Then—static. A piercing, grating noise blasted through the speakers, consuming the room in a wave of white noise.

People shifted uneasily, some rising from their seats, conversations turning into alarmed murmurs.

Steve's gaze shot to Olivia. "What happened?"

Olivia's fingers flew over her tablet, scanning data feeds. She barely looked up as she responded. "I'm not sure Commander."

But something in her voice—that tight edge of uncertainty—made it clear. This wasn't just a technical glitch.

This was interference. Within a few seconds, the screen flashed, and a video feed appeared.

No one could be seen on the screen, but the background showed a cathedral-like setting: wooden walls, colorful stained-glass windows, religious artwork, statues along the walls, and candles lit all over the room.

A large fireplace centered on the back wall had a blazing fire.

Above the fireplace hung a seven-foot-tall Jesus on a cross, covered in blood. In the middle of the room was a large round table with a square section extending from it.

Every seat around the table had two books sitting in front of it.

There was low, soothing church music playing in the background. Olivia spoke, "The video is being transmitted to us Commander, but it is strongly encrypted. It will take some time to find the exact location."

A suspicious smirk coming across Steve's face as he said, "It must be Dresden. But why would he be contacting us is beyond me."

A man wearing a red mask resembling a demon face, with two big horns coming out of the forehead, walked onto the screen from off-camera, wearing a shiny black sweeping robe that flowed with his movements. He walked over and sat down at the square section of the round table.

Twelve men followed, wearing masks and sitting down at seats around the table. The man in the black robe removed his mask, set it down on the books in front of him, and began to speak.

The man stood rigid, his frame worn from age but still carrying the weight of defiance.

His long, scraggly hair framed a face hardened by time, and when he spoke, his yellow-stained teeth—rotted black in places—made the words feel more venomous.

"Commander, it is a pleasure to finally meet you."

Steve held his gaze, unreadable, unshaken. "I wish the meeting had come a long time ago. You must be Dresden?"

The moment the words left his mouth; High Priest Dresden's expression twisted into something hostile. His eyes narrowed into slits, lips pressing together in a tight, furious line.

His hands clenched into fists, barely concealing the storm brewing beneath his skin. The very air around him seemed to crackle with restrained anger as he glared at Steve. "*THAT IS* HIGH PRIEST Dresden to you..... Even I had the respect to greet you as *Commander*."

Steve remained unmoved. "What have you done to possibly earn my respect?"

Dresden's jaw tensed, but his tone remained controlled—measured, almost proud. "Well, to start, *you only exist* as the man you are today *because of us*."

He hesitated before continuing, "If *The Lost* didn't exist, *The Throne* wouldn't exist, and *you*, Commander, would not exist."

A pause, deliberate. Then—"We are writing history.

The story of *The Lost* will be told for generations to come—with everything we have accomplished."

Steve's voice was sharp, cutting through the delusion like a knife. "That is what you call writing history? *Kidnapping people? Stealing their lives? Taking their free will?*"

Dresden exhaled slowly, as if pitying Steve's ignorance. "We sent them to a *much better place.*

Trust us."

Steve didn't flinch. "Where have you been keeping *The Lost*, and what have you been doing to them?"

Dresden's lips curled slightly, but his words remained cryptic. "I would *hate* to spoil the surprise.

I'm sure your agents will be there soon."

Steve's eyes didn't waver. "Which brings us to why *you're* here, talking to me right now."

Dresden's smile returned, this time laced with something unsettling. "Our meeting is *inevitable* Commander, so why fear it? Why avoid it? We have *GOD* on our side."

Steve exhaled sharply, shaking his head. "Your god won't help you when you're *rotting in a padded cell*."

Dresden tilted his head slightly, unconcerned. "We are *proud* of the work we've done in the name of *GOD*. And the *climax* is still yet to come."

Steve's expression darkened. "We are *moments away* from finding your location."

Dresden's grin widened. "And I'll be *right here*, waiting for you when you get here."

Steve's tone sharpened. "I don't think you'll have time for a climax."

Dresden only chuckled. "The *climax* is *inevitable* at this point. You will *soon understand*."

Steve's breath remained slow, measured. But his voice carried finality. "What I *do* understand is that *The Church of the Odyssey* has done *many things* that won't be forgiven—by *me, The Throne, the victims, justice,* or any *god* that is *righteous*."

Dresden inhaled deeply, his posture unwavering. "And the *best* is still yet to come. We are going to bring the *greatest, most paramount divine holy war* to this world."

He paused for a moment. "It is *too late* to stop it. Even *I* couldn't stop it at this point if I wanted to."

Steve's voice was razor-sharp. "Is that supposed to be a *threat*?"

Dresden shook his head. "It's not a *threat*, it's not a *promise*."

He paused before continuing, "It is... *an inevitable reality coming*."

Steve leaned forward slightly, not an ounce of hesitation in his voice. "And when does this reality *become real?"*

Dresden smiled one last time—cold, calculated. *"Very soon*. By the time *you find us*, reality will have *already shifted*.

Steve's eyes locked onto Dresden, unwavering, unreadable. His voice was steady, controlled. "What makes you think we don't know where you are right now?"

Dresden's lips curled into something resembling amusement, but there was something else behind his gaze—calculated confidence. "Your question implies that you *do* know where I am..."

The silence stretched for just a beat too long. Then—a slow shake of his head, the faintest smirk at the corner of his mouth. "...And here I thought we were being *honest* with each other Commander..."

A pause—drawn-out, deliberate, like he was savoring the moment. Then, his voice dipped just slightly, final, absolute. "...See you soon, Commander."

The screen went black, then flickered to static before switching back to the original image that Olivia had displayed. Steve, still seething from the condescending conversation, couldn't hold back his frustration any longer.

The tension in the Command Room had reached its peak. Steve's voice thundered through the space, his fury unmistakable as he demanded everyone's focus. His face was flushed with anger, veins visible at his temples as he shouted, his words echoing off the walls.

"Our current objective is finding Dresden's location. We now know where *The Lost* are, and agents will be there soon. I want *everyone* in this building working on finding Dresden and all relevant information on him and the other *High Priests* of *The Church of the Odyssey*."

A pause—heavy, charged. "Let's *finally* put an end to all of this and bring *The Lost* home."

The moment his command settled over the room, Olivia's voice cut through the air. "I found something Commander."

Her fingers moved swiftly across her tablet. "I don't know if it means anything, but I think *it has to*."

Steve turned toward her instantly. "What is it?"

Olivia tapped her screen, shifting images onto the display for everyone to see.

"I should have noticed this before, but it didn't mean anything at the time. When we were originally investigating *Odyssey Inc*, we found two sets of blueprints from the building's construction—the *original plans* and a *revision approved at a later date*."

Steve narrowed his eyes. "What do the *original* blueprints tell us?"

She zoomed in on a specific section, bringing it into focus.

"In the original blueprints, there was a *46th floor* to the *Odyssey Inc* building—and an *additional elevator* leading to it.

However, in the revised blueprints, both were *removed*."

Then—her voice sharpened. "What I *just* noticed is that the *revision* was approved *after* the building's construction was *already completed*—which makes *no sense*."

Silence filled the room for a second too long. Then—Steve spoke with absolute certainty. "That vacation is coming your way, Olivia."

He exhaled sharply, his mind racing. "That *must be* where Dresden and the other *High Priests* are. Maybe they've been hiding on the *46th floor* all this time, acting as the *board*—handing down directives through *Odyssey Inc* and its investments for the last *twenty years*."

Olivia nodded, her fingers moving quickly over her screen. "We *know* from *Mary's testimony* that the *original* High Priests left the *COTO community* just before *The Lost* started disappearing."

Steve turned toward Mark without hesitation. "Concentrate *all* of our remaining agents *not* in the tunnels on retrieving Dresden and the other *High Priests* from the *46th floor* of the *Odyssey Inc* building."

Then—his voice hardened even further. "Olivia, I want to *shut down everything* we've uncovered."

He listed his demands one by one, his words hammering against the tension in the air. "Lock down *Odyssey Inc's* assets, bank accounts, and *every company* involved. Shut down *COTO Inc, Lionel Trebor,* and *Gerald Randall*."

He continued, "I want the *Odyssey Inc* building *sealed*—no one goes in or out. Our agents *need* to get in *fast* and extract Dresden and the *High Priests*."

Olivia nodded, already bringing up the necessary protocols. "No problem, Commander. I've marked out a path through the *ventilation system* using the *original blueprints*—it leads straight to the *46th floor* in case we can't access the elevator."

Steve's final command rang loud, clear, and absolute. "Attack them *from both sides*. Get agents into the *ventilation shafts* and working on the *elevator*."

The operation was set into motion. The hunt for Dresden had truly begun.

Steve put his head down and covered his mouth to stifle a yawn he couldn't contain. Olivia noticed his weary gesture and a flicker of concern crossed her face.

Despite the intense situation and the high stakes, even Steve's determination couldn't mask the exhaustion that was creeping in.

Olivia said, "Commander, when is the last time you closed your eyes and got some sleep?"

Another uncontrollable yawn he tried to stifle as he spoke, "I couldn't even tell you. We haven't stopped since #64 was taken."

In a motherly tone Olivia said to Steve, "Why don't you go to the residences and get some sleep? There isn't much more to do until the agents get back with Dresden and the High Priests, and that will take at least four hours with the drive time."

Steve felt exhausted, he knew his partner would be too, "Cynthia too. We should probably both rest up before we interrogate Dresden and the High Priests.

I want to be alerted of any updates, and I want to be woken up when the agents are on the way back with Dresden and the High Priests."

Chapter 32 - The Return of Jesus

Jenny was a ten-year-old girl who didn't live within a COTO community, but her family was involved with a Christian church.

Her and her brother had the day off from school and her parents had gone to work. She had just poured herself a glass of fruit punch as her favorite TV show was about to start.

Excited, Jenny sat down on the couch, placing her glass on the table. When the show started, Jenny started dancing to the theme song when it came on like she always did.

A few seconds into her dancing the song stopped, and the TV screen flickered to reveal static.

Her heart sank—her favorite show had vanished.

The static cleared, revealing an image unlike anything Jenny had ever seen.

The screen now displayed clouds, with a majestic throne set in the middle, illuminated by a radiant light emanating from behind it.

The sight was awe-inspiring, filling Jenny with a mix of wonder and confusion as she stared at the ethereal scene before her. The image burned into her mind like an image on a shaken Poloroid picture.

Jenny's heart raced as she grabbed the remote control, determined to switch back to her favorite show.

But no matter how many times she scrolled up and down through the channels, every single one displayed the same mysterious image:

A throne sitting on the clouds, bathed in radiant light. Behind the visual, a low, constant humming filled the room, blending with the sound of what seemed like church music accompanied by angelic voices singing.

The surreal experience left Jenny in awe and bewilderment, as she clutched the remote and stared at the screen, unable to comprehend what was happening.

The silhouette of a man formed within the light, growing larger as it approached the throne.

Emerging from the brilliance, a man in a long white robe, clean-shaven with long flowing dark hair, walked out with a serene grace. His hair and robe swayed in synchronized movements, the fabric shimmering in the radiant light.

He stopped in the middle of the screen, holding a scepter in his left hand with his hands down at his sides. With deliberate movements, he raised his hands to resemble the stance of being crucified on a cross.

He held that position for about ten seconds, the atmosphere charged with a sense of reverence and awe.

Then, he lowered his arms and gracefully sat down on the throne, bathed in the halo of light emanating from behind him. A rainbow formed in the background of the image at the edges of the halo of light when the man sat down,

"I have returned to you in this way, on this day, as prophesized in the Bible within Revelation 1:7: 'Behold, He is coming with clouds, and every eye will see Him.'"

Jesus paused after finishing the verse, letting the words hang in the air, resonating with the viewer. The silence was profound, Jenny processing the gravity of his message.

After a brief moment, he continued, his voice steady and filled with authority, ready to impart the next part of his revelation.

"This message is being broadcast across the world on every radio station and every television channel. Everyone will be aware of my return as prophesized in Revelation 1:7:

I... am Jesus...

And this... is heaven...

A place of perfection and eternal sustenance that I have created, For you.

As you were told in the Bible within John 14:1-3, it says:

Reciting the verse from memory, Jesus spoke with unwavering conviction, his voice resonating with power and authority. The atmosphere was charged with the energy of his message,

"Let not your heart be troubled...

In My Father's house are many mansions;

If it were not so, I would have told you.

I go to prepare a place for you.

And if I go and prepare a place for you......

I will come again and receive you to Myself; that where I am, there you may be also."

Pausing for a second and then continuing his speech,

"Now I have returned to you, and it is time for you to return to me.

Heaven is fully prepared for your coming. Your mansions here in heaven are waiting to be filled by you and the people you love."

Jesus paused; his gaze intense. He raised his right hand and pointed directly at the camera, as if reaching through the screen to the person watching. With a commanding tone, he said, "I want YOU..."

The words hung in the air, charged with significance, making Jenny feel as though she was being personally addressed and called to action.

Jesus lowered his right hand, "The time has come for my return.

The world has become a chaotic and corrupt place filled with Apostates, Heathens, Atheists, and Non-Believers.

Now fully prepared for your arrival, I invite all my followers to come and join me in heaven."

Jesus stood up from the throne, his movements calm and deliberate. He began to walk around the screen nonchalantly, as if lost in thought.

He paced back and forth twice, the hem of his robe swaying gently with each step.

After a few moments of this contemplative pacing, he paused and continued speaking, his voice steady and filled with purpose. "I am calling upon all my devout followers to do the work of GOD, for GOD, which will guarantee you a place in heaven.....

To secure your place here, you must fulfill the request from GOD within 2 Chronicles 15:12-13:"

Jesus started reciting the verse with unwavering confidence, his voice imbued with faith and ultimate persuasion.

His tone was steady and commanding, drawing Jenny's attention and instilling a sense of purpose and determination in her heart.

The atmosphere was charged with the energy of his speech, leaving no doubt about the strength and sincerity of his message.

"And they entered a covenant to seek the Lord, the God of their fathers, with all their heart and with all their soul.

But that whoever would not seek the Lord, the God of Israel, should be put to death, whether young or old, man or woman."

He continued, "And also, you were instructed within Deuteronomy 13:6-10:"

Again, Jesus recited the verse, his voice brimming with ultimate persuasion and conviction.

Every word he uttered carried a powerful weight, resonating deeply with Jenny.

"If your very own brother, or your son or daughter, or the wife you love, or your closest friend secretly entices you, saying, 'Let us go and worship other gods',

Do not yield to them or listen to them. Show them no pity. Do not spare them or shield them. You must certainly put them to death.

Your hand must be the first in putting them to death, and then the hands of all the people.

Stone them to death, because they tried to turn you away from the Lord your God."

Jesus sat back down on the throne, the halo of light bathing his entire body in a divine glow. The radiant light seemed to envelop him, accentuating his presence and reinforcing the sense of reverence that surrounded him.

Jenny watched in awe, captivated by the sight of Jesus on the throne, a figure of divine authority and serenity.

"To be brought here, you must rid the world of Apostates, Heathens, Atheists, and Non-Believers.

When all have been killed and extinguished from your world, I will begin to bring you all here, starting with the followers who destroyed the most.

The time has come for Christianity to show its power within this world. My return, prophesized in the Bible, is finally coming to fruition and will demonstrate our united power as Christians.

I have come to save you all from this chaotic and corrupt world that the Devil and Sin have immersed within man."

Jesus stood up from the throne and positioned himself in front of it.

With a powerful gesture, he raised his left hand, holding the scepter high above his head. The halo of light intensified, casting a divine glow around him. He yelled loudly, his voice echoing with authority and fervor: "SOLDIERS OF JESUS, I LOVE YOU. DEATH TO ALL APOSTATES, HEATHENS, ATHEISTS, AND NON-BELIEVERS!"

The image on the screen disappeared after Jesus said this and changed to static for a second before Jenny's favorite show came back on. Jenny, shocked and very confused by the video she had just watched, felt her mind racing.

She was torn by the impossible choice given by Jesus, someone she loved and wanted to make happy.

The potential horrors the video could incite filled her with fear.

As she became scared and inexplicably thirsty, Jenny's hands shook while she picked up her glass of juice and drank it all in a few big gulps.

She walked to the kitchen, still shaking, put the glass in the sink, and rinsed it with water.

Her eyes then glanced at the wooden block of sharp kitchen knives on the counter.

Jenny left the kitchen and climbed the stairs to the second floor of her house. Jenny's pulse raced as she knocked on her older brother's door.

The strange video had unsettled her in a way she couldn't explain, and there was only one person she trusted to help her make sense of it—her brother Marcus.

He was twelve, only two years older than her, but to Jenny, Marcus seemed far wiser than his age.

After a brief pause, she opened the door and stepped inside. "Marcus, did you see the Jesus video?"

Marcus looked up from his book, his expression neutral but thoughtful. "I did. I thought it was very confusing.

Why would he ask us—his followers—to *kill* people?"

Jenny hesitated, shifting on her feet. "I don't know, but..."

She swallowed hard, then continued with quiet determination, "I would like to be guaranteed a spot in heaven."

Marcus blinked at her, his brows furrowing. "So, what—"

His voice took on an edge of disbelief "You want to become a *Soldier of Jesus* and go around killing Apostates, Heathens, Atheists, and Non-Believers?"

He shook his head. "You are *ten years old* Jenny."

She clenched her fists, frustration bubbling up. "WHAT IF THIS IS ALL REAL AND JESUS HAS COME BACK TO SAVE US?"

Marcus sighed, rubbing at his temple. "I already told you how I feel about that, and you *don't* have to yell."

Jenny exhaled, forcing herself to steady her emotions. This was *so* obvious to her—why couldn't Marcus see it too?

She took a deep breath and tried again. "So even after seeing the video, you *still* have doubts? You *don't* believe?"

Marcus's gaze didn't waver. "Jenny, I have a lot of questions that *no one* can give me a good answer to."

Then, he shrugged slightly, his voice carrying the weight of something unresolved. "It all seems like a *fairy tale*."

The word *"fairy tale"* when referring to the Bible and Jesus had always been a trigger for Jenny, deeply ingrained as part of her upbringing, and indoctrination.

After seeing the video, Jenny had no doubts about its authenticity; every single word felt real to her.

Annoyed, she responded with a frustrated edge to her voice, her conviction unwavering.

Jenny's chest tightened as she stared at her brother, her breath shallow. "Even now..."

She whispered, her voice uneven. "Jesus has come back and *shown himself* to us... How can you still feel it's a *fairy tale*?"

Marcus sat still, his expression firm, unwavering. "I *can't* believe it."

Jenny's heart pounded harder. Her fingers curled into fists as frustration bubbled up inside her. "I wish you *didn't* say that."

Her voice cracked slightly, but she kept going, the weight of her words pressing between them. "You are making yourself an *Apostate, Heathen, Atheist,* and *Non-Believer*."

The air between them felt heavier now—charged with something unspoken, something neither of them truly understood.

But Marcus didn't respond. And Jenny wasn't sure if she wanted to hear what he had to say next.

Jenny, screamed aloud towards her brother and at the room.

Overwhelmed with a torrent of emotions—anger, confusion, and conflict—she desperately wanted to make Jesus happy and had hoped her brother would join her in this.

Hearing her older brother's disregard and disbelief, however, shattered her hopes.

She had prayed that this conversation with Marcus would go differently, that the video would open his eyes to the truth she believed.

Now, standing before her brother, Jenny's heart sank as she realized he embodied everything she was told to destroy—an Apostate, a Heathen, an Atheist, and a Non-Believer.

Tears welled up in her eyes as she understood the gravity of what she had to do to secure her place in heaven.

The weight of the task before her was crushing.

Yet she felt compelled to fulfill her divine duty.

Marcus started to speak, "Jenny just forget about Jesus............."

Jenny, driven by a mix of devotion and desperation, abruptly interrupted him mid-sentence.

In one swift, decisive motion, Jenny swung her arm out from behind her back, wielding a large ten-inch kitchen knife.

She plunged the knife into her brother's temple, and like a hot knife through butter, it slid out the other side of his head.

Jenny feeling the dead weight of her brother drag her down as she held the handle of the knife, she released it.

Marcus instantly collapsed to the floor, and Jenny screamed as blood began to pool around his lifeless body.

She started screaming at Marcus's limp form. "I'M SORRY MARCUS, BUT JESUS SAID... EVEN YOUR MOTHER, FATHER, OR BROTHER."

Tears streamed down Jenny's face as she stared at her brother's body lying on the floor.

The weight of her actions crashed down on her, and she felt a mix of horror, guilt, and a twisted sense of duty.

Knowing she did this for Jesus in the name of God gave her the strength to move on.

The realization that her actions were part of a divine plan bolstered her resolve, even as the weight of her decision threatened to crush her spirit.

Jenny's faith provided her with the courage to face the daunting task ahead, her devotion to fulfilling what she believed was a holy mission unwavering.

She heard people outside and turned to look out the window in her brother's room.

Outside the window, Jenny saw two men in yellow shirts that were walking on the sidewalk, both carrying shotguns.

Another man was jogging on the sidewalk on the opposite side of the street and hadn't noticed the two men as he ran towards them.

The two men rushed across the street towards the jogger; their shotguns aimed directly at him.

The jogger, overwhelmed with fear, dropped to his knees.

One of the men stepped forward, pressing the cold steel barrel of his shotgun against the jogger's forehead.

The chilling touch of the weapon sent a shiver down the jogger's spine, his heart pounding in his chest as he faced the terrifying reality before him. pleading desperately for his life.

His voice trembled as he begged them not to kill him, his eyes wide with terror.

Jenny heard the two men yell: "DO YOU BELIEVE IN OUR GOD JESUS CHRIST?"

The Jogger responded scared shaking, fear in his eyes, "What?????"

The two men said nothing in response but, "Wrong answer."

Both men unloaded their shotguns on him simultaneously and then started running down the street.

Jenny could see what was left of the jogger's body, his intestines pouring out of his midsection looking like a pile of snakes, intertwined with each other.

Half of his skull was missing, nothing but a large empty cavity his insides blown out.

His brain matter could be seen spread about the scene strewn across the lawns, sidewalk, and pieces of him stuck to the cars in the area.

The entire area covered in a crimson red shade that tainted the area with the horror committed.

Seeing the jogger's body put Jenny into a state of shock.

She stood there, frozen, staring at the gruesome sight for what felt like an eternity.

The horror of the scene seared into her mind, but amidst the chaos, a twisted sense of purpose began to take root within her.

Jenny knew that she was now a Soldier of Jesus, and she felt an urgent need to hit the streets and find other Soldiers of Jesus to fight alongside her.

Determined, she went to her room and changed her shirt, putting on a yellow shirt like she seen the two men wearing that proclaimed her love for Jesus.

She grabbed the gold necklace with a cross pendant hanging on it off her dresser and put it around her neck.

With a newfound resolve and a heart pounding with a mix of fear and fervor, Jenny walked out the front door of her house wielding the bloody kitchen knife that she stabbed into her brother's head and started running down the street in the same direction as the men carrying the shotguns.

As Jenny was running past house number 467, she heard a gunshot go off inside.

Looking down at the knife in her hand, she thought she would feel much safer if she had a gun.

She walked inside the house and announced herself. "Hello, is anyone here? I am your neighbor and a Soldier of Jesus.

I need a gun."

An older woman holding a rifle and pointing it at Jenny came rushing down the stairs in front of the door where Jenny stood, holding the knife in her hand still dripping with her brother's blood, and spoke.

"I am Delores, Soldier of Jesus. YOU ARE JUST A LITTLE GIRL. How do you expect to kill apostates?"

Delores glanced down at the knife in her hand she seen a drop of blood fall off the tip of the blade and stain her white carpet as Jenny responded. "I have already killed one, but I only have this knife.

Would you have a gun I could use?"

Delores lowered the rifle, and said, "I have more guns, you can have one, we can hit the streets together.

I just need one minute, I killed my apostate husband, but I still have one more heathen in this house. Follow me."

Jenny followed Delores down the hall.

Delores walked into her fifteen-year-old son's room, carrying the rifle.

Her son was sitting on his bed with headphones on and did not notice when his mother came in.

Delores held the rifle pointed at her son. He looked up from his phone, threw the headphones off his head, jumped up onto his feet, and yelled at his mom. "MOM, WHAT THE FUCK IS GOING ON?"

Delores responded staring into her son's eyes, "I really wish you came to church with us........."

Delores let off two rounds from the rifle into her son's chest.

The look of confusion, shock, and betrayal on Delores's son's face was palpable. Jenny felt a twisted sense of satisfaction as she watched the life drain from his eyes.

She was almost entranced by the scene, the raw emotion of the moment gripping her.

Her son's body fell Jenny watched as the boy fell over smashing his lifeless skull on the dresser before hitting the ground.

Jenny was entranced staring at the boy's body on the floor; Delores's yelled her voice snapped Jenny out of the trance. "LET'S GO, I will get you a gun."

Delores got a handgun and gave it to Jenny as she filled her pockets with ammunition.

They exited the front door of the house and there was a large group of twenty people, all wearing yellow shirts, wielding guns, going door to door, moving down the street, and killing all the Apostates, Heathens, Atheists, and Non-Believers they could find.

Delores yelled out to them. "WE ARE SOLDIERS OF JESUS; CAN WE JOIN YOU?"

This was just the beginning of the nightmarish horrors and viral mayhem that the video would unleash.

Jenny's story mirrored the chaos that erupted in every neighborhood, city, and state across the country, and even in other countries around the world.

Christians from all corners of the globe were joining the fight as Soldiers of Jesus, their resolve unwavering.

And this was only the start.

Over the past week, within the 14,000 communities and 30,000 churches owned by the Church of the Odyssey, the prophecy of Jesus's return with a specific date and time was drilled into the minds of every single follower, priming them for this day.

At the prophesized date and time, within COTO's 30,000 churches, the video of Jesus's return was shown on large television screens mounted on the walls.

Outside the churches, large wooden crates filled with an armory of weapons and ammunition awaited.

Each follower was armed with a yellow Soldiers of Jesus T-shirt, a gun, and ammunition as they exited the church after watching the video.

The gates of all 14,000 communities were left open, unleashing the Soldiers of Jesus upon the world.

All by the directive of Jesus to kill Apostates, Heathens, Atheists, and Non-Believers for a guaranteed spot in heaven.

The terror spread like wildfire. Streets once filled with the mundane sounds of daily life were now echoing with gunshots, screams, and the cries of the innocent.

Families were torn apart as loved ones turned on each other, driven by a twisted sense of divine duty.

The air was thick with fear and the scent of blood, as the Soldiers of Jesus carried out their gruesome mission.

In every corner of the world, the same horrific scenes played out.

Neighborhoods became battlegrounds, cities turned into war zones, and the very fabric of society began to unravel.

The urgency of the terror was palpable, as the Soldiers of Jesus moved with relentless determination, leaving a trail of devastation in their wake.

This was not just a moment of chaos; it was the beginning of an apocalyptic nightmare that would forever change the world.

The prophecy had been fulfilled, and the world was plunged into a darkness from which it might never recover.

Chapter 33 - The Discarded

6 Months Ago

esus sat in a chair, his long hair cascading over his shoulders, and his clean-shaven face set in a look of quiet contemplation. Dressed in a pair of jeans and a white button-up shirt, he stared intently at the couch across from him.

A man lay face down on the couch, his head buried in a pillow.

Jesus felt a familiar surge of anxiety as he prepared to speak with the man, a feeling that always accompanied these moments.

The table in front of the couch was set with an array of three half-filled glasses and three plates of hot, steaming food, as it always was whenever someone occupied the couch.

The aroma filled the room.

Brian stirred on the couch, his body sluggish as he shifted onto his side. The scent of food drifted toward him, pulling him further into wakefulness.

His eyes opened slowly, scanning the dimly lit room.

Plates of food sat neatly arranged, drinks placed beside them. His gaze lingered there for a moment before moving to the man seated across from him.

His voice was sharp, laced with confusion. "Who the fuck are you? Is this a date?"

Jesus didn't flinch. "Brian Stafford, I welcome you and assure you all of your questions will be answered."

His tone was calm, deliberate. "I just need you to drink the three drinks in front of you before I can answer any of your questions."

Brian stiffened, his eyes narrowing. "I AM NOT DRINKING ANYTHING. WHO ARE YOU? WHERE AM I?"

Jesus remained composed, unfazed by Brian's rising frustration. "Brian, I need you to *calm down*, and you *must* drink."

Brian let out a sharp breath, pushing himself upright. "I don't know who you are or *how* I got here."

Jesus leaned forward slightly, his expression unreadable. "You *do* know how you got here, Brian."

His voice was measured, yet unsettling. "You remember the blood *gushing* out the side of your body after being stabbed twice, don't you?"

The words sent a chill through Brian's spine. The *pain*, the *panic*, the *desperation...*

Jesus continued. "Do you recall the ambulance that picked you up? The cold metal, the blaring sirens, the frantic voices..."

A pause. "What do you *think* happened after that?"

Brian's breath hitched. Instinctively, he lifted his shirt, revealing two jagged scars on his abdomen.

His fingers traced the rough edges of the wounds, the memories flooding back—flashes of blood, agony, terror.

His voice came low, heavy. "What the *fuck* is going on here?"

His tone sharpened. "And that is the *last time* I ask before I get violent."

Jesus didn't react to the threat.

Instead, he gestured toward the first door at the edge of the room. "Brian, do you see that door over there?"

Brian scoffed. "Why wouldn't I?"

Jesus's voice carried something deeper now—an edge of finality. "You have brought this conversation to *two choices.*"

Pause. "Option one—you *drink* those three drinks, ask me *any* questions you want, then walk out *that* door."

He nodded toward it. "And have *all* your wants and desires fulfilled."

A heavy silence settled between them. "Option two..."

He gestured toward the second door on the far side of the room. "Do you see *that* door?"

Brian glanced at it, then back at the man. "Yeah."

With a sinister tone in his voice Jesus said, "You *do not* want to know what will happen if *that* door opens."

His voice became cool, detached. "If you choose *not* to drink, or if you *choose to attack me—that door will open.*"

Brian pushed himself to his feet, rolling his shoulders, letting the tension settle into his stance. "Maybe I *do* want to know what will happen."

His lips curled slightly. "I *like* getting answers to mysteries."

Jesus didn't respond directly.

Instead, he spoke—not to Brian, but to the room itself. "DISCARD."

Brian lunged across the table, swinging his fists at Jesus and landing a punch squarely on his face.

The door swung open, and four guards burst into the room.

They detained Brian, surrounding him with a practiced efficiency.

One of the soldiers pulled out a long baton, touched it to Brian's chest, and the room filled with the sound of electrical crackling.

Brian's scream pierced the air for two agonizing seconds before he collapsed, unconscious.

The soldiers picked Brian up and carried him out through the door they had entered.

• • •

An unknown amount of time later

Brian awoke, opening his eyes to complete darkness. Panic set in as he realized he couldn't see anything.

His hands were bound together by cold steel chains. He tried to move and pull his hands free, but it was hopeless. The chains tightened with every attempt.

He tried until the chains were digging into his flesh and he felt the wet blood rolling off his wrists from the wounds he had opened.

A heavy weight pressed down on his back, but he couldn't see or reach around to feel what it was.

He took a few tentative steps, hearing more chains jangle on the floor and feeling the weight on his back pull slightly as he moved.

Desperation mounting, he decided to follow the chain to its source.

He felt around with his tied hands for the chain on the floor, grasped it, and followed it to the wall.

It was connected about four feet from the floor, but he couldn't find a point where the chain was attached.

It felt as if the chain disappeared into the wall.

Exploring further, he followed the wall to the right, running his hands along the cold, smooth steel. He traveled about five steps before coming to another wall, then walked back to where the chain was connected.

This time, he felt around the lower portion of the wall, but found nothing but the same cold, smooth steel.

He followed five steps to the left of where the chain was connected and encountered another wall.

He decided to follow this wall to the left, but when he reached the fifth step, the chain on his back tightened and pulled on his body as it reached its full length.

Brian realized he was being held in a ten-foot by ten-foot cube room, chained up like a dog in a backyard with limited movement.

The chains on his back connected to his hands, which were also bound by chains that linked to his feet.

The intricate web of restraints restricted his every movement, a constant reminder of his captivity.

He could only move around in half of the room, the chains restricting his every step.

The oppressive darkness and the cold steel walls closed in on him, amplifying his sense of isolation and helplessness.

The terror was palpable, his heart pounding in his chest as he struggled to comprehend his dire situation.

Every breath he took was filled with dread, every movement a reminder of his captivity.

Brian Screamed as loud as he could. "WHAT THE FUCK IS GOING ON, LET ME OUT OF THIS ROOM NOW!!!!"

Brian's screams echoed and reverberated within the metal room, amplifying his terror.

Desperation clawed at him as he continued screaming, banging his chained hands on the walls.

The sound of the chains clanging against the metal was deafening, vibrating and echoing through the entire room.

The noise became unbearable, assaulting his ears and causing excruciating pain.

He fell to the floor, writhing in agony as his eardrums throbbed like never before.

The relentless ringing and pounding in his head were overwhelming. He used his tied hands to cover his ears, but it offered no relief.

After what felt like an eternity, the noise finally subsided, and Brian knew he would never try that again.

Curled up on the floor against the wall, clutching the chain attached to his back, Brian screamed again.

His voice was raw and filled with anguish, echoing his hopelessness and fear.

The darkness and confinement of the room pressed in on him, amplifying his sense of isolation and despair. "LET ME OUT OF HERE!!!!! SOMEBODY HELP ME!!!!! I WANT OUT OF HERE NOW!!!!!! I WILL DO WHATEVER YOU WANT PLEASE HELP ME!!!!!! I WILL TAKE THE THREE DRINKS!!!!!!"

A light suddenly flickered on in the room, casting a spotlight on the floor, three feet in diameter, in what seemed like the middle of the room.

The sudden brightness was blinding after the oppressive darkness.

A whooshing noise echoed through the space, followed by the sound of footsteps on the cold metal floor.

Jesus stepped directly into the spotlight; his figure illuminated starkly against the darkness.

Brian just stared at him, his heart pounding in his chest, a mix of fear and confusion gripping him. Jesus spoke,

"You don't need to make so much noise Brian, no one can hear you from inside this room."

Having given up his initial demeanor, feeling defeated, and terrified Brian calmly asked, "Please unchain me."

Jesus staring down at him a few seconds before responding,

"We are way past having any of your wants and desires fulfilled, you were so close, but now so far."

"What is this place?"

Jesus responding in a snarky tone,

"This place....... which you almost became a permanent resident in.........
is heaven."

Confused, and exasperated Brian asked, "How can this be heaven; I am
chained up to a wall?"

Jesus snidely responded,

"Let's just say you didn't get past the entrance......

The pearly gates was our conversation, and you did not pass my
judgement.

You are in a hell of sorts now."

Confounded needing an answer Brian asked. "How, and Why I have
devoted my life to GOD."

Jesus responded as if he was disgusted with Brian's presence,

"Yet when you met me, Jesus your savior, you did not have faith."

Pleading with Jesus trying to receive some relief from his situation
"Jesus......Please I am in pain just take these chains off my hands.

I will do anything."

Jesus snapped back at Brian immediately,

"It is too late for that after how you acted when you woke up on my
couch,

I can't trust that you will keep the perfection here in heaven."

Thinking about the words Jesus had said Brian responded, "On your
couch.... Since when did Jesus have a couch?..... None of this makes any
sense....."

Brian, frustrated, jumped to his feet and ran towards the man in the
spotlight.

Inches from the light, he was violently yanked back by the chain
attached to his back, falling hard to the floor.

Jesus spoke nonchalantly,

"Really, Brian? Why would you even try... And none of it must make
sense Brian... Nothing ever did.

Humans just felt it should because there was a GOD. What I do know
is you have given me no choice."

A low whirring noise filled the room as the chain attached to Brian's back started retracting into the wall, shortening his leash.

The whirring stopped, replaced by a very low humming noise that gradually grew in tone.

Within seconds, Brian's hands were thrust up above his head by an unknown force,

his feet lifting off the ground moments later.

The chains on his hands hit the metal roof with a loud clang.

He could feel agony in his wrists as he hung from the ceiling the chains around his wrist magnetized to the roof.

Jesus spoke, "Me and this light will be the last thing you ever see.

You have now become one of The Discarded."

Brian could hear the sounds of footsteps leaving the room as Jesus disappeared from the light, the whooshing noise of the door opening and closing followed.

The spotlight that was on Jesus turned off the darkness reflecting Brian's new destiny.

Brian was begging and pleading for Jesus to come back,

"WHAT IS DISCARDED?

Jesus, noooooooooo...........

Please come back............

Jesus, I am sorry..."

Chapter 34 - The War in Heaven

Inside The Command Room

The Command Room was tense; every set of eyes locked on the screen as the live feed streamed in from the boat's camera. The ocean stretched endlessly beyond, but now—now there was something else.

Steve rubbed his eyes as he stood, shaking off remnants of sleep. "I hope you woke me up for good news. Have our agents secured Dresden yet?"

Olivia's fingers moved quickly over her tablet, her expression tight with focus. "Not yet, sir. We couldn't get access to the elevator, and the ventilation system has had a few barriers to get through.

They will have him soon."

Mark turned from his station, urgency creeping into his voice. "Commander, the boats are closing in on the signal."

Steve straightened, immediately shifting into command mode. "Make sure they go in *slow*.

We need to find the edge where we lost the helicopter."

His gaze flicked toward Olivia. "Can we get communication with the captain?"

Olivia nodded. "Setting that up now, Commander."

The large screen flickered, then steadied as the boat's camera feed came into view.

The rolling ocean filled the frame, but as the boat advanced, something else glinted in the distance.

Olivia spoke calmly, efficiently. "You are on with Captain Jerome Rheinhold now Commander."

Steve leaned slightly forward, his voice clear and authoritative.

"Captain Rheinhold, this is Steve Hauser, Commander of *The Throne*. We will be assisting you on this mission from the Command Room."

A slight crackle of static, then Jerome's voice carried through. "Welcome aboard, Commander and Command Room."

Olivia tracked the boat's movement, monitoring the narrowing distance. "Captain Rheinhold, you're approaching the borderline where we lost our helicopter.

Take it *really* slow from here."

Jerome's response came through steady but tinged with curiosity. "I'm not sure if you guys can see this on the cameras, but there's something solid here."

A pause. "It has a *reflective surface*. I can see the image shift as I move my head."

Steve narrowed his eyes at the screen.

The ocean's reflection warped as the boat came closer—a distortion, not just water. "We can see the boat being reflected now that you've gotten so close."

Jerome's voice came through again, quieter this time, thoughtful. "I am *touching* it now."

A dull, *thunk* sound echoed through the speakers as Jerome knocked against the surface. "I think it's *really thick glass*."

Steve exhaled sharply, already moving ahead. "Captain, I need you to get through that barrier."

Jerome's response was careful, calculated. "It may take some time, but we've got the equipment onboard to make it happen."

Pause.

Then—"Can you provide reinforcements for when we gain access? I've got *16 men* here and *four boats*. What are our orders once we do gain access?"

Steve's tone remained firm but deliberate. "When you *gain access*, contact us immediately. I will issue further orders at that time. Reinforcements will be on the way."

Mark immediately got to work dispatching reinforcements.

The air in the Command Room felt heavier now, charged with something between anticipation and unease.

They were right at the edge of something unknown. And soon enough, they would see exactly what was waiting for them on the other side.

...

In the Clearing on the Island

The Lost, a sea of almost 7,000 people armed with a various arsenal of guns and ammunition, stood outside the door to Jesus's room.

Jesus, on top of the hill above the door, spoke with an authoritative and commanding presence.

"The time has come to protect heaven and Jesus. I want everyone to stand in a line side by side, The entire island strong standing together, with their guns pointed at that door. When it opens, we all shoot."

Justin, Amelia, and Kevan stood with their guns as everyone started moving to line up. Kevan asked Justin, "So what was this plan of yours?"

"Executing now."

Justin walked over to the door to speak with Jesus.

"Jesus, Kevan, Amelia, and I would like to sacrifice ourselves for you, and for heaven, we will act as a warning to let everyone know when they will be coming."

Jesus studied him carefully, his expression unreadable. "How do you propose to do that?"

Justin didn't hesitate. "We will guard the inside of your room. When they come, our shots will warn you all."

Jesus considered the offer, his gaze flickering with something close to solemnity. "You would sacrifice yourselves for all of us?"

Justin's breath was steady, his resolve unshaken. "We will sacrifice ourselves if it saves you and the other people here from *whatever* is coming."

A long silence stretched between them. Then—Jesus nodded once, finalizing the decision.

"Then I approve. The three of you will go and guard the room."

And just like that, the plan worked. Justin, Amelia, and Kevan slammed the door shut behind them, their breath coming in sharp bursts as they sprinted down the hallway and into the dimly lit room.

Their eyes darted around space, scanning for the weapons that had been there before.

But now—only one crate remained.

Kevan exhaled sharply, glancing between the others. "So, what now? We get to die first when the agents come?"

Justin shook his head, moving toward the far door, inspecting its edges. "I want to find a way to get through the other door.

See if you can find anything we can use to pry it open."

His voice was urgent, calculated. "There has to be more to this place than just this room. We need to stop the agents before they make it this far—before they step out that door onto the island and get *slaughtered*."

Amelia's gaze lingered on the lone crate.

Her voice was quieter but filled with a different kind of certainty. "This room was *just* filled with crates full of guns, and now there's only *one* left."

Kevan frowned. "Ok, what are you thinking?"

She shifted slightly; eyes fixed on the last crate.

"Someone has been *removing* them.

We know it's not Jesus—he's outside. So that means someone should be coming through that door *soon* to get this last one.

I think we just have to *wait* and be ready."

Justin nodded, adjusting his stance near the door. "Kevan and I will watch the entrance and handle whoever comes through."

His gaze flicked toward Amelia. "You make sure that door *doesn't* close once it's open."

The tension in the room thickened, silence settling over them as they took their positions.

After a few minutes of waiting, the door, which looked like a normal wooden door from inside the room, opened to reveal it was a six-inch-thick metal vault door.

The door swung open, and the four men standing on the other side froze in shock. Their hands shot into the air the moment they saw Justin and Kevan aiming their guns directly at them.

One of the men spoke first, his voice trembling. "Please don't shoot us!"

Justin didn't lower his weapon but kept his tone steady. "We will not shoot you, but we need to get through that door."

The man who seemed to be in charge took a cautious step forward, his expression tense but measured. "Please don't shoot my men."

He hesitated before adding, "My name is Torres. I am the lead security guard here. That is all we are—security."

Justin's gaze narrowed. "Then you must be aware that the island is under attack?"

Torres blinked, genuine confusion flashing across his face. "Island? *What* island? Is that where we are—on *an island*?"

Justin exchanged a glance with Kevan before focusing back on Torres. "Yes."

His voice remained firm. "Do you know if there is a radio somewhere, Torres?"

Torres shook his head slightly. "I've never seen one, but there *might* be. I don't know for sure."

He exhaled, glancing back at his men before continuing. "Most of our time is spent in *that room right behind us* and moving supplies around the facility.

At the end of this hallway, there's an *elevator* that will take you *down*. If there's a radio, it would be *somewhere down there*."

Justin studied him for a moment, then slowly lowered his weapon.

Kevan followed suit. They weren't dealing with fighters—just men caught in something far bigger than they understood. "Torres,"

Justin warned, "There will be an *army of agents* infiltrating this place soon. It would be best for you and your men *not* to fight when they show up."

Torres nodded quickly. "I will keep my men safe. Thank you for the warning."

Pause. "What the *hell* is going on here? What were we *involved* with?"

Justin shook his head. "You'll find out soon enough. We don't have a lot of time. We must get moving."

Torres reached into his pocket and pulled out a security card, holding it out to Justin. "Take my security card. It will get you on the elevator and into some other rooms."

Justin took the card without hesitation.

Time was running out.

They escorted them into the only room in the hallway, which was the security office. It contained a table with four chairs, a desk with a computer, and four beds.

They followed the hall to the elevator. Justin kept watch to make sure Torres and his men did not come out of the room behind them.

The metallic hum of the elevator filled the tight space as it descended, each second stretching into uncertainty.

Justin's voice broke through the tension, firm and clear. "Just so we are all on the same page—our number one priority is finding that radio so I can contact *The Throne* and stop the agents."

Silence followed for a moment before Amelia spoke, her voice tinged with doubt. "I don't believe I'm going to see my family again."

Justin turned to her, his expression unwavering. "I *will* get you back to your family Amelia. And *all* of *The Lost*."

Kevan exhaled sharply, leaning against the elevator wall. "Some of *The Lost*, I don't think can be saved."

His voice carried something heavier now—a truth neither of them had wanted to say aloud. "For some, *Jesus* and life on this island... this *hedonistic heaven* has become their reality."

Justin's grip tightened at his side. "As an agent of *The Throne*, I will do *everything* I can to save them."

Amelia hesitated, glancing at the down arrow which sat in place where the floor number was. "The question that's on my mind—how is this elevator traveling *so far down* on an island?"

Justin's gaze remained steady. "We will find out the truth about this place once we *get out* of here."

He turned toward both of them, his voice low but full of certainty. "I promise—I will *fill you in* on *everything* The Throne has uncovered. What happened to us and *who is responsible*."

Chapter 35 – The Underground

The elevator kept descending for over ten minutes before it stopped. And none of them knew what they would find at the bottom.

There were seconds of tense silence before the elevator doors slid open. When they stepped out, they faced three paths: left, right, and straight. Justin directed them through the door on the left first.

They scanned the security card, and the door opened to reveal a large warehouse storage room. Shelves filled the walls, stocked with all kinds of fresh foods, perishables, alcohol, and condiments.

Wrapped skids were stacked high with various types of food products. The room was vast, with aisles stretching into the distance, creating a maze of provisions.

As they walked and explored further, they found a large, refrigerated room. The cool air hit them as they entered, and the room was filled with shelves of various fresh foods, opened wine bottles, and fresh meats.

The sight and smell of the fresh produce and rich meats were almost overwhelming after the tension and fear they had experienced.

It was an unexpected oasis of plenty in the midst of their mission.

Exiting the refrigerated room, they found another door twenty steps away. After scanning the card, the door opened to a large freezer, the cold biting into their skin.

The freezer was filled with all types of meats and frozen foods, neatly organized and packed.

A man wearing a parka spun around in surprise when the freezer door opened, his eyes wide with shock and fear.

Justin asked raising his gun, "Who are you, and what are you doing here?"

The man surprised by their presence, and the sight of the guns in their hands responded, "I am the chef. My name is Garland. I was just getting some ingredients from the freezer. You are the first people I have seen in nine months. Who are you?"

The unexpected encounter added a new layer of urgency and tension to their mission.

The vast storage rooms, filled with resources, stood in stark contrast to the dark and harrowing journey they were on.

Each discovery amplified the mystery and the stakes of their mission, as they navigated through the hidden depths of the island. Justin asked Garland, "Do you know where there is a radio, Garland?"

Shaking his head he said, "I do not. I only have access to my kitchen and this storage room."

Justin responded, "Can you bring us to your kitchen?"

Garland pointed at a door they could not see, "Yes, it isn't far. There is another door just outside this freezer."

They all exited the freezer. Justin got to the door first and scanned the security card, but the door did not open.

The scanner rejecting him beeping while flashing a red light. Garland held his hand out and said, "Here, use my card."

When they scanned Garland's card, the door slid open. "Where did you get that card?"

Justin pointed up, as he said, "We got it from the security guards who directed us to the elevator."

Taken aback Garland shrugged his shoulders, "I didn't even know there were security guards here."

The kitchen gleamed with stainless-steel counters and appliances, meticulously clean and orderly.

The black and white tile backsplash and floors added a touch of classic elegance to the otherwise industrial setting.

Stainless steel pots and pans hung from hooks above the counters, alongside rows of coffee cups and beer mugs, each item perfectly aligned.

The room was a paradox of utility and comfort.

On the opposite side, past the array of culinary tools, was a cozy living quarter.

A neatly made bed with crisp white sheets stood beside a plush couch facing a flat-screen TV. It was clear that this space served as both a workplace and a sanctuary.

Amidst the shiny surfaces and domestic touches, another door stood on the far side of the room, a silent invitation to the unknown. Justin asked, "Where does that other door lead?"

Garland responded, "That door will take you back to the elevator."

Justin walked over and tried to scan the card the security guard gave him and again it did not work, the card reader beeped with a red-light.

Justin asked, "Can you open it for us?"

Garland opened the door; it opened to reveal they were back at the fork in the road. The door to the right of the elevator was the only one left unexplored. "Do you know what is through the other door, Garland?"

Garland shook his head, "My card doesn't work on that door. I only cooked the food and left it outside the elevator. I never even met the people I was cooking for or who was picking it up."

Justin walked up and scanned the security card on the last door, and it opened.

He turned to Garland and said, "Garland, I will take you up in the elevator to the security room. I want you to stay there with the guards."

Justin took Garland up to the security room and then came back down to meet Kevan and Amelia.

They opened the door to the right of the elevator again and walked into another hallway.

The walls were pristine white, with lights spaced evenly throughout the hallway along the corners where the walls met the ceiling, casting a stark, almost clinical glow.

The hallway had an eerie, sterile silence, amplifying their footsteps as they walked.

There were two doors halfway down the hallway, and another at the end.

They approached the first door on the left wall and tried to scan the card, but it would not open.

The sharp beep of rejection from the card reader sent another wave of urgency through them.

Every second mattered now—the radio was their only chance at stopping the agents before it was too late.

Justin tightened his grip on the security card; his jaw set with determination. "I am going to get this door open. Take the card and see if the other ones will open."

Kevan nodded, taking the card without hesitation. "Will do."

Amelia glanced at the sealed door, concern creeping into her voice. "How are we going to get it open?"

Justin didn't waver. "I don't think we have to worry about making noise anymore."

Then—his voice carried finality as he raised his gun. "I am just going to *shoot* the lock off."

Justin let off a few rounds between the frame and the door handle, and the door popped open with a loud crack. He and Amelia rushed inside, their hearts pounding with the adrenaline of the moment.

The room was stark and minimalistic, containing nothing but a table with a computer, a radio hooked up to it, and a flashlight standing upright on the table.

The faint hum of electronics and the dim glow from the computer screen cast an eerie ambiance over the otherwise empty space.

Justin's eyes lit up with urgency as he spotted the radio, his voice filled with relief. "I *knew* there had to be a radio here!"

Amelia stepped closer, her tone edged with concern. "How will you contact *The Throne*?"

Justin adjusted the radio's frequency, fingers moving swiftly over the dials. "There is always a reserved emergency radio frequency that The Throne monitors. I just need to tune the radio to that frequency."

He fine-tuned the signal, then leaned forward, speaking into the microphone. "Mayday, mayday, calling *The Throne*. Agent #64 checking in."

A beat of static—then a voice crackled through the speakers. "This is *Command Room Technician Olivia Techinni. Good to finally hear from you, Agent #64.*"

Justin exhaled sharply, wasting no time. "Olivia, we need to *stop* the agents. They are walking into a *trap* if they come to the island."

A pause. Then—Olivia's response came firm, but grave. "Negative, #64. We have *lost all communication* with the agents in the tunnels."

Justin clenched his jaw, his pulse quickening. "Do you have an *ETA* for when the agents will be arriving?"

Olivia responded swiftly. "The first waves should be there *soon*."

Justin's tone sharpened. "I *need* to speak to the Commander *right now*."

A brief silence followed. "Give me *one minute*, and I will have him here."

Before anyone could speak further, Kevan rushed into the room, breathless. "I got the other doors open. The card *worked*."

Justin glanced at him quickly. "Did you find anything?"

Kevan shook his head. "I didn't even open the doors; I just scanned the card and got *green lights*." He glanced at the radio. "Were you able to contact *The Throne*?"

Justin nodded. "Yes, I'm waiting for the *Commander*."

The radio crackled once more—then Steve's voice cut through, sharp and authoritative. "*Steve Hauser, Commander of The Throne. #64, come in.*"

Justin gripped the microphone tighter. "Commander, we need to *reassess everything*."

Steve didn't hesitate. "Please *explain*, #64. What is the *status* on the island?"

Justin exhaled slowly, knowing the weight of the next words.

"The status on the island is *war*. All of *The Lost* are armed with automatic weapons. They have been tasked with protecting the man here who calls himself *Jesus*."

Pause. "The Lost will do *whatever it takes* to protect *Jesus* and the island, which they believe is *heaven*. Their minds have been *compromised*."

Another silence—thick with the grim reality of their situation. "If we have *any chance* of saving *The Lost*, we *can't invade* the island. We need to go about it *another way*."

Steve's voice remained steady but carried something heavier now. "We have a *war* going on *off* the island too, but I won't worry you with that."

Then—the critical question. "What do you *think* we should do with *The Lost* on the island, #64?"

Justin tightened his grip, his voice carrying conviction. "I think these people just need to be *told the truth*—one at a time."

Pause. "That they *didn't die...* and that the people they *loved* are *still alive*, waiting for them to come *home*."

Steve was quiet for a moment, processing the approach. Then— "We will *stop* the agents at the perimeter in the water, but we need *you* to *stop* the agents coming through the tunnels."

Justin glanced at Amelia and Kevan, nodding. "I have *Amelia Bernhart* and *Kevan Harrison* here with me.

I have *already revealed* the truth to them, and they are *helping me*."

Steve's command came through sharp, final. "Find those tunnels and *stop those agents, #64.* That is your *number one objective.* Over and out."

Justin's hand rested on the radio for just a second before he pushed himself upright, gaze firm. "Let's move on to the next room."

Kevan and Amelia followed without hesitation. There was *no more time* to waste.

When they exited the radio room, Justin took the flashlight off the table, and they entered the door across the hall.

Chapter 36 - Hell

ustin lead the group inside, everything was pitch black. Justin shined the flashlight ahead, revealing nothing but an endless void.

He frantically searched for a way to turn on the lights and found another card scanner beside the door they entered.

After scanning the card and flashing a green light, the lights in the room flickered on and off. After a two-second delay, the lights directly above their head illuminated, continuing in this pattern with a two second delay each light in the room lit up in a line to reveal a vast, cavernous space that seemed to stretch into infinity.

The room was lined with doors, spaced every ten feet along both sides of the walls as far as they could see. These doors extended upward, with metal walkways and stairs providing access to each level, forming a towering grid of confinement.

There were ten levels in total, creating a labyrinth of cells.

The cold, industrial feel of the metal and the sheer number of doors—1,000 in total—stacked side by side and on top of each other, filled the room with an overwhelming horrible sense of dread and despair.

"What *is* this place? It reminds me of a *prison*."

Justin glanced around, taking in the sterile walls, the reinforced doors, the unsettling silence. "I don't know. Let's see what's inside these rooms, and then we can move on. There are no tunnels here."

Amelia ran her fingers lightly over a scanner panel, then turned back to them. "There's a card scanner here. Bring the security card."

Justin and Kevan approached, Kevan's gaze catching on a small plaque beside the door—engraved with a single name.

Brian Stafford.

Amelia's breath hitched, a surge of recognition flashing across her face. "Brian Stafford..."

Her voice wavered, barely above a whisper. Then—more certain. "I *know* him."

Her pulse quickened as the memories rushed back, piecing themselves together. "Brian went to my church—he was one of *The Lost*. He went missing *over six months ago*."

She turned toward Justin, eyes wide with mounting dread. "What in the *hell* is this place?"

Justin exhaled, gripping the security card tighter as he processed the implications. "I don't think we *want* to know."

His voice was low, heavy. Then—finality in his tone. "But the horrors committed behind these doors *need* to be discovered."

And with that, he scanned the card.

The lock beeped. The door clicked open. And the truth waited just beyond it.

Justin scanned the card, and the door slid open to reveal a pitch-black room with no lights.

As soon as the door opened it released a pungent smell, they heard a slight, constant humming coming from the room.

After a few seconds, a light on the roof started to brighten, casting a spotlight on a three-foot circle of darkness that contained nothing.

Justin and Amelia cautiously stepped into the dark room, and Justin shined the flashlight around, revealing a sight that made Amelia immediately run out and start vomiting uncontrollably on the floor.

Inside the room was a man, completely naked, hanging from the roof by his wrists, which were shackled with large chains connected to shackles around his feet. Attached to his back was a heavy chain that extended and disappeared into the wall behind him.

The sight was grotesque and horrifying.

Six tubes, each containing a different colored fluid, ran from the ceiling and pierced into the man's body intravenously. Two additional tubes entered Brian's body one entering through his anus was filled with a brown fluid the other entered the hole at the end of his penis and was filled with a yellow liquid.

The man didn't flinch or acknowledge their presence.

His eyes were closed, and all the skin on his body sagged off his bones, drooping six inches from its original position due to gravity's pull on it.

The air in the room was suffocating, thick with the scent of decay and the weight of something unspoken.

Amelia wiped her mouth; her stomach still twisted in knots from the shock. "What the *fuck* is that?"

She gasped, her voice trembling between horror and disbelief.

Justin stood over the restrained figure, his expression grim. "It's a man, Amelia. I think this is *Brian Stafford*."

His voice was quieter now, edged with something heavier. "Kevan, come in here and help me."

Kevan stepped through the doorway, immediately recoiling. "Aww, that *smell*."

Amelia shuddered, keeping her distance. "I think that's what made me *puke*."

She hesitated, then forced herself to look at the man suspended before them. "Why would there be a man in here *like this*?"

Justin exhaled sharply. "Fuck."

Kevan straightened. "What's wrong?"

Justin ran a hand over his face, his eyes darting to the other doors lining the hallway. "I'm worried about what's in the *other* rooms."

Amelia swallowed hard. "Is he *alive*?"

Justin stepped closer, watching for any sign of movement. Then—he saw it. A faint, rhythmic motion. "His *heart* is beating."

Kevan exhaled slowly, then his voice dropped as a realization settled over him. "I think I *know* what this place is."

Pause. "When I first talked with *Jesus*, he mentioned people *discarded* from heaven."

Kevan's tone hardened. "He said, 'Having died, the *only* place left is what you would know as *hell*. We call it being *discarded*.'"

Amelia's breathing was shallow, her mind racing. "Jesus mentioned being discarded and *hell* to me too."

Her words were barely above a whisper now. "He said, 'If you *combined every story* about the *tortures and torments* of hell, they *still* wouldn't match up to the *true experience. Being discarded* is the last thing you would *ever* want.'"

Justin's grip tightened at his side. "I would say they've created *quite a hell* here."

His gaze flicked to the tubes connected to Brian's body. "I assume these tubes are feeding him, hydrating him. *Keeping him alive.*"

Amelia let out a broken sound, her body shaking with empathy for the man trapped before her. "Why would anyone *do this*? What's the *point*?"

Kevan inhaled deeply, steadying himself. "How long do you think he's been here?"

Justin glanced at Amelia. "I don't know. Amelia said he went missing *six months ago.*"

A faint, low hum vibrated through the air, sending a chill down Justin's spine. He tilted his head slightly. "Do you *hear* that humming?"

Amelia nodded slowly. "Yeah. What about it?"

Justin studied Brian's restraints, the only things tethering him to the ceiling. "I was wondering how he was *being held up* like this since only the shackles on his wrists touch the roof."

Pause. "I think there's a *strong magnet* holding him up."

Kevan shook his head, glancing around the room. "We have no way to *free* him from the chains. What are you *thinking*?"

Justin took a steady breath. "I'm thinking, if I can *relieve this one man's* suffering, even a little bit—I *want* to."

His voice hardened with resolve. "Check outside the room. See if there's a *switch* or something on the wall."

Kevan didn't hesitate. He slipped out of the doorway, scanning the surrounding panels, his fingers moving quickly over controls. Then—his voice rang out. "I *found* one."

Kevan flipped the switch, and over the course of a minute, the humming in the room grew lower until it stopped completely. As the magnet's power diminished, the man was slowly lowered closer to the floor.

His body moved like jelly as it hit the ground, a sickening thud echoing through the room. They carefully spread him out flat, his limbs limp and lifeless.

The man's eyes and mouth opened, and he started to wail slightly, his cries a pitiful whine of pain. The sound was haunting, filled with months of suffering and torment.

He tried to speak, but his words came out as nothing but moans, his voice weak and broken. The sight and sound of his agony were almost unbearable, a stark reminder of the horrors he had endured.

Justin got up and said, "I am going to contact The Throne again and let them know the situation with The Discarded.

Kevan, take the card and flashlight, check a couple of cells, and confirm if there are people in them.

Then take an estimate count of how many cells there are in total. I want an idea of how many discarded people there could be here.

Then we will go through that last door."

Justin and Amelia left Brian lying on the floor in his cell and walked to the radio room.

Kevan started checking the other rooms.

The radio crackled to life as Justin adjusted the frequency, his voice firm and urgent. "Mayday, mayday, calling *The Throne*. Agent #64 checking in."

A brief pause, then Olivia's voice filtered through the static. "This is *Command Room Technician Olivia Techinni*. What can I do for you, *Agent #64*?"

Justin didn't waste a second. "I need to speak with the *Commander* again."

Olivia responded, "Just give me one second."

The line held for a moment before Steve's voice came through, sharp and direct. "Agent #64, have you found the agents?"

Justin exhaled, glancing at his surroundings. "We haven't even made it that far, but they are *still* in the tunnels."

His tone darkened. "We have *another* problem, and it needs addressing *immediately*. I need to explain something called *The Discarded* to you."

A weighted silence. Then—Steve's response came measured. "*The Discarded*? Okay, what is it?"

Justin tightened his grip on the radio. "The *Discarded* are people who were brought here but *didn't pass* the judgment of *Jesus*. They were discarded to a *man-made hell*—kept alive, naked, in a pitch-black room, *hanging* from a *magnetized roof* by their shackled wrists."

He exhaled sharply before continuing. "They are *intravenously* kept alive. They are *tortured* by the *pain* of gravity pulling at their bodies. Additional torture comes from *sensory deprivation*, and the *experience of purgatory*—a state of nothingness that warps the mind."

Kevan entered the room, urgency in his voice. "I checked *five* cells—three on the first level, two on the second. They were *all occupied*."

Pause. "We have *ten levels*. Fifty cells on the left wall, fifty on the right—per level."

Justin's mind raced, calculating the numbers. "So, *about a thousand* cells in total."

Steve's voice returned, tense. "How many *Discarded* are there?"

Justin took a deep breath. "It was something that *always* bothered me, Commander, when I first got here."

Pause. "The Throne found *over 7,000* cases matching *The Lost* criterion, but when I arrived, I was told there were only *6,375* people here."

His voice hardened. "I always wondered what happened to the *rest* of them."

He tightened his grip on the radio. "They became *Discarded*."

A beat of silence. Then—Justin continued, voice laced with urgency. "I just received confirmation that there is a total of *1,000 identical cells*."

Pause. "We don't have time to check them *all*, but we've *confirmed five more* people in a *Discarded* state."

Steve's response was thoughtful but firm. "Why would they be *keeping* these people alive?"

Justin's jaw tightened. "I don't *know* the answer to that question yet."

Pause. "We found *Brian Stafford* in one of these cells. He had been *hung up like that* for *six months*."

Silence on the line. Then—Steve's voice cut through, decisive. "What do you *suggest*?"

Justin didn't hesitate. "We need to *help* these people. It needs to be done *here* though—they will need *immediate medical attention*."

Pause. "I don't think they will *survive* if we remove the tubes *inside* their bodies but *saving The Discarded* needs to be our *number one priority.*"

Steve's tone was sharper now. "There is a *train* in the tunnels. We *lost contact* with the agents before they *found* it, but it *could* be on your end of the tunnel."

A moment of realization passed between them. As Steve Commanded, "*Commandeer the train* and use it to get *you, Kevan, and Amelia* off the island."

Pause. "You have *completed* your mission, #64. *The Throne* can take care of the *rest*. I will have an *army of medical staff* and equipment *waiting at the other end of the track* to be transported to the island to help *The Discarded.*"

Justin nodded to himself, then spoke. "We've found *others* here under the *employ* of the island—four *security guards* and a *chef.*"

Steve responded swiftly. "Tell the *agents* that arrive, and they will *take care of it.*"

Then—final instructions. "Let them know they are to *wait* and *assist* the medical staff when they arrive, *not* to engage the island."

Pause. "After you do that, *concentrate on using that train* and *getting yourself off* the island."

Justin exhaled, grounding himself. "Affirmative, *Commander.*"

Then—his tone shifted. "Commander, *where are we?*"

Steve's response came with an edge of finality. "After your trackers went *offline*, we discovered a *network of tunnels* underground that connect across the *entire country.*"

Pause. "Used by the *phantom ambulances* to transport *The Lost.*"

A moment of weight passed between them. "In those tunnels, we found *train tracks* that go *right under the ocean*—to an island *2,000 kilometers off* the *eastern seaboard.*"

Justin shook his head slightly. "We *knew* they weren't going to make it *easy* for us, or we would have found them *already.*"

Pause. "I will locate the train and give directives to the agents."

Then—another critical question. "How many *agents* are in the tunnels?"

Steve didn't hesitate. "We had a *massive door* we had to get through. The *first wave* of agents will be *on bikes.*"

Pause. "The *second wave* of agents with *vehicles* will arrive in *2–6 hours.*" Final confirmation. "About *1,000* in total."

Justin pressed his fingers against the radio, taking a steady breath. "I will *contact* you again if needed."

Pause. "We *should* get moving. Over and out."

The three of them exited the radio room and headed towards the last door they had not explored yet.

Chapter 37 - Escape

A sense of urgency propelled them forward. When the door opened, it revealed a large, dimly lit tunnel.

Parked within was a train with four cargo cars attached an imposing sight in the gloomy atmosphere.

Peering into the distant darkness of the tunnel, they could see dim lights—tiny specks indicating the first wave of agents still far off in the distance, steadily advancing towards them.

The tunnel stretched out like a cavernous maw, swallowing any semblance of safety or familiarity.

There were two doors on the wall directly in front of where the train was, each one holding potential answers or additional threats.

The air was thick with anticipation and a faint buzzing echoed ominously from the motor bikes in the tunnels, reminding them of the enormity of their task.

Kevan asked, "Do you think we have time to explore the last two doors?"

Justin thought about it for a second and responded, "We should, but just to be safe, will you stay here and wait, while Amelia and I check it out?"

Nodding his head, and pointing at the train he said, "Yeah, not a problem. I will check out the train while I wait."

Justin and Amelia approached the first door and opened it with the security card.

They took a cautious step inside, and the door closed behind them with a soft click.

Inside was a meticulously organized chemistry lab, rows of counters laden with scientific equipment.

Vacuum chambers, microscopes, glass jars, beakers, flasks, and funnels filled the room, creating an intricate landscape of experimentation.

The air was filled with a mix of chemical scents, some jars and beakers being heated by a Bunsen burner, others cooled by various liquids.

The gentle hum of machinery and the occasional clink of glass added to the room's scientific ambiance.

Amidst this orderly chaos, a man stood behind one of the counters, pouring a liquid into a flask using a funnel.

His concentration was intense, but the sudden intrusion startled him, causing him to pause and look up in surprise.

In the corner of the lab, another man lay on a bed, deep in sleep, oblivious to the disturbance.

The man behind the counter stiffened, his hands frozen mid-task.

His wary eyes flicked from Justin to Amelia, then to the guns strapped across their chests.

The tension in the room thickened as uncertainty pressed against him. The man asked, "Who are you? Why do you have guns?"

Justin took a measured step forward, his voice steady but firm. "Everything here is coming to an end. Your work here is no longer needed. What is your name?"

The man swallowed hard, his posture rigid as he finally spoke. "My name is Francis Latere. I am a chemist."

He hesitated. "What is going on?"

Justin studied him carefully. "How long have you been here?"

Francis frowned, thinking for a moment. "Two and a half years."

Justin glanced at the sleeping figure in the corner. "Can you wake up your friend? He needs to hear this too."

Francis sighed, moving toward the cot. "Yes, though we aren't exactly friends."

He placed a hand on the man's shoulder, shaking him gently. "His name is Ulrich Sanguis."

Ulrich stirred, grumbling incoherently as he slowly sat up. His groggy confusion written on his face he spoke with a very thick accent. "What—What? Why do you disturb my sleep?"

Francis nodded toward Justin. "We have guests."

Ulrich rubbed his eyes before blinking at Justin and Amelia. The man had two different colored eyes one brown, the other slightly green. His gaze locked on their weapons, and a surge of tension passed through him. He spoke with a thick accent, "Eh... Hands up. Don't shoot me."

Justin held his ground. "Ulrich, how long have you been here?"

The older man's brows furrowed as he gave his answer. He kept his hands raised, exposing a large birthmark at the base of his right wrist as he spoke. The mark curved around the joint, snaking along the underside of his forearm—neither random nor decorative, but something older, etched into him before memory. It wasn't just a mark. It was a name he hadn't yet learned to speak.

"Over five years."

Justin exchanged a glance with Amelia, then turned back to the two men. "Have you heard of *The Lost* and *The Throne*?"

Francis leaned against the counter, nodding slowly. "Of course. It was all they talked about on the news before I was brought here."

Ulrich crossed his arms, his expression darkening. "Yes, I've heard of it."

Justin pressed forward. "What were you two working on here?"

Francis exhaled, rubbing his hands together absentmindedly. "It was something called the *Three E's*. We don't know what it was used for; we just did our jobs and made it."

Justin's gaze sharpened. "What does *blood* have to do with the *Three E's*?"

Ulrich straightened slightly, his voice carrying a new weight. "I don't know. I did work on blood that was populated with *MRNA, amino acids, proteins,* and *enzymes.*"

Francis sighed, shaking his head. "Ulrich's and my work were always separate; we just did it in the same lab. The security guard made pickups each week."

He paused. "So, we really don't know what happened *after* the security guards took it from the lab."

His eyes met Justin's, curiosity flickering in his gaze. "You mentioned *The Lost* and *The Throne*, why?"

Justin's voice carried a quiet intensity. "This place is where *The Lost* were being taken, and *The Throne* will be here *very soon*."

Francis paled, the realization hitting him like a wave. His fingers curled into his palms as his voice wavered. "What are we supposed to do?"

Justin's tone was firm but measured. "I recommend *waiting* and telling *the truth*—especially if you had *no idea* what was going on here."

Pause. "There are *other employees* we've found here waiting in the *security office* together. I think you should go there to wait."

Francis glanced at Ulrich before nodding slowly. "Can you show us where it is?"

Justin gestured toward the exit. "You'll need the *security card*. So, follow me."

They stepped out of the lab and into the tunnel where the train stood waiting. As they entered, Justin's gaze landed on Kevan—who stood deep in conversation with another man.

The low hum of their voices echoed off the concrete walls. Kevan turned as they approached, his face tense with urgency. "I found the train conductor. He has *agreed* to operate the train for us. The agents are *getting closer* too—you can *hear them now*."

The conductor straightened, offering a curt nod. "My name is *Alexander Stypence*. I am the *conductor and engineer* of this train. I am *happy* to help."

Justin gave him a firm nod. "Nice to meet you, Alexander, and thank you."

He turned back toward the scientists. "I'm just going to take them to the *security office* so they can *join the others*—I'll be *right back*."

With that, Justin led Francis and Ulrich away, when he returned—there was still one last room left to check. Justin ran over to the last door, swiped the keycard, opened the door, and walked into the room.

He was horrified as he looked around, seeing an infirmary with 48 occupied hospital beds lining the walls.

The people in the beds were all asleep, and the only movement in the room was the rhythmic rise and fall of multiple breathing machines. The mechanical noise filled the air.

Chuuuuuuuuu-Cheeeeeeeeeee

Chuuuuuuuuu-Cheeeeeeeeeee

Chuuuuuuuuu-Cheeeeeeeeeee

Justin navigated around the room, carefully examining the people in the hospital beds.

Their faces were pale, and they looked frail and ghostly under the harsh fluorescent lights.

In the far corner of the room, a doctor was lying on a bed, sleeping.

Justin walked over to the man and stood over him, taking a moment to gather his thoughts before speaking. "Time to wake up."

The doctor blinked up at Justin, his groggy confusion shifting into cautious awareness.

He sat up slowly, rubbing at his face, as though trying to shake off the weight of an uneasy sleep. "Who are you? What are you doing here?"

Justin remained steady, watching him closely. "We have come to get you—and *everyone*—out of here. We don't have much time before *reinforcements arrive*."

He held the doctor's gaze, firm but reassuring. "I need you to come with me."

The doctor's expression darkened as unease settled into his features. "Where are you taking me?"

Justin's voice carried certainty. "To the *security office*."

The doctor exhaled sharply, glancing around the dimly lit room, the weight of the unknown pressing against him. "What is happening? What about my patients?"

Justin didn't hesitate. "Everything that was going on here is *over* now. We will take care of your patients."

He gestured toward the door, ready to move forward. "You will be *free* from this place. Let's go."

Justin guided the doctor out of the infirmary to the security office; his steps brisk and purposeful. After ensuring the doctor was safe, he quickly rushed back to the train, urgency driving his every movement.

He arrived just in time, a mere two minutes before the first agent on a motorbike rolled up.

As the agent dismounted, Justin stopped him, his voice urgent and commanding as he asked, "I am Agent #64. I have been in contact with The Commander. Who is the commanding officer here?"

The agent responded, "There is a commanding officer that should be arriving soon if we wait."

Minute by minute, more agents on bikes arrived, joining the growing group at the train.

The scene became increasingly bustling with activity as the agents dismounted, the tunnel walls lined with their bikes, their faces determined and focused on the task at hand.

Justin took a deliberate step forward, facing the assembled agents and spoke out to the group. "I need to speak with the commanding officer here."

An agent stepped forward from the group, his expression serious. He cleared his throat and spoke, his voice steady and authoritative as he addressed Justin and the assembled team. "Agent Malik Thompson. I have the highest rank here."

Justin met his gaze, nodding once. "I am *Agent #64*. I have spoken with *The Commander*, and the *mission objective has changed*."

He didn't waste time on pleasantries. The situation demanded urgency. "Under *no circumstances* are any agents to leave this underground.

Above ground, on the island, *all The Lost* are waiting—armed with automatic weapons and *orders to kill* anyone who sets foot there."

Malik's jaw tightened slightly, but he didn't react with alarm—just sharp understanding. "What are our orders then?"

Justin exhaled, gripping the security card firmly before speaking. "You are to *wait here*, in the underground.

We have orders to take *the train* to the *other end* of the tracks, where *medical personnel* will load it with *supplies* and equipment."

A pause—just enough for the weight of the moment to settle over them. "This train will transport *everything* back here, and your orders will be to *assist the medical staff* with their objective."

He looked around the gathering, ensuring every agent understood the gravity of their new assignment. "There are *people* here who need *immediate medical attention*."

Malik remained stoic, absorbing the information. Justin continued, "There is a *radio room* where *The Throne* can be contacted if needed, and a *fully stocked storage room* with food, drinks, and alcohol."

The security card gleamed under the dim overhead lights as Justin extended his hand. "You will need *this security card* to open the doors."

Malik took it, his grip firm, his nod slow but resolute. The weight of responsibility was clear in his eyes. "I will convey the orders to the rest of the agents."

His voice remained steady, unwavering.

A flicker of relief crossed Justin's mind, but it was short-lived. "You do what you need to *complete your objective*. We will take over from here."

Malik shifted, glancing toward the tunnel as more agents on bikes approached. "Just let me know where *those people* are, and where *that storage room* is."

A pause—then his next words revealed something deeper. "Our food rations ran out *over twenty-four hours ago*."

His voice lowered just slightly, enough for the exhaustion to creep in. "Everyone is *starving*."

Justin briefed and gave Malik a tour of the underground, showing him where The Discarded were, the employees in the security office, and then brought him to the storage room. Some of the agents followed them.

Alexander got the train started, warmed up, and ready to go. Justin came back through the door into the tunnels.

As they were climbing the steps of the train, Justin said to Kevan and Amelia, "Are you ready to get off this island and back to the real world like I promised you?"

Chapter 38 - How to Save a Lost

About four hours later, the train came to a halt at the other end of the tracks. As the doors opened, they were met by an organized and bustling scene—an army of doctors, nurses, medical equipment, and Throne agents awaited them. The platform was a flurry of activity, with medical personnel preparing and loading medical equipment to tend to The Discarded.

Justin, Kevan, and Amelia stepped off the train and were greeted by Commanding Officers Harris Langdon and Gary Lachlan, who stood at attention, their faces a mix of relief and determination.

Harris stepped forward, his presence commanding as he addressed Justin with precision. "Agent #64, we were sent by *The Commander* to collect you and your companions. We have a vehicle waiting."

Justin inhaled deeply, glancing at Kevan and Amelia before turning back to him. A small, knowing smile crossed his face. "I don't think you need to call me *#64* anymore."

Gary chuckled, shaking his head slightly. "*Congratulations*, Justin, on a *successful* mission. This case got cracked *wide open* as soon as you went missing."

Justin exhaled, shaking off the weight of everything that had led to this moment. "The Commander's plan *worked*. I had *no doubt* it would—once they took one of our agents."

Harris nodded, cutting straight to business. "The *Commander* is waiting for all three of you. They have a plan to rescue *all of The Lost*—ready to execute."

He looked at each of them in turn, his voice carrying urgency. "And having *firsthand knowledge* of the island and the people there, *The Commander* wants to run it by you three."

A brief pause—then, his final words sealed their next steps. "So, let's get moving."

The urgency in Harris's voice propelled them forward.

They quickly loaded into the vehicle, their minds racing with the weight of the mission and the relief of having made it this far. The drive to The Throne building was tense, filled with anticipation.

Arriving at The Throne building, they took the elevator up to The Command Room. As the doors opened, Olivia greeted them with a warm smile and enthusiastic applause. Soon, the entire room joined in, clapping in unison.

Steve walked up to the elevator and spoke. "Congratulations on a successful mission, Justin."

Looking to each of them as he spoke, "We will start with a debrief of you, Amelia, and Kevan. We will share everything that we have found, and you will share with us all the information that was learned on the island."

Justin responded as they exited the elevator, "I couldn't have done it without the help of Amelia and Kevan."

The debrief was intense, revealing the full picture and scope of what The Church of the Odyssey High Priests had accomplished through murder, identity theft, shell companies, and Odyssey Inc Investments. The original 13 High Priests of The Church of the Odyssey were manipulating the world like pawns on a chessboard to achieve their goals.

Justin asked, "What is the plan to rescue The Lost?"

Motioning to Justin Steve said, "In time it will be revealed, for now follow me."

They walked to the center of The Command Room, and met the rest of the group, Steve started speaking "Before we talk about The Lost we need to speak about something that is happening right now everywhere and growing as a problem. It was left out of the debrief for this reason. Olivia, please put on the Jesus video for Justin, Kevan, and Amelia."

They played the Jesus video. With each viewing, its emotional impact intensified, knowing that more lives were being lost by the minute because of it. The weight of the video's consequences hung heavily in the air, amplifying the urgency and gravity of the repercussions this video could cause.

The weight of the situation pressed down on Justin as he leaned against the table, staring at the screen.

"This video would cause *chaos* everywhere if it were ever shown."

Steve's tone was grim as he responded. "This video *was* shown across the *world*, overriding every cable channel. On the internet, it's going *viral* everywhere."

Pause. "The problem *continues to grow*, and a *war* is inevitable. People are taking up arms. The government has had the *military* evacuate civilians not joining the war from cities and neighborhoods, barricading roads, and confining the *Soldiers of Jesus* within the cities."

His voice hardened. "This is happening *everywhere*, and there aren't enough resources to *save* everyone."

Then—the harshest truth yet. "Within the *first hour* of the video being shown, there were *over 100,000 murders*. And with *every hour*, more are murdered and more people *join* the *Soldiers of Jesus*."

He exhaled, shaking his head slightly. "We are *almost certain* that Dresden and *The High Priests* are responsible for this video."

His next words carried unmistakable warning. "The *streets are not safe*. We have been using the *tunnels* to travel when necessary."

Justin's fingers tightened at his side. "What did they plan to *accomplish* with all of this?"

Steve's expression remained unreadable, but his answer came without hesitation. "I think Dresden and *The High Priests* will be the *only ones* who can answer that question."

Pause. "I think it's their way of *flipping the board* in a game when they know they've *lost*."

Justin scoffed under his breath. "A little *childish*, if true."

Then—he straightened, shifting the conversation forward. "What is the plan to *rescue The Lost*?"

Steve didn't miss a beat. "We have *agents* who have *breached* the dome around the island and are *awaiting orders* offshore in the water."

He gestured toward the map on the screen. "The underground is *also* filled with agents, as you know."

Then—the answer to the operation itself. "Our plan is to bring *The Lost* back to the *real world* the same way they were *taken* to the island."

Justin's eyes narrowed. "How do you mean?"

Steve tapped a few keys, pulling up detailed schematics. "Our plan is to *fill the dome* with a *gas* that will *knock out* everyone on the island *without hurting them*."

Pause. "Once *everyone* is *incapacitated*, we will *invade, sedate,* and *evacuate*."

Justin took a breath. "How do we plan to *deal* with their mental health state?"

Steve nodded slightly, already anticipating the question. "Much like *you* told us from your experience *on the island*."

His voice was steady. "They will individually wake up *alone* on a *couch*, with a *mental health professional* there to explain *everything*—that *none* of it was real or true."

Pause. "We will have their *families* there to help if needed. Or—when they are *ready* for that."

Justin weighed the plan in his mind, then gave a slow nod. "I think that might *work*."

Then—the final question. "When do we *execute* the plan?"

Steve glanced at Olivia. "The plan is *ready* to be initiated *now*."

Justin straightened fully. "So, what are we *waiting for*?"

Steve's gaze darkened slightly. "We wanted to wait until after the *debrief*—in case there was *any* additional information *Amelia, Kevan,* or *you* could supply that might *change* or *alter* the plan."

Pause. "Also, we wanted to give the *medical teams* time to *extract The Discarded safely*—which will take *2–3 days*."

His eyes flickered toward Olivia. "Olivia, the moment The Discarded have been evacuated Project Resurrection will commence."

Olivia's fingers moved swiftly across the controls. "I will *execute Phase One* of *Project Resurrection* at that time Commander."

Justin took a breath, grounding himself. "How long will it take to *extract all The Lost* from the island?"

Olivia adjusted the calculations before responding. "Best-case scenario—that should take *a week*."

A notification flashed across the screen, and Doris leaned in slightly. "I just *received confirmation*—the agents have accessed *the 46th floor* and have *detained Dresden*."

Steve exhaled sharply, his voice unwavering. "What about the *other twelve High Priests*?"

Doris hesitated before answering. "They were *all dead* when the agents got into the room—sitting at the *table, masks* on their faces."

Pause. "Dresden was *the only one left*."

Her voice lowered slightly. "They are bringing him *back here now*."

Steve's jaw clenched for a moment. Then, with an exhale, his voice carried something final. "Finally—this is all *coming to an end*."

Chapter 39 - The Interrogations

All the captives discovered in the island's underground were escorted back to The Throne and confined in a holding cell for over a week. Steve was determined to complete the interrogations and uncover every secret to fill in the blanks.

However, he prioritized channeling all their resources towards the safe extraction of the discarded and The Lost, the victims in all of this before commencing the questioning.

The weight of his decisions bore heavily on him, knowing that he yearned to speak with them more than anything else. The unspoken words and unanswered questions gnawed at his conscience, leaving him restless and tormented.

The moment had finally arrived for Steve to uncover the answers he had been seeking for the past six years, ever since the investigation of The Lost began.

Every lead, every clue, had led to this critical juncture, and the anticipation of truth weighed heavily on him, filling him with a mixture of hope and dread.

Deep down, Steve harbored a deep-seated fear of the answers he might receive from everyone involved.

The looming truth held the potential to unravel everything.

The detainees sat nervously in the dimly lit interrogation rooms; anxiety etched across their faces as they awaited Steve and Cynthia's arrival.

Each of them was haunted by their roles in the island's dark secrets and The Lost's suffering, except for Dresden.

Steve and Cynthia entered the room where Chef Garland Streisor was confined. Garland's eyes flickered with a mix of fear and defiance as they approached. The weight of his past actions bore down on him as he fidgeted in his seat.

Steve and Cynthia took their places across the table from him, their expressions unreadable.

Steve leaned forward, breaking the tense silence. "Can you please state your name?"

The man across from him straightened, his expression wary. "My name is *Garland Streisor.*"

Steve nodded, studying him carefully. "Can you tell us how you ended up on the island?"

Garland hesitated before responding, his gaze flickering with distant memories. "I came across a *job listing online.* It sounded *too good to be true*—a *one-year contract* as a *personal chef* at an *undisclosed location,* paying *$1,000,000.*"

His voice lowered slightly. "I applied and was given the job. When the time came for me to start, I received a text with a *time* and an *address* on my phone."

A pause. "I went to the address, but the *next thing I remember* is waking up on *a bed in the kitchen.*"

His jaw tensed. "I *didn't even know* we were underground—*let alone* on an island."

Steve exchanged a glance with Cynthia, who suddenly stiffened as realization washed over her. "He ended up on the island *the same way The Lost did*—minus the phantom ambulance."

Garland exhaled, his voice quieter now. "I *never* saw anyone the *entire* time I was there until your agents showed up."

His fingers tapped against the chair absently as he continued. "When I *woke up* on the bed in the kitchen, there were *instructions* on the table and a *key card.*"

He gestured vaguely. "The instructions said I would be preparing food for *ten people* each day—including myself."

Another pause. "I was free to *cook whatever I wanted* for the ten people, but I was *instructed* to prepare *different meals each day* and *not to repeat* meals within the same week."

His eyes darkened slightly. "I was also instructed to *cook three personal request meals* each day. *Mealtimes* were at *8 AM, 12 PM,* and *5 PM.*"

Steve remained focused. "How did you know what to cook for the *personal request meals?*"

Garland nodded toward an unseen point in his memory. "There was a *small mailbox* on the wall *outside the door* by the elevator. The meal requests would be in the mailbox *every morning.*"

Steve leaned forward. "How did the food *get to the other people?*"

Garland exhaled, shaking his head slightly. "Food was to be *ready* on *wheeled carts* beside the elevator at mealtimes."

Pause. "After I delivered the carts to the elevator, I was *instructed* to go back into the kitchen to *start prepping* the next meals."

His voice tightened as he added. "The *personal request meals* were to be on the *12 PM cart.*"

Steve's gaze sharpened slightly. "So, you *didn't* deliver the food yourself?"

He tilted his head. "Do you know who *did?*"

Garland sighed. "Like I said—I *never* saw anyone else while I was there."

His voice held an edge of frustration. "No one had to *deliver* my meals to me. My meals *never* made it on the cart; they *stayed in the kitchen.*"

Pause. "My *key card* only accessed the *kitchen* and the *two doors* to the storage room."

A flicker of unease passed through his expression. "The storage room was *restocked every week...* but I *never* saw who was *restocking it.*"

Steve took a moment before asking his final question. "Are you a *religious* man, Garland?"

Garland shrugged slightly. "I would say *more spiritual.*"

He hesitated before adding, "I don't *follow* any particular religion."

Steve nodded. "I think that's *all the questions* we have for you *right now.*"

He and Cynthia rose from their chairs, exchanging a silent look of determination. Each step toward the door carried the weight of what they had just learned.

Cynthia exhaled, shaking her head slightly. "So, the chef was *just* that—a *chef*. He was an *unknowing* and *unwilling* participant in the island."

Steve nodded in agreement. "It does *seem* that way."

They moved toward the next room, the air thick with anticipation. "Let's see how many more were just *puppets*."

Cynthia flipped through the names. "Who do we have next?"

Steve scanned the list before answering. "The *train operator*."

His voice carried a certainty that neither of them dared question. "I feel like this one will be *quick*—if it follows the same pattern."

His gaze darkened slightly. "Our train operator *probably never even stepped off* the train."

Steve and Cynthia opened the door and walked into the room where the train operator was waiting. The operator's face was etched with worry, his hands fidgeting nervously on the table.

The weight of the situation hung heavily in the air as Steve and Cynthia settled into their seats, preparing to uncover yet another layer of the island's secrets.

Steve's voice was warm and welcoming as he spoke, "I would like to start by thanking you for operating the train and helping our agents."

Alexander smiled and said, "Not a problem Commander."

Steve's voice was firm but measured. "Can you please state your full name for the record?"

The man across from them straightened slightly, his expression guarded but cooperative. "My name is *Alexander Igor Stypence*."

Steve nodded. "How long have you been operating the train on the island?"

Alexander's gaze flickered with something unreadable. "For *one year* now."

Steve leaned forward. "How did you *end up* on the island as the train operator?"

Alexander exhaled, shifting in his seat. "I came across a *job posting* on the internet for a *two-year contract* as a train operator, paying *$1,000,000*, and I applied."

Steve's expression remained unreadable. "Did you ever *meet* with anyone during the hiring process?"

Alexander shook his head. "No, I didn't even have an *interview*."

He hesitated, recalling the details. "I was *instructed by phone* to go to an address to meet someone for an interview, but I *never* saw anyone there."

A pause. "The next thing I remember is *waking up* on the bed *inside the train*—and that was *over a year ago*."

His voice took on an edge of resignation. "I had access to *maps of the train tracks* and *information* about the train itself. There was a note saying I would receive *instructions* on the computer screen *inside the control station*."

Steve narrowed his eyes slightly. "What did you *do*?"

Alexander let out a dry chuckle. "I started *freaking out* at first."

He rubbed his temples, as if remembering the panic. "I got *off the train* and started *exploring* the area, but I couldn't *open* any doors I found."

A bitter sigh. "I walked down the tunnel for *hours*, looking for an *escape*... but I eventually *gave up* and went back to the train."

He gave them a wry look. "I had been there *ever since*—just making the trips *when the computer told me to*."

Steve exchanged a glance with Cynthia, then asked, "What were you *transporting* to the island on the train?"

Alexander shrugged. "I'm not sure but everything was in the same *Wooden boxes*. I didn't know what was in them."

Steve raised an eyebrow. "You *never* opened the boxes?"

Alexander shook his head. "The boxes were *nailed, latched,* and *locked,* so no, I never got to open them."

Steve tapped a finger against the table thoughtfully. "Were the boxes *heavy*? How did you get them onto the train *by yourself*?"

Alexander nodded. "*Very heavy*."

His voice remained practical. "The boxes had *large handles*, and the train car has a *winch*. I would just *hook* the winch onto the boxes and *pull them onto the train*."

Steve considered the logistics. "How many *trips* up and down the tracks would you make *each day*?"

Alexander hesitated before answering. "At least *once* every day. But some days *two or three times*. Whenever the *computer* gave me *instructions to go*, I went."

Pause. "I *lost track* of the days after a while, so I couldn't tell you."

Cynthia's brow furrowed as she glanced at the documents in front of her. "The *train tracks* are *2,000 km*."

She looked up, skeptical. "How is it *possible* to make *three* trips *in a day*?"

Alexander let out a small, knowing smile. "It is *not* a *normal train*."

Pause. "It *looks* like an *old train*, but it has been *outfitted* with some of the *newest technologies*."

He leaned back slightly. "Being a *straight track* helps too."

Then—the shocking reveal. "I have had this train going *500 km per hour*."

Steve let the number settle before asking his final question. "What about your *meals*? Did you see *who* was delivering them?"

Alexander shook his head. "There was *some food* on the train—because I wasn't always there *for mealtimes*."

He shrugged. "But when I *was* there for mealtimes, I was *usually sleeping* and ate the food *later*."

He Paused. "So, I *never* saw *who brought the food*."

Steve glanced at Cynthia before turning back to Alexander. "I think that's *all the questions* we have for you *right now*."

Alexander straightened slightly, offering a small nod. "I am *glad* to help."

Steve and Cynthia rose from their chairs, exchanging a glance before stepping out of the room, leaving Alexander behind.

The corridor stretched before them, dimly lit, its silence pressing in.

Cynthia's voice broke the quiet, edged with urgency. "Is this even *possible*, Steve? That all the people *underground* on the island were just *doing their part* without even realizing what they were a *part of*?"

Steve exhaled, his gaze distant as he considered her words. "I think everyone was just being used as *pawns* by Dresden."

He shook his head, the weight of the revelation settling over him. "The *other High Priests*, their *churches and communities, Odyssey Inc,* all their *companies—The Lost—everyone involved.*"

His voice carried something final. "It *all* leads back to *Dresden*—especially now that *all* the other High Priests are *dead.*"

Cynthia's expression tightened, her mind already moving ahead. "When will we be *talking* with him?"

Steve straightened, his tone firm. "We will be talking with him *last.*"

Pause. "I want to get *as much information* as I can from the other *interrogations* before talking to *him.*"

He glanced at the notes in his hand, then met Cynthia's gaze. "Next will be *the doctor* we found in the *infirmary—Cooper Blained.*"

His words settled between them, thick with anticipation. "Let's go."

And with that, they moved forward—toward yet another truth waiting to be uncovered.

They walked into the room, their footsteps echoing on the cold floor. As they entered, they saw Cooper Blained sitting, his posture rigid with tension.

Steve and Cynthia took their seats across from him, the air thick with anticipation as they prepared to uncover yet another piece of the intricate puzzle.

The atmosphere in the room was thick with tension as Steve and Cynthia sat across from Cooper, their expressions measured, seeking answers.

Steve's voice carried a mix of authority and quiet understanding. "How are you doing, doctor?"

Cooper exhaled, shifting in his seat. "I would be better if you could remove these handcuffs."

Steve glanced at Cynthia and gave a slight nod. "Cynthia, please take care of that for Cooper."

As she moved to unlock the cuffs, Steve continued, his tone firm but inquisitive. "So, how did you end up on the island?"

Cooper rubbed his wrists, the freedom unfamiliar. "I *woke up* there one day after a shift at the hospital I worked at.

I don't know *how* I got there. I was *locked* in that infirmary for *three years*, tending to the patients."

Steve's eyes darkened slightly. "How did your supplies get *restocked*?"

Cooper shook his head. "*Weekly*, the *security guard* would drop off a crate full of *supplies* to restock the infirmary."

Pause. "*Daily*, he would arrive with a *large, heavy crate* that contained a *new patient*."

Steve straightened slightly. "Did you have *any idea* where the patients were coming from?"

Cooper sighed, shaking his head. "I did *not*. They just kept *coming* every day, *injured*, and I would *fix them up*."

He exhaled, a flicker of frustration crossing his face. "All the patients were *sedated*, so after I *fixed their injuries*, it was just *healing time* for them."

A weight settled over the conversation. "The infirmary was *always* full. Patients arrived in the *crates daily*, and the *longest resident* in the infirmary was *put in the same crate* and picked up by the *security guard* later that day."

Steve folded his hands on the table. "Is there anything else you would like to add?"

Cooper hesitated, then met his gaze. "I had *no idea* these patients were *The Lost*."

His voice was laced with quiet frustration. "I am a doctor, and I was just *trying to help them*."

Steve considered him for a moment, then gave a slow nod. "I think we are *done* here for now Cooper. If we think of any *other questions*, we may be *back* to talk to you again."

With that, Steve and Cynthia stood, their expressions somber as they prepared to move on.

Once out of the room Cynthia let out a thoughtful exhale, shaking her head. "Well, at least we *learned* how *The Lost* were being *healed* before they were *awoken by Jesus* on his couch."

Steve scoffed slightly, shaking his head. "Quite the *miracle*."

Pause. "Next will be *Francis Latere*, one of the *chemists* working in the *underground*. Hopefully he can inform us what The Three E's were."

His voice carried finality. "Let's go."

And with that, they stepped out—toward yet another mystery waiting to be unraveled.

Steve and Cynthia entered the interrogation room where Francis Latere sat. His hands trembled slightly, and beads of sweat formed on his forehead.

They took their seats across from him, the tension palpable. Francis's voice quivered as he finally spoke, breaking the heavy silence.

The interrogation room was quiet except for the steady hum of overhead lights.

Francis sat across from Steve and Cynthia, his posture tense, his expression wary. he asked, shifting uncomfortably. "Are these handcuffs really necessary?"

Steve leaned forward slightly, his gaze steady. "Tell us what you know, and then we can determine their necessity."

Francis exhaled slowly. "What do you want to know?"

"You can start by stating your name and professional title."

"My name is *Francis Latere*. I am a *2nd Class Chemist*."

Steve nodded, jotting something down. "How did you end up on the island, working in the lab underground?"

Francis shook his head; his expression clouded with uncertainty. "I *don't know* how I got there. I was *inquiring about a job* at a company, and the next thing I knew, I *woke up in the lab*."

Steve narrowed his eyes slightly. "Were you and *Ulrich* working together in the lab?"

"Our work was *kept completely separate*."

Steve glanced at Cynthia. "Cynthia, please undo Francis's handcuffs."

She rose from her chair, moving toward Francis with a determined look. Carefully, she undid the cuffs securing him to the steel bar on the table.

The sound of metal clicking open echoed in the room—a momentary relief in the midst of uncertainty. Francis rubbed his wrists, exhaling softly. "Thank you."

Steve wasted no time. "You were working on something called *The Three E's*. Do you know what it is and what it was being used for?"

Francis nodded. "I *know* what it is. I received *chemical blueprints* on how to make it when I arrived and have made the concoction *thousands* of times while I was on the island."

A slight pause. "What it *does* and *is used for*, I do *not* know."

Steve tapped his fingers against the table. "Let's start with *what it is* then."

Francis sighed, his voice taking on a mechanical precision. "The *Three E's* was a mix of chemicals—most *naturally from the body*, some *not*."

Pause. "It contained *hormones, neurotransmitters, vitamins, minerals, supplements, psychedelic* and *sexual dysfunction drugs*. They were all put into a *stable liquid formula*."

Cynthia raised an eyebrow. "That is *quite* the concoction of ingredients."

Steve remained focused. "Where did you get the ingredients for *The Three E's*?"

"Most ingredients were delivered *weekly* to the lab by one of the *security guards*."

His tone was flat—just facts. "Each week, the *same security guard* would drop off what was needed for the next week and tell us *the quota* for the next week."

A pause. "He would also pick up mine and *Ulrich's* completed work for the prior week. Once our work *left* the lab, we *didn't know* what happened to it."

Steve leaned back slightly. "What if I told you *The Three E's* was a *drink* given to *The Lost*? What would the *side effects* be?"

Francis exhaled, shaking his head. "I *don't* see a *natural* way for the *hormones* and *neurotransmitters* to distribute throughout the body if it were *ingested*. They would just be *flushed out* of the system."

His expression darkened. "If they *found* a way to *make that happen*... The amount of *ingredients*—also the *drugs, vitamins, supplements, hormones*—were *extremely large* enough to *kill* someone."

Pause. "So, I *don't* see how that would be *avoided* either."

His voice lowered, thoughtful now. "But—hypothetically—if someone had *high levels* of the *hormones, neurotransmitters, and psychedelic drugs* involved, they would be put into a *euphoric, blissful stupor* of sensation within *every nerve* of their body."

A beat. "And with the enhanced effect of the *sexual dysfunction drugs*, they would *want sex all the time*."

Steve nodded grimly. "That sounds about right."

Pause. "That's what the island *was*—a *sexual heaven* created for *The Lost*. *The Three E's* was used to *make it all seem real* to them." His gaze sharpened. "Did you ever get to *leave the lab*?"

Francis shook his head. "*Never.*"

His tone was bitter now. "Our *food* was delivered *daily* by the same *security guard*."

Pause. "That *security guard* was the only other person I ever saw—until your agent, *Justin Standone*, came through the door of the lab."

Steve absorbed the information before asking, "What was your *relationship* with Ulrich *Sanguis*?"

Francis shrugged slightly. "He was already there when *I* was brought to the island."

His voice was detached. "We spent *all* our time together in the lab, but we were working on *completely different projects* and didn't have much *free time* if we were to make our *quotas* for the weekly deadline."

Pause. "We *ate* at the same time each day but had *little to no conversation* while we ate."

Steve pressed further. "Do you know what *he* was working on?"

Francis shook his head. "I *don't* know what he was doing."

His fingers tapped absently against the table. "Even when the *security guard* came to *restock* us, he gave *me* what I needed and gave *Ulrich* what *he* needed."

His brow furrowed. "I don't even *know* what they gave him to *have an idea* of what he was working on."

Then—a small revelation. "I *know* he was doing *work with blood* though—because he is a *hematologist*."

Steve took in the answer, then leaned back. "I think that will be *all* the questions we have for now."

He watched Francis carefully. "Is there *anything* you would like to *ask us* or add that we may not have covered?"

Francis hesitated, then asked, "What is going to *happen* to all of us?"

His voice dropped slightly. "I was *kidnapped* and *forced* to do this work. I *never* would have *participated* if I *had a choice* or *knew* what I was involved with."

Steve sighed, resting his hands on the table. "To be *honest* with you, Francis—I *don't know* right now."

Pause. "If what you and the others say is *true*, and you are *a part of The Lost*, I will do *everything* in my power to ensure you *don't* receive *punishment*."

A longer pause. "An extensive *investigation* into your *past* will be conducted, and if we *don't* find *anything suspicious*, I am *sure* you won't have *any liability* to the island."

Francis exhaled, his shoulders easing slightly. "Thank you, Commander."

Steve nodded once. "We may have *more questions* for you, Francis—after we talk to *Ulrich*."

Francis offered a faint smile. "No problem."

And with that, the interrogation moved to its next target.

Steve and Cynthia rose from their seats and left the interrogation room, quietly closing the door behind them.

As soon as they were outside, Cynthia's voice carried the sharp edge of frustration as she turned to Steve. "Why would anyone *do* all this, Steve? What could *Dresden* possibly *gain* from what was accomplished on the island?"

Steve exhaled, his expression unreadable. "I *don't* know."

Pause. "But I am starting to think Dresden was just trying to take the *cult community* to the *penultimate level*—because he *could*."

Cynthia shook her head, disbelief clouding her features. "It just *doesn't make any sense*."

Her voice hardened. "How could someone *rip people from their lives*, *brainwash* them, and *enslave* them into believing they *died* and went to *heaven*?"

Steve's lips pressed into a thin line. "It *does* sound like a *horror movie plot*."

His voice lowered slightly. "Every *immoral action* is committed for one of *four reasons*: *money, power, passion,* or *control*—with *millions* of variables falling into all four categories."

Pause. "We *know* Dresden doesn't care about *money*."

His gaze darkened. "I think his motives fall under *power and control*."

Cynthia furrowed her brow. "Is that *true*? That *money, power, passion,* and *control* are responsible for *every crime* and *immoral action*?"

Steve nodded slowly, a flicker of certainty in his expression. "It is within our *human nature*."

Then—a challenge. "But think about it—prove me *wrong*."

His voice carried something firm now. "Find a situation where *those four categories* are *not* responsible for the actions."

Silence stretched between them as Cynthia considered his words. Finally, she spoke. "Should we continue on to *Ulrich Sanguis?*"

Steve straightened, already moving forward. "Let's go."

And with that, they stepped toward *the next piece of the puzzle*. Steve and Cynthia entered the room, their footsteps echoing off the walls. They took their seats across from Ulrich, who had dozed off.

Their sudden entrance startled him awake, causing his handcuff chains to rattle against the steel bar.

The sound drew their eyes to his wrist, where a birthmark—broad and curling—peeked out from beneath the cuff, winding upward and vanishing under his sleeve.

The fluorescent overhead light buzzed softly as Ulrich blinked rapidly, shaking off the remnants of sleep.

His eyes darted nervously between Steve and Cynthia, awareness slowly settling in. "Do we *need* the cuffs? You treat me like *criminal*, in cell, in handcuffs."

Ulrich had a thick accent, but it was only prevalent when he pronounced certain letters. It was evident when words started with W or T, his accent was prevalent. His W's were pronounced with a V, and his T's were pronounced with a Z.

Steve remained firm. "We will keep them on *for now*. If you *answer our questions truthfully*, we will see about taking off the handcuffs."

Ulrich exhaled sharply, his posture stiff. "What questions you have?"

Steve didn't hesitate. "To start, *state your name* and *your professional title.*"

Ulrich adjusted in his seat, his voice measured. "My name is *Ulrich Sanguis.* I am a *1st Class Chemist,* specializing in *Molecular Virology* and *Hematology.*"

Steve nodded slightly. "How long were you *on the island*?"

Ulrich frowned. "Like I told your agent, I have been in the lab for *five years.*"

Steve leaned forward. "How did you *get to the island five years ago*?"

Ulrich's brow furrowed as he rubbed at his temples. Cynthia noticed the green tint in his left eye as he spoke, "My mind has been on nothing but my work for the past five years. My memory of getting there is faded, but I came on the train."

Cynthia crossed her arms. "You *rode* on the *train* five years ago to get to the island?"

Ulrich's lips pressed into a thin line. "Like I said, my memory is *faded.* But *how else* could I have got there?"

Steve remained focused. "What have you been *working on* for the past five years, and *what did it have to do* with *The Three E's*?"

Ulrich shook his head. "I don't know what the Three E's are."

Pause. "I was experimenting with and creating plasma cultures from blood samples, injecting, creating, and coding new MRNA molecules."

Steve's expression hardened. "Where did the *blood* that you worked with *come from*?"

Ulrich exhaled, shaking his head. "I *don't know.*"

Steve's gaze darkened. "There was a *tap* in your lab that *poured fresh human blood.* You *must* know where it was coming from."

Ulrich shrugged. "I made the *plasma* I used from the blood supplied. I just do the work, I don't ask the questions—like you."

Steve inhaled slowly before asking, "What was done with the *finished product*?"

Ulrich shifted in his seat. "It was *given* to the *security guard* each week."

Cynthia tapped her pen against the table, considering his answers. "You said you were *creating and coding.*"

Her gaze sharpened. "What was the *MRNA being coded for* in the plasma cultures?"

Ulrich hesitated, then exhaled. "It was *many things.*"

Steve narrowed his eyes. "Give us *some examples.*"

Ulrich's voice lowered slightly. "One example—I was doing work on *MRNA*, coding it to form *small malignant tumors* within their reproductive organs to achieve *sterility* in both *males* and *females.*"

Cynthia added, "That is probably why none of the women on the island were getting pregnant!"

Steve smiled and then stiffened, absorbing the weight of the statement. "What was this *MRNA being used for*?"

Ulrich lifted his hands slightly before dropping them onto the table. "I *don't know*. I just do my job and give samples to the security guard."

Steve's jaw tightened. "What *else* were you working on?"

Ulrich sighed. "I was also *working with hemoglobin, mass-producing* genetically manipulated hemoglobin."

Steve pressed further. "What were they *genetically modified* to do?"

Ulrich nodded slightly, explaining. "Normal hemoglobin *resides inside our red blood cells* and *transports gases* like *oxygen* and *carbon dioxide* throughout the body."

Pause. "I *modified* the hemoglobin *proteins* to *target* and *carry different things* within the body."

Cynthia tilted her head. "What *other things* did you modify them to carry?"

Ulrich shook his head, his voice flat. "I *don't know* what they were."

He shrugged. "I was *given the instructions* with what needed to be done from the *security guard.*"

Cynthia leaned forward slightly. "When were you *given these instructions* from the security guard?"

Ulrich furrowed his brow. "When I *came to the lab* for the *first time.*"

Cynthia pressed further. "Was it the *same security guard* you were *brought back with*?"

Ulrich nodded quickly. "Yes, yes, it's him. Torres"

Steve leaned back, his gaze unwavering. "Did you have *anything else* you wanted to add, Ulrich?"

Ulrich's lips curled slightly into a humorless smirk. "I only add when I do math."

Steve gave a slow nod before standing. "I think we are *done* here for now. We will be back to ask you *more questions.*"

Pause. "I'm also *sorry* you will have to *keep* the handcuffs on—like a *criminal.*"

Ulrich scoffed, his expression sour. Steve and Cynthia quietly walked out of the room, the door clicking softly behind them. Steve turned to Cynthia, his expression contemplative. "Did you *catch* it?"

Cynthia's lips curled into a faint smirk. "Like the *curveball* it was."

Chapter 40 - The Resurrection of The Lost

Inside of The Command Room

The Command Room was no longer full of people. All the Forensic Accounting Investigators were gone, and the additional desks and workstations had been removed.

The room now contained only six people: Doris, Olivia, Mark, Justin, Kevan, and Amelia. The Command Center buzzed with quiet intensity, every eye fixed on the unfolding events.

The interrogation with Ulrich Sanguis played live on the monitor, the weight of his words settling over the room like a thick fog. The sudden ring of the phone cut through the tension.

Doris answered swiftly, while the others remained glued to the screen. Amelia exhaled sharply, shaking her head. "How can *so many people* be involved, and yet *no one knows anything*?"

Justin leaned back slightly, his voice thoughtful but firm. "The whole operation used *fake identities* and *Odyssey Inc* to funnel money into the *communities* and *churches*."

Pause. "With the churches being *non-profit organizations* that are *tax exempt*, I don't think they were ever *investigated enough* to be found out."

Amelia's brows furrowed as she thought back. "I saw how much *money* ran through my *one church* when I was doing their *accounting*."

Her voice carried an edge of frustration. "I always found it *funny* that they were *100% tax exempt* and *didn't* have to report to *revenue services* like *every other entity* in existence—*person* or *business*."

Kevan scoffed, shaking his head. "I agree. They are *no different* from any *business*."

Justin ran a hand over his face, processing it all. "The *plan* to make the *island* happen was *very intricately done* and *planned.*"

Pause. "I don't doubt their *tax-exempt, sovereign nation,* and *private communities' status* played a *big part* in *hiding the money.*"

Doris hung up the phone, turning toward the room.

Her voice cut through the discussions. "Everyone to *The Command Center.*"

Movement rippled through the group as they gathered, drawn together by the gravity of the moment. An unspoken bond had formed among the key players in the investigation—a shared burden, a collective determination. Anticipation hung thick in the air.

Doris took a breath before speaking. "The *medical mission* to rescue *The Discarded* from the island was *successful.*"

Pause. "Thirteen of *742* of *The Discarded died during transport* and could *not* be helped, but the *remainder* have made it to the *hospital* and are in *intensive care.*"

Justin inhaled deeply, his expression tense. "That is *good* to hear we were able to save so many."

A flicker of hesitation crossed his face. "I don't know what kind of *life* they will be able to have after *what has been done to them.*"

Amelia's voice broke through the moment. "What about the *people on the island*?"

Pause. "Have they been able to *get them*?"

Doris checked her notes before responding. "I just received *confirmation* that the island has been *fully cleared.*"

Her voice carried finality. "*The Lost* have been *rescued,* and *Jesus* is on his way *here* for *questioning.*"

Justin exhaled, pressing his fingers against the table. "I hope *The Lost* can be *acclimated* to being *found*—and having a *resurrection* from the *death* they *thought* they *experienced.*"

Olivia spoke up, her tone measured but assured. "We have a team of the *best mental health experts* from around the *world* putting together a *so-called Resurrection Plan* for *The Lost.*"

Pause. "It's designed to help them *acclimate* and deal with the *trauma* their minds are *bound* to go through."

Doris nodded, adding, "They will be *resurrecting The Lost* starting with the people who have been on the *island the least amount of time.*"

Her tone turned strategic. "They will be *easier* to break than someone who has been on the island for *years.*"

Olivia tapped at the keyboard, pulling up the data. "There will be *live feeds* and *recordings* available, with many experts *studying* the *resurrection interviews.*"

Pause. "They will be conducting the *first 32 resurrections* in the *next thirty minutes.*"

Doris glanced at her screen. "Steve just finished *interrogating Ulrich Sanguis.* He is *on his way* to *The Command Room.*"

Amelia walked closer to Olivia, her tone curious but edged with apprehension. "Can I see the *list of 32 people?*"

Olivia nodded. "Yes, I will *put it up* on the screen."

Her eyes scanned the list, pulse quickening with each name. Every entry was a potential link to her time on the island—people she had known, people she had left behind. Then, abruptly, she stopped. Her breath hitched in her throat.

Number 29. *Simon Cartwright.*

Amelia's fingers trembled slightly as she pointed at the screen. "Can we watch *number 29*—Simon Cartwright's *resurrection?*"

Olivia turned toward her, curiosity flickering in her gaze. "If you would like. Did you *know* him?"

Amelia swallowed hard, nodding. "Yes, he was my *guide* when I *first* got to the island."

A shadow of something unspoken passed over her face. "We had a *special relationship.*"

Her voice dipped lower. "In the end, I *wasn't sure* if I could *trust him* after *Justin* told us the *truth* about the island."

A pause—heavier this time. "And we *left him behind.*"

Doris folded her arms, glancing toward Olivia. "Steve mentioned he wanted to *watch a couple* of the resurrections before he goes back to *finishing the interrogations—the security guards, Jesus,* and finally *Dresden.*"

Olivia's fingers tapped against the console. "I will get *Simon's video feed* ready."

Amelia exhaled, forcing herself to steady. "Thank you, Olivia."

Then—the soft hum of the elevator filled the room. The doors slid open. Steve and Cynthia stepped inside The Command Room, their expressions composed but alert.

Olivia turned toward them, her voice edged with anticipation. "Perfect timing *Commander*—the *Resurrection* is just about to *start*."

Steve nodded, shifting his weight slightly. "Who will be *conducting* the Resurrection?"

Olivia adjusted the screen, pulling up the relevant files. "*Clayton Trilling* will be the psychologist."

Steve's eyes flickered with recognition. "I have *heard* of him?"

Olivia let out a quiet chuckle. "*Almost* everyone has."

Her voice grew more precise, more measured. "*Clayton Trilling* is the *Director General* of the *World Health Organization*."

Pause. "He is one of the *most experienced* and *qualified professionals* in the fields of *brain function, psychology,* and *brain therapy*."

She pulled up a profile. "He has held this *prestigious position* for *several years*."

Her gaze flickered toward Steve. "Prior to his current role, Clayton *trained* some of the *world's leading experts* in these fields."

Pause. "Before joining the *World Health Organization*, he ran his *own practice* and worked as the *lead profiler* for the *National Bureau of Investigation*, handling some of the *most extreme cases*."

Her voice dropped slightly. "He *literally* designed the *Resurrection process* that will be used for *all of The Lost*—after *studying the case* and the *process* they were *brought to the island*."

Then—a final detail. "He was born an *autistic savant and* used his savant *abilities* and *knowledge of the brain* to *heal himself* of his *autism*—something that has *never been done*. He is a true prodigy"

Steve exhaled, shaking his head slightly. "It will be a *privilege* to see him at work."

Olivia turned back to the screen, making a final adjustment. "*Simon Cartwright's Resurrection* is *starting now, Commander*."

And with that—the screen came to life. They turned towards the large screen on the wall, and all the screens in the room changed to show the view inside an all-white room with a couch and a chair sitting five feet apart in the middle of the room.

A table between the couch and the chair held a steaming hot plate of food and a glass full of liquid.

The screens displayed four different perspectives: from the left, the right, above the chair, table, and couch, and from the point of view of the man that was sitting in the chair, wearing a black suit with grey pinstripes, he had his hands resting on his lap twirling his thumbs looking at the man on the couch.

Laying on the couch, Simon Cartwright was asleep. After a few minutes, he awoke, rolled over, and caught the enticing aroma of the food on the table.

Sitting up with his back to the man in the suit, he spoke. "Oh my god, what is that smell?"

Clayton responded in a calm tone, "The food is for you, if you want it. I know you are hungry."

Simon turned around and sat on the couch, looking at the man in the suit.

His eyes glanced around the all-white room with smooth white walls and his mind flashed back to when he awoke in Jesus's room.

The surreal similar feelings, the aromatic food, and the all too familiar drink beside it, starting to feel a rise of panic, and confusion within him he asked, "What is going on here? Where is Jesus?"

Clayton stopped twirling his thumbs, shifting slightly as he made a motion with his hands. His voice was measured, gentle yet firm. "Just stay *calm*, Simon. You have been *lied to* for a *long time*, and I am here to *reveal the truth* of what has happened to you."

Simon's posture stiffened, his eyes narrowing. The island had warped his perception of truth—shattering any certainty of what was *real* or *fiction*. His response carried the weight of that instability. "And *what* is the truth?"

Clayton remained composed. "I *guarantee* you—before you leave this room, I will answer *all* your questions."

He folded his hands in front of him. "My name is *Clayton Trilling*, and I am here to *help guide* you through this *difficult time*."

His gaze flickered toward the plate on the table. "Let's start by having you *eat some food*. And when you're *done*, I will answer *all of your questions*—I will tell you *exactly* what has happened to you."

Simon hesitated, curiosity flickering in his expression. "Where *am* I?"

Clayton's tone remained steady. "I will be able to answer *all* your questions—*after* you eat."

He gestured slightly. "You haven't eaten *solid food* in *almost two weeks*. I *know* you are hungry."

Simon blinked. "*What*? *Why*?"

Clayton didn't waver. "Eat your food, we will talk after and I will tell you a story."

Simon hesitated for only a moment before picking up the utensils. He took the first bite cautiously, then another—each one savored as if it were the *best meal* he had ever had.

Clayton sat back, watching. Calm. Patient. Within minutes, Simon had cleared the plate. He drained the drink in front of him, then leaned back on the couch, eyes sharp, posture tense.

He stared intently at Clayton. "The *first* thing I want to know is... *Where is,* and *what happened* to Jesus?"

Clayton tilted his head slightly. "Why do you *care* about what has happened to this *Jesus person*?"

His voice carried a deliberate pause. "Don't you *care* about yourself? Don't you want to *know* what has happened to *you*? Jesus is *not* the star of your story."

Simon's jaw tightened. "We were *supposed* to *protect Jesus*—and keep the *intruders* out of heaven."

Clayton studied him carefully. "What if I told you that the *last few months* of your life were *not real* in the way you have *perceived* it?"

Simon's breath hitched—then his anger flared. His voice was sharp, laced with frustration. "HOW DO YOU HAVE *ANY IDEA* WHAT I PERCEIVED—WHAT I *EXPERIENCED*—WHAT IS *REAL*?"

Clayton didn't react to the outburst. Instead, his voice remained unwavering—calm, reassuring, edged with empathy. "I have *no idea* what you experienced Simon—by *any* means."

His words held weight but not force. "I *do* know that the *heaven* you perceived was *not real*."

A pause. "I would *love* if you could *prove me wrong*. Let's *talk* about it."

Simon exhaled sharply. "You still haven't answered my *question* about Jesus."

Clayton nodded slightly. "In time, you will know the *destiny* of Jesus."

Then—the shift in tone. "How did you *get* to heaven?"

Simon straightened, his response carrying conviction. "Jesus brought his *chosen people* there."

His voice deepened with certainty. "After I *died*, I was brought there—by *Jesus*."

Clayton's brow lifted slightly in surprise. "After you *died*?"

Pause. "You look *alive* to me."

Simon's breathing slowed. "I was brought to *heaven* after *dying* in a car crash."

Clayton kept his gaze steady. "Who *told* you that you *died*?"

Simon frowned. "Jesus did. But I was *in heaven*. I *saw* it. I *experienced* it."

His voice tightened. "How else could I have *gotten* to heaven?"

Clayton exhaled, shifting slightly forward. His tone softened—but held firm authority, like a father revealing a truth that would *shatter* his child's world. "The *death* you experienced was a *lie*."

Pause. "And the *heaven* you perceived... was an *illusion*."

Simon's body tensed. His arms shot upward, frustration boiling over. "HOW IS THAT *POSSIBLE*?"

Clayton didn't raise his voice. He simply held Simon's gaze. "Let's *keep* the conversation to a *talking tone*, Simon."

Pause. "There is *no reason* to *yell*."

His voice remained measured. "How it was *accomplished* is *still under investigation*, but in time, we will get *all* the answers."

Simon inhaled deeply, fighting to steady himself. "What *can* you tell me?"

Clayton offered a nod. "Now *there* is a question that will *advance* our conversation."

His voice took on the tone of strategy. "Do you know what *The Lost* and *The Throne* are?"

Simon exhaled slowly. "Of *course* I do."

Pause. "It was *all over the news* about those *missing people*."

Clayton's gaze sharpened, studying him. "What if I *told* you that you were *one of The Lost*?"

Simon's breath faltered. His shoulders sank. His eyes fell to the floor. *It made sense.* The island. The deception. The Lost. His voice was quiet now. "I think I would need a *little more information*."

Clayton remained composed. "Have you heard of the term *Phantom Ambulance*?"

Simon shook his head. "I have not. What is it?"

Clayton's voice carried weight. "There was a *network* of *fake ambulances* working across the country to make *The Lost disappear*—after their *accident* or *injury*."

Simon's breathing hitched. His mind—unraveling. His voice wavered. "So, I was *kidnapped*?"

Clayton nodded. "Yes—*sedated* and taken to the *island* to *meet Jesus*."

A pause—deliberate. "Much like *now*, you were sedated by *The Throne* and *rescued* from the *island*."

His voice was firm. "And here we are now—trying to *resurrect* you, in a *sense*, from the *death* you thought you *experienced*."

Simon swallowed hard, his voice barely above a whisper. "So, I *never* died... and the island *wasn't* heaven?"

Clayton's response was simple. "The island was *just* an island—with a man named *Jesus* on it."

Simon's gaze flickered between Clayton and the door, the weight of everything pressing against his mind. The truth unraveled before him, and yet, its edges still felt raw—uncertain.

He exhaled, forcing himself to steady. "Do you know what happened to *Amelia Earhart*?"

Clayton offered a small smile. "I think she *went missing* flying over the *Pacific Ocean* almost *one hundred years ago*."

Simon chuckled, shaking his head at the memory of Amelia's stupid joke about her name. "Sorry, *not* Earhart. *Amelia Bernhart*. She was *on the island*."

Clayton gave a nod, leaning back slightly. "She is *safe*. She is *here*, if you would like to *see* her when we are *done talking*."

Simon's breath hitched slightly. "She is *here*?"

Clayton's voice carried certainty. "Yes. *The Throne* has *rescued everyone* from the island."

Simon swallowed, processing that revelation. His next words came with a quiet urgency. "I want to *see Amelia*. And if I *never died*, can I see my *wife, Cheryl*?"

Clayton's expression softened. "You *can* Simon. They are *both* here."

He gestured slightly toward the room's exit. "I just want to make sure you *don't* have any *more questions* before you *walk out that door*."

Simon hesitated, thoughts swirling. Then—he considered something familiar. A question he once posed to Jesus. His voice was quieter now, laced with reflection. "Can we *meet again* like this and *talk* if I do have *more questions*?"

Clayton offered a reassuring nod. "Of *course*, Simon. *Anytime* you need to or *want* to talk—I am *here* for you."

He reached into the inside pocket of his suit jacket, pulling out a business card. With deliberate movement, he placed it on the table between them. "What has happened to you, Simon, can have *extreme effects* on your *mental health*."

His voice carried quiet authority. "You can *call me anytime*, Simon. *Don't hesitate*. I am *here* to help you *assimilate back* to your life."

Simon exhaled, the tension in his shoulders easing slightly. "Thank you, Clayton."

Then, with certainty, he spoke again. "Right now, I think I would like to *see my wife*."

Clayton nodded. "I *thank you* also Simon—for making my job *here easy*."

A pause. "Some of *The Lost* have been on the island for *over twenty years*."

His gaze darkened slightly. "I don't know if I will be able to *help* them."

Simon's tone sharpened slightly, a lingering question still burning in the back of his mind. "Who or *what* was responsible for *all of this?*"

Clayton exhaled, offering a measured response. "Like I said, the *investigation* is *still ongoing.*"

Pause. "All *The Lost* will receive a *debrief package* with *all* the information once the investigation is *finalized.*"

Simon gave a slow nod, his expression steadier now. "I think I am *ready* to see my wife—and *go back* to living my life."

Clayton gestured toward the door. "*Walk out* whenever you are *ready.*"

A quiet understanding settled between them. "There will be *someone* to guide you to your wife on the *other side* of the door."

Simon stood up from the couch and walked out of the door to meet the guide waiting for him. Clayton remained seated in the chair, awaiting his next resurrection to come through the door.

The atmosphere in The Command Room was charged with anticipation as the group processed what they had just witnessed.

Conversations murmured across the space, reflections unfolding in quiet contemplation. Justin leaned forward slightly, arms crossed, his voice steady. "Well, that went *well.*"

Amelia exhaled, shaking her head. "I feel *even worse* now for not *trusting* him."

Steve glanced at Olivia, hopeful yet measured. "I hope the rest of *The Resurrections* go as *easy* as that did."

Olivia scanned the monitors, her focus unwavering. "I am seeing *good results* so far."

Pause. "Including *Simon Cartwright, 22* of the first *32* resurrections have already been *completed*—and are *with their families.*"

Doris folded her arms, her voice carrying a weight of caution. "We are about to see how *difficult* these resurrections *can get.*"

Steve turned toward her, brows furrowed. "What do you *mean?*"

Doris glanced at her notes, then met his gaze. "They wanted to see how the *resurrections* will go with *long-term* residents of the island."

Her tone sharpened. "So, *Clayton* will next be attempting to *resurrect* the *man who started our investigation.*"

Steve straightened, momentarily taken aback by her words. The weight of the statement settled over him, leaving him speechless for a few beats before he finally spoke. "*Really?*"

Doris nodded. "I got a call, and they asked me to pick *one* of *The Lost* who had been on the island for *more than five years* for *preliminary observations.*"

She exhaled, considering the enormity of the task ahead. "I figured there will be *over thousands* of these *Resurrections*, and we will *not* be able to see or watch them all."

Pause. "So, who better than the *man who started this investigation* and *formed The Throne?*"

Cynthia's voice broke through, carrying an undeniable poetry to the moment. "It's *almost poetic.*"

She glanced at the others, realization settling in. "We finish where we started—as *The Throne.*"

Chapter 41 – Leonard Chance

teve and the others stared at the screen waiting for the next Resurrection to start. Olivia checked the monitors once more before speaking. "They are bringing *Leonard Chance* into the room *now*. He should *wake up* in a few minutes."

They all turned towards the screens showing the different camera angles inside the resurrection room as two men carried Leonard Chance into the room and placed him on the couch across from Clayton Trilling, who sat watching the two men as they walked out of the room.

Then he focused his attention on Leonard Chance, asleep on the couch. Leonard stirred on the couch, the familiar scent of food washing over him as consciousness settled in.

The sensation was immediate—comforting, recognizable. It felt like *home*. It felt like *Jesus*. His voice cracked through the quiet. "JESUS!"

Clayton's response was calm but firm. "Jesus is *not here*."

Leonard rolled over instantly, sitting upright, his breath shallow as he scanned the room. His pulse quickened—white walls, structured stillness, control.

It was all too familiar, yet all *wrong*. His panic took hold, words spilling from his mouth faster than his mind could process them. "Where is *Jesus*? What *is* this? Where *am* I? *Who are you?*"

Clayton sat back, unshaken by the barrage. His tone was reassuring but measured. "Just *relax*, Leonard. One question at a time."

A pause. "My name is *Clayton Trilling*. I am here to *help* you, Leonard."

His gaze didn't falter. "You have been *lied to* for a *long time*—and I have been chosen to *reveal the truth* to you."

Another pause. "You can *trust* me, Leonard."

Leonard scoffed, shaking his head, his voice laced with condescension. "The *truth... Trust you?*"

He leaned back slightly. "I *don't even know* who you *are.*"

Clayton didn't miss a beat. "You may *not* know who I am."

His voice remained steady. "But you can be *assured*—I am being paid a *lot* of money to *help you.*"

A subtle smirk. "So, that is what I am going to do."

Leonard's frustration deepened. "*Help* me?"

His fists clenched slightly before he exhaled sharply. "I just want to *know* what is *going on* here."

His gaze flickered, searching for some fragment of familiarity. "I was in *heaven* with *Jesus.* Now I don't even know *where* I am..."

Pause. "But I *know* I am *not* in heaven *anymore.*"

Clayton nodded, his expression unchanged. "You are *correct.*"

His voice softened just slightly. "This is *not* heaven."

He gestured toward the food. "Take your time and *eat* what's on the *table.* I *know* you are *hungry.*"

Leonard scoffed, brushing off Clayton's words. His tone carried defiance. "You *know* I'm hungry?"

A pause, a sharp inhale. "What *else* do you *know* about me?"

Without hesitation, Leonard picked up the utensils and began eating. Clayton watched, patient, allowing silence to stretch before he spoke again.

"I *know* on *August 21st, 2029, at 2:12 PM*—over *six years ago*—you were *stabbed twice* for *no reason* while walking down the sidewalk."

Leonard stiffened slightly, but Clayton continued. "You were stabbed on the *upper left side* of your *abdomen*—and your *left shoulder*—by someone wearing a *black hooded sweatshirt* and *black pants.*"

A pause—intentional. "You managed to *call 911* and were picked up by what is called a *phantom ambulance.*"

The spoon in Leonard's hand stilled, hovering midair. Clayton continued, unwavering. "You *disappeared.* You went *missing*—never to be seen *again* until *now.*"

Leonard's hand trembled slightly, the spoon still suspended between his plate and his mouth. His voice was quieter now. "I *never* went missing."

He swallowed hard, his mind clashing violently against the truth that threatened to break through. "I *died* when I was *stabbed*."

Clayton didn't argue, didn't push. Instead, his response came measured—controlled. "Finish *eating*—and we will *talk some more*."

And for the first time—Leonard *hesitated*. A little more intrigued by what Clayton had to say Leonard started to eat the food on the plate a little bit quicker. Leonard finished the food on his plate, picked up the glass, drank it down in three swift gulps, and slammed it onto the table with a satisfying exhale. "That was *really* good."

Clayton folded his hands, his expression calm, unwavering. "So where would you like to *start*?"

He gestured slightly. "You can ask me *anything*, Leonard—one question at a time."

A pause. "You can *trust* that I will be *honest* with you."

Leonard wasted no time. "Where is *Jesus*?"

Clayton met his gaze. "Jesus is in the *custody* of *The Throne*."

Leonard shook his head, his confusion mounting. "What is *The Throne*?"

"The Throne is an *organization* that was formed to *find* the people who were taken to the *island*."

Leonard's expression hardened, frustration simmering beneath the surface. His voice rose. "WE WEREN'T *TAKEN* TO THE ISLAND."

He pressed his fingers against the table, leaning forward. "That is *not* how it works. We *died*."

Pause. "Why is *Jesus* in custody?"

Clayton remained composed. "You're *right*, Leonard. You weren't *taken* to the island."

His voice held firm clarity. "No one was. Everyone was *kidnapped*—the same way *you* were."

Leonard scoffed, shaking his head as Clayton's narrative clashed violently with his own memories. "I WASN'T *KIDNAPPED*!"

His fists clenched at his sides. "I *died* and went to *heaven*—along with *all* the other people who were there."

His voice sharpened and raised in volume. "WHY IS *JESUS* IN CUSTODY?"

Clayton's voice dropped slightly, quiet but firm. "You never *died*, Leonard. You were *kidnapped*."

Leonard shot upward, barely containing his frustration. "I CAN'T *BELIEVE* THAT!"

His voice cracked with disbelief. "My *whole* life I *followed GOD* and His *only son Jesus*—and then I was *stabbed twice* and woke up in *heaven* with *Jesus*."

His chest rose and fell rapidly as he struggled against the unraveling reality. "HOW DO YOU *EXPLAIN* THAT?"

Clayton didn't flinch. Instead, his voice carried quiet empathy. "That is what *The Throne* has been trying to *figure out* for over *six years*."

Leonard threw his hands up in exasperation, dismissing Clayton's words. His voice dripped with frustration. "Again, *with* this *Throne*."

He scoffed. "Am I supposed to be *happy* with *being here*—and *not* in heaven, where I *was*?"

Clayton studied him carefully. "Why *wouldn't* you be happy *being here*, Leonard?"

Leonard exhaled sharply, shaking his head in disbelief. "In *heaven*, I was *surrounded* by women who *wanted* to have sex *all the time*."

Pause. "Nothing was *off limits*. It was every man's *ultimate fantasy*."

He narrowed his eyes at Clayton. "Wouldn't *that* make *you* happy?"

Clayton's voice remained even, resolute. "I am happy with my *wife*—and having a *committed monogamous relationship*."

Leonard scoffed. "I *thought* you said I could *trust* you to be *honest*."

His tone was laced with condescension. "Any man would *give up* their life to live the life I had in *heaven*."

Pause. "We had *unlimited food, water, drugs, alcohol,* and *sex*. We *didn't* have to *work*. No *stress*. No *worries*. No *cares*."

His voice darkened. "I would have *sex twenty times a day* in heaven—only stopping to *eat*."

Clayton inhaled deeply, steadying his words. "This *heaven* was *not real*, Leonard."

A pause. "Think about this—if I were *telling you the truth*, and you *didn't die*, and *heaven wasn't real* as an *afterlife*..."

His tone turned deliberate. "What would your *wife* and *little daughter* think *of that*?"

The words hit like an unexpected blow. Leonard's smirk faded. His shoulders stiffened. His response was quieter now—uncertain. "I *haven't thought* of my wife in *years*."

His breath shallowed. "She left my memory *long ago*."

A moment passed before he added, "She was *pregnant* when I *died*."

His voice cracked. "Wait, she had the *baby*?"

Clayton softened just slightly. "Can you *imagine* what it was like for your *wife*—for the last *six years*—thinking you were *dead* and *raising* your *little daughter* all by herself?"

Leonard's jaw tightened. His mind clawed desperately for the truth—*his* truth. His voice sharpened. "I *was* dead."

Clayton didn't hesitate. "You *didn't* die Leonard."

His voice carried certainty. "How do you *explain me*, this *room*, and our *conversation*?"

Pause. "How did you *end up here* when you were in *heaven*—in an *afterlife*?"

Leonard exhaled sharply. "Jesus *said* there were *people* coming to heaven who *wanted to destroy it*."

He shook his head. "So, I *don't even have* a *good idea* at where I am now and what this could be."

Clayton nodded slightly. "The people you *speak of* were *The Throne*."

Pause. "They *found the island*—and *rescued* all of *The Lost* that were *kidnapped* and *taken there*."

A beat. "They *did destroy* it—*in a sense*—as the *heaven* it was."

His tone turned heavier. "Did you know that *you* are the *reason* The Throne was *started*?"

Leonard's mind reeled. He shook his head slowly. "I have only *heard* of The Throne *from you*—so *no*, I didn't know *that*."

Clayton folded his hands. "Your *missing person investigation* started *it all*."

Pause. "The Throne was started by a man named *Steve Hauser*—who is now *The Commander* of *The Throne*."

His voice remained steady. "He has been running the *largest missing persons investigation* for the *last six years*."

Another pause. "He found *your* missing persons case had *a lot in common* with *thousands* of others."

A weight settled over the room. Leonard barely managed to speak. "I *don't feel so good*."

Clayton nodded, unfazed. "It is probably your *withdrawals* from *The Three E's*."

He exhaled and continued, "Over the last six years, you have drunk The Three E's every 90 days, about 24 times. The Three E's were riddled with hormones, neurotransmitters, vitamins, minerals, supplements, psychedelic, and sexual dysfunction drugs.

Your body will take a while to adjust back to its normal levels, which is what is causing the withdrawals.

They were using The Three E's on the island to keep you in a euphoric, sexually aroused state, with high hormone levels, and to cause sterility within the men and women.

This is why you were having sex twenty times a day instead of trying to understand the situation you were truly in. It is also why the women never got pregnant on the island."

Leonard clenched his fists, his breath uneven as the weight of realization settled over him. His voice carried quiet fury, edged with the need for justice. "Who *did this* to us?"

Clayton remained composed, his voice steady. "The *investigation* is still *underway*, but I will tell you *what I can*."

He met Leonard's gaze. "The *Church of The Messianic Christ*—the *community* you were a part of—was *part* of a *network* of churches and communities that were being *used*."

Pause. "Everyone on the island was *handpicked* to be *taken*—from within that *network*."

Leonard exhaled sharply, frustration lingering in his voice. "How has it taken *six years* to *find me*—if people were *looking* the entire time?"

Clayton folded his hands. "There is a *network of underground tunnels* that were being used—*just recently discovered*."

Pause. "They connected *all over the country*—and even *utilized* a *shallow section* of the ocean."

Leonard's brows furrowed as Clayton continued. "The tunnel *extended 2,000 km under the ocean*—all the way to the *underground* of the island."

Leonard shook his head slightly, muttering. "Holy *fuck*."

Clayton exhaled, his voice measured. "You will receive a *full debrief* with *all the details* once the investigation is *finished*."

Leonard took a slow breath. "So—where *am* I *now*?"

Clayton's tone softened. "You are *alive* and *well*, Leonard."

Pause. "And you are *back home*."

He leaned forward slightly. "I *know* you said you haven't *thought* of your wife and family."

His voice carried quiet certainty. "Does anything I've said *change that*?"

Leonard hesitated, emotion flickering in his expression. Clayton continued, carefully. "Your *wife* and your *six-year-old daughter* are *here*—and they *would like to see you*."

Leonard's breath caught in his throat. "They're *here*?"

Clayton nodded. "Your *family* is *waiting* for us to *finish our conversation*."

A pause—then, with emphasis: "What you have gone through, Leonard, has been *very traumatic* to your mind. You may *not* realize it *yet*."

His voice remained steady. "But I am *here*—for you—whenever and *wherever* you need me."

Clayton reached into his jacket pocket and placed a business card on the table. "Anytime you *feel* you want to or *need* to talk—I want you to *call me*, with *no hesitation*."

Leonard picked up the card, turning it between his fingers. His voice was quiet now—uncertain but sincere. "I will."

He swallowed. "Can I *see* my *daughter* and my *wife*?"

Clayton gave a reassuring nod. "You can *leave* this room *whenever* you are *ready*, Leonard."

A pause, then a softer tone. "Did you have *any other questions* for me before you do?"

Leonard hesitated before shaking his head. "I *don't* have any questions."

A beat of silence, then—"I just think I need some *time*."

His voice cracked slightly. "I'm *not ready* yet."

Pause. "Can we just *sit* here *quietly* for a bit—so I can *gather my thoughts*?"

Clayton offered a reassuring nod. "We can do *whatever* you want Leonard."

The room fell into silence, thick with unspoken thoughts.

Clayton twirled his thumbs, mirroring a familiar gesture.

Leonard's head drooped, his eyes fixed on his lap, his hands held together.

Then—a single tear rolled down his face, landing onto his hands. Clayton watched quietly before speaking. "What is *troubling* you, Leonard?"

Leonard looked up, his eyes now a river of silent grief. His voice cracked, breaking through the quiet. "WHAT IF THEY *DON'T WANT ME*—OR *LOVE ME ANYMORE*?"

Pause. "I AM *NOT* THE SAME PERSON I WAS."

His breath hitched. "HOW CAN I WALK *BACK INTO THEIR LIVES*—AS IF NOTHING *HAPPENED*?"

Clayton didn't hesitate. "You do *not* have to do *anything* you do *not want to*, Leonard."

His voice carried quiet reassurance. "If it *helps*—I spoke to your wife and daughter *yesterday*."

Pause. "Your wife *never remarried*—and they are *very excited* to *see you*."

Another pause. "Your *daughter* is *very excited* to meet her *daddy*—from all the *pictures* and *stories* her mother has shown and told her."

Leonard swallowed hard, his voice barely audible. "It *does* help. Thank you."

His hands shook slightly. "I wish I could have been *there*—for the *first six years* of my daughter's life."

Clayton exhaled, his voice weighted with understanding. "The situation is *difficult* for *everyone involved*, Leonard."

He leaned forward slightly. "We *can't reverse* what has happened. But we *can* make the *best* of the *bad situation* we were *put in*."

Pause. "I will prescribe you *some medication* that will help with that."

Leonard wiped his face, his breath slowing. "I feel *violated*."

Pause. "I had my *freedom and family stripped from me*, my *brain washed*—and *enslaved* to contribute to someone else's *objectives*."

Clayton nodded. "That is *all true*, Leonard—and you should feel *that way*."

His tone turned heavier. "But—realize—you are *not alone* in this *feeling*."

He gestured toward the door. "Everyone from the *island* will *share* those *same feelings* that you do."

Pause. "The *entire country* has been *violated*—and *very scared* that they could be the *next person* to *go missing*."

His voice dropped slightly. "It is *all over now* Leonard."

A final reassurance. "We can *all* get back to *normal*."

Leonard scoffed under his breath. "*Normal?*"

Pause. "More like *stepping into a life* I *never lived*."

His voice cracked. "My *normalcy* has *never* been *having a daughter*—or being a *father*."

Clayton softened. "Leonard—you will be an *amazing husband* to your wife *Cecilia*, and *father* to your daughter *Virginia*."

Pause. "I have *no doubt* in that—and you can *call me anytime* you need *help* or to *talk*."

Leonard exhaled sharply. "I *think* I am *ready* now."

Clayton gestured toward the door. "All you have to do—*is walk out*."

A final breath. Leonard stood up, straightened his shoulders, and inhaled deeply. His voice steadied. "I'm *ready*."

And with that—he stepped forward *toward the rest of his life*.

Leonard turned and walked towards the door, stepped through it, and it closed behind him.

The Command Room buzzed with quiet anticipation, the team gathered closely around The Command Center. The weight of Leonard Chance's resurrection lingered in the air, heavy with significance.

Steve exhaled, shaking his head in mild disbelief. "He *did* it. *Six years* on the island, and *Clayton* was able to *turn* him."

Justin nodded, his voice firm with conviction. "The Lost just need to be *told the truth*."

Steve folded his arms, his mind already moving forward. "Can we schedule *Clayton Trilling* to *join us* in the room when we interview *Jesus and Dresden?*"

A pause. "I think it will be an *asset* having his *observation and input.*"

Doris checked the latest reports on her console. "All *32 preliminary resurrections* have been *completed.*"

She scanned the data, continuing. "The *secondary set* of *64 resurrections* are *almost completed.*"

A pause, heavier now. "Going forward, there will be *192 psychiatrists* working *8-hour shifts, 24 hours a day*, until *all* of The Lost have been *resurrected.*"

Steve nodded slightly. "They should all be *completed* within a *couple of weeks*—as long as there are no *unforeseen complications.*"

Olivia tapped a few keys, running calculations. "Using the *average* of *1 hour per resurrection*, it should take *12 days* or so—give or take a *couple of days* for longer resurrections."

Doris suddenly stiffened, scanning an incoming update. "I do have *an update* from the *agents on the island* that might help."

Steve turned toward her. "What is it, Doris?"

Doris glanced at her screen, her voice carrying an undertone of quiet shock. "The agents have found that the *blood on tap* that was being used by *Ulrich Sanguis* in the lab..."

She hesitated slightly. "...was being *directly piped in* from the *tubes* that were *plugged into The Discarded.*"

The tension in the room tightened. Cynthia's brows furrowed, the realization settling over her like a cold weight. "Could that be *why* they were *keeping The Discarded alive?*"

Her voice dropped slightly. "They needed a *fresh supply* of *plasma*—which was made from the *blood*—for Ulrich to *work with* for The *Three E's.*"

Steve exhaled sharply. "That *sounds* about right, Cynthia."

A pause. "Blood harvesting, but *why?*"

Olivia straightened. "It could have *something to do* with what *Francis Latere* said—about *not knowing* how The *Three E's* would *absorb* into the *system.*"

Her voice turned analytical. "And how the *amounts* were *enough* to *kill* the person who *drank it*."

Doris glanced at her reports. "We have been doing *a lot* of research into this."

She tapped the screen. "We have *many chemists* working in a *lab* to *reverse engineer The Three E's*—to see what we can *learn*."

Steve took a breath, nodding firmly. "*Great* work, everyone."

He turned toward Cynthia. "We are *going to get back* to the *interrogations*."

A final instruction. "Make sure *Clayton Trilling* is *ready*—after we interrogate the *security guards*."

Chapter 42 - Jesus

The elevator doors slid shut behind them as Steve and Cynthia walked down the corridor toward the interrogation rooms. The tension of the unfolding investigation loomed over them.

Cynthia broke the silence with a smirk. "So, who's on first?"

Steve didn't miss a beat. "WHO... is on first."

Cynthia blinked confused at his response. "What!?"

Steve chuckled, shaking his head. "You've never seen that old Abbott and Costello act, *Who's on First*?"

Cynthia tilted her head. "Who are Abbott and Costello?"

Steve sighed dramatically, as if mourning an era long gone. "They were an old comedy act from *75 years ago*."

He waved it off, a playful smirk tugging at the corner of his mouth. "It's *not important*—I was making a joke *way before your time* that went *right over your head*."

He straightened, all humor fading as his voice turned serious. "I want to see the *lead security guard* first."

Steve and Cynthia walked into the interrogation room where Torres Deltera, the lead security guard, was handcuffed to the table.

They took their seats across from him. Torres had his head down and his eyes closed, his hands and fingers intertwined, holding them about six inches above the table in front of him.

Steve and Cynthia settled into their chairs, the weight of the conversation pressing down on them. Across the table, Torres lifted his head, his weary expression revealing a deep exhaustion that lingered beneath the surface.

His voice was quiet, almost apologetic. "Sorry, I was just *praying*."

Steve offered a small nod. "Do you mind if we *ask* you a few *questions*?"

Torres exhaled, shaking his head slightly. "*Ask* me whatever you would *like*."

A pause. "I will be *truthful*. I am just *happy* to have been *taken away* from that *place*."

Torres had revealed himself to be no more than a pawn—just another captive in a system built on deception. Like the others discovered in the island's underground, the security guards had been kidnapped and brought there against their will. Torres was the exception: the only one granted free movement throughout the facility.

His duties were logistical, almost mundane on the surface. He unloaded crates from the train and delivered them to designated locations. But the horror crept in when he discovered what some of those crates contained: The Lost—human cargo, arriving in silence. Torres also handled meal deliveries, restocked rooms weekly, and distributed supplies to the other workers. He was, in essence, the lifeline of the facility's daily operations.

The weight of what he'd become part of crushed him. He confessed that upon arrival, he and the others were greeted by Jesus, who issued strict instructions. Torres was appointed lead security guard and given a key card. The others were confined to the security office, only permitted to leave under two conditions: if Torres summoned them, or if the word "Discarded" was spoken within the office. In that case, they were to rush to Jesus's room and protect him at all costs.

Torres's voice trembled as he admitted his role in escorting the Discarded to their cells—chaining them up, locking them away. He also exposed Ulrich's lies: Torres had never given him orders upon arrival. Worse, Torres had seen Ulrich inside the rooms with the Discarded, confirming suspicions that ran deeper than anyone had feared.

Steve absorbed the revelations in silence. The truth was unraveling, but speaking with the other security guards now felt redundant. Their stories would only echo Torres's. He decided to bypass them entirely and go straight to the source: Jesus.

The tension in the corridor was palpable as Steve and Cynthia moved toward the next interrogation room. Their pace was steady, their minds focused on the unraveling mystery that had brought them here. Cynthia glanced at Steve, her tone inquisitive. "So, who's next?"

Steve exhaled, running a hand through his hair. "I *believe* what Torres is telling us."

His voice carried certainty. "I *don't think* we need to *speak* with the *other security guards*—I *don't think* they'll have any *new information*."

A pause. "So, all that's *left* is *Jesus*—and *Dresden*."

Cynthia folded her arms, thinking it through. "Are you going to *talk* to Ulrich *again*?"

Steve nodded. "I *want* to speak with *Ulrich* again—to ask him a few *more questions*."

A beat. "But if I do that—it'll be *after* I speak with *Dresden*."

Cynthia's brow furrowed slightly. "Ulrich is the *only one* who we have *confirmation* has *lied* to us."

Steve's tone sharpened. "*Yes*—I want to see what *Dresden* has to say about *Ulrich's participation* in *all of this*."

Cynthia nodded slowly. "So—we're *speaking* with *Jesus* next?"

Steve's gaze darkened slightly. "*Yes.*"

A brief silence stretched between them before Cynthia asked, "Do we want to *wait* for *Clayton* to get here?"

Steve shook his head. "*No.* Let's go in *without* him."

A pause. "Olivia will have him *here soon.* She probably wasn't *expecting us* to *skip* the *other security guards*—but they're *watching all* the interrogations *live.*"

His lips pressed into a thin line. "So—Clayton will arrive *shortly after* we go into *Jesus's room.*"

And with that, the interrogation pressed forward—toward *the men who had shaped the illusion of heaven itself.*

Steve and Cynthia walked into the interrogation room that contained Jesus, handcuffed to the table. They sat down in the chairs across from him.

Steve said, "So finally we meet the man Jesus who was running the island."

Jesus was adamant and spoke sternly, "I was not running an island. I was the curator of GOD's kingdom of heaven."

The door creaked open, and Clayton Trilling stepped into the room.

His presence commanded attention, and all eyes turned to him as he walked with deliberate strides.

He made his way to the end of the table and settled into a chair; his expression unreadable. He nodded to Steve and Cynthia and said, "Sorry I am late Commander."

Steve before continuing said to Clayton "Feel free to give your input or ask any questions, Doctor."

Clayton leaned back in his chair ready to observe saying, "Thank you Commander."

Steve looking to Jesus again asked "Jesus, what is your real name?"

Jesus spoke with the only truth he had ever known. His voice was steady, each word carrying the weight of his unwavering conviction. "My real name is Jesus."

Scoffing Steve said, "I find that hard to believe."

Jesus spoke casually, "It is the only name I have ever known my whole life as a human."

Steve surprised at his response retorted, "As a human????? Why were people being brought to the island?"

Jesus spoke with pride in his voice, "The island as you call it was heaven. They were being brought to heaven, not an island. Given salvation by me, their lord and savior, in the kingdom prophesized to all of my followers."

Starting to feel annoyed with Jesus's answers, Steve's frustration boiled over. He could no longer contain himself and blurted out, "You call that salvation? Being kidnapped and having your freedom stripped from you, being taken away from your loved ones?"

Jesus spoke casually with authenticity and confidence in his tone, "Death is a part of life. After death, they came to me. I was bringing them to a better place."

Jesus's answers doing nothing but making Steve's blood boil as anger rose up in him, "A BETTER PLACE???? You trapped them all on an island. How long have you been on the island?"

Jesus, his patience wearing thin, felt a surge of annoyance and anger rise within him, when Steve referred to heaven as just an island again.

His eyes, usually calm and composed, now blazed with intensity. His jaw clenched, and a vein throbbed visibly on his forehead. Jesus yelled, "I WAS IN HEAVEN! For twenty of your years."

"My years?"

Reverting back to his calm demeanor, Jesus took a deep breath and steadied himself. The storm of emotions that had flared moments ago was now under control, "Time is different for me. It is not measured in years."

Steve shook his head at Jesus's response and asked, "Why were you keeping The Discarded alive on the island? Why didn't you just let them go free?"

Jesus responded immediately, "They failed the test. Once chosen, if they don't make it into heaven, they go to a hell."

Steve, trying to maintain control, felt his anger reaching a boiling point. His knuckles turned white as he gripped the edge of the table, every muscle in his body tensed.

His voice, though low and steady, carried a dangerous edge as he sternly said, "What gives you the right or the power to create a hell and force people to go there? You can't play with people's lives like this."

Jesus Calmly responded and with ultimate conviction he spoke, which only invoked Steve anger and annoyance, "I am and have been since my birth a man imbued as GOD. I came to earth to bring salvation to all of my followers."

Cynthia, unable to contain herself any longer, cut in sharply. "WHAT? You came to earth?"

"Yes, I was GOD reborn through a virgin, to finally return as I prophesied in the bible. I rebuilt heaven and was bringing all of my followers there."

Unable to listen to any more of the nonsense spewing from Jesus's lips, Steve's patience snapped, his fists clenched at his sides. "Mind my language, but nothing you are saying makes any sense. What the fuck are you talking about?"

Cynthia elbowed Steve lightly, her eyes glinting with both concern and determination.

Cynthia whispered, "Probably not helpful, Commander. Let me try."

Cynthia continued, taking over for Steve, hoping he could get his emotions in check.

Her voice was steady and composed, a stark contrast to the tension that had just filled the room. "Where did you grow up, Jesus?"

"I grew up within The Church of The Odyssey."

Cynthia asked with a caring tone, "Who was your mother?"

Jesus emotionless with a straight face responded, "I was taken from my mother after birth, but her name was Maria."

He paused, "She was not important. She was just the vessel used to bring forth my resurrection."

Cynthia tilted her head to the side a little as she asked, "Who took you from your mother?"

Jesus continued, "It was at birth, so I do not know the answer to that question. But I grew up inside the church, I was being educated by the high priests and cared for by Mothers of The Church."

Cynthia asked, "What were the high priests teaching you?"

"They taught me about the kingdom of heaven I would inherit. They taught me the doctrine of the church, and brought forth my true potential as the resurrected GOD."

He paused before continuing. "They brought the prophecies in the bible to fruition, seating me at the throne in heaven when I became eighteen years old."

Confused, Cynthia asked inquisitively, her brow furrowing as she tried to make sense of what Jesus had said, "If you were truly the resurrected Jesus, why would you need to be taught the doctrine of the church, and need humans to seat you in heaven?

Couldn't you do that yourself, and wouldn't you know the information already?"

Confidently speaking what he believed to be the truth; Jesus's voice rang out with conviction.

His eyes locked onto Cynthia, unwavering and intense. "As a human vessel, I lost my omniscience I had as GOD, so no, I would not know the information they taught me."

Turning to Steve and Clayton, Cynthia's expression was resolute. Her voice carried a sense of urgency as she addressed them. "I think they brainwashed and raised a baby to become this Jesus."

Hearing Cynthia's words, Jesus cut in immediately. His voice was sharp and insistent, his eyes burning with intensity. "Why do you choose not believe?"

Cynthia retorted back, "You do not choose your beliefs! You either believe what can be proven and shown to you, or you will trick yourself into believing something created by other humans or your own imagination."

She paused, "One thing I have learned in my life Jesus, is that something as horrible as what The High Priests did to you—taking you from your mother—and what was happening to The Discarded and The Lost are evils that are always executed by humans."

Jesus responded as if he didn't hear a word she said, "I am sitting here in handcuffs in front of you, and you still do not believe."

Cynthia immediately responded, she was losing her patience, "What makes you believe it? That you are God in human form? What have you been shown that proves it to you?"

Jesus sat in silence for a few seconds before saying, "I don't need to be shown proof! I have known it since the day I was reborn!"

Clayton after doing nothing but listening and observing the entire time leaned forward in his chair and looked towards Steve and Cynthia and spoke, "Can I speak to you both outside, please?"

Steve, Cynthia, and Clayton all rose from their seats. Clayton needed to speak with them in private about Jesus. Without a word, they exited the room together, Steve asked, "What are you thinking, Clayton?"

Clayton spoke sternly but there was a lingering of worry in his tone, "I think we need to look at this subject from a different perspective than we are."

He paused, "What if what Cynthia said is true, that he has been brainwashed to believe all of this since birth?"

Another pause letting his theory settle in their minds, "If what he is saying is true, he is one of The Lost too. He just went missing way before all of this started."

Empathically he said, "I think we need to handle this situation with the utmost care."

Steve asked, "What do you suggest?"

Clayton knew what needed to happen and spoke his thoughts, "I would like to have him classified as one of The Lost Commander, and I would like to be personally responsible for his resurrection."

Steve confused asked, "Why would we do that?"

Clayton explained his thoughts, "At this point, to tell you the truth, Commander, I don't even think he can be helped. If true, he is too far gone from actual reality; he would not survive in society.

If he was thrown in a jail cell, he would not know why."

He paused before continuing, "Let's keep him here and let me work with him; otherwise, his entire life would be wasted. If he can't be fixed, his life can have some worth through what we can learn from studying him and his mind."

Steve respecting Clayton said, "If that is what you think is best, I will approve that."

Clayton assuring Steve said, "I will find out if he is lying quite quickly. We will be able to have multiple qualified people observing and studying him behind the scenes also."

Cynthia cut in realizing something, "You know what that means, don't you?"

At the same time, Steve and Clayton said, "What?"

Cynthia continued her thought, "It means that every single person involved except for the only High Priest still alive has been a puppet in this."

She paused before continuing, "Every single person on and off the island. Jesus, The Lost, The Security, The doctor, the chemists, the chef, the train operator, The Transporters, The phantom ambulances, the hitmen, Odyssey Inc, the communities, the churches, the real estate companies, the car rental businesses, the construction companies.

Not all of them were innocent of committing crimes for money but not knowing the extent of what they were involved in. They could never be held responsible for The Lost."

Steve hung his head, "Let's not forget about all The Soldiers of Jesus, and the innocent lives lost to the video."

Clayton spoke out loud, "The human mind can be transformed in infinite ways, especially from birth. Whoever is responsible for this has perfected that skill."

Steve responded, "I think it is time we speak to the man responsible, at least the only one left."

Cynthia asked, "How can one man be responsible for all of the crimes, psychological tortures, and deaths that have been unleashed on the world with this case over the last twenty years?"

Steve said with a hint of excitement in his voice, "Let's go and find out!"

Chapter 43 - Heaven's Creator

As the door swung open, Steve, Cynthia, and Clayton stepped into the room. The tension was palpable, and the atmosphere thickened as Dresden immediately erupted, sneering at the Commander.

His face twisted with contempt, and his voice dripped with derision. "You have made me wait so long Commander, the anticipation is at its peak, and finally we meet in person."

The three of them sat down in the chairs at the table, their silence speaking volumes as they stared at Dresden. His demeanor changed as they sat down, he had a look of jubilation, his eyes gleaming with excitement.

Steve leaned forward, breaking the silence. His voice was calm but firm as he started the conversation. "I have learned everything about how you made heaven become a reality on earth.

Dresden, the only question I have for you is why? What has been the point of all of this?"

A touch of disappointment crossed Dresden's face. His voice rose and fell in volume as he spoke, accenting certain words to make his point.

The frustration evident in his tone he began, "You still refuse to address me as HIGH PRIEST Dresden! You disappoint me, Commander. I have EARNED MY TITLE THE SAME AS YOU have."

Steve erupted at Dresden's response, his patience at its end. he shouted, his voice echoing through the room. His face flushed with anger, and his eyes blazed with intensity. "AFTER WHAT YOU HAVE DONE! Your title is meaningless to this world."

Resuming his calm demeanor, Dresden's smile slowly returned. His eyes glinted with a mix of amusement and something darker.

He began, his voice smooth and controlled. "My name and title as High Priest Dresden will be remembered for centuries to come.

The Story of The Lost will be talked about, be written about in books, become a nightmarish horror story told to children, imbued into culture, and the historical timeline of reality."

He leaned back in his chair, and the corners of his mouth rose into a big smile as he stared at Steve and said, "You, Commander, are the hero of this story. You will be imbued into history in the same way."

Not understanding how being a part of the story was something special, Steve replied, "I would have preferred if The Story of The Lost was never created rather than play a part in it."

Dresden started speaking the moment that Steve stopped. "We all must play our part whether we like it or not. The world is a theater with different acts playing out in different perspectives everywhere, creating new stories to be told at every moment of existence."

He paused, "Few stories will gain the reverence of the Bible and be remembered forever, like The Story of The Lost that we have created."

Steve's anger surged as Dresden wove him into the narrative of The Lost. His jaw tightened, and a flush of red crept up his neck.

The way Dresden casually included him as a key player in this twisted tale was infuriating.

His fists clenched at his sides, and his eyes burned with a mix of frustration and indignation. He yelled, "THE STORY YOU CREATED DRESDEN!!!!"

Shaking his head, "I played no part in making this happen."

He paused before continuing, "You and the other High Priests needed to be stopped! THE STORY NEEDED TO BE STOPPED!!!!"

He gripped the edges of the table, "My goal for the past six years has been to put The Story of The Lost to an end, close this book, and today we will."

Responding with a snarky attitude, Dresden's words were carefully crafted to crawl under Steve's skin. His tone was dripping with sarcasm, and a sly smile played on his lips as he spoke.

He knew exactly how to push Steve's buttons, and he reveled in the visible frustration that flickered across Steve's face with each pointed remark.

"You can close a storybook Commander, but that will never take away the reverence, remembrance, and horrors of The Story of The Lost contained inside."

He paused, "The empathy the reader of this story will feel and know the impact of all affected in the story, bringing those horrors to life every time it is told or read."

Frustrated and ready to end the conversation, Steve felt a wave of defeat wash over him. He was at his wits' end with Dresden's evasive and provocative responses. His shoulders slumped, and a heavy sigh escaped his lips.

The spark of anger that had fueled him earlier was now dimmed. He spoke calmly, "So that is why then, you wanted to create a story? You haven't really told us anything."

Excited, Dresden almost hopped in his chair, his handcuffs clanging against the cold metal. The sound echoed through the room, mingling with his enthusiasm. His eyes sparkled with a disturbing gleam, and a wide grin spread across his face. He spoke not yelling but at a high volume from his excitement,

"I AM THE OPEN BOOK, COMMANDER. What part of The Story of The Lost do you want to know? Ask me a more specific question. The why changes and evolves throughout the years to bring us to this meeting today."

Dresden's response put a cap on the anger that Steve was feeling hoping the conversation would steer in a way to give them some answers, he calmly asked, "How did this all start? Where did the idea for this story come from?"

Feeling the tension drift from the conversation Dresden started to show more jubilation now that Steve was interested in hearing the story,

"The Story of The Lost, like the why, changes and evolves and continues to evolve until it gets to the point where the story is its own creation and continues to grow and to write itself, adding new characters to the story, even though there is no author at the pen anymore."

He paused, "It all started with wanting to create a new community hidden from the world. Somewhere the elites of our community's hierarchy could be rewarded with a heaven.

After Brian Schersinger's death and using his name to create an empire and unlimited stream of money, we started to expand the church, starting new communities, and the ideas evolved."

Interested in learning more about The Story of The Lost, Steve realized he had to leave his emotions out of it, to learn about the story he had to listen to it unbiased. Steve asked, "So you started with a smaller operation in mind?"

Dresden continued, "We had the idea to build a community underground. We secured the real estate, mining, and construction companies to build tunnels and roads underground for the community. Once the Tunnels started the tunnel idea evolved, and the tunnel network continued to grow until it was complete and encompassed the entire country.

We learned about a shallow section of the ocean in which the tunnels could be continued beneath the ocean. We secured an island within line of the ocean tunnels. Construction started on the island to build the underground, deforest areas of the island, and seed the land to be filled with fruit-bearing plants. We also started to build the train tracks and the train underground in the tunnels."

Driven by curiosity, Steve inquisitively asked, "How did you get the dome over top of the island?"

Excited to share how it was accomplished Dresden almost jumped in his seat again when Steve mentioned it, his handcuffs clanging on the bars as he spoke,

"The dome was a miraculous feat it was constructed in an underground facility. The mirrored exterior made it almost invisible to satellite surveillance.

Weighing in at over one million pounds, it had to be airlifted by a fleet of 40 transport helicopters and placed over the island, extending to the bottom of the shallow ocean. If you have the money, you can have anything accomplished in this world, Commander."

Steve asked, "How did you get that area of ocean registered as restricted space from water and air?"

Dresden waving his hand at the notion that it should have been hard he said, "That was easy. A simple report of an endangered species of ocean coral that layered the shallow bottom and built up off the shallow ocean floor had that area shut down overnight."

Steve seeing their plan as complete said, "That is around the time when people started going missing twenty years ago, I assume."

Dresden responded with a proud smile on his face, "You know the timeline well, Commander."

He paused, "Yes, shortly after that, we started bringing elite followers from our communities using the ambulances and the tunnels."

Wondering Steve asked, "Why did you have to make them think they died and went to heaven?"

"Another evolution of the idea due to the money and connections we had. If we truly wanted somewhere for our elites to go to what better than a heaven."

He Paused, "Also, if we wanted to keep the place hidden, we couldn't just bring people to the island, so we kept them in a sedated coma until they woke up with Jesus. Our elite followers getting to experience a true simulation of heaven."

Steve asked, "What about Jesus?"

Excited joy washed over his face with a large smile at the mention of Jesus's name as he responded, "Jesus and The Lost are the perfect example of how the human mind can be transformed in ways to see reality through a kaleidoscope of distortion."

He paused and smiled, "Jesus is my best work; it was imperative for him to believe who he was, and what was taught to him."

Clayton cutting in needing some input from Dresden, "Does he really believe everything he says?"

Nodding his head Dresden continued, "Jesus was my son. He was taken from his mother and raised as the resurrected Jesus."

Dresden let an extended silence settle over them as they contemplated his words. "He spent every waking moment until his 18th birthday in darkness suspended unable to utilize his body, like The Discarded. The High Priests would teach him in darkness speaking as the voice of GOD within his head, about his purpose, and destiny to inherit heaven.

The Mothers of The Church cared for him washed and fed him in the evenings. He was locked away in the church basement his whole life until his eighteenth birthday when he was the first person to wake up on the island. Which fulfilled the prophecy he was indoctrinated to believe."

Cynthia disgusted by what she had just heard blurted out, "I'm sorry but that is fucking horrible, how could you do that to your own son!!??"

Dresden snidely responded, "It is what GOD does to his children every day."

Cynthia offended and taken aback by his reasoning, "I don't believe in this god, don't you think that is a little twisted?"

Speaking with a slight rasp in his voice for effect, he leaned in closer, his eyes narrowing. The added texture to his tone gave his words an eerie, almost haunting quality, as he said,

"GOD is twisted. I learned that a long time ago. A twist of good and a twist of evil randomly delivered through every variable action of every living creature with the free will to act."

Steve jumping back into the conversation wondering how this god can be so evil and twisted as Dresden had said this, Steve asked, "So this god you speak of is not a moral agent?"

Dresden scoffed, he made a motion waving his hands, his handcuffs clinking as he did this,

"Morality is not an issue for GOD. Morality is a human thought. All actions are just, to enact GOD's action. I was supposed to kill myself at the same time the other High Priests did, but who would be here to tell The Story of The Lost if I did that?"

Wondering why Dresden would not have just ended it when the other High Priests did Steve sarcastically said, "I really wish you did kill yourself and put an end to all of this, so why didn't that happen?"

Dresden smiled, "The Lost was all my plan. The High Priests were puppets just like everyone else. I used the High Priests, the church, their communities, and all their followers.

Who do you think brought forth the idea for us all to kill ourselves before you found us?"

Still needing to know the answer why they were having this conversation, Dresden avoiding the question, Steve asked again, "But you didn't kill yourself. Why? Just to take on all the liability?"

"The liability is of no consequence. Life eventually will come to an end. It is the mark you leave on the world, and the minds remaining in existence that matters.

It is so I would be the one man that will be remembered through all of this, along with you Commander.

We are the key pieces that will be attributed and spoken about as the good and evil in this story."

Confused and wanting to know Steve asked, "Why would you want to be remembered for the evil you unleashed on the world?"

"Good and evil are always subjective terms. We wanted to create the ultimate community hidden from the world, and not one person on that island would view it as an evil place."

Steve unsatisfied with Dresden's answer said, "You can't really believe that...... the good of the island was all a lie!!!!! There is nothing you can do or say that will change that."

Dresden stared directly into Steve's eye's as he said, "The truth of a lie is in the eye of the beholder. If the beholder believes they know the truth, then that truth becomes fact within their mind.

Who are you to take these people away from what they believed is heaven?"

Steve shot back, "We will ask the questions here. These tables cannot be turned to view us as the villain."

Dresden voice was laced with condescension, "If I am an open book Commander, you should be too. What are you afraid of Commander, answer the question."

Steve's temper started to rise again, Dresden pushing his buttons, "I am not afraid of you, or your questions Dresden. That I know! Without Odyssey Inc and the money, you are as worthless as you were thirty years ago when you killed Brian Schersinger."

Staring at Steve in silence for a few seconds before he responded, "You still didn't answer the question."

Annoyed, his anger rising even more, he struggled to regain control. His jaw tightened and his eyes narrowed, determined to steer the conversation back onto a productive path. Raising his voice, "I DO NOT NEED TO ANSWER YOUR QUESTIONS DRESDEN!!!!!"

He paused for a moment and continued, "If you do not see what you did as evil, your subjective opinion does not matter because what you did is OBJECTIVELY EVIL to every subjective mind in existence but yours!"

Cynthia cut in when Steve paused, feeling the tension rise again within Steve and the conversation, speaking calmly Cynthia said, "Why don't you tell us about The Three E's?"

"What do you want to know?"

Cynthia started to explain, "We know what was contained within The Three E's and we already understand why, but how did it work?"

"Ulrich came up with the method a long time ago."

Happy Cynthia had taken control of the conversation and got it back on track, Steve was surprised to hear Dresden give up Ulrich's involvement so easy, Steve repeated what Dresden had said, "Ulrich came up with the method?"

Dresden excited again to explain, "Yes, Ulrich devised a groundbreaking method and delivery system. Ulrich also designed and patented multiple strains of mutated hemoglobin capable of carrying more than just oxygen. These strains had varying deterioration time spans, allowing for precise control over the release of their contents.

By utilizing the stomach lining and fat, the plasma he used in The Three E's allowed transfer and storage of the ingredients within the bloodstream's hemoglobin without affecting the body until the hemoglobin naturally deteriorated."

He paused before continuing, "This revolutionary hemoglobin was employed to store and gradually transfer the ingredients of The Three E's from the stomach lining to the bloodstream over time.

It was a pioneering discovery that enabled the introduction of substantial amounts of substances into the human body, to be released slowly in small doses over the course of three months.

Steve asked, "How long was Ulrich on the island?"

"Ulrich has been under my employ since the beginning, before the island.

Perfecting The Three E's was imperative to heaven being real to its occupants. The first one hundred people we brought there showed us that."

Interested to learn something they didn't know Steve asked, "What do you mean?"

Dresden explained, "The first 100 we brought there resorted back to their human tendencies over time, tribal fighting, violence it was not heaven.

We wiped the island clean like GOD did when he washed the world with Noah's flood, the first 100 became the first Discarded.

It was Ulrich's idea on how to keep them alive to utilize them for their blood, so we had a never-ending supply of plasma for The Three E's. I wouldn't know how to do that just had the money to make it happen."

"Ulrich says he was on the island for five years."

Dresden scoffed, "An obvious lie. He was the only person who was not expendable due to his skill set.

Without The Three E's, it never would have worked. We cycled new security guards, chefs, train operators, doctors, and chemists every couple of years, or if they became a problem."

Cynthia's disgust with Dresden overcame her, "How could you do that to people discard them?"

Dresden's response stern and void of emotion, "Their existence did not matter anymore, but we needed a continuous supply of blood so we could continue to make The Three E's."

Steve wanting more answers steered the conversation back, "Who was responsible for connecting the tubes in their bodies?"

"Ulrich did that. He had a secret door in his lab which would take him to The Discarded.

When someone was Discarded, he would sneak off in the night to hook the tubes up to them."

Steve still confused by their motives asked, "I still am not hearing why you did this."

Dresden shrugged his shoulders, "Does there have to be a why? I feel every step, and choice within the story is the why because free will was used to make a choice when the convenience of the choice suited our goals."

Steve shook his head as he spoke,

"So just because you could...

That is fucking disgusting Dresden!"

Dresden offended by Steve's disgust, "I gave those people everything they needed all in one place in an unlimited supply. What allowed them to be controlled so easily was supplying them with the three things that humans need and always want."

He paused, "Any human can be controlled fully if they are given food, water, and most importantly, free willing access to the opposite sex. The psychedelic drugs in The Three E's always kept everyone on the island in a catatonic state, and the sexual dysfunction drugs kept them filled with pure lust and ecstasy, so most people would have sex or orgies to pass the time."

He paused before continuing, "They never asked for much other than drugs and alcohol, even though Jesus told them he could give them anything.

They were supplied with everything they needed on the island, and most got caught up in a routine of being addicted to drugs or alcohol and having sex multiple times per day with many different people, and sometimes multiple people at the same time. When you supply humans with all things they need for survival, they revert to their animal state... fucking whatever is in their path."

Steve snidely responded, "It sounds like the path we had to follow to find you, except we saw it after your selfish fucking ego fucked every other being in existence along the path."

Dresden spoke sarcastic and condescending, "That is very poetic, Commander!"

Seeing Steve's temper started to rise even higher after Dresden's sarcastic response, Cynthia cut into the conversation again. "Over one million people have been murdered across the country so far because of The Video. What was the whole point of that?"

Dresden smiled and spoke, "You won't like the answer.

It was always our church's ultimate goal to amass an army of followers and rid the world of atheists, apostates, heathens and nonbelievers.

I never realized how easy it would be until then. We had a hasty decision to make when we found out you were inside the tunnels and going to find the island.

It was all coming to an end, and we were angry you had destroyed the heaven we created over the past 20 years. We needed to end it all with a big bang, like it started."

Losing control at Dresden's blatant disregard for human life, Cynthia abruptly stood up from the table. She leaned closer, staring directly into Dresden's eyes. Her face was flushed with anger, and her voice was filled with fury as she yelled, "ONE MILLION PEOPLE HAVE BEEN MURDERED!!!! How can you not ca-ca-care?"

Dresden pulled his head closer to his hands when she stopped speaking and wiped the specks of saliva off his face echoing the words she spoke.

Cynthia started to break down as a tear formed and started to roll down her face, thinking about all the innocent people that had been murdered.

Seeing Steve's anger rising when Cynthia started crying, Clayton jumped into the conversation and calmly said, "Dresden, have you ever loved another human being?"

Dresden shot back, "Only the true Jesus Christ, not my imposter of a son."

Clayton trying to get an understanding of who Dresden was, "Were your parents around while you were growing up?"

"What kind of question is this?"

Clayton explained, "I am a doctor, a psychiatrist, a profiler I just want to understand you and your brain. Will you divulge that part of The Story of The Lost to me, so I can understand the brain that wrote it?"

Dresden's face lit up with a smile, his eyes twinkling with approval, as Clayton's idea sparked a genuine sense of enthusiasm within him being able to reveal more of the story.

"My parents died in a car crash when I was a baby. I ended up in a foster care system run by a church when I was four years old."

Clayton continued the unseeming interrogation, "Were you in the car when it crashed?"

Dresden smiled, "Yes, I was."

He paused for a moment, "I survived the crash; my tiny little baby skull had cracked open in the accident. I was told I was in the hospital for six months after the accident before I woke up."

Clayton shocked asked, "How could you survive such a damaging accident?"

Dresden sat up and with pride in his voice said, "It was a miracle from GOD. None of the doctors could explain it."

Dresden's answers triggered a memory in Clayton's mind, reminding him of something he had read a few years ago. As Dresden continued to respond, each piece of evidence seemed to align perfectly, stacking up with every question answered.

Clayton's eyes widened slightly, the puzzle pieces clicking into place as he recalled the crucial information from his past readings. "You said you were put into foster care. Was it The Church of The Holy Divine foster care?"

Dresden nodded, "Yes, how did you know that?"

Clayton came to a realization and asked, "Are you... The Hopewell baby?"

At the same time, Dresden, Steve, and Cynthia, after having gained their composure, said, "What is The Hopewell baby?"

Clayton explained the dots he connected, "He was a very special baby in the mid-1960s who survived a car crash, flying out of his car seat and through the windshield, shattering his developing skull and brain.

The baby's frontal lobe was obliterated, the baby's forehead being the impact point when it hit the already smashed windshield. The doctors were baffled at how he had survived.

They never expected him to ever wake up, but the baby was kept on life support and one day, he did wake up."

Intrigued with the story Steve asked, "What happened when he woke up?"

Steve said, "As long as Dresden can't hurt anyone anymore, I don't care what they do with him."

Cynthia cut in asking, "Is there anything we are forgetting to ask him?"

Steve thought for a second and said, "I think we have covered everything about the operation we didn't know about fully.

I don't even think Dresden knows why he did it or maybe his brain doesn't need a why."

Clayton looked to Steve and said, "It would be good if we could keep him for neurological testing and observation.

Seeing The Hopewell Baby's brain 65 years later would be a so-called miracle for the field of neurology. We could learn so much from Dresden's brain."

Steve's phone started to ring, and he picked it up. It was Olivia calling him. "Olivia, what can I do for you?"

"Dresden just ate something inside of the interrogation room."

Steve exclaimed, "Are you sure?!"

"He pulled something out of the sleeve of his robe and put it in his mouth."

Steve responded, "Send medical, Olivia."

Steve rushed back into the room, Cynthia and Clayton following him, as Steve yelled out. "SO, YOU ARE TAKING THE COWARD'S WAY OUT DRESDEN!"

Dresden calm and collected, "My Godly work here is done, The Story of The Lost is done and has been told; it is time to move on and be rewarded by the one and only true Jesus Christ when I meet him in the real heaven."

Steve scoffed, "What if that is all a lie too, like the heaven you created?"

"You will find out the truth when it is your time, I know where I am headed."

Steve responded, "You may have to wait a little longer. As much as I would like to see you dead, it would pleasure me to keep you alive when you want to die.

The doctors that are coming will do whatever they can to keep you here with us."

Dresden exclaimed, "They better hurry Commander!"

He paused for a moment, "The story is about to come to an end. You can finally close this book,"

He looked directly at Steve, "You will never be able to unwrite the story within it. It was an honor having the polarity of you being the good to my evil."

Struggling to maintain his voice, he attempted to speak, but his words emerged through choked gurgles as he was drowned by the rising fluids in his throat.

Dresden started convulsing violently in his chair, his hands and arms flailing within their restraints, banging and clanging on the metal bar on the table.

His eyes rolled into the back of his head, and he began to foam a mix of saliva and blood from his mouth. The scene was chaotic and horrifying.

A doctor and a nurse rushed into the room and over to Dresden's convulsing body.

Cynthia quickly removed the handcuffs, and the doctor laid Dresden down on the floor where he continued to convulse.

The medical team worked frantically, trying to stabilize him, but the situation looked dire. The Doctor asked, "I think we are too late. What did he take?"

"We have no idea."

Dresden's convulsing slowed and then stopped. The doctor was checking his heartbeat with a stethoscope. "He is gone Commander. His heart was beating extremely fast, and it stopped with the convulsing."

Steve turned and walked out of the room, feeling a tumultuous storm of emotions all at once. He felt peace, satisfaction, and relief that the ordeal was finally over.

Happiness flickered briefly, only to be overshadowed by overwhelming disgust and sadness for the lives affected.

Fear and anger surged within him, and disappointment lingered at the edge of his consciousness.

He felt a sense of confusion, panic, and betrayal, feeling cheated by the twisted reality he had uncovered. Offended by Dresden's actions and disturbed by the horrors unveiled, Steve truly understood what it felt like to be one of The Lost in that moment.

Cynthia and Clayton followed Steve out of the room, leaving the doctor and the nurse with Dresden's lifeless body.

The weight of their collective experiences hung heavily in the air, a grim reminder of the darkness they had confronted and the human cost of Dresden's twisted story.

Cynthia glanced at Steve, concern flickering across her face. "You okay Commander?"

Steve exhaled slowly, his gaze distant. "He is *where he belongs* now—in a place he *can't hurt anyone.*"

A pause stretched between them. "I am just *glad* we *finally* put an *end* to the *story* that Dresden *created.*"

His voice lowered slightly. "I am *not nearly as happy* as I thought I *would be* when this ended."

Cynthia gave him a small, knowing nod. "Let's go *back* to *The Command Room* Commander."

Her voice was steady, reassuring. "The *feeling* will *pass.*"

And with that—they stepped forward, carrying the weight of an ending that felt *anything but victorious.*

Chapter 44 - The Book Can be Closed

teve, Cynthia, and Clayton stepped out of the elevator into The Command Room. The atmosphere was thick with unspoken emotions—relief, exhaustion, and a lingering weight that none of them could quite shake. Everyone was huddled around The Command Center, their faces illuminated by the soft glow of the screens.

Olivia broke away from the group as soon as she spotted them, her stride purposeful as she met them at the elevator. "Not the ending to the story we would have *hoped for,*"

She said, her voice measured but carrying the weight of closure. "But it is *over* Commander."

Steve nodded, his expression unreadable. "Thank you, Olivia. I am *glad* it's over."

The words felt hollow, lacking the satisfaction they were supposed to bring. Amelia crossed her arms, exhaling slowly before asking the question lingering in the air. "So—*what happens now?*"

Steve turned toward the group, his tone steady but carrying a subdued edge. "The Lost can finally *go back* to their lives—before *all of this started.*"

A pause. "We really *owe it all* to agent #64, Justin Standone."

Justin shook his head, his stance casual despite the praise. "I was just *doing my job.*"

A faint smirk. "It could have been *any agent* with *any number.*"

Steve held his gaze. "But it *wasn't* just *any agent*, Justin."

A beat. "You got to *play that role* in the *story Dresden created.*"

Olivia straightened slightly, glancing between them. "I *realized something* while we were putting together the *timeline*—something that wasn't *exactly explained* in our presentation."

Steve raised an eyebrow. "What *was it?*"

Olivia exhaled slowly, choosing her words carefully. "How we ended up in the *position we are today*—having *solved this case*—was really a *stroke of luck.*"

Steve narrowed his eyes. "*How?* We all *worked extremely hard* to solve this case over the last *six years.*"

Olivia's gaze didn't falter. "Let's *face it,* Commander. *Now* that we *know* the *scope* and *depth* of what was *going on*—we were *always ten steps* from anything *substantial*—until *#64 was taken.*"

Steve tilted his head slightly. "I won't *question* you, Olivia. *Explain yourself.*"

She nodded, organizing her thoughts before speaking. "We had *2,000 undercover agents* within the *COTO communities*—and if they hadn't *decided* to take *#64*—if they had taken *any other agent*—I think we would *still* be trying to *solve this case today.*"

A pause stretched between them. "The *information* that allowed us to *solve this case* was *finding* the name *Brian Schersinger*. If we hadn't found that *when we did*—we might *never* have found the name *at all.*"

Steve exhaled, absorbing that truth. Olivia continued, "We *only found* the name *Brian Schersinger* because *#64 was taken*—and brought through the *tunnel* in the *warehouse in Prudence.*"

Her voice sharpened slightly. "Out of *all 1,072 tunnel entrance warehouses*—that *warehouse in Prudence* was the *only existing link* in *all of this*—to The Lost, The Church of The Odyssey, and *Brian Schersinger.*"

A beat. "If our agent had been taken through *any other tunnel*—we would have found the names *Lionel Trebor* and *Gerald Randall*—giving us *no link* —and *no leads* to *Brian Schersinger* and *COTO.*"

Doris crossed her arms, nodding slightly. "We might have put *all the pieces together eventually* Commander—but finding the name *Brian Schersinger* expedited the process *exponentially.*"

Justin let out a short laugh. "It's like we *won the lottery*—with *those odds.*"

Steve smirked, shaking his head slightly. "We *drew #64*—and the *ticket paid off.*"

He turned toward Justin, his voice carrying quiet gratitude. "You will be *rewarded greatly* Justin—for your part in *putting an end* to all of this."

Justin met his gaze, his tone unwavering. "Just *knowing The Lost are home*—is *reward enough* for me."

Amelia leaned forward slightly, curiosity flickering in her expression. "If *The Throne's objective* was to *find The Lost*—now that they've *been found*—what's *in store* for *The Throne* in the *future*?"

Steve exhaled, stretching his shoulders back. "To start—everyone *here* deserves a *nice, long vacation.*"

Olivia chuckled, glancing toward Doris. "I've *already planned* and *booked* mine and *Doris's one-month vacation* to *Mauritius.*"

Steve raised an eyebrow. "Isn't that an *island*?"

Olivia grinned. "It is. And it's *beautiful*. I *can't wait.*"

Justin shook his head with a smirk. "I think I'll *stay on the mainland* for my vacation."

A beat. "I've had *enough* with *islands* for now."

The group let out quiet laughter, the tension in the room finally beginning to ease. For the first time in years, they could breathe again.

Doris said to the group, "There is an update coming on the news about the Soldiers of Jesus situation."

The big screen inside The Command Room flickered to life, casting an artificial glow across the gathered group. Conversations quieted as everyone turned toward the broadcast.

The news anchor sat rigid, his gruff tone carrying the weight of authority. His serious expression didn't waver as he stared directly into the camera. "I am *Dick Johnson*, and this is the *six o'clock news.*"

His face shifted—as if the weight of the tragedy lifted momentarily—his demeanor brightening as he delivered good news for the first time in weeks.

"The *tables have finally turned* on *The Soldiers of Jesus*—as the *military* has *taken control* of the situation."

A pause, thick with the gravity of what came next. "What *started* with a *video* brought on *more death* than the *worst pandemics* in *human history.*"

Clayton continued, "The baby had suffered extensive brain trauma, most of which healed over the six months of care while in a coma. Even most of his frontal lobe regenerated and healed.

What the doctors found later was that the middle of the baby's brain never healed and parts of his limbic system did not develop or exist.

The limbic system plays a big part in controlling motivation, emotion, learning, and memory."

He paused before continuing, The Hopewell baby became a neurological study, and doctors came to experiment on him from around the world. After four years, the studies were deemed unethical and were shut down.

The lead researcher was scared, nervous and destroyed all the records of the experiments that existed. Until more recently, when some of the files resurfaced, I read about it almost two years ago."

Steve needed to know more, "What happened after the study was shut down?"

Clayton finished, "The Hopewell baby, who was no longer a baby, was given over to The Church of The Holy Divine, which ran a foster care service."

Steve looked towards Dresden and asked, "Is that your real name, Dresden Hopewell?"

"Not a name I ever went by."

Clayton cut in, "Hopewell was his parent's last name. He was given a new name and identity. He grew up under a completely different name once in the church's care. He may not even know what his real name is.

Can I talk to you outside, Commander?"

"Of course."

They all got up from their chairs and exited the interrogation room. "Do you understand what this means, Commander?"

Steve had a confused look at the question, Clayton continued "With Dresden being The Hopewell Baby, all he has to say is the word insanity, and no judge or jury would ever convict him.

The worst punishment he will get is to be locked up in a padded room for the rest of his life."

Olivia glanced at him, a hint of confusion flickering across her face. "Your *father* isn't *here*."

She hesitated. "The files said he is *deceased*."

Kevan exhaled sharply, his gaze darkening slightly. "I *know* that."

A beat of silence. "It's a *long story*—and it is *personal*."

As the elevator doors slid open, Amelia's heart skipped a beat. Inside stood her husband, Jacob, and their three sons—John, Thomas, and Michael. The moment Michael saw his mother, his tiny frame burst forward, his voice ringing through the room.

"Mommy! Mommy! Mommy! *Where you been?*"

Amelia barely had time to react—she ran toward him, arms outstretched, scooping him up with a spinning embrace. She squeezed him so tightly, as if she could make up for every lost moment in a single hug.

Michael squirmed, laughing breathlessly. "Hug *too tight* Mommy."

Amelia loosened her grip but held him close, her voice raw with emotion. "I'm *sorry*, baby boy. I just *missed you so much!*"

Jacob stood beside them, his eyes glistening, his entire body trembling with emotion.

"I *still* don't believe you are *back*."

His voice cracked. "We have *missed you so much*."

A pause—thick with the weight of grief. "We *grieved* for you, waited for you—never *expecting* to *see you again* Amelia."

Tears spilled over as he exhaled, shaking his head. "I am *so happy* you are *home*—and *still alive*."

John and Thomas, standing close together, chimed in, their voices overlapping with excitement. "You *missed* our *choir rehearsal*—and the *big show* me and Thomas *headlined*!" John's words spilled out with barely-contained energy.

Amelia wiped at her tears, looking at them with pure love. "Your mommy is *back now*—and I will *never* miss another *minute* of your life."

Thomas grinned. "We did *so good* Mom—they asked us to be in the *Halloween choir*!"

Amelia pulled both boys into her arms, holding them tightly, kissing their heads. Then, without hesitation, she turned to Jacob and wrapped herself around him.

Jacob's arms tightened around her, and before long, John and Thomas joined, until they had formed a five-person family hug—whole again.

Amelia turned to Kevan, offering a gentle smile. "Kevan, this is my family."

Her voice softened. "They mean *everything* to me."

Kevan nodded, the weight of their shared history resting between them. Amelia exhaled deeply, holding onto the moment before speaking again. "Is there somewhere we can go—where my family can have *some privacy*?"

Her eyes flickered toward Kevan. "I'd like you to *come with us*."

Doris didn't hesitate. "Take the elevator to the *73rd floor*. It's *under renovations*—but *no one* will be *there now*."

Amelia nodded, taking Kevan's hand briefly before stepping toward the elevator. Her family followed closely behind, their movements synchronized by hope and relief.

As the doors slid closed, Steve turned toward the rest of the group, his voice firm. "I have a surprise for you Cynthia.

I couldn't have asked for a better partner while Mark was busy taking my place."

Steve offered a knowing smile, his eyes glinting with quiet anticipation. Cynthia tilted her head, curiosity flickering across her face. "A *surprise* for me?"

She smirked slightly. "What *is* it?"

Steve held up a hand, his voice steady but teasing. "Just *give it a second*."

The air in The Command Room was thick with anticipation—a silence so deliberate, so heavy, that every heartbeat felt amplified.

Then—within moments—the elevator doors slid open.

Standing just beyond the threshold was Esther Rollins—the sister Cynthia had lost when she became one of The Lost over three years ago.

Cynthia's breath hitched, her entire body freezing in place. The shock lasted only a second before she yelled her sister's name, her voice cracked with raw emotion. "ESTHER!"

She didn't hesitate—didn't even think—before running toward her, her arms reaching, desperate to close the gap between them. They collided in a tight embrace, bodies trembling, the sheer force of relief and love washing over them both.

Esther clung to her just as tightly, her voice shaking as she whispered, "I am *so glad* you are *home*."

A breathless laugh escaped her, filled with something between disbelief and overwhelming joy. "I *knew* you were *still alive* this whole time. I *never* stopped *looking* for you."

Esther exhaled, her grip tightening before pulling back just enough to meet Cynthia's gaze. "Not a *day went by* on the island that you did *not* cross my mind."

Her voice cracked slightly, overwhelmed. "I am *so happy* to be *home*."

Cynthia turned toward Steve, her eyes filled with gratitude. "Thank you again *Commander*, for the *opportunity* to be a *part* of this investigation."

A pause—then, a warm but firm nod. "I'm going to go *spend time* with my *sister*."

Without another word, Cynthia and Esther walked back into the elevator, hands still clasped as if neither was willing to let go again.

The doors slid closed, and with it, a chapter ended.

Inside The Command Room, only Olivia, Doris, Mark, Justin, and Steve remained—watching, absorbing the moment. And for the first time in years—something felt whole again.

Steve said to the group, "So where does that leave us five?"

Olivia interjected immediately, "Doris and I are going home to pack. We are leaving in three days. Great work, everyone."

Justin responded, "Like The Lost, I can finally get back to my life too, so I am going to do that."

As Doris, Olivia, and Justin stepped onto the elevator, the doors slid shut behind them, leaving only Steve and Mark in The Command Room. For the first time since their mission began, the air was quieter, but no less heavy.

Mark turned toward Steve, his voice carrying careful curiosity. "How are you *Commander*—now that it's *all over*?"

Steve exhaled, his words hanging in the space between them, filled with emotions too complex to unravel in a single breath. "*Unsatisfied. Disheveled.*"

A pause. "I thought I would *feel different* once it was *over.*"

His gaze darkened. "The way *Dresden* ended it for us—by *taking his own life*—left *blank spaces* on some of the *pages* of the story."

His voice dropped slightly. "Pages that will *never be filled in.*"

Mark studied him for a moment before placing a reassuring hand on Steve's shoulder. His grip was firm but steady, an anchor amidst the storm of exhaustion. "I *understand* why you feel that way *Commander.*"

A pause—then quiet certainty. "But remember—*WE* put a *stop* to it."

His voice strengthened. "*WE* saved almost *everyone* that *Dresden* was able to *unleash his evil on*—that we *could.*"

The truth was bitter, but undeniable. "Dresden was a *psychopathic sociopath*—and the world is a *better place* with him *dead.*"

A beat—then finality. "He *can't hurt* anyone *anymore.*"

Steve nodded slightly, though his expression remained clouded with something deeper, something unfinished.

"Yet—the *pain* he has caused will be *permanent* within the *minds* of *everyone affected* by his story."

His voice held weight—a promise he wasn't willing to let slip away.

"I have a *plan*—to make some *good* come out of *all of this.*"

A pause—then conviction. "To *give back* to the *people of the world.*"

His eyes sharpened. "To *fund The Throne indefinitely*—and to *help billions.*"

Mark's brows furrowed slightly, his intrigue deepening. "I don't *doubt* you do, but—*how* do you plan on *accomplishing that*?"

The tension between them shifted—not in uncertainty, but in the weight of what Steve's plan was.

"I am going to make a deal with Ulrich Sanguis that he can keep his life if he will work for The Throne under our conditions. I am also going to make him give us the patents he created for The Three E's."

He paused, "Once The Throne has the patents, we will lease them to pharmaceutical companies so they can turn their pills into a drink for slow release over three months and if they don't want to distribute it, we will produce it ourselves."

He paused before continuing a determined look on his face,

"I will not let them hide this helpful technology, it will revolutionize the pharmaceutical industry, and The Throne will make money on everything they sell."

Mark thought over what Steve had explained, "That is genius Commander!"

Steve continued, "Ulrich will work for us improving the patent and hemoglobin to slow release over longer periods. He will also come up with new ideas and patents to sell; The Throne will have more money than Odyssey Inc and The Church of the Odyssey."

A big smile came across Mark's face, "The Throne won't have to worry about money ever again."

As they stood there, the reality of their accomplishment began to sink in. They had faced unimaginable horrors and emerged victorious, bringing hope and healing to those who had been lost for so long.

The Command Room, once a hub of frantic activity, now felt like a place of quiet reflection. The weight of their success and the gravity of their actions would stay with them, but so too would the knowledge that they had made a difference.

Steve responded, "You're right, Mark."

The elevator doors slid open behind Steve and Mark, capturing their attention.

They turned around and saw Domenic Cirrone, the President of Odyssey Inc, stepping out of the elevator.

His presence commanded attention, and the air seemed to shift as he entered the room.

A look of determination on his face hinted at the importance of his arrival, Steve glanced up as Domenic entered The Command Room, his unexpected presence bringing a subtle tension to the air.

His expression was tightly wound, a visible strain etched into his face.

Steve's voice held curiosity, though a hint of caution crept in. "Domenic—what do I *owe* this *surprise visit*?"

Domenic's shoulders rose in a slow inhale before dropping. "Can we *sit down* and *talk*?"

The simple request carried weight, an unspoken urgency that Steve didn't ignore. Without hesitation, Steve, Mark, and Domenic settled at the desk, their movements measured as if bracing for what came next.

Steve leaned forward, his voice carrying both urgency and quiet empathy. "What is *wrong* Domenic?"

Domenic exhaled sharply, his hands folding together as he struggled to contain his distress. "The Throne has *frozen* all of *Odyssey Inc's accounts*."

His voice wavered slightly before steadying. "I have *millions* of employees *across the country* that are *unemployed*—because we are *unable* to do *business*."

A pause—he swallowed hard before continuing. "I have received *word* that the *board of directors* is *no longer around*."

His gaze darkened. "And I suspect your *suspicions* were *right*—Samuel Constant was *not real*."

Steve's expression remained unchanged, but his voice carried the weight of quiet certainty. "You are *correct*."

Domenic shook his head slightly, his breath uneven. "I *do not know* what *Odyssey Inc* was *created for*—or the *purpose* it was being *used*."

A sharp inhale. "I am *sure* you have *figured all* of that *out by now*."

His tone shifted, pleading but firm. "Allow me to *appoint* a *new board of directors*—and for *Odyssey Inc* to go *back to business*."

Pause. "If you want *Odyssey Inc* to be *overseen* by *The Throne*—I am *fine with that*—but *please* let my *people* go *back to work*."

His hands trembled slightly. "Imagine if *The Throne* was *dissolved*, Steve—and *all* of your *employees* were out of a *job*."

A single tear slid down Domenic's face—he wiped it quickly, almost embarrassed—but Steve saw the genuine emotion behind it.

It tugged at something deep, something that forced him to reevaluate the situation. Steve exhaled, his decision coming swiftly. "I will *allow* you to *resume business starting tomorrow*."

A pause, firm. "You will be *under supervision*—and *every transaction* that *Odyssey Inc* makes will be *scrutinized*."

Domenic let out a shaky breath, his relief visible. "At this point, Steve—you could *put a camera* in my *office* and come *be my boss*."

His voice cracked slightly. "I just *want my people* to be able to *go back to work*."

Steve softened, offering a slow nod. "I *thank you* for *coming to me* with this Domenic. Just the ask can change millions of lives, and I respect that you would put yourself out there to accomplish that."

His voice steadied. "It is *no longer detrimental* to our *investigation*—so we can *all go back to normal*."

Domenic's shoulders slumped slightly, as if a weight had lifted. "Thank you, Commander."

His voice dropped lower, quieter. "*Thank you*."

And with that—the course of Odyssey Inc shifted again. Domenic got up and made his way towards the elevator; he was happy almost strutting a dance as he walked.

Steve felt good being able to be the one man who could allow millions of people to go back to work.

He said to Mark, "That felt good, it's time to focus on healing and moving forward. We've closed this chapter, but our work is never done."

Mark responded to him, "It is over Commander, The Story of The Lost is done, the wounds inflicted can be healed, and the book can be closed."

And with that, they turned their attention to the future, ready to face whatever came next, as they approached the elevator to exit the Command Room it slid open to reveal two men wearing black suits, carrying briefcases.

The waves within the flow of their hair glistened as they stepped out of the elevator and the bright lights of the Command Room were reflecting off their foreheads.

One of the men extended and raised his hand towards Steve and said, "Steve Hauser—*Commander of The Throne*—it is an *honor* to meet you."

The man's voice carried an air of authority, measured but unwavering. "My name is *Percy Shellving*—and my colleague here is *Stanley Manning*."

Steve met Percy's handshake, his gaze sharp with curiosity. "It is a *pleasure* to meet you."

A pause. "What do I *owe* this *pleasure?*"

Stanley stepped forward, his expression unreadable. "Can we *sit down* and *talk* Commander?"

Steve nodded, leading them toward one of the desks inside the room. The four of them settled into their chairs, the air between them thick with unspoken weight.

Steve folded his arms, leaning slightly forward. "So—what is this *about*?"

Percy exhaled slowly, his voice measured yet deliberate. "We are from a *classified division* of the *government*—and that is *all* you need to *know right now*."

A pause—then quiet certainty. "We had a *question* for you Commander—now that *The Throne* has *completed* their *one objective investigation*."

His gaze didn't waver. "We were *wondering* if *The Throne* might *want to take on another case*—one *matching The Lost's grandeur*?"

Steve didn't hesitate. His response was firm, final. "If *The Throne* is needed—The Throne will *be there*."

A pause. "*However*—we are *shutting down* for a *month*."

His tone sharpened slightly. "*Everyone* at *The Throne* is getting *paid vacation*—and that is *non-negotiable*."

Percy exchanged a glance with Stanley before nodding slightly. "This investigation has been going on for *many decades*."

His lips pressed into a thin line. "I don't think *another month* will *hurt*."

A pause and he continued. "We are *hoping* The Throne can *bring it to its end*."

Steve smirked slightly, tapping his fingers against the table. "Then we will *meet again* in a *month*."

Stanley straightened, offering a firm nod. "We will *explain* what our *organization is*—and *break down the case* for you *then*."

A pause—then quiet certainty. "See you in *a month*."

And with that—the conversation paused, the weight of a new mission lingering in the air.

They stood up and shook hands standing beside the desk, Stanley and Percy made their way to the elevator leaving Steve and Mark in the Command Room.

Steve turned to Mark and said, "Well I guess we found our next case, let's get started on that vacation before it's too late."

The End

From the Author
Thank you for joining me on this journey. If this book resonated with you, good or bad I'd be incredibly grateful if you left a review on Amazon, GoodReads, Book2Read, or your preferred platform. Your thoughts help others discover Nevaeh The Story of The Lost—and as the author your experience of the story means the world to me.

Epilogue

I began writing this book on January 14, 2024, and today, on August 6, 2024, writing this Epilogue, I've completed the rough draft. It's time for a thorough read-through and much editing.

On January 14, 2024, the idea for this story came to me in the shower, as many good ideas do.

By the end of my shower, the concept had expanded, and I had to make notes of the idea. Immediately afterward, I jumped onto my computer and started plotting out the ideas, and I didn't stop.

The story you just read came to me in pieces that day in the shower. I could envision the narrative and its main setting vividly.

I knew exactly what it was, where it was, and the role it would play in the story.

I could see the factions and characters, even though they didn't yet have names.

The ending was also clear in my mind, all centering around the main setting of a fake heaven created by men.

Eight months later, after writing 36 chapters while writing this does the story match my original vision?

For the most part, the main themes and the central setting are an exact match to my initial idea.

Over the past eight months, I created the world within this book, its story, and precisely how I wanted to tell it.

I needed characters to fill roles, and as I continued writing, everything seemed to come together and fall into place perfectly.

I completed editing Nevaeh to my satisfaction on January 4th 2025 almost one year after I started writing it. I sent this book to over 40 literary agents before I decided to self-publish under my own imprint.

Now October 2025 I have written two additional books to launch my author career with one of those books being book #2 to The Throne Epic Mysteries Series, and I am prepping the final version of Nevaeh which has gone through much more editing and formatting.

I always felt some of the best entertainment I have found in my life regardless of the medium it was in, always kept me on the edge of my seat and wanting more all the way through.

I found many different mediums which I could find entertainment like this be it through amazing books like The Dark Tower series.

Graphic novels like The Walking Dead, and Y the Last Man or even Tv shows like Lost, From, and Breaking Bad.

I found with this book and story I wanted to create something like that.

There are obvious tributes I have given to some of my favorites like the chapter called "Behind the Curtain" a tribute to one of my early life cinematic loves The Wizard of Oz.

There are blatant throwbacks to the TV show Lost having the story revolve around "The Lost" is an obvious one. Brian Schersinger's business account was the magic numbers 4 8 15 16 23 42 from the TV show.

A chapter called The Others.

The Lost being on an island always was my original thoughts in the shower the other pieces just fell and fit into the story as I was writing it.

How to save a Lost is a tribute to the song by The Fray, how to save a life.

The life of Brian is an obvious throwback to Monty Python's religious parody movie.

I hope with this story I was able to give you something original, creative, enticing and exciting to keep you wanting to know more about Nevaeh and the other elements of the story to keep those pages turning from Amelia's death at the beginning to the revelations at the end of the book.

About the author Mathew J. Shaw

Mathew's journey as a writer began with curiosity and defiance—sneaking onto his family's first computer, a Windows 95 running WordPerfect, despite his mother's warnings not to touch it.

What he discovered there was transformative: the power to breathe life into characters and shape worlds with words. That spark became a lifelong passion.

Born in Mississauga, Ontario and later moving to and growing up in North Bay, Mathew began writing his first book, *A New Life*, at a young age.

Though many of his early works remain unpublished, the act of writing became a constant companion—a creative force he's never stopped nurturing. With no formal education beyond high school, he's taught himself through reading, reflection, and relentless creativity.

By day, he commands a crew of twenty heavy equipment mechanics with precision and grit. By night, he transforms—pen in hand, mind ablaze—into the architect of twisted worlds and genre-defying tales. His dream? To let the stories take over, sustaining his every day so he can write full time, twisting narratives into something unforgettable.

An avid reader across genres, Mathew draws inspiration from the likes of Stephen King—especially *The Dark Tower* series—S.E. Hinton, Tamara Siler Jones, and countless others. His bookshelf spans, many genres of books, graphic novels, philosophy, holy books of all faiths and educational texts, each one feeding the ideas that shape his writing.

Whether crafting bold fictional worlds or exploring the deeper questions of life, Mathew writes with the beats of his heart, the lyrics of his soul, a curiosity, and the belief that stories have the power to transcend.

Other Books by Mathew J. Shaw

Don't miss a word.
The Mind of Clayton Trilling Series
The Next Step - The Controller's Game Book #1 – February 2026

Clayton trilling, a brilliant profiler with an unparalleled grasp of the human psyche, faces his most formidable opponent yet. A ruthless mastermind who never hides, never retreats, and always dictates the next move. When a cryptic envelope arrives, everything changes. inside lies the first move in a psychological game orchestrated by something only known as The Controller

Unravel the untold.
Experience the unexpected.
<u>Sign up for Twisted Storylines Publishing's email list</u>

You'll get exclusive content, sneak peeks, and future updates—straight to your inbox.
<u>twisted-storylines-publishing-i52y3q.mailerpage.io</u>

Manufactured by Amazon.ca
Bolton, ON

53809211R00240